COLDBLOODS

HOTBLOODS, BOOK 2

BELLA FORREST

"*R*UN!" Navan roared.

It was already too late. As I lunged out of the way, the coldblood who had sensed me clutched the fabric of my suit.

"Invisibility suit," he snarled.

I tried to wrench myself away, but his grip held. His arm didn't even budge. Now, the other rebel coldbloods were circling me, like panthers about to pounce.

The next thing I knew, Navan was throwing all of his body weight forward. The chair he was tied to crashed into the legs of the coldblood gripping me, and in the millisecond in which his grasp slackened with surprise, I managed to rip myself free. My legs jerked into motion, sending me racing between two coldbloods with their wings spread wide.

"Leave me!" I heard Navan yelling at me from behind.

His request tore me apart, but I pushed my emotions aside. I darted through the open door, and out in the hallway, running as fast as my shaking legs would carry me. Overhead, the fluorescent lights seemed to flicker in time with the word repeating in my head: *Run. Run. Run.*

I heard the wrenching of metal behind me. A quick glance back revealed a silver door hurtling my way, and I hurriedly ducked—though I didn't miss the door's sharp corner, which grazed my cheek in its thundering path down the hallway.

Laughter echoed after it.

"Don't you know it's only a matter of time?" a shrill voice called, and I turned to see a coldblood approaching from the end of the hall. He was advancing slowly with his muscled arms out, his hands feeling at the air.

Breathe, Riley, I reminded myself. *You're wearing an invisibility suit, which blunts the ability of regular coldbloods to smell you. This coldblood is probably less powerful than the one back there. Just keep quiet and he won't find you.*

I clapped a hand over my mouth to muffle my terrified exhalations. The coldblood was advancing at a rapid pace, swiping his hand across everything in his path. Painstakingly, I tiptoed forward. The door was only ten feet away, but if he heard me and flew ahead...

Crouching, I scanned the ground. I spotted a tiny, rusty nail and closed my fingers gingerly around it. With one rapid flick of my wrist, I chucked it across the floor. Seconds later, the coldblood had slammed into the wall where the nail had landed. Trembling overtook my body at the sight of the wall's now caved-in form. If he had heard me, then *that* would've been me.

The coldblood grunted as he recovered and strode closer to me than before, only a few feet away, and advancing fast. As he moved, his silver-haired head roved like a searchlight, his bulging brown eyes set into a glare over his wide, aquiline nose, while his arms lashed out violently. Heart pounding, I tiptoed ahead as quietly and rapidly as I could.

When I reached the set of double doors, I paused. There was no way around it: once I opened them, the coldblood would know exactly where I was.

Now only a couple of feet away, the coldblood had paused too. His roving head stopped to face right where I was. His mouth spread into a fang-toothed smile. His wings unfurled, and I took off.

Bang! The wall where I'd been a second ago bent.

Bang! The door I had just raced through burst off its hinges.

Outside, the harsh wind swiped across my cheek, and I flattened myself against the wall a few feet away, on the left side of the exit.

The remaining door whined as it swung open, and the cold-blood's head appeared, swiveling slowly, a furious scowl overtaking his features. He lunged forward to the right of the door, the side opposite me, striking his arm out at nothing.

By now, my whole body was one trembling gasp away from being discovered. If I moved, he'd find me. And if I didn't, well... I couldn't hide for long.

I lifted my foot, then froze as the coldblood threw himself in my direction, stopping mere inches away from me. My heart stilled as he paused. He took one sniff, then another, his nostrils flaring.

And then he shook his head, and swore under his breath.

"You guys going to help or what?" he yelled over his shoulder, presumably to those back in the bunker, and a second later, he raced away, back into the building.

I let out a ragged sigh of relief, and wasted no time finding out whether the other coldbloods would take him up on his request. I staggered away from the bunker, my footsteps picking up speed over the hardened Siberian snow. Only once I'd put a few yards between me and the squat stone structure did I stop and take a look around. I swallowed hard.

While the bunker's immediate surroundings had been thankfully deserted, here, closer to the main camp, was a different story. A yard or so ahead, it was bustling with activity: coldbloods and shifters threading in and out of brown tents, as well as loitering and talking to their own kind in groups. This tent village extended both ways as far as the eye could see. If I wanted to get around it, the trip would take hours, maybe even longer. Right now, I needed to head back to the ship and alert the Fed using the ship's comm device. To do that, I had to find the edge of the camp's invisibility shield. That meant navigating my way directly through the camp, around coldbloods and shifters alike.

My decision reluctantly made, I turned back one last time, fists clenched.

I'll come back for you, Navan, and get you out of there. Just like I promised.

My fingers rose instinctively to my lips. They were tingling with the memory of our passionate, doomed kiss. I sucked in another deep breath before continuing. If I got caught standing here like a melodramatic idiot, that was not going to help Navan. I had to make it through the camp, and I had to do it now.

As I neared the camp's border, I practiced taking shallow

breaths and light steps. The snow was thankfully not soft, but the frozen ground was muddier around the camp, which would not be that easy to pass over quietly. I also had to hope that I wouldn't bump into any more highly sensitive individuals like that imposing coldblood back there. If I was heard, smelled, or felt again, there'd be little to no chance of escaping.

A large structure a dozen feet away caught my attention. It was cylindrical, almost like an overgrown metal silo, and it was emitting a low, ominous creaking sound—as if it had something inside it that was turning slowly. My gaze moved to the top of the structure, and I stilled.

Billowing out of the top of the silo-like building, in great big red puffs, was smoke. Deep, red smoke. I'd never seen red smoke before.

That... That can't be from...

I turned away, a wave of nausea overtaking me at the thought.

Humans. That's who the coldbloods and shifters have been stealing. Humans like me.

Even as I hurried on, I couldn't tear my eyes away. I didn't know the science behind how smoke *could* even be red like that, but the sight played on my worst fears... and what else could be going on in there? Where were all the humans they'd been bringing to this place?

The questions both terrified me and motivated me. Getting back and telling the Fed about this camp wasn't just for Navan—it was for all humans, too. If the coldbloods and shifters got their way, we'd be nothing but cattle for their factory farming, with them using our blood to fuel their immortality elixir obsession. I couldn't let that happen.

At the edge of the tent city stood an old picnic table, with relaxed coldbloods crowding around it and playing some kind of board game. Everyone I passed wore the same ice-blue uniform, while no one seemed to be on the lookout for danger. Apparently, word of my escape hadn't reached them yet. The whole camp seemed distracted—some stirred up with talk of Navan's recent capture.

"Jareth's son—really!" one pudgy shifter woman remarked, her long, bony finger scratching at her veiny neck.

"So they'll kill him?" another shifter woman asked, her slit eyes blinking rapidly with excitement.

I hurried on before I could hear their answer, but as I continued weaving my way past tents, I took a deep breath. *That shifter woman is an idiot,* I told myself. I had heard the higher-up coldbloods talking; they wanted to *use* Navan, not kill him.

Consumed with worry nonetheless, I nearly walked into the muscular arm of a broad coldblood, and I scrambled out of the way with seconds to spare. Luckily, he trudged by obliviously, his footfalls thudding on the frozen ground.

A quick look around bolstered my spirits. Although my head was pounding, I was nearly through the camp. Already, the tents were growing sparser, as were the coldbloods and shifters I had to sidestep.

From what I'd come across, if these coldbloods were anything like the ones on Vysanthe, I could see why Navan didn't like them. Maybe I was biased, knowing what they were doing to humans, but the coldbloods I passed seemed arrogant and cruel. Some would shove each other as a way of greeting, others merely to assert their dominance. Shifter and coldblood would exchange a few words when necessary, although both mostly kept to themselves. Evidently, old divisions died hard, even when the two species were working together.

Hearing the sound of running feet behind me, I quickly moved to one side.

"The captured coldblood's human companion has escaped! It may be in the camp now!"

I swore beneath my breath. The speaker was a small, quick-footed shapeshifter, whose thin lips were open wide with what he was yelling: "We can't let it escape!"

As nearby coldbloods threaded out of their tents and around the little shifter, I gulped. Getting out of here wasn't going to be as easy as I'd hoped.

"What do you mean 'escaped'? And how do you know it's still here? You're always running around crying about one thing or another, Haldorf," a female coldblood jeered as I crept by the small group. Other coldbloods, judging by the expressions on their faces, seemed to share her annoyance and skepticism.

"The human has an invisibility suit," Haldorf responded in an equally biting tone. "It is probably headed back to its ship. Right now, it could be anywhere—even here."

As I continued, a coldblood a few feet away commented, "Oh come now, my senses are more powerful than that. If there was any human within a hundred miles of here, you can bet your wee little shifter ass I'd know about it."

I hurried on, stifling a dry chuckle. Now definitely wasn't the time to get complacent; I hadn't made it through yet, though I was at least getting close to the invisibility shield.

I recognized the far-off tent as one of the last things I'd seen before Navan had been snatched. It had all happened so fast that I hadn't even processed our surroundings. But now, here, half a yard away from it, I recognized the structure, an ice-blue tent that towered above the rest. Housed on top was a camera, its head roving in a way reminiscent of the coldblood that had chased me. A metal skeleton frame supported the tent, wires threading in and out of it. The place was probably some sort of surveillance center. I kept my distance from the tent as I continued—who knew what that hulking high-tech camera was capable of seeing.

Step by step, I neared the spot of thin air that I was pretty sure was the shield. My breathing grew more labored the closer I drew. This was it.

I darted forward, and a quick glance back confirmed that the shimmering globe of the invisibility shield was behind me. I launched into a sprint, and didn't stop until I reached Navan's and my broken-down ship.

But as it came within view, I paused. Although its metal exterior looked innocuously intact, the crashing and cackling coming from inside told a different story. Shifters had taken it over.

And with the ship infested, I had no way to contact the Fed. Which meant I had no way to save Navan.

I breathed deeply, trying not to let a looming sense of despair overtake me.

The ship's door slammed open, and two shifters emerged, snickering and chattering between themselves. I backed away before they got too close. I needed someplace safe to think—somewhere I could formulate a new plan of action.

My gaze scanned the horizon and stopped on a rocky-looking hill in the distance. It probably wasn't that much safer than where

I was now, but it was more out of the way, and at this point, I was in no position to be picky. So, with one last, forlorn look at the ship, I trudged forward.

I was panting heavily as I arrived at the hill, weighed down by emotions as much as physical exhaustion, and I discovered with some relief that it contained a rocky cave. It would at least protect me from the wind. I made my way inside and found a flattish rock, where I sat down.

I pressed the button on my wrist, allowing my body to materialize. I didn't know why, but I felt the urge to see my legs and feet. It was strangely reassuring. I opened and closed my hand, which was white with cold. Then, leaning so that my back was resting on the rock wall, I closed my eyes.

Immediately, my mind was flooded with everything that had just happened. My escape, our capture, our kiss... The coldbloods had hurt Navan earlier when they'd found him—was that what they were doing now? With their fury at my escape, would they take out their anger on him?

Exhaling sharply, I got up and started walking from one side of the small cave to the other. Thinking about Navan being in more pain because of me was practically unbearable.

What am I going to do now?

The answer was as murky as the cave I was in. Without question, rescuing Navan was my number one priority, and the easiest way to accomplish that would be with the Fed's help. But the ship had been my only means of contacting them. I could try to take out the shifters... but without my throwing knives, I didn't need to be a Seer to know that wouldn't end too well for me.

But even if I did somehow contact the Fed, then what? I'd tell them about what I'd seen, and trust that their main priority would be rescuing Navan and not just attacking and destroying the base? What were the odds of that?

I stopped pacing, nodding to myself. If I rescued Navan, together we could probably fight our way onto the ship, if it hadn't been seized by the coldbloods by then, and get an urgent message to the Fed via the ship's comm device. But the whole coldblood base was on high alert now—I would need at least one weapon to stand any chance of getting to him.

Sitting back down on the flat rock, I took a deep breath. Really, it didn't matter what the most logical or safest option was; I couldn't just leave Navan in that bunker without trying to rescue him. Now was my best chance. Even if I somehow found an alternative way of reaching the Fed, the coldbloods could have sent Navan somewhere else or badly hurt him. I had to try to reach him myself one more time.

And this time I could try stealing a weapon while I passed through the camp. It might not even be hard—all I'd have to do was stash it in my invisibility suit. That way I could at least defend myself and Navan, when the time came. Plus, I had the advantage of invisibility, and I doubted the coldbloods were expecting me to walk right back into their midst right after escaping. What kind of idiot would do that?

Me, apparently.

I tamped down the feelings of doubt threatening to paralyze me, and rose to my feet. I was desperately low on options, and this was the only course of action my brain could settle on.

I steadied myself against the rock wall, though it didn't help much. My head was throbbing; my belly was rumbling. After all that had happened, I felt like I might throw up, burst into tears, or both. But I didn't have time for that. Not now.

Outside, it was growing dark. The setting, grayish sun was visible on the horizon. By the time I reached the base, it would be night. I hoped that would somehow work to my advantage as I pressed the button on my suit.

As I neared the base, I tried not to think. Instead, I focused on the steps my feet were taking. One after another, then another, then another. As soon as one harried thought would emerge, I would return my focus to my advancing feet.

Right now, I didn't have to figure out exactly how I was going to complete this impossible task—I just had to focus on the next step my foot took.

This time, I didn't pass by our ship. Instead, I headed for a part of the invisibility shield that was safely away from it, out of earshot. Although the shifters hadn't caught me earlier, I didn't want to take any chances.

When I reached what seemed to be the invisibility shield, I paused. Sucking in a deep breath, I steeled my nerves. I held out a hand, and the air shimmered, the huge protective dome appearing.

I'm coming for you, Navan. I conjured up the image of his handsome, smiling face in my mind and focused on it as I took my first step through the shield.

But before I could lay my second step down on the ground, a sharp female voice pierced the cold evening air.

"Who's there?" a female coldblood called, and as I gazed in her direction, I realized she was looking straight at me. She was a terrifyingly burly creature, with thick brown eyebrows and snarling, downturned lips.

"Shifter, you know it is forbidden to camouflage yourself when at the base," she continued when I didn't answer. "Especially now that we have a red alert about an intruder."

I looked left, then right. The whole invisibility shield was bordered by coldbloods standing in wait. If I wanted to get by, I'd have to sneak by this coldblood now.

As quietly as I could, I set my foot down on the ground.

"I mean it, shifter," she snapped, jutting out a mechanical-looking spear. "Take another step and just see if I don't impale you."

I froze. Another desperate look left and right found the situation as impossible as the last time I had looked. If I wanted to get by, I had to make it past coldbloods who were already primed for my possible arrival.

Offering a small mental prayer to the universe, I surged forward. I heard a whizzing sound behind me, and ducked just in time. The spear slammed into the ground ahead of me with an electrical fizzle.

I froze, staring at the spear for a few seconds, expecting the coldblood who had thrown it to immediately come chasing after it to retrieve it. When she didn't, I cast a glance over my shoulder, and saw her distracted with throwing another spear in a different direction.

It seemed like one of my prayers, at least, had been answered. I now had a weapon. I had no idea how to use it, or if it was even safe for a human to wield, but... I glanced from the now-blocked invisibility shield to the direction of the coldblood guards, then crouched down and gingerly poked at the spear.

As soon as my finger touched its metal surface, I realized that was a mistake. A shock of electricity passed through me, and I cursed, realizing my whole body was suddenly visible. In a panic, I jammed the button of the invisibility suit, but it only made a light hissing noise. The spear had messed up the suit.

Keeping down low against the ground, I prayed the coldblood guards were still distracted. My eyes frantically returned to the damned weapon, and I knew I had to make a last-minute change of plan.

I poked at the electrical spear again, and when no electrical surge passed through me this time, I grabbed it, and immediately crawled as fast as I could back through the invisibility shield. I had to get away from those coldbloods now that I no longer had an invisibility suit to protect me.

I'd have to try to board the ship again—facing the shifters instead. At least I had a weapon now... though I was without my invisibility suit, so I wasn't sure if those two advantages canceled each other out.

Whatever the case, I stood a better chance against a handful of shifters than a camp of coldbloods *and* shifters.

As I neared the ship, its smooth surface looked almost eerie in the fading light, but all was silent. Maybe the shifters had torn through it to their satisfaction and left. Hopefully they hadn't wrecked the comm technology in the process. That would be a blow I wouldn't survive.

I shuddered, a chill running down my spine at the thought.

There was only one way to find out.

I peered through the door, cautiously turning my head left, then right. To my relief and surprise, everything inside looked untouched. Navan's bag was missing, along with the weapons we'd had inside the belly of the ship, but there was no sign of the shifters.

And the control panel was right in front of me. All I had to do was flick that green switch, and I could transmit a message to the Fed.

Excitement welled in me as my hand descended for the switch, but when my fingers were a split second from touching it, something slammed into my head.

Ear-splitting cries filled my ears as four shifters materialized within the small chamber. They leapt out from the walls, un-camouflaging themselves as they flung their bodies toward me.

I staggered backward and out of the ship, a scream stuck in my throat, my body half numb from the shock as I tried to fight them off with my spear.

I had no choice but to retreat, as they all launched at me at once. I ran away from them, from the ship, toward the direction of the village—and the opposite direction from the coldblood base. As I raced, my legs pumping faster than I'd ever thought them capable of going, a pain bit into my shoulder. One of the bastards had landed on me, was digging its nails into my back.

I skewered the hideous, pale-skinned creature, stabbing the spear into its flesh and harpooning it into the snow. And then the next that came launching for me, and the next. I found myself descending into a panicked, slashing frenzy, until they all lay bleeding on the ground... and then I noticed three more shifters popping their ugly heads out of the back of the ship.

Oh, for God's sake.

I had to run. I didn't have time to withdraw my spear from the last shifter I had harpooned—that would be allowing too short a distance between myself and the shifters now darting toward me.

I pounded ahead, and, thanks to my head start, managed to put a safe distance between myself and the shifters that had followed me; they were considerably smaller than me, after all. But, as far off as they were, I could still see their little bodies running for mine.

So I kept sprinting, slamming my feet into the ground with all the strength I had left. Where I was headed didn't matter, so long as it was away from the ship and the harrowing cries emitting from it. I sprinted over rock, snow, and ice, not slowing until the ship was a speck on the horizon behind me. Only then did I stop, shooting the tiny thing a forlorn look. It was my last point of reference. Without it, I had next to no idea where I was. But right now, I had no other choice. I'd have to make my way to the nearby village on foot.

At the mere thought of more walking, my legs collapsed under me. The adrenaline was finally leaving me, and as I sat, my butt aching from the cold, hard ground, I gazed drearily into the wilderness ahead. Last time I had wandered off by myself in search of something, it hadn't gone well. But now I didn't have any other choice.

2

It took nearly all my strength to clamber back onto my feet. I took a deep breath, then set my gaze in the direction of the town, or at least where I thought it was.

As soon as I started walking, my head throbbed with an ache that spread to my whole body. What was a full-body ache called— a way-too-tired-because-I've-been-attacked-by-just-about-every-thing-ache?

"Shut up, Riley," I muttered to myself.

When I got crazy-tired, I tended to get crazy-hysterical too. I tried to think of what Angie or Lauren would say to soothe me. But, as my legs stumbled ahead, I came up with a big fat nothing. Usually, I was the one comforting them.

No, all I could think about was the same useless, repeating word as before: *run, run, run.*

I kept my gaze on my feet to ensure that I didn't fall. Under my boots, the snowy ground swirled. A glance across the landscape revealed that the air all around me was swirling with snow.

I groaned. A snowstorm. Just what I needed right now. Every step I took was beginning to feel heavier than the last, while my eyes seemed to be blinking slower and slower...

I barely registered my body collapsing onto the ground. When I struggled to open my eyes, all I saw was white. They fluttered closed, and a warm, comforting blackness swallowed me.

PINGGGGG.

My eyes snapped open. My hands went to my ears as I wrenched around. Blinding fluorescent light. Flat gray stone walls.

Where was I?

I leapt up, the blood rushing from my head as I raced to the door—which was also made of stone. I yanked uselessly at the handle a few times, trying to get a grip on the momentary dizziness that came from standing up too quickly.

"Back away from the door," a husky voice boomed from the ceiling.

I looked up, my eyes coming into focus. The entire ceiling seemed to be one big speaker, its black surface dotted with tiny holes. My gaze swept around the room, my heart pounding as I realized that I recognized this place. A Fed interrogation room.

There was a beep, and then the door slammed into me as it opened. I tumbled to the floor, and someone chuckled. With their boot, they pushed me away.

"You were told to back away from the door," a cold voice said.

I craned my neck to see a gnarly, clawed hand dipping for me. I jerked away instinctively, but it managed to grab me.

"Don't try to escape. It won't work," the masked lycan said.

He lifted me up and placed me on a stone chair as easily as if I were a feather, then lowered himself onto the chair across from me. Folding his hands on the table, he addressed me.

"So, human, tell me the truth. Tell me what you and your cold-blood master have done."

I gaped at him. It was hard to focus when I was face-to-face with the sight of my own distended, terrified face in the steel of his mask.

"I-I don't know what you mean."

His fist slammed on the stone table so hard it sent a crack snaking through the top. "Lies," he hissed.

The door opened behind him.

"What is the meaning of this?"

The new speaker was a lycan I recognized—he was the same head of interrogation with whom Navan and I had spoken days ago. Right now, however, he was baring his wolfish teeth in rage at the lycan sitting across from me.

"Commander Sylvan, sir, I apologize," the masked lycan said. "You were in a meeting. I thought I could interrogate her before-hand. See what else we could get out of her."

Sylvan strode forward, grabbing the stone chair he was sitting in and pulling it to the door. It scraped loudly on the floor as it moved.

"You thought wrong," Sylvan growled, gesturing out the door.

The masked lycan rose and advanced so that he and Sylvan were nose-to-nose.

"Are you going to believe anything that human slave will say? After what we've found?"

Sylvan turned his back on the other lycan.

"What I do is no business of yours. Farl, you have a compromised interest in this case and are therefore not permitted to speak to the human. I am the head interrogator, and you will listen to me, or face the consequences."

"Commander, with all due respect, I won't just take this sitting down."

"You're right," Sylvan snarled, storming forward and shoving Farl out the door. "You'll take this standing up."

He pressed a button on his suit, and the stone door slid closed. He turned to face me.

"I would apologize, but we haven't yet established exactly what it is you're guilty of."

As he went to sit down, I sputtered, "I don't know what... I just got—"

He dismissed me with a wave of his hairy hand. "I haven't asked you a question yet."

I shut my mouth, directing my glare to the door over his shoulder.

He clasped his fingers together, his long claws coming to rest on the backs of his hands. He directed a piercing look at me.

"Tell me how you came to be here."

Now that I finally had the chance to tell my side of things, I paused. Doubts from before crept into my head. What if telling him the scope of the rebel coldblood camp made him focus on attacking it, instead of saving Navan?

"Today, human," Sylvan barked.

One glance at his intelligent coral eyes made up my mind for me. Lying or leaving things out now was too dangerous to risk it. I'd finally gotten what I'd desperately wanted, back there in the snow—contact with the Fed.

So I told him everything. From flying in the Fed-equipped ship, to picking up the sneaky shifter, to discovering the coldblood camp. At the last, Sylvan's deep-set eyes bugged out.

"You say there were *how* many of these rebel coldbloods and shifters?"

"I don't know," I replied honestly. "The shifter had said there were a few hundred shifters there when Navan asked him, but I don't know if he was telling the truth. Combined with the coldbloods, to me it looked like a few thousand... maybe even more."

He bowed his head, as if considering what I'd said, then shook it fiercely.

"No, no," he said. "Impossible. A camp of that scope passing under our notice? Impossible! When we sent you on that mission, our intel indicated the base likely numbered from a few individuals to fifty, tops."

"They had an invisibility shield," I reminded him.

But now his thin lips were set in a firm line.

"Impossible, human. For something like that to slip by our notice, that would mean one of our own was betraying us, changing the data in certain reports. What you're suggesting is a traitor inside our very own ranks." His voice lowered. "It's out of the question."

"I know what I saw," I replied in a steady voice, not lowering my gaze.

Sylvan paused, scratching at one of his ash-brown sideburns, and I could have sworn there was a flicker of genuine worry in his eyes. "And what is your story for how you came to be a mile or so away from this camp, practically frozen to death?"

"How did you pick me up, anyway?" I countered, wanting answers to some of my own questions first.

I noticed suddenly that I was wearing a plain black robe. My broken suit had been taken from me, although I supposed it wasn't all that surprising, given that the suit was theirs in the first place. Maybe that suit had helped them find me, somehow, even though it was dysfunctional. They'd said it was expensive, so I guessed it was possible they had installed some tracking tech inside it for security.

"Answer the question, human," he said coolly.

"I tried to rescue my... friend, Navan. The coldblood who was sent with me on the mission," I said. "The rebels captured him, and even with my invisibility suit, I couldn't do anything. I couldn't save him."

My voice hitched at the last part. The guilt over what had happened washed over me, making my gut churn. I'd gotten out. Navan hadn't, in spite of what I'd promised him.

"And then?" Sylvan prodded.

"I was going to call for your help on the ship, but it was infested with shifters. They attacked me, and I barely escaped. I was exhausted with nowhere to go, so I tried to make it to the nearest village, but I collapsed on the way. The last thing I remember is losing consciousness, before waking up to... this."

Sylvan's vibrant eyes narrowed as I spoke, his mind seemingly scanning and dissecting every word I said.

"And that is all?" he said after a minute.

"That's everything I know."

"I see," he said, rising from his chair.

"So what are you going to do?" I asked.

He paused, his bushy brows rising. "That remains to be seen."

"Can I at least contact my friends?" In particular, I needed to speak to Bashrik. When he didn't respond, I added, "It's not like I can tell them where I am—I have no idea."

At this, a smile played on his angular features. "True. You do not."

He strode out without another word.

I watched the door close behind him with a sinking heart.

How long was I going to be kept in here? What if they didn't believe me? And what would they do with the information I'd given them? Navan was still out there, and based on the vibe I'd gotten from Sylvan, the likelihood of a rescue mission seemed slim. Why would they care to rescue Navan, anyway? That would be a tricky, risky, and time-consuming endeavor. If they were going to act based on what I'd told them, I feared they'd just move in to attack the entire base, and who knew what would happen to Navan then.

I had to find another way to infiltrate the rebel base, but to do that, this time I desperately needed backup. Angie and Lauren's cellphones wouldn't be working out in the country, and I hadn't the faintest clue how Bashrik's comm device worked, but I did have one other way to contact them.

A few minutes later, the door opened to reveal a different lycan. This one was thinner and bonier than Sylvan, while his eyes were a lime green.

"I've been sent in with this," his husky-yet-melodious voice said. He lifted a device that looked like a phone.

"Is that..."

He nodded solemnly. "An iPhone X."

As I gaped at him, he swiped a gray curl off his face.

"What?" he asked drily.

"Just... I don't know," I said. "I figured that you lycans would have different technology, something more advanced."

"This is the newest model available, I'll have you know," he said huffily. "Human technology will suffice for your needs. You do know how to use one of these, don't you?"

"It's fine," I said, reaching for the sleek black phone. Once my fingers closed around it, however, he didn't release his vice-like grip. His lime eyes found mine.

"I'm supposed to inform you that you're to indicate that you are safe, but nothing more. Nothing about the Fed—no funny business. I will be here to ensure that."

I was waiting for the "or else" part of his statement, but he seemed content that his warning would be enough.

"Okay," I promised. "Nothing about the Fed."

I didn't mention that I was going to try to see if I could swing a visit with them... and ask permission from the Fed later. Something told me that admitting that in advance would not go over well.

He released the phone, but seconds later, his hand had grasped mine. He took a long sniff, and then his nose crinkled.

"Hm," he said, releasing me.

"Uh, can I call now?" I asked.

"What is your name?" he asked.

"Riley."

He took another sniff, and then, before I could respond, said, "And they say you and your coldblood comrade discovered a base of thousands of coldbloods and shifters, who've been living in Siberia right under our noses?"

"Yes. Although your friend doesn't seem to believe me."

Another closed-eyed sniff.

"Interesting," he muttered to himself, then directed a wry smile my way. "Not all of us lycans are 'friends', by the way. We are duty-bound to each other and to our cause, yes, but nothing more." He stepped back and gestured at me with his arm. "Now you may call. You have ten minutes."

It felt odd dialing the Churnleys' landline number in such weird circumstances. I hoped I remembered the right digits, even though I'd memorized them before leaving home. Part of me was afraid that no one would pick up at all, especially since the old machine ran on solar power or something, and I'd never heard it ring once while I was there. What time was it back in Texas, anyway?

On the eighth ring, just as I'd started to lose hope, Mrs. Churnley's cautious voice came through the line. "Hello?"

A strangled cry came out of my lips. I hadn't realized just how much I missed human contact up until now.

"Who is this? Whatever you're selling, we're not buying," she snapped.

"Wait, Mrs. Churnley—it's Riley!" I said. "Sorry. Could you put Angie or Lauren on the line?"

"Oh, Riley, dear! So nice to hear from you." Mrs. Churnley's tone warmed instantly. "I hope that new boyfriend of yours is treating you right."

My chest ached at the thought of Navan being tortured and beaten, trapped inside the rebel camp. "He always puts me first," I said, then, with a glance at my lycan companion, added hurriedly, "I really need to speak to my friends."

"All right, dear. I think Angie's upstairs."

Each moment that passed felt like an eternity. My ten minutes were ticking away.

A gasp erupted on the other end of the line, then came a shaky voice: "Riley, is that really you?"

"Angie! Oh man, does it feel good to hear your voice!" I said, sighing with relief and leaning back in my chair. The lycan looked less than impressed and was tapping his finger on his wrist. I kept talking. "So much has happened, but I don't have much time. I just wanted you to know that I'm okay, but... Navan's not."

A stony voice called out in the background. "What is she saying, Angie? Why didn't they call with Navan's comm?"

The pit in my stomach grew three sizes.

"Put my brother on the line," Bashrik said, his voice now a dismal croak. I wasn't even sure what he was doing hanging around at the Churnleys'—I'd expected one of my friends to have to rush and fetch him.

"Bashrik, I—" I said.

"He's dead, isn't he!" he burst out.

"No, I—"

"I told him not to go. I told him it was a suicide mission," he continued. "I should've gone there myself to stop him!"

"BASHRIK, HE'S BEEN CAPTURED BY REBEL COLD-BLOODS!" I cut in. "But he's alive." *For now*, I mentally added.

There was a long pause, in which my heart slowly broke. "Oh," a small voice finally spoke from the other end of the line, and I could hardly recognize it as Bashrik's. "Wh-What happened? H-How did you get out? How... How could you leave him?"

The last question broke me completely. "I-I tried my best to save him, Bashrik," I said quietly, my chest aching, tears rising to my eyes, "but there were too many coldbloods and shifters. They've been keeping a hidden base."

"What? There were coldbloods and shifters working together? H-How many?"

I put my elbows on the table, and my head in my hands. This was playing out just as horribly as my conversation with Commander Sylvan had.

I swallowed hard. "Bashrik, I'm sorry. I'm so, so sorry. But I don't have time to go into those details now. Can you please just—"

"No," he cut in, the strength suddenly returning to his voice, though it was still hoarse—and I could tell that his shock was giving way to panic. "I'm coming over there myself! And this time I won't take no for an answer! Where are you?"

I breathed out and glanced at the lycan, who was shaking his head.

"I don't know," I said truthfully.

"How can you not know? No matter. Wherever you are, I'm coming there! Both Ronad and I have healed decently enough. Ronad knows the ins and outs of coldblood technology—and our devices' tracking capabilities are far superior to anything you can imagine on Earth."

I cast a nervous glance to the lycan, whose teeth were bared.

"No, no need," I said, trying to keep the fear out of my voice. "I can meet you near where they captured Navan. The coldblood base is in remote Siberia, but we could meet at the nearest village."

Silence.

"Bashrik?"

"I'm listening," he said.

"If you're really determined to save Navan, then all of us can meet there."

I determinedly kept my gaze off the lycan, who, out of the corner of my eye, I could see was shaking his head back and forth in a furious "no".

"Hm..." Bashrik said.

"The name of the village is Borscht," I said quickly.

As I hung up, I could hear Bashrik's voice go frantic. "I meant what I said about tracking—"

The lycan snatched the phone out of my hand. "That wasn't—in any way, shape or form—what we discussed."

"Sorry," I said. "But you heard him—he was going to track the call anyway. The coldbloods do have really advanced technology."

The lycan grimaced, then handed the phone back to me. "Whatever the case, you'll have to call your friends back and tell them that unfortunately you made a mistake and you won't be meeting them at all."

I shook my head. "If I don't meet them in Siberia, they're going to track the call and find me anyway. Do you really want to gamble with those odds?"

The lycan's face spread into a series of stoic lines. "Killing some interfering coldbloods won't be the worst thing I've done."

I snatched the phone back. "Oh yeah? What about innocent humans? Because my friends haven't done anything to hurt anybody."

His face remained unmoved. "Any human who works with a coldblood can't be innocent," he maintained with a decided shake of his head.

"Then why didn't you rip the phone away and tell Bashrik to go to hell?"

The lycan didn't respond, only frowned deeper.

"Because you know I'm right," I said, realizing it as soon as I said it.

At that, his green eyes flashed, and he grabbed the phone again. "Regardless of what I know, the idea of you going to Siberia to meet your friends is, well, impossible," he said. "You're a prisoner under suspicion, not a tourist free to come and go. It's out of the question."

"Maybe the commander wouldn't authorize it," I agreed.

The lycan frowned. "What are you saying?"

Truth be told, I wasn't sure why I'd responded that way. I guessed I was just trying anything at this point to get a positive response out of the odd lycan, and my reverse psychology seemed to have given him pause.

"I don't know," I said. "But at least... please just think about it overnight. I'd be extremely grateful if you could convince your higher-ups to let me have this meeting with my friends."

At this, he looked at me curiously. "All right," he said finally, with a slow nod of his head. "I'll take you to your room then."

"I have a room?" I asked, surprised.

Rising, he chuckled. "We may be harsh here, and you may be

our prisoner, but that doesn't mean we wouldn't provide you with the basic necessities of life."

"Thank you," I said uncertainly, standing.

"Oh, don't thank me," he said, with a dismissive wave of his hand. "I'm only following orders." He cast a dark look at the iPhone before tucking it into a pocket. "For the most part."

My room was pretty much as described: basic. It was somewhat cell-like, with a stone door, floor, and ceiling, stone walls, and a toilet and bed made out of—you guessed it—smooth gray stone.

"I will come to you tomorrow with my answer," the lycan said, lingering at the door. "Until then, sleep well, human."

It was only once he'd closed the door behind him that I realized I'd never found out his name.

The door was shut firmly, as expected, while the bed was just as uncomfortable as it looked. The sad scrap of a rag for a blanket seemed like a cruel joke. Nonetheless, I settled onto it, and, despite it being about as comfortable as a coffin, exhaustion claimed me, and my eyes dropped closed.

3

I woke up to a scraping sound, but before I could open my eyes, something covered them. Striking out my arms only resulted in them being grabbed. My cries were muffled by a cloth gag. As I thrashed, I was lifted into what felt like a cloth bag and dropped in, and I hit the floor with a smack. My body smarted with pain as the cloth bag was dragged across the floor. Tears came to my eyes. After all I'd been through, now I had to be kidnapped *again* and taken to who-knew-where?

Worse still, whoever had taken me, judging by how they'd thrown me to the floor, didn't much care if I was hurt.

I was carried out of my room and down steps—to where, I had no idea—and then I was put down, shoved onto what felt like a wooden chair. My blindfold was ripped off, and when I saw who I was facing, my blood ran cold.

"So, human, let's try this again," said the same harsh, masked lycan I had originally woken up to, and whom Sylvan had driven out—Farl. "Sylvan can't save you this time. He and some other fools left to look into your lying claims. No, there will be no getting out of this. Tell me what you and your coldblood master have done and I'll consider sparing you."

I gaped at him, as panic rushed through my body. There was a deadly edge to Farl's words, and I didn't doubt for a second that he'd hurt me if it came to it. But still, what did he want from me? Did he know about the Fed agent Navan had killed?

"N-Nothing," I stammered, "I was telling the truth."

There was a long, measured silence. Farl stepped back and began pacing in a circle around the table at which I was seated. His impassive eyes darted from his companions, who also wore black clothes, to the room's only door. We appeared to be in the basement, as the floor here was dirt. The walls were stone, although lined with something much more ominous—long, curved pikes, metallic-looking spears, a spike-covered bed leaned vertically against the wall...

Farl sat down on a wooden chair, turning to me with a terrifying fanged smile.

"Let me tell you a story, human." His mouth became a sneer. "I had a brother—once. Lyon. He was a good lycan, a loyal agent, a compassionate brother. He was just and brave. He performed his job flawlessly. One day, he didn't report to headquarters. He was last seen in Alaska. Days passed, weeks..." Farl's coral eyes flicked to me. "I bet you already know how this story ends."

I took a deep breath, praying that Farl couldn't see the truth in my eyes, as I was already guessing how this story might end. A shiver of fear danced across my skin.

"They sent a few lycans over to investigate, and my brother's body was found," he continued in a low voice. "His bloodied corpse was discovered in the middle of the snowy tundra—frozen, a bullet in his brain, his mouth twisted open wide. He died yelling, you know."

Now Farl's coral eyes had gone lighter, filmed with tears. "They promised to investigate," he continued, "But you know how it is. We aren't exactly booming with agents here on Earth at the moment—we have to make do with what we have. That was why they assigned you and your coldblood master to that coldblood base investigation in the first place. We just don't have the manpower for it. So, the investigation was juggled from one date to the next, until it was put off indefinitely. That was when I decided to go there myself, see what I could find."

Farl smiled bitterly. I felt at once sorry and scared. There was a pitiable, yet dangerous, fire in his eyes.

"You know what I found?"

He slammed his fist down on the table, an inch from my hand, sending it flying up. Out of the corner of my eye I took note of my surroundings—we were encircled by the other masked lycans, all of whom were armed. There was no way out. Whatever Farl was going to do to me, there would be no escaping it.

But he wouldn't actually... kill me—not when he wanted information out of me—right?

I took a deep breath. "No," I said, trying to keep my voice steady.

Farl's eyebrows contorted in rage. He snatched up my hand and squeezed with his powerful fingers. Pain ratcheted through my arm.

"N-No—stop!" I cried.

He dropped my hand onto the table.

"I found a bunker. I kept an eye on it for a few weeks, and, what do you know, I saw its owner come back."

Now Farl was leaning in uncomfortably close, his rank breath wafting into my face. My hand was still throbbing, and now my head had started to throb, too. My eyes darted about the room again, desperately seeking a way to escape, a way I might have missed before.

"I saw him," he hissed. "And I saw you."

Farl leapt up and grabbed the metallic spear off the wall. It glinted dully in the light. On the wall were other weapons, but they were too far away for me to grab one to defend myself. The other masked lycans would get me before that. It was too late now. Farl had returned and was pressing the sharp tip of the metallic spear into my lower arm.

"Deny it again, I dare you."

The spear's tip crackled with electricity, burning hot, horrible pain into me. Dammit—I couldn't die here. Navan still needed me.

He twisted the spear, and my whole lower arm went numb with pain. What would it feel like if he actually... No, I couldn't think about that. I wasn't going to let Farl win this game. I shook my head, set my jaw. Yes, Navan had killed Farl's brother, but it had been an act of self-defense. I had a feeling that Farl wouldn't buy that reasoning, but I refused to implicate Navan, no matter what this psycho wolfman did.

Farl leaned in even closer, his eyes boring into mine. His voice was now deadly quiet. "You'd be dead now, you know, if I hadn't lost track of you, that night in Alaska. I followed you to the nearby village, waiting to catch you all in a moment when your two coldblood companions had their guards down. But it seemed someone else was following you, too—on an unrelated mission. After the gunshots exploded, you took off, and I lost the chance of finding you. Still, I held out hope we'd meet again, and this time, I'd get the Fed itself to serve you justice... but instead they set you free on a mission. A mission during which you betrayed them again. Now, tell me what you did to my brother—I want to hear you say it yourself."

I said nothing.

"Admit it!" he roared, jabbing the tip in deeper, sending explosions of pain all over my arm. "Admit that you and your master killed him."

"I'm sorry!" I cried out. "This is all a misunderstanding. Navan—"

"What is the meaning of this?"

Hearing the familiar voice, I practically fainted with relief. It was the green-eyed lycan from before. He'd come to find me early.

"A mere questioning session, Galo," Farl replied coolly. He lifted the metal spear off my arm, where it had left an angry purple bruise.

"In the torture chamber? In the middle of the night?" Galo asked in a voice laced with skepticism.

"There were doubts as to her story's veracity," Farl replied.

"And yet you weren't questioning her story about the cold-blood base," Galo stated.

Farl sprang up, spear still in hand.

"Her coldblood companion lied to us. He killed my brother—I saw him less than a hundred yards from the scene of the crime myself!"

Galo strode forward and took my hand. "Then you should be speaking to him. This one is a human—a mere girl at that."

Farl grabbed my other hand, although he kept his furious gaze locked on Galo.

"Humans can be swayed to commit crimes as heinous as any coldblood. We both know that."

"That may be so, but right now you are defying a direct order from our authority, Commander Sylvan, not to interfere with the investigation," Galo said in a forceful voice. "Stand down or face the consequences."

Farl didn't move.

"Careful," Galo warned.

Farl spat on the ground, then let go of my hand.

As Galo led my trembling self over to the door, Farl called after him: "This isn't the end of this."

Galo paused to toss him a dark smile. "Oh, I don't doubt it." His gaze swept around the room, to the other motionless, masked lycans, whom I'd almost forgotten were there. "You all ought to be ashamed of yourselves. Farl mourned his brother. What's your excuse?"

"We're ready for a new legislature, one that's harder on coldbloods and their ilk," Farl answered for them, practically spitting.

"Thankfully, Farl, you are in the minority. This will be reported to Commander Sylvan, as I'm sure you know good and well. Farewell."

Just before the door closed, Farl hissed, "Damned veritas."

I had no idea what he meant by that, but as we walked along the corridor, I was too grateful to still be alive to think about it. I kept having to inhale and exhale deeply—it felt surreal, walking freely down the same place I'd been dragged through.

Galo patted my back almost gingerly, and I noticed only then that he had on a big backpack made of a thick black nylon-like material.

"Well, hello again. And I apologize for my... Hm, 'comrades' is too generous a word," he said. "Some Fed agents aren't worthy of the name. Certain lycans can be extremely territorial and vengeful, regardless of the vows they take when they join the Fed."

All I could do was nod as we continued. My nerves were still on edge, half of me expecting Farl to come charging back for me. I'd feel safer once we'd put more distance between ourselves and that room.

"Anyway, all that did was further prove that you can't stay here. With the commander gone, it's not safe. I stole some invisibility suits, and now I'm taking you to your friends. We'll rescue Navan together," the lycan said.

I stalled and stared at him, stunned. "Wh-What?" I asked, hardly daring to believe my ears.

He sniffed, and then said simply, "I've decided it's the right thing to do. Not to mention that Navan would make a valuable ally in the fight against these rebel coldbloods."

"Wha... Okay," was all I could respond with. I had been hoping he'd help me out, but what I hadn't been expecting was for him to shoulder the responsibility *himself*. I was hardly going to interrogate him now, though. "Thanks," I breathed.

"Come along, we've no time to waste."

We continued up a stone staircase, until we emerged in a huge chamber of floor-to-ceiling white marble rippled with green. I paused to take in our impressive surroundings. The room was filled with ships that resembled the one Navan and I had used: small, compact, and made of what looked to be chrome.

"Hurry—if we take too long, they won't let us leave at all," Galo said.

Truth be told, I wasn't sure that this odd lycan would even be able to fly a ship. Farl had called him a "veritas", whatever that was. He was clearly different from the other lycans, with his thin, gangly frame, and he was visibly getting on in years.

"Are you sure this is a good idea?" I asked tentatively. As much as I was glad for his help, a part of me still felt this was too good to be true, and I wanted to be sure of our safety.

"Not now," Galo said, his bushy brow furrowed. "I need to concentrate. We're stealing a ship." He said it matter-of-factly, the same way you'd say, "I brushed my teeth last night."

He strode up to one ship, put his hand on it, then shook his head. "No, no..." he muttered. At the next ship, his face lit up. "Aha!"

He turned to me with a toothy grin. "To answer your question about whether this is a good idea, my answer would be 'probably not.' However, the result of us being caught and us doing nothing at all are about the same—you won't be able to see your friends."

He gave the ship he'd chosen two taps, and the door slid open, revealing a compact interior. We climbed in, and once we were both seated in the cushy seats and the steel door had shut behind us, I realized the obvious problem: getting the ship out of this room. There was no visible way of flying the ship out of here—the room was made up of four marble walls, as well as a marble floor and ceiling. Unless Galo planned on somehow squeezing the ship through a doorway, I wasn't sure how we were going to lift off.

"So, uh," I began.

"Don't worry," Galo said absently. "Just watch."

With that, he pressed a small, round blue button. Seconds later, the ship was disappearing under his hands.

"Drat!" he cursed, jamming the button again, bringing the ship out of invisibility.

Next, he hit a triangular green button. Both of us held our breath for a second, until the ceiling shuddered and a hole in the roof opened up.

"Ah, yes," Galo said, his yellow teeth spread in a victorious smile. "Knew it." Seeing my dubious look, he admitted, "It's been a while. Anyway, now for up..."

He pushed a curved red lever, and next thing I knew, we were blasting upward. A countless number of levels flashed by, all at a speed too fast to really make out anything, and I only let out a breath when we broke into the sky.

Now we were hovering over a big octagonal stone pyramid, where we had presumably just been. I gazed around at the surrounding area, taking in the snow-and-pine-tree-covered mountain it was housed on with interest.

"So... this must be a pretty remote location, for the Fed to be able to escape human notice," I said, casting a sidelong gaze at Galo.

"Yes, yes indeed," Galo said impatiently. "Now, where was it you said we were going?"

I exhaled. It looked like I wasn't going to get details of the Fed's

location out of the wily old lycan. But that wasn't exactly important now anyway. We had to concentrate on getting to my friends.

"Um, so I told them to meet me in Borscht," I said. "At least, I
think that was the name of the place." I closed my eyes and tried to
remember the jumble of letters on the town sign, but only came
up with an image of Navan's smile as he danced with me under the
stars and held me close in the cold.

"Borscht is a Russian stew," Galo said after a pause, sounding
less than impressed.

"Well, it was something like that," I retorted. "Can't you look up
similar names on your iPhone or superior Fed technology?"

"Never mind," he replied, "I've just found it. *Borscha* is what
you're looking for. I've set the coordinates into the ship's location
database. Now, I'd rest up if I were you."

I hoped that Bashrik hadn't been overconfident about Ronad's
tracking abilities, and that they'd find the right village.

I turned to Galo. "So, this whole illegal escape thing," I said
tentatively. "I'm guessing this pretty much rules out any help from
the Fed?"

Galo snorted, turning his gray curled head my way. "What do
you think?"

I sighed. Truthfully, I'd pretty much counted on the Fed's help.
But at least I had Galo and his ship. And besides, it wasn't like
staying at the Fed's HQ would have been a better option,
surrounded by hostile lycans. I'd had too many close calls already
—there was no guarantee I'd last another day there.

I gave Galo a grateful smile. "Thank you. You know, you didn't
have to do all this, and honestly I wasn't expecting it."

"I know I didn't," he said with a dismissive wave of his hand.

After a pause, he turned to face me. "Truth is... I once had a grand-daughter like you. Not so long ago. Anyway, she's not here anymore, but you remind me of her in some ways. And also, as I said before, it was the right thing to do." His thoughtful gaze far off, he shot me a rueful smile. "So don't let it go to your head or anything. You should really get some sleep."

I nodded, feeling a strange mash of emotions surge through me. But I was just too tired to voice what I was feeling, or express my full gratitude to Galo—I could hardly make sense of what I felt myself. After everything I'd been through, as soon as I closed my eyes, it wasn't all that hard to take Galo's advice.

"It's been fourteen hours, and I've been waiting four." A male voice entered my consciousness from somewhere above me. Firm hands gripped my shoulders and shook me.

Groaning, I opened my eyes to see Galo frowning at me from his seat in the ship. I stretched, then sat up. Immediately, a wave of memories from the past few days washed over me.

In particular, something I had stupidly forgotten to do.

"My friends!" I said, slapping my hand to my forehead. "I never told them we were coming. Bashrik could be at the Fed Headquarters right now!"

"There, there," Galo said, with a little wave of his hand. "We'll be meeting them at a tavern in about forty-five minutes."

"What? How'd you get in contact with them?" I paused. "Does it have to do with you being a ver... What was it that Farl called you?"

"I am hungry," Galo said with a peevish wag of his head, "but I suppose I can at least sate your curiosity. No, me contacting your friends has nothing to do with me being a veritas. It means I am a 'truth-smeller.' There's about one of us born for every thousand lycans, so we're quite rare. We could be compared to your human seers, although as I said, our truth ability comes from our sense of smell. In any case, that's why I believed you... if you were wondering. Because I knew you were telling the truth. Not due to your oratory prowess."

"Oh... I see," I said, the pieces falling into place. "So that's what all that sniffing was about."

He nodded wryly.

I smiled, shaking my head. Well, it seemed that I'd just encountered yet another mystical creature that transformed my entire perception of how the world was supposed to work.

"I have parked the ship a mile or so away from town and cloaked it with an invisibility layer," he said, changing the subject. "So now we can go eat and meet your friends."

"So wait, how did you get in contact with them then?" I asked Galo as we exited the now-invisible ship. If they were at a tavern, I guessed it would be the same one Navan and I had visited on our first night in Siberia. My heart fell just as it did a flip. I felt a renewed pang of guilt in thinking of him, but soon I'd be reunited with our friends—and hopefully... our rescue team.

"Your coldblood friend Bashrik has a comm device that I figured out how to connect with," Galo said. "I messaged them, pretending to be you."

I frowned. "Can I see what you said?"

He handed me his own comm device, and when I looked at

what he had typed, I couldn't help but smile. Ten hours ago, he'd written: "Borscha is where we'll meet."

Then, an hour or so ago, he'd written: "Greetings and salutations dearest friends. This is Riley. I will meet you at the tavern and I am greatly anticipating this most joyous reunion."

"You have no idea how young human women speak, do you?" I said.

Galo sniffed. "I'd say I did a pretty good job."

I decided not to correct him. Despite being a lycan, Galo was proving to be a pretty good ally—someone from the Fed I could finally trust. I hoped my friends would, too, because we'd need his help if we wanted any chance of saving Navan.

4

*T*he trip into town took a good half hour. I tried getting Galo to move faster, but he was determined to keep his consistently moderate pace.

"If we rush ourselves and it's a trap, we'll have no energy to flee," he said with a determined nod of his head.

I rolled my eyes. "What kind of trap could it be? Bashrik holding us hostage to find out where his brother is, the same brother he needs our help to rescue?"

Galo shrugged. "Has it never occurred to you that those cold-bloods could have tortured information out of Navan, namely concerning your friends, their appearances and whereabouts?"

I shivered. "No," I said decidedly. "Navan would rather die than endanger his brother and friends."

"I certainly hope so," Galo said.

His words filled me with a cold sense of longing, and we walked the rest of the way in silence. Galo's gloomy statement had ruined my mood. Even as I was opening the wooden tavern door, I was bracing myself for what was to come.

"RILEY!" Lauren and Angie cried.

I only had a few seconds to register their relieved, overjoyed faces, before they were throwing themselves onto me in a hug.

"You're okay! What happened?" Angie said.

"I've been so worried. I haven't slept more than two hours," Lauren gasped. I could see the dark circles behind her purple glasses that proved her words.

"And what was with that text?" Angie asked. "We figured you'd been captured or something. Bashrik was prepared for an ambush."

"Oh, that." I grinned. "That was Galo. Anyway, I'll get you guys up to speed soon enough." Their gazes went over my shoulder to Galo, who had wisely chosen to wear a hood that mostly obscured his striking face.

"Oh yeah, sorry, this is Galo," I said, gesturing to him.

He made an attempt at a smile, which looked more like a scary grimace, and when he waved, Angie and Lauren waved back tentatively.

"Bashrik's over there," Lauren said, stabbing her thumb behind her at a table in the corner, where he and Ronad were sitting. The difference between them was night and day. Before, Bashrik had been the one who appeared in better health. Now it was a completely different story. Ronad's youthful face had a slight rosy tinge, and his skin looked sun-kissed, while his brown hair was glossy and neatly swept back. Bashrik's dark hair, on the other hand, had a serious case of bedhead, and his sapphire eyes were enclosed by dark rings. His skin looked slightly gray, as if he'd been only half-heartedly taking his chameleon potion.

"He's been a pain in the ass the whole time," Angie said with a sigh. "We're both ready to kill him, so don't be surprised if he gets on your nerves, too."

"It's only been an hour?" I asked. "How'd you get here?"

"Let's sit down first," she said.

As we approached the table, Ronad waved politely, while Bashrik's frown deepened.

"So, Angie and I told the Churnleys and our parents that we were going to spend a few days in Austin. We dipped into our savings and took a plane," Lauren explained. "But those two... well..."

"We figured the security body scan would be a bit of an issue," Angie said, cracking up. Everyone joined in, except for Bashrik.

"I held onto Bashrik, and he flew," Ronad added with a rueful smile. "Although he wasn't much of a talker during the trip."

I studied Ronad as he tried patting Bashrik's tensed back. Now that Navan was out of the picture, it looked like Ronad was trying to take on the role of the calm "brother", despite the fact that he was clearly stressed too. It was likely Navan and maybe even Bashrik had done the same for him after his love, Naya, had died.

"Can you really blame me?" Bashrik was grumbling. "With my most beloved brother in the hands of vicious rebels, how can I chitchat and laugh as if everything's all right?"

"Hey," Ronad said, "you know Navan means the world to me too." His determined smile wavered, then fell, showing the real sorrow behind his steadily-voiced words.

"About that, Bashrik," I said, pausing to try to find the words to say. Bashrik's face was set in hard lines—like he wasn't going to buy whatever I did say.

"I really am sorry," I continued. "Like I said, I tried everything I could. I-I..." My voice shook as frustrated guilt welled up inside me. For failing Navan. For failing Bashrik—I'd promised him I'd watch out for his brother. For even failing myself here and now, not able to express to Bashrik just how sorry I was.

Bashrik's face softened—maybe he saw the anguish on my face —and he exhaled. "Well, the important thing is that we're all going to try to rescue him now. Right?"

He looked to me with narrowed, expectant eyes—eyes that, although a slightly different shade, reminded me painfully of Navan's.

"So are you going to introduce me?" Galo asked.

"Ah, yes, of course." I smiled and proceeded to introduce the eccentric lycan and fill them in on what had happened to me since I'd left Navan with the coldbloods—from trying to rescue him myself, to being picked up by the Fed, to how we'd ended up escaping the Fed's HQ.

When I had finished, Angie and Lauren looked at me, dumb-founded.

"Girl, you sure have been through the mill," Angie said.

I grimaced. "Yeah."

Galo adjusted his hood. "Now that introductions are out of the way, shall we talk business?"

"So you're really certain there's no hope of the Fed helping us now," Ronad said. It was more of a statement than a question, since I'd already told him it was unlikely, at least while Sylvan and his team were away.

Galo nodded. "I'd say that's accurate, boy. Going back to try convincing anyone else would be dangerous at best, lethal at worst, and I don't have access to Sylvan's direct line. I'm not high enough for that, unfortunately."

"Here's a suggestion," Bashrik said. "We rescue Navan now, with whatever force necessary." He slapped his grayish palms down on the table, causing it to shake.

Ronad put a hand on Bashrik's shoulder. "Seriously? Rush into a camp filled with countless coldbloods and shifters, without any actual plan? Riley already tried that, and it didn't work out too well for her."

I felt a blush rise to my cheeks, recalling that stupid incident.

"I didn't say that exactly," Bashrik said, crossing his arms across his chest. "Although the longer we wait here, the more likely it is that they've hurt Navan—or worse."

"You're right," Ronad said gently. "So that means we should act quickly but intelligently." He turned to me. "By the way, I assume your blood is still on its way to Vysanthe?"

Fear tingled at the back of my spine. So much had happened since then, I'd practically forgotten about the whole blood problem. "Yeah," I said hoarsely. "I guess it is."

"Well…" Ronad wet his lips nervously. "Hopefully, we'll still have time to do something about it once we rescue Navan."

"Continue your story," Bashrik urged. "You haven't filled us in on exactly how Navan got kidnapped. I want to know everything that happened since that last comm I had with you, right after you first arrived in this village. I also feel like I'm missing out on a bunch of details of what happened before then, too. Navan's comms were always so brief, in between the two of you traveling."

"You're a glutton for punishment, aren't you, Bashrik?" I said grimly. But I acquiesced. I told them the rest—the whole grisly story—filling them in on every detail to the best of my memory. The one thing I didn't mention was just how close Navan and I had become... Sharing that hotel bed together, how he'd heated me with the hot wax, our lips touching in those last, fevered seconds we had together. Those memories felt somehow sacred, and I wanted to keep them all for myself—those moments that made me feel warm and whole.

"You really care for Navan, don't you?" Ronad asked in a low voice once I had finished.

I shot him a startled glance. "How did you know?"

He smiled sadly. "He called me one night when you were sleeping—extremely agitated. He made me promise not to tell Bashrik because he knew he would worry too much. He begged that I didn't ask any questions, that I just remind him what the punishment for interspecies mingling was back on Vysanthe. It had been so long since a case was reported that he'd forgotten what punishment was doled out, he claimed. I think he remembered, just hoped it wasn't true. Anyway, I told him: the punishment was death for both involved. He thanked me, and then he hung up."

Butterflies danced in my stomach at the thought of Navan already putting that much thought into... whatever it was we had. They were shaky, sputtering butterflies that brought tears to my eyes. God, Navan had been so stoic... and yet he'd clearly cared so much for me. I wished I had known sooner.

Everyone's gaze was now on me, and I felt the heat rise in my cheeks. "I do... care for him very much," I stammered.

Bashrik eyed me. "I hope you realize just how taboo this is. It's comparable to you or your friends coupling with... well, a dog."

Anger flared through me, but Angie and Lauren exploded into disapproving objections before I could make my thoughts heard.

"You're comparing humans to dogs?" Lauren said, her eyes goggling out at him.

"Don't be so hard on yourself," Angie said to Bashrik sarcastically. "You guys are better than dogs."

A pink tinge appeared in Bashrik's cheeks, and he bowed his head. "I apologize. My statement was a bit rash. I just wanted Riley to understand the seriousness of her... possible relations with Navan."

"I do," I said. "I... I didn't plan for any of this to happen, and I don't have any idea what will happen once Navan's free. All I know is that I'd do anything to save him."

"So let's get him back!" Bashrik said forcefully.

"Okay, okay," Ronad said. "Although I think we should be making these plans back at the bed and breakfast we're staying at. We're not exactly alone here."

He cast a glance at the kitchen door, where a boy who looked to be about twelve ducked out of sight. A group of rowdy teenagers had also arrived while I'd been talking and had seated themselves on the opposite side of the room.

"Good point. But first I'm ordering some food," Galo said, his belly rumbling out the seriousness of his statement. He turned his gaze to me. "You want to order, or should I scare the poor waiter into good service myself?"

I rose quickly. "I'll go."

I walked up to the kitchen door and gently knocked. The boy poked his shaggy brown-haired head out.

"My friends and I were wondering if we could be served—just stew or anything hot you have, really," I said to him as gently as I could, hoping he, like many in this old tourist town, spoke English.

I wondered why he was ducking down like that, what he'd seen that had scared him so much—whether it was Bashrik and Ronad's hulking forms or Galo's angular face. Or maybe he was afraid of the *tonrar*, just how people had been when I was here with Navan.

The boy gave a quick nod before scurrying off and fetching a cauldron-like bowl of soup. I followed him back to the table, where he plopped it in the center. After shakily handing out four wooden spoons, he moved swiftly back to the kitchen.

"My friends and I can share," I offered, handing a wooden spoon to Lauren.

"Good," Galo said. He grabbed a spoon and took a few hearty slurps. Halfway through one, he raised his shaggy, still half-hooded head. "There's nothing like food in the belly to get the brain going. Anyway, where were we..." He did a figure-eight in the air with his spoon, stopping it to point to me. "Ah yes. We'll make the plan back at the bed and breakfast. Luckily for us, I brought some invisibility suits and some other superior Fed technology, too —one of the best ships we have."

"We have superior technology, too. We just don't have access right now—it's back on Vysanthe," Ronad pointed out with a grumble.

"Yes, yes, I'm sure you do," Galo said patronizingly, as if he were consoling a child.

Bashrik was fiddling with his spoon, eyeing Galo with apparent distrust. "How do we really know that you're telling the truth, and not trying to betray us so your other Fed agents can pick Ronad and me up?" he said. "I've seen how your kind treats mine."

"And I've seen how your kind treats every other kind in the galaxy," Galo replied smoothly. "But as to your question: you don't know. I can only assure you that I believe I am supporting Riley because of the noblest of reasons."

"Is that so?" Bashrik said.

"Yes," Galo declared stoically. "Because it is *right*."

This had a less-than-impressive effect on the table—Bashrik scoffed outright, while Angie and Lauren whispered tensely between themselves.

"I'm a veritas," Galo declared. "So when I say that I know it's right, I'm not kidding."

Ronad and Bashrik stared at him for a long moment.

"No," Ronad said, shaking his head. "Veritas are a myth among the lycans—no one's ever met an actual truth-smeller."

Galo lowered his hood partway so he could direct his lime-eyed gaze at Ronad.

"Not many, I'm sure. Except for you now."

This brought a hush over the table, which was broken by Bashrik. Directing his glare at Galo once again, he said, "So let's just say you're telling the truth and that we can trust you. What do we do now? Just march you to where we're staying and have you help in the plan?"

Galo smiled sanguinely. "Yes," he said. "That's exactly what you'll do."

"And Riley, what do you think?" Angie asked.

Everyone's heads swiveled in my direction.

I exhaled. "I think Galo's right," I said slowly. "I do trust him, and I think he's our best chance at rescuing Navan. He's already proven his loyalty by rescuing me. If he were going to betray us, it wouldn't make sense for him to steal a ship, steal invisibility suits, and take me out of the Fed Headquarters. Navan's deep in that coldblood camp, and there are thousands of them in there. We have to give this a shot—for Navan."

There was a span of silence. Ronad nodded, while Bashrik had stopped outright glaring at Galo.

"Okay," Bashrik sighed. "Let's head somewhere quieter and hash out this plan."

We paid for the meal, and as we all left and walked through the village to the bed and breakfast, I hurried ahead to join Galo. As he removed his hood, I glanced at his wizened face. Although I really did feel that I trusted him, something in me just couldn't help but ask him quietly, "Did you mean everything you said back there?"

"Every word," he said, gliding ahead quickly. "The trouble with always smelling the truth is that it predisposes you to want to tell it most times, too."

He was already a few feet ahead of me, and he cast a derisive glance back as I fell farther behind to join Lauren and Angie.

"Now hurry up, we have a bed and breakfast to get to."

5

The bed and breakfast looked pretty dingy from the outside—walls of dirty off-white bricks and a crumbling roof. Nevertheless, the inside was surprisingly homey. It was in Lauren and Angie's room, all of us flopped on their bed's multicolored quilt comforter, that we formulated our plan. With the help of a pad of paper Lauren had brought, we laid out what we were going to do.

"We have only two invisibility suits," Ronad said. "So the safest option would be that only two of us go into the camp, keeping in contact with the others, who will be nearby, with the comm devices."

We all agreed on that one. Even Bashrik gave a begrudging nod. "The real question of the hour is who those two will be," he said. "Considering Ronad and I have the most experience dealing with coldbloods, we'd be the best bet. Not to mention that I'm easily the strongest of you all."

"That may be so," Galo remarked drily. "But you aren't the most reliable."

"What do you mean?" Bashrik said, his eyes flashing.

"What I mean is—what's stopping you from making a deal with the rebel coldbloods if it means your brother gets free? How do we know you wouldn't betray us to save him?" Galo said. "Anyway, I'm the one who best knows how to use the Fed weapons and suits, and I'll die before I trust a coldblood."

"Oh really?" Bashrik said, glowering at him.

From the way his chest had started to heave, I sensed Bashrik might be about to do or say something he'd regret. He was so stressed out by Navan's situation that I feared any provocation might cause him to snap. I stood up and positioned myself between the two men.

"Guys—please. We're on the same team," I said.

Both men pursed their lips, but remained glaring at each other.

"Riley's right," Ronad said. "This is only wasting valuable time we could be using to work on saving Navan."

This seemed to calm Bashrik down somewhat. When Angie softly added, "Please," he nodded, leaning back in his chair.

"I apologize, lycan," he said gruffly. "Sometimes my concern for my family makes me a bit... difficult to deal with."

"I understand," Galo said, though he didn't take his eyes off the coldblood.

"Okay, so, we need to make a decision," I reminded them as I sat back down.

"You're right," Angie said. "But I should be the one to go with Galo. You've been through enough as it is, and Lauren, well...."

"I'd probably collapse with terror at the sight of the camp," she admitted, looking terrified at even the thought.

Angie and I gave her a reassuring squeeze as Galo stroked his chin thoughtfully.

"Yes, yes. That will do. Riley and I will be the ones to go."

The whole room erupted into angry noise.

Angie was the angriest of all. "What? That's not what I said—!"

Galo waved his hand. "Yes, I'm aware. And while your concerns do take into account the wellbeing of Riley, which is important, they do not take into account the success of the mission. Riley has the most experience with the invisibility suit; not to mention, I have received word that she has an uncanny skill for knife-throwing. What can you offer us that she can't?"

Angie's hazel eyes were set into an expression of exasperated surprise. "I'm in better shape, so I can run faster," she said, mouthing a "sorry" at me, "and I once took out this big guy who was trying to mug me."

"Hm," Galo said. "Good points, but sadly still not quite enough. I think we can all agree that Riley is more suited to the task. After all, she's infiltrated the base once before—she might have failed in her mission, but she knows the area now better than any of you."

All eyes went to me. They looked as uncertain as I felt. After all, the mission would be a dangerous one. Not to mention an incredibly important one, and I'd already failed at saving Navan once before. And yet, once again, Galo was right. I'd been there in the coldblood camp—I knew where Navan was; I knew the layout of the bunker. And more than from a merely logical standpoint, there was the whole heavy sense of responsibility I felt about

Navan's capture. I'd left him *there*, with those brutal monsters, and I wanted to be the one to rescue him from them. I wanted to be the first one he saw when he was freed. I wanted to see his lit-up grateful face—and kiss it.

I exhaled and rose. "I have to be the one to do this. I'm the only one who was there at all. More than that, I won't be able to rest unless it's me in there saving him."

Lauren took my hand. "Are you absolutely sure, Riley?"

I nodded, giving her a sad smile. "Absolutely sure."

Silence fell between us.

"I suppose Riley is right. She does have the know-how," Bashrik said. He glanced at Angie, who, frowning, nodded her agreement. "And as for Galo accompanying her instead of me... I'll admit I'm not of the most stable mindset right now, so perhaps it is for the best."

Galo nodded in appreciation, and it seemed we'd finally come to an agreement. Now that we'd established who was going into the camp, we laid out the rest of the plan: together we'd fly into the Siberian wilderness, landing the ship a safe distance from the coldblood camp. It was in this ship that the others would wait while Galo and I snuck into the coldblood base. We were to keep in contact whenever we could using the comm devices, and to turn back at the first sign of trouble.

"And I mean the first, slightest, tiniest, eeny weeniest sign of trouble," Angie said, looking me sternly in the eye.

"Yes, yes," Bashrik replied impatiently, although I could tell he was thinking, *Yes, turn back at the first sign of trouble—as long as you have Navan, that is.*

"Agreed," I told Angie, managing a wan smile.

The more we talked about the mission, the more nervous I was getting. It was just me, a weak human, and Galo, an elderly lycan, going into a base filled with thousands of merciless killers—cold-bloods and shifters alike. Sure, we had our invisibility suits, but I'd barely made it through the camp undiscovered last time. And what if Galo got himself caught? Was I really willing to leave him behind if the mission called for it?

"You okay, Riley?" Lauren asked, looking at me with concern.

"Yeah, I'm fine," I said, the strain audible in my voice. "I'm just going to drop off these mugs downstairs."

Hurriedly, I gathered up the tea mugs we'd been drinking from and rushed out of the room. On the top of the staircase, I took a deep breath. Some air—that's what I needed. If I kept running through the mission and all that could go wrong in my head, I was going to explode.

After I'd dropped off the mugs on the kitchen counter and returned to the room, everyone was on their feet.

"There's no time to waste," Bashrik said, as he heaved every article of clothing his hands came into contact with into a beefy duffel bag.

"Yeah, except when you're packing my bra," Angie pointed out with a grimace. She lifted a slinky red lace balconette out of his bag. "What did you think it was?"

"My apologies," Bashrik said, eyeing it with a wary sort of curiosity. "I thought it was a fancy doily."

At this, Lauren, Angie, and I burst out laughing. Bashrik's face went red as he upped his pack-heaving pace.

"Really, we do have to get going!"

"He's right," Ronad said, with a rueful smile of his own.

I zipped about the room, helping them finish packing their bags, and then we all but ran down the stairs and out of the bed and breakfast, saying a quick goodbye to the owner on our way out.

When we reached the ship, we rushed to clamber inside, and as soon as we were all piled in, Galo lifted off.

Angie was the one who broke the silence. "So it's awesome that we got out of our bed and breakfast super duper fast, but for how long are we going to be squished together like this?"

I glanced back to see her, Bashrik, Ronad, and Lauren all side by side behind us, looking uncomfortably squeezed. Clearly, these ships had been designed to comfortably fit two lycans— and not one person more.

I smirked. "It's not very far."

"And seeing as Riley and I are the ones risking our lives, undergoing a cramped-but-brief trip is a minor price to pay," Galo said, not looking up from the ship's steering wheel.

"Yeah, maybe, but you're not stuck beside some glaring monosyllabic jerk," Angie said, making a face at Bashrik, whom she'd ended up beside in the melee.

"I could rip apart your stuffed rabbit again," Bashrik offered.

"And I could solidify your eyes shut with Lauren's coconut face mask again, but we agreed to get along better," Angie shot back.

I resisted the urge to laugh. Clearly, Angie hadn't been kidding when she'd said that Bashrik was driving her crazy. And I knew all too well how swift Angie's justice was when it came to her enemies. I remembered how she'd slipped several spoonfuls of the spiciest chili sauce into the soup of an unsuspecting Andrea, a girl who'd bullied me in junior high. I could still remember her little cheeks puffed out like a squirrel's as she held her mouth and raced to the bathroom.

"In any case, for how long in this direction am I expected to fly?" Galo asked.

"I'm not sure," I said. "I lost the map Navan and I had while trying to escape. But, like I said, the camp's not far; we weren't flying for long before the ship broke down. I'll recognize the area when we reach it."

"Okay, so maybe... in another ten minutes or so, we'll land," Galo said. "Better to be a bit too far than a bit too close."

The ten minutes dragged on like half an hour. Everyone was tense, quiet. But sure enough, I recognized the area when we reached it—it wasn't difficult, thanks to Navan's and my broken-down ship still parked there in the snow—and it ended up being about eleven minutes away. When we landed, we wasted no time in hurrying out of the cramped quarters.

"Thank God," Angie said, sucking in several breaths of fresh air.

"Oh please," Bashrik replied, looking down his nose at her. "I'm sure you've had worse travel companions."

"You'd be surprised," Angie replied, deadpan.

"So," Galo said, clearing his throat.

Everyone quieted down, turning to look at Galo and me.

"Be careful, okay?" Lauren said, approaching me with teary eyes.

As she and Angie wrapped their arms around me, I hugged them back tightly. "I will," I promised.

When we separated, Bashrik gave me a tensely nodded "Good luck," while Ronad shook my hand with a kindly "Stay safe."

"We will," Galo commented, with an odd little laugh.

When I glanced at him, his eyes looked even greener than usual, perhaps from nervousness.

As we walked away, I looked over my shoulder one last time. I took in the scene carefully, trying to memorize every detail I could —Angie's blond head held erect as she tried to look tough for me, Lauren adjusting her glasses with a sad smile, Bashrik, with his muscled arms folded across his broad chest, Ronad, waving, his lips set into a worried line.

I waved my hand once more, then turned and continued walking.

"I didn't indicate this to the others," Galo said in a low voice, "but you should probably know that our chances of success are not good."

Out of the corner of my eye, I glared at his still-calm face. "Was that supposed to make me feel better?"

"No," he replied. "It was supposed to inform you of facts. I am simply doing this—helping you on this mission—because it is right. Not because it is likely to be successful."

"Okay, well how about this," I said a bit testily. "You can think that this is a long-shot, and I'll go on thinking that we *can* do this."

I was stressed enough about what we were about to do; I didn't need Galo making his dire, loopy predictions.

"As you wish," he said. "Although we should probably put on the invisibility suits soon."

"You're right," I said, pausing. "But for putting on the suits..."

"Yes, yes," Galo interrupted, getting my drift immediately. "I'll go over here, and you'll go over there, and we'll change without looking at each other."

"Okay," I said, sighing and walking off a few paces, before turning my back to Galo.

Really, I'd just made a point about the changing thing because I was irritated with Galo for being so calmly pessimistic in the face of our upcoming mission. For whatever reason, I trusted the man —not only in not being an old pervert, but also in having my back during this mission. It was weird—and maybe it was because of what Galo had said back on the ship—but I was feeling more and more like Galo was a sort of wise grandfather, one who had my best interests at heart. And I'd need that. This mission wasn't important, it was essential. I had to rescue Navan. I hadn't admitted it to my friends, but I was more in agreement with Bashrik than I'd let on. I wasn't sure I could leave the camp without Navan. Not again.

And he'd be there. I'd heard them talk about using Navan as a pawn—he had to be alive. Or maybe hurt. Maybe they'd even sent him away, and if that was the case, I'd find out where and I'd go there. Whatever it took, that's what I'd do to save Navan. I'd seen the protective look in his eyes when we'd kissed. I knew he'd do the same for me.

"You ready?" Galo asked from a few paces away, breaking through my thoughts.

"Ready," I said, clearing my throat.

"Good," he replied. "Let's go."

I took a deep breath. It was time.

*a*s soon as my fingers closed around Galo's hand, he pressed the button on his wrist. Immediately, he disappeared from view. I pressed the button on my wrist and did the same. It didn't take long before we were passing by Navan's and my old ship, and the sight of it made my heart droop. If only Navan and I had known what we'd find here when it first broke down...

"Best not go near it," Galo said, voicing my thoughts. "We've got enough to worry about without getting mixed up with ship-dwelling shifters."

As we passed, a gray wolf padded out of the ship. It sniffed at the air, then turned its furry head toward us.

"Keep moving, slowly," Galo said in an undertone.

I did as told, and, though the disguised shifter advanced a few paces, it disappeared back into the ship.

"Good job," Galo said. "Now for our actual mission."

My smile fell. The old lycan was right—we were just now reaching where the invisibility shield had been around the camp.

"You said that Navan was in a bunker separated from the main camp?" he asked.

"Yeah," I said. "You just have to walk through the dirt path in the middle—it cuts straight through the camp. Then there's some empty space, and we'll come to the bunker where they were keeping him. I can lead us in."

"No, no," Galo said. "If there's anyone who should be caught, it's me. I'll go first."

Although I worried about the old man, I didn't argue. Galo stood a better chance of fighting off any coldblood guards, and I couldn't afford to be captured again, not when the rebels would use me to coerce Navan into doing their bidding.

Galo stopped, and I heard a sniffing noise. A foot ahead, the air shimmered, presumably because Galo had touched the shield.

"Yep, we're here," he said. "And no, I can't sniff invisibility shields, if you're wondering—it's only habit." He paused. "Now would be a good time to tell your friends that we're here. And I'm sure I don't have to tell you that once we get inside you must stay completely silent, and not let go of my hand unless completely necessary. If I'm caught, you should of course continue on your own, but otherwise we must stay together. Since we're both invisible, finding one another in a crowded base camp would be nearly impossible."

"Okay, I won't let go," I said, before taking the comm device out of a pocket on the side of my suit. "We've reached the bunker— we're going in," I whispered into it, then turned the device off and tucked it back into my pocket. "Ready," I told Galo.

"All right. Hey ho, let's go," he said.

Together we stepped through the shield, and I held my breath, expecting a shifter or coldblood to greet us on the other side with a spear—but there was no one. The camp itself was almost empty and fairly quiet, with hardly any coldbloods or shifters milling about, and no guards around this part of the border.

Galo squeezed my hand, and I was pretty sure I understood his message. So far, this looked good.

As we ventured farther into the camp, we saw that the atmosphere was much the same. The few coldbloods and shifters who were outside mingled about casually—the tension of earlier seemed to have died down. Even when I accidentally brushed a shifter woman's arm, she paused, glanced around suspiciously, but then shrugged it off.

In fact, going through the entire camp was easy, to my massive relief. Galo navigated us through the tents and around the odd coldblood or shifter, keeping as firm a hold on my hand as I kept on his. When we finally broke out of the main part of the camp, and the last tent was a good yard away, Galo stopped. After what sounded like him looking around, he whispered, "Let's give your friends an update."

I took out the comm device. Normally, it would've been funny to see the little round thing floating in my invisible hand, but these weren't normal circumstances.

I pressed the button. "Hey, guys, just an update. We've made it through the camp and are on the way to the bunker." I breathed so softly I could barely hear myself—but it seemed to be loud enough for the comm's sensitive mic to pick up.

"Hey, Riley—Bashrik here." The reply came almost instantly. "Okay, good. Stay safe, and give us the next update when you can."

With that, I clicked the device off and put it away. As we continued, we passed by the far-off silo-like building, which was thankfully not currently spewing red smoke.

"This place is disgusting," Galo muttered, mostly to himself. I could hardly blame him. It had been a shock enough for me, let alone a lycan Fed agent who belonged to an organization expressly designed to be aware of places like this.

As we neared the bunker, we saw that its surroundings were deserted. We reached the building's doors, one of which was still wrenched off its hinges, and Galo paused again.

"You ready?" he whispered.

"No," I said.

He chuckled. "Good. Me neither."

And then he squeezed my hand, and we walked through the doors. He paused there, and I understood—he wouldn't know where exactly in the building Navan was, but I did. Keeping our hands clasped, we switched positions so that I was leading him, and continued advancing. My heart hammered in my chest as we neared the end of the hallway, toward the room I'd escaped from last time. The last time I was here, I'd nearly been captured. This time, however, there wasn't the slightest sign of any coldbloods.

A chilling thought suddenly occurred to me as my hand closed around the room's doorknob. Had they moved Navan somewhere else? *Are we too late?*

Something about this situation felt very, very wrong.

"Where did they all go?" I breathed.

I didn't hear Galo's answer as I entered the room and spotted a chair in the middle of it—more specifically, as I spotted who was in it. He was tied with the same red intestine twine as last time, his face looking even more slack and hopeless than before.

Navan.

I released Galo's hand and sprinted forward so I could pull off Navan's blindfold. Surprised, he looked around as I lowered his gag too. In my excitement to see him, I had forgotten that I was still invisible.

"Navan, it's me," I whispered, my voice shaking with relief at the sight of him alive.

Navan's eyes widened with fear. "Get out of here," he said frantically. "They left me unguarded on purpose—it's a *trap!*"

My heart leapt into my throat, and I twisted around just as two uniform-wearing coldbloods appeared in the doorway.

7

"Search the room. Someone's here," one of the coldbloods said.

He locked the door as the other strode ahead, arms out and a glassy, rifle-like weapon raised.

"Show yourself," he barked.

As quietly as I could, I backed away from Navan.

To my horror, I recognized the coldblood at the door as the same silver-haired one who had chased me last time.

Sneering, he advanced toward Navan and pointed his gun at Navan's arm. "Show yourself—or I'll pull the trigger."

I scanned his scowling, sculpted face. *Would he actually shoot Navan?*

A glowing blast exploded from his gun. Navan ducked his shoulder away just in time.

The coldblood hadn't been bluffing—that shot would've

injured Navan badly. My heart was nearly pounding out of my chest. I had to surrender.

"I'm warning you," the silver-haired coldblood snarled.

This time, he aimed the gun between Navan's thighs.

"Don't fire!" I cried out. "I'll show myself."

"Don't!" Navan shouted, just as I pressed the button on my suit.

When I materialized, I lunged out of the way, but the silver-haired coldblood was too fast. He tackled me onto the ground. As I struggled, he kicked me, then, straddling my waist, pointed the gun at my right thigh.

"Struggle again and I'll shoot you this time. After all," he said, smiling with yellow teeth, "you don't need legs to talk."

Ahead of us, there were sounds of a scuffle. The other coldblood cursed in irritation as he was thrown backward.

"Whoever you are, invisible idiot, stop, or I'll shoot her!" the silver-haired coldblood roared.

There was a pause, then an "Oh bollocks" from Galo as he materialized too.

"Gotcha!" the other coldblood cried triumphantly.

Galo and I eyed each other anxiously as the coldblood threw him to the ground as well. My hand dove into my suit for the comm device. I jammed the button, just as the silver-haired coldblood snatched it out of my hands.

"Nice try—but did you really think a human could outsmart coldbloods?" He chuckled and tossed the comm device onto the stone floor, crunching it under his foot. He moved his boot onto my chest. "What other things do you have hiding in that suit of yours?"

Cold fear cut through me. Would he actually strip me down completely? What else was he going to do to me?

"Nothing," I said, glaring at him. I'd just have to wait until he was distracted... and then I could stab my knife into his stupid evil back. Stab and keep stabbing until he'd stopped moving entirely. It was the least they deserved.

But now he was squinting at me, pressing his foot harder against my chest. My breath came out in shuddering gasps.

"We'll see about that," he said softly.

He felt me up and down, while I squirmed, until his hand clasped triumphantly on the knife in my pocket.

"You lying little bitch," he growled.

With his knee digging into my shoulder, he raised the knife, then slashed it down. It connected with the button on my suit with a great crackling shudder. He repeated the motion, over and over again, until my whole suit sputtered and shuddered into permanent visibility. He tossed the knife to his companion to do the same to Galo's suit, then turned his sneering attention to me.

"You really thought that would work? For Rask's sake, humans are getting dumber every day. In any case, you won't be needing those suits anymore."

"What should we tie them up with?" the other coldblood asked once he'd disabled Galo's suit too.

His long brown hair flicked back and forth as he turned his head to look around the room, before his gaze stopped on a chain hanging from the ceiling. He glanced at the silver-haired coldblood, who nodded.

"Bingo."

"By the way," the silver-haired coldblood said as he advanced to grab it down, "in case you haven't gotten the message yet—if either of you moves or tries to escape, I'll shoot one of you."

I glared fiercely back at him, once more picturing myself stabbing him with the knife over and over again. These coldbloods were nothing like Navan—they were a different species entirely, one that didn't deserve to exist at all. Hot tears rose to my eyes. I knew it wasn't fair to blame myself for failing again, but I couldn't help it. I'd been so eager to free Navan, so overjoyed to see him, that I hadn't stopped to consider that this could be a trap. And it had cost both of us our freedom this time.

I glanced at Navan, who was looking at me as if I had actually been shot, with tormented, longing eyes. "Don't struggle," he mouthed at me sadly, and I nodded. As soon as they'd threatened to hurt him, I had stopped struggling.

By now, the two coldbloods had pulled down the chain and brought it over to Galo and me.

"There's not much of it," the other coldblood pointed out, eyeing the metal thing dubiously. "Not sure if there'll be enough for two."

The silver-haired coldblood looked from me to Galo to Navan, then back to me again. A menacing smile came over his face. "Oh, don't worry. I've got an idea."

I gulped. Did that mean what I thought it did? That if there wasn't enough chain for two... then he'd have to get rid of one?

He advanced toward me, with his hands out.

"If you hurt her..." Navan growled.

The silver-haired coldblood grabbed Navan by the throat. "Shut up, human-lover."

Letting him go, he shoved me down next to the chair and

gestured for his companion to do the same with Galo. Then, he wrapped the chain around both of us and the chair several times. This resulted in Galo and me being on the floor, chained to the front legs of Navan's chair.

I exhaled in relief. Maybe they weren't going to kill off one of us after all.

The two stepped back to admire their creation with cocky grins.

"The real question is," the brown-haired coldblood said, "what happens if the chair falls over?"

They chuckled. The silver-haired coldblood gave the chair a kick, which made it tip back uncomfortably. Laughing, he crouched down in front of me and took my chin in his rough hands. "You were the same intruder as last time, weren't you? I got in big trouble for letting you slip out."

"Leave her alone," Navan snarled.

The silver-haired coldblood kicked Navan in the leg, sending the whole chair shaking.

"You're not exactly in a position to make demands, fool," he sneered.

Navan glowered at him, his eyes burning with the promise of a painful death.

"Shouldn't we tell Ezra that we've captured them?" the brown-haired coldblood asked.

"True," the silver-haired one replied. "I've had enough of looking at these pathetic creatures anyway."

Together, they strode out.

Navan only spoke when the sound of their footsteps had

quieted to silence. "Please tell me that this is somehow part of your plan."

"It's not," I said hoarsely. "I'm so sorry."

He exhaled sharply. "You shouldn't be here," he said, and I winced at the anger lacing his words. "You shouldn't have come. What were you *thinking*?"

"I couldn't just abandon you!" I said.

"She does have a point," Galo interjected.

"And you have a Fed agent helping you? What about the others?" Navan demanded.

"Galo was the only Fed agent who believed me," I explained. "Bashrik and the others are outside the invisibility shield, on another ship." That last sentence, I mouthed, not wanting to say the words aloud in case we could be heard.

Silence fell. After another minute, Navan murmured, "You shouldn't have come."

"I'm sorry," I snapped back, furious tears flowing down my cheeks. I felt ridiculous, stupid, like I wanted to sink into the floor. Our plan had not only utterly failed—it had actually caused Navan to be hurt more.

"Stop it." Navan said the words in a leaden voice. When I looked up, his stormy eyes were now sorrowful too. Evidently, he had picked up that I was crying.

"What difference does it make?" I asked. "Now we've been caught. We're screwed. We'll probably never make it out of here alive—if that's not reason to cry, then I don't know what is."

"It makes all the difference to me," he said.

I glanced up to see him looking down at me with a tortured expression. When our eyes met, he looked away.

"Riley, please..."

"Look at me when you're saying it," I said.

Grudgingly, he leaned down so that our faces were closer. His blue-gray eyes were tormented, his cracked lips parted.

"I was so worried about you," I said in a choked whisper.

"And now I'm so worried about you," he replied. His gaze flicked to my lips, then back to my eyes. "If you see a chance of escaping on your own, promise me that you'll take it. And that you'll stay somewhere safe this time. No more rescue missions. Okay?"

I shook my head. "I'm sorry, Navan."

His brows set into a scowl, and his fiery eyes bored into me. "Promise me."

I glared right on back at him. "I'm not leaving here without you."

"Dammit, Riley!" Navan stomped his foot, sending his whole chair shaking. "You've got to stop putting yourself in danger like this. What if they torture you? What if they... I can't protect you now. If anything bad were to happen, I'd never forgive myself because I—I care about you. Don't you get that? I can't let you get hurt."

Navan's tone had turned frantic. He was leaning so far forward that the strain was visible in his face. I reached my head up as much as I could, then leaned it on his knee and closed my eyes. The close contact felt nice, although I wished I could be wrapped in his arms instead. Despite everything, I felt somehow safe, now that Navan was by my side.

Galo's voice snapped me out of my happy reverie. "I hate to break this up, but we have company."

I opened my eyes and drew back to see the same coldbloods as before. They were smirking, striding into the room with the imposing, mud-brown-eyed coldblood I was pretty sure had been named Ezra—he had been the first to interrogate Navan after he was captured. Ezra was frowning, looking both repulsed and annoyed. Clearly, he'd seen our affectionate moment.

"You shouldn't have tied them up like that," his curt voice declared.

"Why not, sir?" the silver-haired coldblood asked.

"You've given the lovebirds room to be disgusting," Ezra snarled, crouching down to look me in the eye. "This the one from before?" he asked, turning his dark gaze toward the silver-haired coldblood, who nodded.

"I'm pretty sure."

Frowning, he returned his gaze to me. "Are you the human from last time?"

I glared back at him defiantly. Maybe it would work to my advantage to have him worry that there were more of us.

"Okay, we'll try this a different way," Ezra remarked calmly.

Without warning, he punched Navan in the jaw. It gave an ominous crunching sound.

"Yes!" I blurted out.

"Don't tell them anything," Navan said, his voice sounding both wet and wooden.

Ezra smashed his fist into Navan again. "What was that? I don't think I could hear you over the sound of your face crunching under my fist."

Navan's whole body shuddered as he choked out a cracking

cough, his face tensed into a heartbreaking stoicism the whole time.

Giving his hand a casual shake, Ezra turned his dark-eyed gaze to me. "Now, why don't we come to some sort of understanding?"

I gaped at him stupidly. Words jumbled in my brain, nonsense syllables slapping around in my mind. All I could see—over and over and over again—was his horrible muscled fist slamming into Navan's slack face. I couldn't think—I could barely breathe. My throat had closed up with fear.

Ezra raised his fist again, and my whole body started trembling.

"Do I need to make myself clearer?" he asked.

"N-No," I gasped out, my heartbeat rocketing up to a thousand. "I'm the one from before. Just don't hurt him anymore—please."

A sickly-sweet smile passed over Ezra's face. "Yes, yes, of course," he said, stroking his hands along the chain that bound me. "You help us, and I'll help you."

Reaching for the chain wrapped around the chair leg, he grabbed it with both hands and bent it apart. The chain snapped. Holding one severed chain end up, Ezra turned to the other two coldbloods.

"That's why you shouldn't have tied them up like that."

The silver-haired one opened his mouth like he was going to protest, but then closed it, probably thinking better of it. Ezra tugged the chain so that I was pulled upright, then used it to lead me to the brown-haired coldblood, handing me over to him.

"Don't bother trying to question the lycan—he'll never talk. The human, however, we may just have a chance with. See that she's put in a cell," he said.

"Riley, I mean it," Navan said, a note of panic in his voice now. "Don't tell them anything."

Smiling, Ezra strode over to Navan. "Yes, Riley," he said, punching Navan in the face so hard that his head lolled to the side, rendering him unconscious. "Don't tell us anything."

"No!" I yelled, straining to reach Navan.

As I struggled in the coldblood's grasp, I searched Navan's face. He was still breathing, but damn, I worried about how many more blows he could take. As Ezra advanced right in front of me, his eyes were glittering. "Don't worry, your paramour will be fine—as long as you tell us what you know."

Ezra waved his hand at the brown-haired coldblood, and, before I could respond, he'd tugged me away. We traveled down several floors, until we reached a room full of cells. Here, the ground was damp dirt, and the whole place was filled with an eerie quiet. The cells appeared to be surrounded by stone walls, with a small window too high up for me to look through. It was unclear whether the cells were empty, or whether their occupants had long since given up bothering to speak. At one cell near the middle, the coldblood opened a steel door, unfurled my chain, and flung me inside, causing me to trip.

"Wait—please," I said.

But he strode away without the slightest pause.

On my hands and knees, I crawled over to the stone wall and leaned against it. More useless tears spilled down my cheeks as I thought of Navan, of how much they'd already hurt him and what they were going to do if I didn't talk. I closed my eyes and saw it— them stringing him up in more chains, lashing his bloodstained, broken body with knife-tipped whips, laughing as he groaned. I saw them gathered in a circle and kicking him until his hunched-over form didn't have the strength to tremble anymore. I saw them spitting in his tormented face and jabbing his already ripped-up torso with spears, mocking him for trying to protect me. I lay there, my vision blurred with horror, until I grew too tired to cry.

It was in this dull, fuzz-sighted haze that the door of my cell opened and then shut.

A coldblood had entered. He had a tall, stooping form, which was topped with a severe buzzcut colored with spots of gray. His mouth was a cruel, thin-lipped gash, and yet... the hazel eyes behind his golden spectacles looked kind.

"I need you to tell me what you know, so that Navan won't be harmed," he spoke up in a low, gruff voice.

I didn't look at him. He came to sit beside me, the navy cloak he wore billowing out as he did so. "Believe me when I say that I'm not your enemy. I want Navan unharmed as much as you do."

I turned my head slightly to cast the coldblood a derisive look. "If you work with these coldbloods, then you're my enemy."

He frowned. "No, no. You've only seen their bad side. Renegades have to be harsh and strict in the beginning—otherwise, they'll never get anywhere. We're all working together for a good cause."

I said nothing. I wasn't exactly in the mood for talking, let alone arguing with a coldblood. And as logical and convincing as his words sounded, he was just trying to butter me up. This coldblood was probably just like Ezra—except he introduced his good face before his bad one.

Scanning me with cold eyes, he said, "Do you really want to see how far us coldbloods are willing to go to get what we want?"

His words sent a chill down my spine. Tears pricked at my eyes, but I angrily blinked them back. So what if this lying coldblood had been just as heartless as I'd feared? Was it really that much of a shock that he'd just been pretending to be decent? But if he had been alluding to more of the nightmarish torture I'd been imagining for Navan…

"I apologize," he was saying now. "I didn't mean to frighten you, only to stress the seriousness of the situation. My name is Lazar."

Now his eyes had gone kind again, but I wasn't buying it. He'd revealed himself to me—he was cruel, just like all the other coldbloods here. Still, it wouldn't hurt to play the game.

"So, Lazar," I replied, glaring into his eyes. "Why do you care what happens to Navan?"

He frowned. "Why would I be here talking to you if I didn't?"

I scoffed. "Because Ezra or whoever else sent you. Because since they'd tried intimidating me for information, they figured why not try to nice-talk it out of me."

Lazar shook his short-haired head. "I can assure you that's not the case. Anyway, just tell me what you know—and why you were traveling with a Fed agent," he continued, "and everything will be fine. You two will be reunited, and Navan won't be harmed." Seeing my emotionless face, Lazar clasped my shoulder anxiously. "Please, Riley, don't test Ezra. I've seen for myself what he's capable of."

I jerked away with a shiver. Lazar was doing it again—trying to manipulate me. Even so, what if he was right?

But then I thought of the silver-haired coldblood, how he'd kicked Navan for almost no reason at all. Saving Navan from Ezra's wrath was no guarantee that he'd be saved from the other cold-bloods. Besides, telling them everything I knew would give away the one advantage we had—that of the Fed's involvement. Well, only if those investigating Fed agents hadn't been captured and interrogated already.

"Would you prefer I left you alone?" Lazar finally asked.

"Yes," I replied.

"As you wish," he said, rising with a sigh. "But please at least consider my words. Ezra will stop at nothing to get his way. I know him."

Lazar lingered for a minute, searching my face for a response I wouldn't give him. Then, with a disappointed frown, he turned and left, shutting the door behind him.

I glared at the door, trying not to imagine what they'd do to Navan as a result of my refusal to cooperate. They wouldn't actually inflict any permanent damage on him, would they? I reminded myself that they wouldn't, not when they were planning to use him as a pawn. Then again, once that strange, higher-up coldblood had found out that Navan was Jareth Idrax's son, he'd referred to him as a "bargaining chip" in the coming conflict with Queen Gianne. Bargaining chips didn't have to be fully unharmed, or even whole, did they? All Navan would have to be was alive for his father to want him back. In the meantime, that meant the cold-bloods could do just about anything they liked to him...

My head spun with horrible images of Navan twisting with pain, until I could take it no longer. I closed my eyes and tried to doze off, or at the very least, lose myself in that peaceful place between sleep and consciousness.

Resting my head against the wall, I couldn't fall asleep, but I had no way of knowing how much time passed. It must have been quite a few hours, because I became more and more aware of the hunger in my stomach, and how parched my mouth was.

By the time the door opened again, I felt too feeble to even look and see who it was.

"I'm here to show you something."

Surprised at the cool, feminine voice, I looked to see a coldblood woman standing by the wall. She had braided, ashy hair and heavy-lidded eyes.

She placed what looked like a small TV in front of my face.

"Watch," she commanded.

The screen flickered to life. On it, Navan was in the same chair as before, surrounded by uniformed coldbloods and Ezra. I closed my eyes.

The woman pressed her cold hands to my face and wrenched apart my lids, holding them open.

"Watch."

And so, trying in vain to twist away, I did. As Navan sat on the chair, behind him some coldbloods had hooked up a cord to a metallic cylinder in the corner. Ezra had the other end of this cord attached to Navan's arm with a clamp. He looked at the camera and smiled.

"Time to play."

At his last word, the cord—and then Navan—rippled with electricity.

Ezra gave a thumbs-up to the camera. Gritting his teeth, Navan at first held strong, refusing to move or make a sound. Beside him, Ezra nodded to the coldbloods by the metallic cylinder, who pushed a lever on it. This must have upped the dosage of electricity, because seconds later, Navan was writhing, his mouth twisted with painful yells. As I watched, horror-stricken, trying to twist away myself, his body convulsed more and more.

With every added convulsion, I felt my own stomach convulse in turn. This wasn't happening, couldn't be. Even the glaze of tears in my eyes wasn't enough to block what I was seeing. Nothing would ever erase that heart-rending image from my retinas.

As the convulsions continued, it became clear that this wasn't just painful for Navan, it was potentially deadly.

"Stop!" I cried to the woman, shrieking now. "Tell them to stop!"

My whole body was writhing back and forth too, wracked with sobs and hyper-ventilating breaths. And still, the woman said nothing, just held me there and made me watch.

On the screen, Ezra stepped in front of Navan. Baring his teeth in a smile at the camera, he said, "You help us, we'll help you."

Then the screen went black.

8

*M*y hands were still trembling, but after a minute of staring numbly at the blank screen, a different emotion rose up in me. Rage.

How dare *these monsters do this. How* dare *they keep us captive.*

I was *sick* of being the victim—of being a helpless pawn in these monsters' hands. I didn't know how I was going to do it, but I had to take back some control.

Seizing on that fire, I whirled on the coldblood woman next to me with a glare. "Fine, I'll tell you rebels everything," I spat, "*if* you take me to your boss. Not Ezra—I want the guy in charge of this whole place."

The coldblood woman's eyes widened slightly at my outburst, and she raised a brow. "You want to see Chief Orion?"

"Yes, whatever his name is."

"Very well. Come with me." She grabbed my arm and led me to the door.

I shook her off with a scowl, and cast another glare at her when she gave me a warning look. "I'm following," I said bluntly. "Just do your damn job and lead."

Her nostrils flared, and I could see she wanted to retaliate, but she bit down on her lip, apparently thinking better of it.

She sped up along the corridor, and I kept pace, my blood pounding in my ears. I was still shaking, but now it really was more from anger than shock.

We took a staircase and descended two flights, then stopped in front of a single towering metal door. I clenched my fists together, steeling my nerves for the man on the other side.

My escort knocked gently on the door. There was a pause, before a familiar, deep voice commanded, "Enter."

The door clicked open automatically, and as it moved, it revealed a surprisingly bare room—bare except for a desk, a chair, a long tank filled with the strangest array of flora I had ever seen, and, of course, the coldblood chief himself.

He was standing in front of the desk, towering what must've been seven feet above the floor, his powerful arms crossed over his chest and his giant wings folded behind his back. I took in the deep scar that ran down the side of his face, then met his almost-black gaze head on. His expression was calm, near inscrutable, and I wasn't sure if he was surprised to see me. Judging from the slight upward curve of his mouth, he wasn't displeased.

"Stop torturing Navan," were the first words to blurt from my lips as I dared take a step closer to him. "Just stop it. There's no need. I've come to tell you everything."

He gazed down at me, a spark of interest in his dark eyes, and I once again sensed that ancient aura coming from him. He didn't look particularly old, but there was something about his gaze that told me he had lived far more years than his appearance let on.

A second later, he reached down into a drawer of his desk and pulled out some sort of comm device. He switched it on and said, "Ezra, no more until I say."

He then switched the device off, planted it down on the table, and returned his full attention to me. "Well," he said, his voice both soft and ominous, "what do you have to say?"

He pulled up a chair and gestured for me to seat myself. I looked at it uncertainly, and decided that I wanted to remain standing. I felt like I was barely half his size, and sitting down wasn't going to help with that. Right now, I needed all the boldness I could muster.

I drew in a breath, and, although Navan's warning not to tell any of these coldbloods anything was ringing in my ears, I did. Well, not quite everything. I explained to Orion how I had come across Navan in the first place, through to how we came to arrive here. I told him that the Fed were aware of shifters in the location, and had sent Navan and me to investigate. What I left out was Bashrik and my friends' involvement, though I did mention Jethro and Ianthan at the start of the story since, well, they were dead. I was praying that the coldbloods hadn't found Bashrik after they'd discovered the comm device on me. Hopefully, even if coldbloods or shifters had gone out to scope the area, to see if anybody had been accompanying Galo and me as backup, Bashrik or Ronad would be able to escape in time and fly our group to safety.

When I was done with my story, I paused, planting my hands on my hips and narrowing my eyes at the chief. He was watching me closely, that glint of interest still there in his eyes.

Silence stretched for several seconds, until he spoke. "I must say, you have guts for a human."

I set my jaw harder, accepting the compliment.

"And it's interesting to hear how and why you came here... First you with your coldblood friend, and then with the wolf. My men thought you and the lycan might be a little backup sent to look for those other agents we captured recently," he continued, and my stomach dropped. "But according to you, that's not the case?"

I shook my head, even as my throat went dry. Sylvan and his men had been captured. Though, given the sheer number of shifters and coldbloods in this place, I probably shouldn't have been surprised. Still, it was a punch in the gut. Sylvan and his team had been the only ones who'd taken my intel seriously, and it made me all the more anxious about Bashrik, Ronad, and my friends. *Please, guys, be smart and stay alive.*

But I couldn't think of them right now. I had to focus on myself and Navan, both of whom I also very much wanted to stay alive.

"So," I said, clearing my throat and trying to sound businesslike once again. "I understand that you want to... cooperate with Navan in some capacity." I had been about to say *use*, but could not quite get the word out. "I'm sure I can speak to him and get him to come to some agreement with you regarding your plans, if you're upfront with me about *your* mission."

"Naturally," Orion replied. A slight amusement played across his lips as he gripped the edges of the desk and leaned gently against it. "Though, I believe you overheard much of what Ezra told your coldblood friend when you first came in here."

My cheeks flushed slightly at the memory of him calling me out from under the bench.

"Put simply," he went on, "all we really want is a place to call home. And isn't that what everyone wants?"

"Well, it's not just that, is it?" I cut in bitterly, almost scoffing as the vision of that billowing red smoke flashed across my mind.

"Yes and no," Orion replied coolly. "We want to restore Vysanthe to the home it should be for all coldbloods, regardless of political affiliation. Those child queens had no right to drive us out, and Vysanthe is suffering under their petty, divided rule. It could be ten times the nation it is today if it were handed back over to the people, and that is really what we're all about. The immortality elixir is merely a means to help us achieve that."

"Oh, really? How?"

Orion smiled. "That's a good question. You're right that merely prolonging our lives wouldn't help us win a war. But we're seeking to create a *true* immortality elixir—one that not only extends life indefinitely, but preserves it. One that protects us from disease and fortifies our physical strength far beyond that of a regular cold-blood. Immortality wouldn't be true immortality if we could be as easily killed as any old coldblood, now would it?"

I bit my lip, but didn't respond. The logic made sense, though.

"If Navan were to agree to help us," Orion continued, "he could go down in Vysanthean history as a hero, be remembered for generations into the future. He could play a pivotal role in all of this. He could be the key to Queen Gianne's downfall." Here he paused, and glanced casually over at his tank, his eyes fixing on a particularly vivid plant with purple, tentacle-like leaves. "If he were to agree," he repeated softly, "it would also mean that we would spare your lives, not to mention, give Navan a real purpose to his life. I'm sure he'd rather be a hero than the lackey boy of some impetuous young queen?"

I nodded stiffly. I wasn't buying his speech, but I couldn't miss the underlying threat in his words. I kept my voice bold as I replied, "You clearly have a lot of conviction for your cause, and while I'm not going to pretend to agree with your methods, I will agree to talk to Navan and get him to hear out your proposition—*if* you agree to a few terms of my own. Trust me when I say that he is way more likely to listen to me than you." At that, I intensified my glare, but if anything, it only seemed to amuse him.

"I don't doubt that."

"Then you will grant me three requests," I stated. "First, untie Navan. Second, release him and give the two of us a decent room with some privacy. And third, provide us with enough potions to fix whatever damage you have done to him—as well as something to heal his wing," I added, remembering the wound that the traitorous shifter had inflicted on Navan just after we'd discovered the coldblood base. I wanted to demand Galo's safety as well, but knowing how much the rebels despised the Fed, I knew I couldn't push my luck. If I asked for too much, then there was a chance Orion would grant me nothing—given that he didn't exactly need to bend to any of my demands in the first place—and that would help nobody. I needed to tread carefully to not blow my chances, and somehow figure out a way to help poor Galo later. *One step at a time.*

Orion drew in a light breath, but I could already see from the look in his eyes that he was not going to deny me. If anything, he looked curious as to whether I, a little human girl, could really pull this off—could really bend a stubborn beast like Navan to my will.

"Pernixa," he said sharply, his eyes moving to the coldblood woman who was still standing behind me, close to the door. "You heard the girl. Grant her requests."

The woman nodded and then opened the door, gesturing that I follow her.

I looked back at Orion one last time, at his unnerving gaze that seemed to be X-raying my brain, and then I nodded curtly before turning and following the woman out of the room.

As we ascended the stairs and returned to the corridor, I couldn't ignore the writhing feeling in my stomach. I didn't trust Orion, not one bit, and the last thing I wanted to do was try to persuade Navan to have any kind of dealings with him. But... I just had to take this one step at a time. At the moment, it was all I could do.

9

The coldblood woman stopped outside a door on the highest level of the bunker, away from the cells and torture chambers. This was a residential part of the building, judging by the coldbloods milling casually about. They cast both glares and curious glances my way, but I ignored them all, my mind focused on only one thing: making sure I got my end of the deal.

As my escort pushed open the door, it seemed like one of Orion's promises, at least, had been fulfilled. I stepped inside and found myself looking at a much more pleasant room than any I had seen so far in this building. There was a single bed in one corner, along with a bedside cabinet that held a clock and a bottle of water. There was even a thick, albeit grubby, carpet lining the floor. It wasn't going to win any TripAdvisor awards, but it would do.

I turned expectantly on the woman, who was already heading

for the door. "And you're going to fetch Navan and the medicine now?" I asked.

She grunted, apparently not wanting to give me the satisfaction of more of a response than that. It was probably too humiliating for her as it was, to be put at the service of a human.

As she disappeared down the corridor, I pulled the door closed. I felt like downing the bottle of water in a few gulps, but something told me Navan would need it more than me, so I ignored my thirst and sat on the bed instead. I waited nervously, listening to the footsteps pounding outside. I got anxious more than once as they swerved a little too close to my door, worrying that some unruly coldblood was suddenly going to burst in. But none did, and, as I watched the seconds tick by on the clock, I managed to relax a bit and settle into my own thoughts.

Navan. I was going to see Navan again. Properly this time, without any of that inselo twine crap stopping him from holding me. What was more, I was going to be alone with him... completely alone. How long we would have, I didn't know, but for now, the thought of seeing him again was enough to lift my spirits. I had still barely had a chance to process the kiss we'd shared. A part of me couldn't believe we actually *had* kissed. Everything had happened so fast, and I'd been trapped in a relentless nightmare ever since. The one thing I did know was that we needed to make every second we had together count.

There was a rapping at the door exactly two minutes later. It swung open, revealing the coldblood woman carrying a tray of familiar-looking silver vials, and behind her... Navan stepped into the room.

As his eyes fell on me, I felt the breath leave my lungs. I could barely wait for the coldblood woman to back out of the room before I raced over to him and launched into his arms.

"Riley." He groaned softly, hugging me back, but as I caught a glimpse of the side of his face I realized he was wincing. I pulled away, fearing I was hurting him. If I thought I'd been to hell and back... I didn't know where he'd been.

The last thing I wanted to do was place distance between us, but I took a couple of steps back, eyeing him from head to toe. As earlier, he was in his full-on coldblood form, with grayish skin, bruises scattered across his face and arms, and his clothes were tattered. I caught his hand and pulled him to sit on the bed, then immediately brought the tray of vials over and presented them to him.

"Uh, you need to drink this stuff. It's supposed to fix you, and your wing." I was relying on him knowing what to do with these substances.

But he wasn't looking at the vials. His slate eyes were glued to my face, his expression a mixture of concern and confusion.

"What happened?" he asked, his voice painfully scratchy. "Why have they brought us here?"

I reached out to grab the bottle of water, unscrewed the cap, and handed it to him. "Drink, Navan. You need it."

He took a few sips, while I took a deep breath. I knew that he wasn't going to like what I had to say, but he wanted answers.

"Navan I... I got a meeting with Orion—that chief coldblood who sniffed me out— and, in exchange for telling him our story, I bought us some time, and this medicine for you."

"You... You told him everything?" he asked, his eyes widening.

"Everything except your brothers' and my friends' involvement," I said, feeling a flare of impatience. "And I'm pretty sure you would've done the same if you were forced to watch me being electrocuted to death."

He swallowed hard, then leaned back, pinching the bridge of his nose. "I get it," he muttered.

"Now, will you get to work on some of these potions? I don't know how much time we have."

"What happened with Orion, exactly?" he asked, as he started examining the vials.

"By the way, you seemed to recognize him back there," I said. "Have you seen him before?"

"Orion is pretty infamous back in Vysanthe," Navan replied, downing one of the vials. "He was a known rebel leader back in the day. I guess I was just... surprised he's still at it."

"Well, here's the bad news," I said. "He didn't do all of this for us for nothing. I told him that I would talk to you and persuade you to hear out his plan. He wants to involve you in their mission—he mentioned you playing a key role in bringing about Queen Gianne's downfall."

Navan grimaced. "Yeah. I guess that's not really surprising to me. Ezra already hinted as much."

"Orion also said they're trying to develop a 'true' immortality elixir. One that not only extends their natural lifespans, but fortifies their strength as well, so they become close to invincible."

"I didn't realize that." Navan's brows rose. "That takes my father's theory to a whole new level. I'm not even sure how it'd be possible... but it makes perfect sense Orion is trying. If they want to build an army powerful enough to take on Vysanthe's military, they're going to need every last scrap of strength they can find."

"Orion wants to meet with you to talk about everything, and he wants you to actually cooperate. Honestly, Navan," I said, looking at him worriedly, "I don't know whether you're going to have a choice in this. I can't stand for them to take you back into that... into that room and..." I paused, trying not to choke on my words. "If you refuse to help, I honestly don't think you'll make it out again. The only thing that's keeping you alive right now is their perceived value of you."

He set down the vial that he had been about to drink from and reached out to touch my hand, apparently sensing I was close to tears. Our eyes met, and he nodded stoically. "I know, Riley. I know. I'm stubborn, but I'm probably not stubborn enough to want to die." He withdrew his hand and ran both hands down his face, letting out a low groan. "I'm going to have to meet with him, and... Well, we'll take it from there."

I nodded, even though I was terrified what this mission was going to mean for Navan.

"Honestly," he went on, "I've got to return to Vysanthe at some point soon anyway. Remember I'm a Chief of Exploration—I don't want any of my team getting suspicious as to my whereabouts. But yeah, before I agree to anything, I want more details."

He set me with another look, one that told me he was also worrying about my safety in all of this, about what his involvement would mean for me. I sensed he was about to bring it up, but I didn't want to talk about me right now. He needed to get himself fixed up while he had the chance.

I stood up and hovered over the tray of vials he had resting on his knees. "One of these is supposed to be for your wing. Maybe an ointment? Do you know which one?"

He sighed, but allowed me to distract him. He opened each vial and sniffed its contents, before finally settling on one that was slightly larger than the others. "Yeah. This one is an ointment. This other stuff is supposed to be drunk, mostly for bruises and general post trauma."

I waited for him to finish downing the other liquids, and then lifted the tray away from his lap. I took the ointment vial from his hand, trying to ignore the tingle that ran up my arm as our fingers brushed.

"So, you gonna get out those wings, or..."

He had stood up, pulled off his shirt, and spread out his wings before I could finish my sentence. I felt my breath hitch involuntarily as his back, in all of its full, toned glory, came into view. I would've taken more time to admire it, had I not been distracted by the myriad of dark bruises and scars.

I swore beneath my breath. "Navan... I'm so sorry," I whispered.

He said nothing, while my eyes spanned the length of his long wings, until I spotted the shifter gash that had impaired his flight before. But it was pretty high up for me to reach while he was standing.

"Hey," I said softly. "Could you sit on the bed?"

"Oh. Yeah." He moved to the bed, and I climbed onto the mattress behind him. I perched on my knees, placing one hand gently on the nape of his neck, while I used the other to begin dabbing the vial's applicator against the leathery surface of his wing. I felt his neck muscles tense, and I worked as gently as I could until the whole wound was moist with the stuff.

His skin was cold, in spite of the moderate temperature in this room. It occurred to me that his "chameleon" potion—the potion that allowed him to absorb the sun's rays during the day and become human-like, as well as adjust to the temperature around him—was starting to wear off. He had lost his own stash of vials, so he had no way to keep up that treatment. Not that he exactly needed to now.

I moved to leave the bed and set the vial down on the tray with the others, but before I could place any distance between us, his arm reached around and he caught my hand.

"Riley," he said, his voice low as he pulled me in front of him. His gaze met mine, and my other hand forgot it was holding a vial. The sealed bottle dropped onto the mattress. My heart skipped a beat at the longing I saw in his eyes, etched across his lips.

His Adam's apple bobbed as he swallowed. "We haven't talked about..."

My hand reached up, my finger pressing against his lips, and before I really knew what I was doing, I was placing his hands on my waist, coaxing him to pull me flush against his chest, while my mouth found his.

"Rask, Riley." It was half moan, half whisper.

"Shh," I said.

"You're right," he breathed. "There's nothing to talk about."

His firm lips closed around mine, enveloping them and caressing them softly, slowly, as if he were relishing every second of their contact. I closed my eyes, pressing myself harder against him, even though I knew I probably shouldn't with his wounds. His hands dropped to the small of my back, then made their way up along the curve of my waist until his thumbs settled just beneath the cup of my bra.

I kissed him harder, wanting to absorb his pain, drown it out, if only for a few minutes. I knew his embrace was overwhelming whatever pain I had been feeling, and I desperately wanted to do the same for him.

My drowning attempts seemed to be working—perhaps a little too well—because he fell back on the bed, withdrawing his wings and pulling me on top of him. I trailed a line of kisses from his forehead, down his nose, before meeting his lips again, while his hands were beginning to tug at my clothes and move places that felt dangerously close to setting me on fire.

"Navan," I whispered, as I realized that my own hands had started moving toward his waistline.

He didn't respond, just kept kissing me, until we both realized we were beginning to near a point of no return.

He groaned against my lips, before removing his hands from my pants' waistband. My heart was still galloping in my chest, and my blood felt like it had been replaced with liquid heat, but I didn't protest when he rolled me off of him and onto the mattress by his side.

This was moving too fast. As much as I was overjoyed to see him, too much had happened—and at the same time, not *enough* had happened. We'd only just shared our first kiss, and, here in this coldblood bunker... it seriously wasn't the time.

Our heads rested against the pillow as we stared at each other. His lips were slightly swollen, his grayish cheeks flushed. I could only imagine how much *I* was blushing.

"You okay?" he said.

I nodded, still trying to catch my breath. Then a small smile crept onto my lips. "Who the hell is Rask?"

My smile spread to his lips, causing his beautiful eyes to sparkle with amusement. It felt like it had been an eternity since I'd seen Navan smile, and the sight made my heart expand, everything around me falling away.

"I'll tell you another time," he murmured through his grin, moving in to press another kiss to my lips.

"Huh? Why?"

Before he could respond, there was a sharp rap at the door. Our safe little bubble shattered, and Navan and I were so startled we almost bashed heads as we leapt out of bed.

My hands moved down my clothes, smoothing them out, while Navan tugged his shirt back on.

"Come in," he growled, irritation lacing his baritone voice.

The door swung open. I was expecting it to be the female coldblood, but to my surprise, it was the male coldblood with hazel eyes and buzzcut hair that I'd met earlier. The one who'd been trying to convince me to talk before Navan got tortured.

What surprised me more was Navan's reaction to the man. Hell, he looked like he'd seen a ghost.

His jaw slackened, his mouth dropping open as he stared.

"U-Uncle?!"

10

"What?" I blurted, while Navan stalked closer to the man and grabbed him by the shoulders. He blinked several times, as though he couldn't quite believe his eyes. Lazar averted his gaze to the floor.

"Uncle Lazar. Wh-What are you doing here?" Navan gasped.

Lazar swallowed, then stepped around Navan and into the room to create a little more distance between them both. "Yes, Navan. It's me."

Navan shook his head, stupefied. "What? How?"

Lazar sighed. "I'm a rebel, nephew. Have been for a long time."

Navan staggered backward. "You've been playing both sides? All this time? Why?"

Lazar shuffled his feet, still looking slightly uncomfortable. "Because I believe in the cause, Navan. I believe that our great nation was never meant to be severed in two, and I believe that we are long overdue for a rehaul of the system. I believe in the power of the people."

Navan went silent. Then his hands balled into fists. His breathing became sharper, a muscle in his jaw twitching. "And you believe in... this?" He gestured a hand around the room. "You believe in capturing and imprisoning innocent people? Stealing and slaughtering humans?" His voice rose. "Letting your own family members be tortured?!"

His chest was shaking now, and I realized, just as had happened to me barely an hour ago, his shock was transforming to rage. I had seen how Navan acted under the influence of rage before... and it had not been pretty. I half expected him to fly at Lazar and rip his head off like he had done to Jethro, but he held himself in place, for the moment.

Lazar held up his hands in a peaceful gesture. "I don't expect you to accept it's a necessary evil, Navan, even though to me, it is. I don't want to get into an argument with you. Really, I don't. Neither did I want you here in the first place, for the record. But you ventured here of your own accord, and now, well... I'm not in charge. Orion is."

"So I take it you haven't come here to help us escape, then," Navan scoffed, a part of him still appearing to be disbelieving.

"I'm afraid I haven't."

The words sounded incredibly harsh coming from an uncle to his nephew, and yet, even as he spoke, his air of discomfort remained. It made me recall my earlier encounter with him, and I realized that perhaps his motives for getting me to talk were more virtuous than I'd initially thought. Maybe Lazar had been trying to prevent his nephew from getting hurt more.

But apparently his good intentions didn't stretch much farther than that.

"Then why have you come here?" Navan spat.

"Orion feels he's given you enough time to talk and wants to finalize the agreement. He... sent me to bring you to him."

"Oh, excellent," Navan said. "Thanks so much for that. Just what family is for."

He turned his back on Lazar and faced me, his expression positively seething. It looked like it was taking all he had to keep himself in check, so much so that I felt compelled to say to his uncle, "Can you just wait outside for a minute?"

Lazar nodded, not meeting my eyes, and moved swiftly out of the room.

As the door clicked, I moved to Navan and clutched his hands. "Are you okay?"

"I just..." He pulled a hand from my grasp and ran it through his hair in exasperation. "I can't believe it."

"How is your uncle even getting away with this?" I asked. "I thought your family was, like, really high ranked back on Vysanthe. How is he doing this unnoticed?"

Navan blew out. "Uncle Lazar is kind of the black sheep of the family—though not for reasons even remotely related to treason. He's an alchemist, like my father, but he's published some shoddy studies over the years that have discredited him as a scientist and lost him favor with the queen."

"I guess that explains why Orion is interested in you over him? Otherwise, Lazar could have done whatever job Orion wants you to do."

"True. My status back home is greater, and I have more influence and access to things in general."

We fell silent, and for a long moment, the only sound in the room was that of the footsteps, drifting in from the corridor.

"I was never that close to him," Navan said finally. "If I were, then this would hurt a lot more. But I never could have imagined he would stoop to this." He glanced sullenly toward the door, then back at me with a look of deep resignation in his eyes. "You ready to leave?"

I hesitated, not feeling ready to leave this little haven in the slightest, but then nodded. "If you are."

He took my hand and led me toward the door. "I'm not sure I'll make it halfway down the corridor before I decapitate him, but let's see how this goes."

11

*A*s we descended the staircase to Orion's office, Navan walked in stony silence, refusing to say a word, even when his uncle spoke to him. His way of dealing with the situation seemed to involve pretending that his uncle didn't exist. Which was fine by me.

He had let go of my hand after we left our little room, evidently not wanting to draw more attention to us than necessary. Still, I wished he hadn't. There was comfort in the feel of his cool skin against mine, and right now, I needed something to hold onto, to ground myself in the moment. I still couldn't believe I'd managed to get us into this situation—how could everything have crumbled so fast?

I kept my gaze on Lazar's lean frame, trying to garner a hint of family resemblance somewhere in the older man's face. Perhaps there was something in the glint of his eyes, though Lazar's were hazel, where Navan's were the color of a winter storm. Scrutinizing him closely, I couldn't help but wonder what Navan's father might look like—did he look more like Navan, or was he closer to this man, with aging features and only a hint of a likeness? How could the two brothers have ended up on such opposite sides of the spectrum? One, the queen's trusted advisor. The other, a rebel against the crown.

Keeping close to Navan's side, resisting the urge to take his hand in mine again, I walked with him the rest of the way toward the grimly familiar entrance of Orion's office. Up until the very last moment, Lazar made attempts at enticing Navan into conversation, but Navan was having none of it. I didn't blame him. His uncle's moral compass was screwed up, and I could see the frustration Navan felt at Lazar ending up so far down the rebel rabbit hole. I had never believed in the idea of "necessary evils", and I wasn't about to start believing in them now. No, if a handful of people suffered for a cause, then that was a handful of people too many.

Besides, the "necessary evil" that Lazar was trying to pass off as acceptable was so far beyond the line of righteousness that I doubted he could even see the line anymore. Judging by the harrowing sight of the red smoke billowing from the strange metal silo, more than a handful of innocents had already suffered for this supposed cause. Lazar was either kidding himself, or he'd been conditioned by the rebels to believe that what he was doing was for all the right reasons. I didn't know which was worse.

I'd seen it before. It was history, repeating itself, over and over again. I was just surprised that an apparently superior race was not immune to the same mistakes that felt so deeply human to my mind.

Even so, the sight of Lazar's earnest eyes, practically pleading with Navan to turn and look at him, or to at least answer him, made me feel a slight twinge of pity. Not that I had any leg to stand on when it came to ignoring certain family members. I could understand the impulse to push them away, yet the soft plea in Lazar's voice tugged at some sympathetic string in my heart. There wasn't time to bridge the rift between them, to figure out the minutiae of what had led Lazar into this world, but I hoped there might be a moment later in which Navan might sit down with his uncle and hash out their differences. I didn't know why; I just did.

Lazar gently rapped on the door of Orion's office, a dull thud echoing into the room beyond.

"Come in," called the baritone voice I now recognized so clearly. I could already picture the broad-shouldered, imposing figure of Orion awaiting us behind his desk, his dark eyes hungry for the information I had promised.

"It will be easier if you agree to his terms, Navan. And please, do not lie to him," Lazar whispered, just as we were about to set foot in the room.

Navan shot him a dirty look. "I will do whatever I feel comfortable with, Uncle," he spat, "but I will never be a turncoat. I will not agree to something I do not believe in."

"You are still so young, Navan." Lazar sighed remorsefully. "There is so much you do not understand."

Angry fire burned in the depths of Navan's slate eyes. A muscle twitched in his jaw, his shoulders squaring as if to strike. Stepping quickly beside Navan, pressing my palms gently to the firm rise of his chest, I looked up into his eyes and demanded that he look back. I would not be ignored, not now, not when there was so much we still needed to do. This was so much bigger than any family dispute. My blood was still whizzing its way toward Vysanthe, but we couldn't even begin to think about chasing it down until we bartered our way out of this invisible compound.

Instantly, his features softened, the flames dying down in his glowering gaze. Feeling the rapid beat of his pulse begin to slow beneath my palms, I watched as he lifted his gaze away from mine and back to Lazar for the briefest of moments.

"No, Uncle, it is *you* who does not understand," he said in a low voice. "There is *never* an excuse for *this*."

With that, he placed his hand on the small of my back and ushered me into the office to greet the waiting stare of Orion. As I had imagined he would be, he was standing behind the desk, his stature just as imposing as it had been the last time we'd met.

I turned back to glance at Lazar. He was loitering at the threshold of the door, his hazel eyes peering toward Orion with an almost eager look in them.

"You may go, Lazar. Thank you for fetching your nephew for me," Orion said calmly, folding his arms across his vast barrel chest.

Evidently having been hoping he would be allowed to stay, Lazar's expression sank as Orion spoke. With an awkward nod, he retreated without another word, disappearing into the hallway beyond, his footsteps fading into the distance.

"You've had a chance to think about my offer," Orion began, skipping straight to business. His eyes were trained on Navan. "I met your... friend's requirements. I have upheld my end of the bargain, and now I ask that you do the same for yours." There was a warning look in the chief's dark eyes, and I could tell he was the kind of man who didn't like to lose.

"To be honest, Orion, it's all been pretty vague," Navan said, his mouth set in a grim line. "I hear these words—'offer', 'agreement', 'bargain'—being thrown around, but without terms, I can't possibly agree to anything. Not that you've put me in a particularly accommodating mood," he sniped, gesturing to the bruises that had blossomed across his ashen skin. They were beginning to fade, thanks to the vials he'd taken, but they still dappled his strange flesh.

I reached out and rested my hand on Navan's forearm, to calm him. Things wouldn't end well if he lost his temper in front of Orion, not when our lives hung in the balance. I could tell Navan knew the power Orion held over us, but he'd been through so much—there was no telling how much more it would take for him to snap. I was determined for that not to happen, not if I could stop it. Besides, by the look of the thick-set, dark-eyed Vysanthean, I wasn't confident Navan could even take him on. Navan was big and strong by any standard, but this guy looked like he could do some serious damage with just his little finger.

"I suppose that's one way of seeing it," said Orion, a hint of amusement in his voice. "Although, you're not exactly in a position to argue, are you?" he baited, flashing his dark eyes at Navan. There was a clear taunt in the action, but my hand remained firm on Navan's forearm.

"Don't rise to it," I breathed.

"You should take your friend's advice." Orion smirked. I cursed silently, forgetting that a breath no doubt sounded like a booming shout to the Vysantheans' superior senses.

"What is it you want from me?" Navan asked, not falling for Orion's taunt. "I might be more open to agreeing if you'd get on with it and tell me what I'm actually here for. I know you all have a bit of a thing for my dear old Pa, and think he'll give you something in exchange for my safe return, but I don't think he'd be up for paying the kind of price you guys might want. I wouldn't be surprised if he left me to figure things out on my own, to be perfectly honest." A flicker of something rippled across Navan's eyes, but it wasn't there long enough for me to scrutinize properly. It looked like a glimmer of hurt.

"It's not your father I want, though his alchemy skills are far and above those of the meager alchemists I have working day and night here. His help might prove invaluable, but I know men like Jareth Idrax." Orion sighed. "I think your judgment is likely correct. Jareth would never betray his position to save anyone, unless it was his own skin."

"Can't argue with you there," Navan said tightly.

Orion smiled. "Well, we know of your troubles with Ianthan and Jethro, and we are just as eager to ensure that this young woman's blood does not end up in the wrong hands. If either queen were to find the key to immortality, then this rebellion would be doomed before it even began." A tight laugh escaped his throat. "As much as you might not like it, in order to retrieve that sample, you are going to have to play on our team for a little while. Who knows, you might end up liking it..." He winked, but Navan was clearly not amused.

"Do you have details, or are you just going to talk my ear off?" Navan asked.

Again, Orion laughed. He seemed to do a lot of laughing for a man in such a high-powered position. I had expected him to fall into a mask of stern seriousness, but there was an undeniable humor about him. He was more amused by himself than anyone else, but it was still surprising.

"If you do this, Navan, we both might get what we want," Orion said. The smile that tugged at the corners of his lips made the deep scar that ran down the side of his face crinkle, curving it into almost an S-shape. "If you do what I ask—with no errant detours or foolhardy escape plans—there will be enough time for you to track down the pod Ianthan and Jethro sent to Queen Brisha. I don't want it reaching her any more than you do. It would take the wind right out of my sails if she managed to synthesize that elixir before I got the concoction just right."

Navan pulled a sour face. "So I'd be doing two favors for you, for the price of one."

"Look, neither of us wants Vysanthe to find out about Earth, though my reasons are a little less beautiful than yours," Orion continued, with a wink at me that made the veins in Navan's temples bulge. "In return for letting you go, to track down this pod and save Earth from imminent discovery, all I want you to do is head back and meet with Queen Gianne. Explain to her what has happened on your latest little vacation to the far reaches of the universe. Tell her of Jethro and Ianthan's betrayal—tell her you killed them, as punishment for their treason. You know, really butter her up. Tell her that they were planning to join Brisha's side. Make up a reason for it."

"Anything else?" Navan retorted. "Doesn't sound too tricky, you know, just wander into the queen's court and make up a bunch of lies to save the skins of some people I don't care about."

"But you *do* care about one person, don't you?" Orion replied, gesturing toward me.

My insides twisted up in anger. How dare he put me in the center of all of this? How dare he use me as a pawn in his big plan? I felt a stab of guilt, too—I was fast becoming the chink in Navan's armor, and I hated the idea of it, that what was growing between us could be exploited by anyone who cared to.

Navan fell silent.

"I thought so," Orion mused. "Speaking of those people you don't care about, however, I'm going to need you to feed Queen Gianne some more lies. I know she thinks there are rebels regrouping, somewhere beyond the rule of Vysanthe, and you are going to mislead her for us. She fears an uprising— both of them do. They know their hold on Vysanthe is tenuous at best, and you are going to bolster that fear. Tell her you found a rebel base on your travels, in some dusty corner of the universe, and we were few when you came across us, eking out the rest of our sad existence with our tails between our legs. Tell her you managed to win a small group of us over to your side, and you have brought them before her, with information she will be gagging to hear."

Navan's expression shifted, and I could sense he was examining possible loopholes in his mind. "You'll give me my own ship, then—"

"And I'll be sending Lazar with you, to oversee matters, and there will be three more of my most trusted coldbloods joining the ranks," Orion said, with a tight-lipped smile. "Two shapeshifters will also be coming with you, to keep you in check."

Instantly, Navan shook his head. "None of those pasty little maggots. No way."

"There *will* be two shapeshifters coming along, because you will need them when the time comes. You're not really getting that this isn't negotiable, are you?" he asked coldly. "You will need the shapeshifters so you can tell Queen Gianne that these are creatures who have joined the rebellion, whom you have convinced to come over to your side."

"Queen Gianne will kill those shifters the moment she sees them," Navan bit out. "And I wouldn't blame her," he added, bitterness dripping from his words.

At some point, I was going to have to ask to see a book, or something, on the various ins and outs of interplanetary species and why they were so at odds with one another. It wouldn't hurt to be a bit more clued-in.

"Not if you stop her," Orion interjected. "Tell her the shifters know important information about other rebels. Plead for their lives in exchange for information about the rebel base, its size, its location."

Navan's forehead furrowed in a frown. "She'll just send a squadron after the base. When she realizes it's not where these shifters said it was, or where I said it was, I'll be dead meat."

"The shifters are coming with you, whether you like it or not. If any issues arise, if you are forced to kill someone of importance, the shifters can take their place. Their presence will make your life a whole lot easier. Do I make myself clear?" Orion said coldly. Navan remained silent as the chief continued. "You will tell Queen Gianne that the rebel planet is lightyears away, in a far-off quadrant of the universe that will take at least a year to reach. You found these individuals at an outpost, closer to Vysanthe, with word that this imagined rebel base is far larger. She will be so focused on finding this place, and nipping the rebellion in the bud, that she won't see us coming. By the time she realizes her error, we'll have swarmed upon her like Horerczy butterflies."

I raised an eyebrow. "Horerczy what?"

"They live in the swamps of our homeland," Navan muttered. "Vampiric insects that smother their victims and eat them alive, gnawing them down to the bone in seconds—like tiny piranhas with wings."

I shuddered. Vysanthe really didn't sound like the friendliest of places.

Orion leaned forward. "While you're at the queen's palace, I want you to keep a lookout for any weakness in her queendom—any good spots we might strike from, or find our way into, to make the coup go all the smoother. Do all this, and you can consider yourselves free people. If you desire, we can arrange for rebel transport to return you to Earth, or anywhere else you might want. I hear Caro is nice this time of year."

"We will owe you nothing for the rest of our lives?" Navan asked.

Orion nodded slowly. "That is correct."

"I'll go," Navan said quietly. "I'll go without a fight—if you let Riley go back to her family today."

My heart sank. I looked up at Navan's face, but he wasn't returning my gaze. Even though I had known what his answer would be from the start, given what Orion would do otherwise, it didn't make it any easier. Standing so close to him, I couldn't help remembering the way those lips had felt upon mine, and how I might never touch them again. Once he left for Vysanthe, he might not return, and I'd never know what happened to him... My body went numb at the thought, though I tried not to let my reaction show on my face.

Orion said nothing, his curious smirk seeming to invite Navan to elaborate.

"She won't breathe a word of this to anyone," Navan continued. "Besides, she'll be no use on a journey like this."

Orion's smirk morphed into a malicious grin, and a chill ran down my spine. "Actually, my dear boy, I think she could be of great use indeed."

The next thing I knew, Orion was a blur, moving like lightning across the room—and something cold pressed against the side of my neck.

12

*H*ardly daring to turn, I saw that Orion held a gun in his hand, the barrel nuzzling the fragile flesh at the curve of my throat. I gulped, feeling the cold barrel more intensely.

"No!" Navan roared, but it was too late.

Orion's finger pulled the trigger. A sharp pain shot up through my neck, bursting through every cell and nerve ending like wildfire, the agony excruciating, making my voice cry out in an incoherent scream. This was it... This was the way I died. It had come out of nowhere; I didn't know whether to be happy or sad that it had come upon me so suddenly. At least this way, I didn't have time to agonize over the things I'd never had the chance to do, before the searing pain took over my brain, fogging it over in a mist of pure torture.

Willing my death to be quicker, given the unbearable agony boiling away within me, I was surprised when the fog in my head began to clear, and the pain began to ebb slightly. As it faded, I became aware of strong arms around me, and Navan's slate eyes looking into mine with such anguish, I thought my heart might break.

"Riley," he whispered, tilting my chin upward.

"Still here... I think," I choked out, wanting to kiss the lips that rested so close to mine. After a brief glimpse into the jaws of certain death, I wanted to feel alive again.

The sound of Orion stepping backward distracted me. He was standing a short distance away, evidently eager to put some space between himself and Navan's furious aura. Even though Orion was likely the stronger man, I knew there was a lot to be said for adrenaline, or whatever the coldblood equivalent was. In his arms, I could feel Navan shaking with what looked like rage and despair.

"What did you do to her?" he spat, almost crushing me against his hard chest. I clung on, regardless. I could catch my breath later.

"I inserted a chip into her neck," Orion explained calmly. "Riley going on this mission is a necessary part of the bargain, I'm afraid. You're an unpredictable creature, at best. Did you think I'd send you with a troop of my men, and not have safeguards in place?" A cruel smile twisted up the corners of his lips, his scar twisting with it.

I could feel Navan's heart thundering in his chest, the vibrations reverberating through my palms, which I had pressed against him. No matter how closely I held him, I could not get him to calm down.

"I said I would go," he snarled, his fangs flashing for a moment, reminding me of the first time he'd shown his true self to me. Up close, it really was frightening.

Orion shook his head. "I can't simply take your word for it, that you will go through with what I ask, and not harm any of my men on the way. This makes matters much easier," he said, tapping the barrel of the gun he still held in his hand. I didn't know where he'd been hiding it, or how he'd whipped it out so quickly.

"Take that thing out of her neck, now!" Navan demanded, but I knew there was no point. Orion didn't seem like the kind of guy who ever went back on his decisions.

"I'm not going to do that, Navan," Orion said silkily. "You see, if at any point I find out you aren't toeing the line, or there's so much as a whiff of betrayal, I will activate the chip, and I will kill Riley. That goes for trying to remove the chip, too, or telling anyone about it," he added. "It's not the kind of technology I like to go around boasting about, but it serves its purpose." An almost remorseful expression crossed the scarred man's face, but it didn't make sense to me. Surely a man like this, who was so used to war and bloodshed, could not feel bad about one little, manipulative chip?

"I said I would go," Navan seethed. "Why do this? Why push me?"

"Because, although *you* may be too important to kill, given who your father is, Riley is not," Orion said slowly, giving a casual shrug. "If you slip up, she'll be the one who suffers, and you will see every second of it on her... delightful face." He eyed me like a vulture circling, and I felt a shudder run down my spine. Whether it was due to the after-effects of the chip he'd placed in my neck, or the malevolence creeping beneath the surface of his face, I wasn't sure.

"I would have done it anyway!" Navan shouted. "You must be

insane if you think I can just waltz a human into Vysanthe and not have anyone notice. You're only putting us in more danger!"

Orion smirked. "Let me be straight with you: I don't trust you, Navan. The Idraxes have never been the most trustworthy of families, and I need to ensure my requirements are being met."

"I am not my father," Navan spat, and I could see the venom burning in his eyes. Boy, he really must hate his father, to feel such fury. Not for the first time, I wanted to know more about Jareth and the life Navan had lived on Vysanthe, before taking to the skies. What had pushed him away, so fiercely, from his own people? I knew, to some extent, but there had to be more to it.

Orion shrugged. "Perhaps not, but you have his blood running in your veins. Besides, I'm sure you'll figure out a way to keep her safe, if you wish her to live. You could always tell Queen Gianne that she's an unknown specimen you found on your travels, and felt like keeping her as a slave, for your own... needs. From the look of her, nobody would blame you. She looks strong and lively —the perfect pet. We coldbloods take on pets so often, Queen Gianne would barely bat an eyelid."

I looked at Navan in horror, hardly believing my ears. I knew they took resources from other planets, but to steal beings and use them as slaves? Did they think everyone else so inferior that they could just do that? It pained me to think it, but I knew they probably did. These Vysantheans clearly had some sort of superiority complex.

"She'll know," Navan grated out.

Orion shook his head. "She won't. Nobody would be insane enough to take something, or someone, important into the fray of Vysanthe. It's the perfect ruse," he stated, grinning at me like a wolf. "You just have to keep your eye on her, make sure she doesn't get into any trouble that could blow everything wide open. Which, if you know what's good for you—and her, for that matter—you will do."

For a long moment, nobody said anything. There was too much going on in the room, and my head was spinning. The pain in my neck had ebbed, but shots still fired up my nerves every few minutes, startling me. Each time, I felt Navan's strong hand around my waist, gripping me tight.

"Is there anything else?" Navan said, at last, his tone bordering on defeated.

"I don't think so," Orion replied coolly. I wanted to smack that stupid, superior look off his stupid, superior face.

"Then may we go?"

Orion nodded. "I've had a nicer room prepared for you," he said, suspiciously kindly.

As we turned to go, Navan's hand steering me toward the door, I heard Orion's voice calling us back.

"Oh, there is one more thing," he noted.

Before either Navan or I could speak, I felt a jolt of electricity spasm through my body, ricocheting through every muscle and sinew, feeling as though it was snapping each one as it coursed through me. I caught a glimpse of Orion's hand, pressing a button, but then my eyes filled with black spots, my knees buckling as I crumpled to the ground.

The pain and lack of control lasted only a few minutes, but it was enough to see that Orion was serious. His point was well and truly made. Putting his arms around me, Navan helped me back onto my feet, though they were wobbly to say the least. Propping me up, he glowered in Orion's direction, but the chief merely gave a cold, amused smile.

"That is just the beginning of what this device can do," he said, "so I urge you not to try me."

Turning to Navan, I felt my insides twist. I knew Orion wasn't bluffing. If that was only a taste of what the chip could do, I didn't want to find out the impact of its full force. If that moment ever came, I had a feeling death would be a blessing in comparison.

s we walked out of Orion's office, my knees were still trembling from the effects of the chip. Navan's arm was around my waist, helping me along, and I clung to his side, longing to be anywhere but here, with the dark cloud of the mission to Vysanthe looming over us both.

A guard walked slightly ahead of us, ensuring we moved in the right direction, but I could barely look at him. Unless it was Navan, I didn't want to see another coldblood until I had to. I was done with their superiority, and their penchant for aggression and manipulation. I was done with the way they thought they could control everyone and everything, to meet their own ends.

My attention snapped to the sound of footsteps approaching. Glancing up through still-foggy eyes, I saw a small group of cold-bloods walking straight toward us. Grimacing, I wondered if this was another of Orion's tricks—had he granted us a moment of peace, only to dash it with violence? These coldbloods looked particularly grim, their faces crosshatched with scars and black tattoos that webbed across their skin. It was then that I noticed the familiar figure in the center of the nasty-looking trio.

Galo.

He looked surprisingly unhurt compared to Navan, but the grim expression on his coldblood escorts' faces made me worry how much longer that would be the case. If Galo was experiencing fear, however, his posture wasn't giving it away. He was standing tall, his chin held up almost defiantly—as though he'd rather die than give the coldbloods the satisfaction of seeing him cower— and as he spotted me, his face softened.

"So, we meet again," he said as we drew closer, his lips spreading in a faint, crooked smile.

"Galo," I breathed, concern for his safety setting my nerves on edge. Impulsively, I ran forward on wobbling legs and tried to reach out to grasp at him.

"Stay back," one of the coldbloods snarled.

"You have to let him go!" I shouted, unable to take my eyes away from the lycan who had been so surprisingly kind to me. I remembered how gentle he had been when he took my hand in his as we traveled through the compound, like someone's much-loved grandfather. Part of him must have known he was walking into a trap, but he had come along anyway—and suffered for it.

"Ah, there's no use bargaining for an old goat like me, Riley." Galo sighed. "You'd better stay back—these coldbloods are party poopers. They won't let me go."

"I'm not going to leave you here," I said, tears pricking my eyes. Navan tried to pull me back, but I jerked away from him.

"Just take care of yourself, kid," Galo said as the coldbloods pushed him forward. He set Navan with a stern look. "Take care of each other."

Navan's expression remained stoic. "Thank you."

The coldbloods marched him around the corner and out of sight. Even to the very last second, Galo kept his chin up, that soft smile upon his canine lips.

"Galo!" I choked back a sob, hardly daring to imagine what would happen to him.

Navan pulled me toward him, enveloping me in his arms. I couldn't muster the energy to fight him this time.

"Galo's right," Navan whispered. "Orion would never allow his release. He has complete control over us, with the deal we made, and..." His fingers brushed the back of my neck, where the chip was embedded beneath my skin, and I shivered at his touch.

"You have to promise me that we'll come back for him," I said, my voice firm even though it was shaking. "He risked so much to save you."

Navan held me closer to his chest. "Once we return to Earth, I promise that I will do everything in my power to repay our debt to him."

"Keep up!" our coldblood guard barked, having turned at the end of the corridor to see us lingering behind.

Navan pulled me forward, keeping his arm around me, though all I could think about was Galo's face, and what punishment might lie in wait for him. I'd already seen what they'd put Navan through. To know that there was a species out in the universe that relished such brutality, and wielded such enormous power... I shook the thought away. If I continued down that mental path, I knew the figure standing next to me might start to shift, morphing from beautiful to terrifying in the blink of an eye. Navan was not his father, nor a true representation of his people, but there *was* a darkness in him. He was Vysanthean, after all.

The coldblood guard stopped in front of a door, and opened it wide for us to enter. As soon as we were inside, he loomed in the doorway, a nasty look on his face.

"While the chief makes his preparations, the pair of you are to stay here," he said. "Don't try to escape. We'll know about it, if you do."

With that, he slammed the door shut, my ears picking up on the faintest beep as it closed. We were locked in. Usually, I wouldn't mind the idea of being locked up in close quarters with Navan, but right now I wanted to feel fresh air on my face, and see daylight on Earth once more, in case it was the last time I ever got the chance.

The room itself was much nicer than the one they'd previously kept Navan hostage in, but claustrophobia shivered through my veins, constricting my chest with panic. There was a sofa and a bed, with another door leading to a bathroom, but that was about the extent of it. The lack of windows underscored the fact that we were trapped.

"Are you okay?" Navan asked, his arms still around me, his eyes gazing down into mine. He paused, a grim smile turning up the corners of his mouth. "Stupid question."

I nestled into his chest, wanting to feel the solidity of him around me. If I closed my eyes really tight, I could pretend none of this was happening. I could pretend we were in my childhood bedroom at home in New York, and he was there, comforting me over something stupid, something ordinary.

"I will keep you safe," he promised, murmuring into my hair.

"If anyone can, my bet is on you," I replied, keeping my eyes squeezed shut. It was hopeless. I couldn't push the mission out of my head, no matter how hard I tried. There was too much at stake—too much that could go wrong. "What if, after all of this, the queens still find Earth, Navan? What if I mess up—what if they find out what I am, and what my blood can do, and come looking for my species? What will they do to humankind if they find us?"

It was a question that had been bugging me through everything that Orion had said. There were too many lies to keep juggling at one time. Surely, one would slip through, ruining everything? I was the evidence the queens needed that an immortality elixir could be created, and I was about to walk right into Vysanthe.

"I won't let that happen," Navan said, lifting my chin. "I swore I'd keep Earth safe, and I'm still going to."

"You're one man, Navan. And you told me yourself that it's only a matter of time before one of the queens' engineers cracks the technology that'll enable them to find Earth."

"We can't worry about that now. Don't be a defeatist," he said, a little coldly.

I withdrew from him, surprised by the tone in his voice. Instantly, his features softened, his arms reaching out to pull me back into his embrace.

"I'm sorry." He sighed. "It's been a long day."

"Tell me about it," I muttered, trying to keep the hurt out of my voice.

"I'm just worried about taking you there, to Vysanthe," he

explained, his words tightening as he uttered the name of his home planet.

I let myself relax back into the closeness of him. "I understand," I whispered. "I'm worried too. Seeing Galo in the hallway —I feel like I keep putting people in harm's way. Orion would never have been able to make you go, if it wasn't for me," I admitted, pushing away tears. I didn't want him to see how much it was getting to me. I was stronger than this, but at this moment, I didn't feel it. In fact, I'd never felt so scared and vulnerable, fearing for the lives of those I cared about. If I messed up on Vysanthe, it wasn't just Navan and I that I'd have to worry about—it was everyone on Earth. Everyone I loved. Angie, Lauren, Roger, Jean... All of them.

"Galo will be okay," Navan promised, though I didn't know whether or not he was saying it just to comfort me. "They'll likely keep him to trade for one of their own, if the Fed were to capture a rebel coldblood."

"Sometimes, there are things worse than death," I reminded him, thinking of the chip in my neck, and the power Orion now wielded over me. Over us both.

Slowly, Navan lifted my head up, forcing me to look in his eyes. There was an oath in them, a promise that everything was going to be all right. It must have been hard for him to appear so confident, when I knew the insecurity he felt when it came to protecting other people. It stemmed from losing his sister, Naya, even though her death hadn't been his fault.

Gratitude swelled in my heart for him, that he was being so strong for me. Seizing the moment, I looped my arms around his neck, my hands running through his hair, and pulled him to me, my lips crushing against his in a desperate kiss. Fireworks went off inside me, my mind emptying of everything but him. I wanted to feel his warmth surrounding me, strengthening my resolve for what was to come. This had to be worth fighting for, right?

It was frantic, his hands on my hips, running up the curves of my waist, bringing me as close to him as possible. His kisses weren't soft or delicate, but that wasn't what I wanted anyway. I wanted passion and fire, to remind me I was alive. As his mouth fell to my neck, planting fierce kisses along the fragile skin of my throat, I knew how easy it would be for him to taste the blood that ran in my veins. He never would, but the thought crossed my mind. My pulse quickened as his lips returned to mine, his tongue exploring my mouth. I felt the world fall away. It was just me and Navan, unified.

Like this, we could take on anything Orion and Vysanthe had in store.

About an hour later, the door burst open to reveal two guards. I had been sitting next to Navan, holding him, and immediately drew away, but the smug look on the faces of the two coldbloods told me they already knew what had been going on between us. Feeling my cheeks flush, I scowled at them, determined not to let them sully what Navan and I had.

"The ship's ready," one of them said.

"Best not keep them waiting," the other added, flashing a fanged grin in my direction.

With that, Navan took my hand and led me out of the room, following the two guards through a labyrinth of hallways. We exited through a seemingly innocuous door, out into the bright light and fresh air of the real world. I had never been so glad to draw crisp oxygen into my lungs, or see the sun gleaming overhead, casting its warming rays down through the invisible barrier of the compound and onto my face.

The gentle caress of a light breeze on my skin felt almost heavenly. It seemed I would get to take one last look at Earth, before I left it... for who knew how long. There was a good chance I would never make it back.

"What if this all goes wrong?" I whispered urgently, gripping Navan's hand.

There was a gleaming ship, similar in structure to Navan's *Soraya*, standing in the middle of the open expanse of ground, the shimmering, liquid-metallic surface shifting beneath the light of the sun's rays. It was all getting too real now. Never in a million years had I thought I'd leave Earth. A painfully short time ago, such a thing hadn't been possible for someone like me. An astronaut maybe, after years and years of training, but not me.

"I'll make it work. Trust me," Navan replied, so casually I wanted to scream. How could he be so calm, in the face of something so life altering? I had a feeling he was doing it to spare my feelings, to show he was confident of our success, but that just led me to wonder what he was really thinking, beneath that stoic façade.

As promised, there were four coldbloods and two shifters waiting on the field in front of the ship, their eyes all turned toward us. I shuddered at the sight of the shapeshifters in their natural form, their pale flesh hanging from their limbs like melted pools of skin. I quickly looked elsewhere, taking in the faces of the four coldbloods. Lazar was there, though I couldn't say it was particularly nice to see his familiar face. The other three were burly males with the same shaven buzzcut, though one had a shock of white-blond hair, while the other two had jet black. Three sets of impenetrable, dark eyes looked over me, making my skin crawl.

"Welcome aboard the *Asterope*," Lazar announced, gesturing at the ship behind him.

Pressing a button on the side of the ship, Lazar prompted a gangway to slide out from the underbelly of the vessel, as a door shot upward with a click. With no time to waste, everyone entered, though Navan and I hung back, not wanting to be the first on board.

As soon as I stepped into the interior of the vessel, my heart sank. It was much smaller than I'd anticipated, with barely enough room for Navan to stand upright. I wasn't sure what I'd been expecting, but it certainly wasn't something so tiny. I mean, where were we all going to sleep? Were there hidden pods somewhere, where we could rest our heads on the trip? I didn't even know how long it was going to take, but I knew it would definitely be long enough to need to eat and sleep and move around a bit.

"I suppose we should get down to business—who is sleeping where, and who is sleeping with whom?" the blond-haired coldblood spoke up, a curious glint in his dark eyes, which, upon closer inspection, were actually a very deep shade of brown. His voice was gruff, with a hint of mischief in it.

Lazar shot him a look. "Not now, Kalvin," he warned.

Kalvin shrugged. "Why not now? It's a long journey, and I'm

going to need some shuteye at some point. Might as well get it out of the way now, before we set off."

Lazar sighed. "Well, I'm going to get us off the ground. You can talk amongst yourselves for a while. I'll be sleeping in the cockpit, so don't think to include me in your game of pairs," he said, before disappearing through a door at the far end of the ship's cramped main room. I watched him go, not feeling comfortable being left alone with three strange coldbloods and two shifters.

"So," purred Kalvin, turning his intense stare in my direction, "who gets the girl?"

14

𝒶 t the sound of Kalvin's words, my blood ran cold. I didn't want to share with anyone but Navan. Clearly feeling the same, Navan stepped a little in front of me, his arm slipping around me.

"There are only three sleeping pods, and there are seven of us," Kalvin continued. "So, who gets the girl to keep him warm on this long, cold trip?" He winked, my stomach turning.

"She is staying with me," Navan growled.

Kalvin grinned. "Now, now, let's not get ahead of ourselves. These things need planning," he taunted. "Obviously, those two will sleep together, since I'd rather pull out my fangs with tweezers than get up close to a shifter," he remarked. The two shifters made a sour face at him, though they said nothing in retaliation.

To my surprise, the two shapeshifters drew closer to one another, nuzzling each other with the flabby pouches that might have served as their cheeks. I didn't know whether to find it cute or repulsive.

"Are they... an item?" I asked quietly, not knowing how to phrase it. I'd never seen anything like it, though it made perfect sense. I'd already been told that interspecies relationships were frowned upon, at best, so why wouldn't shifters find love with other shifters?

Navan nodded, his own face showing revulsion. "They are mates, yes."

"How do they..." I trailed off, feeling embarrassed.

"You don't want to know." Navan smiled, though it didn't reach his eyes, which were fixed on Kalvin's arrogant face.

"But where do we put everyone else?" the coldblood asked, evidently enjoying the game of toying with Navan.

"I'm not sleeping next to Nestor," one of the dark-haired cold-bloods announced suddenly, shoving the other coldblood in the shoulder. "His snores could start quakes!"

"Yeah, well, I'm not sleeping next to you either, Cristo!" the coldblood named Nestor snapped, pushing Cristo so hard he stumbled up against the back wall of the ship.

Kalvin grinned. "Boys, boys, you're missing the point," he murmured, his gaze on me. "I think Riley here should sleep with me and Cristo, since we're the highest ranking on board this ship, after old man Lazar over there," he said, flicking his wrist in the direction of the door Lazar had gone through.

I froze, hating the sound of my name coming from Kalvin's lips. Orion or Lazar had no doubt told them all who I was, but it still didn't make me like it. It turned my stomach, to hear the way they spoke it, always with a hint of something untoward. I could already feel Kalvin undressing me with his eyes, making me want to back out of the ship that instant, and put as much distance between myself and these hungry coldbloods as possible.

"She stays with me," Navan snarled. "Don't make me say it again."

"It would be a nice idea, if the two of you could be trusted—which you can't. Who's to say the pair of you won't come up with some escape plan the moment you're alone together? Nope, not gonna happen. So, sorry, but think again," Kalvin said.

I realized then they didn't know about the chip in my neck, keeping Navan in line. Orion really must not have wanted anyone to know about the technology, if he hadn't even told his "most trusted" men.

Navan looked at me, evidently thinking the same thing, but I shook my head discreetly, keeping him from invoking Orion's wrath.

"She stays with me," Navan repeated, his words dripping venom.

Kalvin ignored him, his eyes still fixed on me. "You know, I've never tasted human before," he said, licking his lips licentiously, "but I bet you're delicious."

I held onto Navan's arm, certain that he was about to lunge for Kalvin. Beneath my hand, I could feel Navan's muscles spasming as he fought back the urge to strike at the obnoxious, lewd cold-blood. I shared the sentiment, but I knew that getting into a fight here would do us no good. Besides, there was no space for a brawl.

For a moment, I thought about bursting Kalvin's bubble, telling him that my blood would have to be synthesized before he could get his filthy jaws on me, but then I realized something.

They *knew* about my blood. Kalvin was just trying to rile Navan up, and scare me in the process. Well, not today. I'd had enough of coldbloods trying to frighten me.

"I could tear that pretty neck of hers wide open, and drink until there was nothing left." Cristo laughed coldly, his leering eyes wandering over my body.

Nestor nodded. "I'd bathe in her blood. I'd bottle it up and sell it to the highest bidder." With all three coldbloods staring at me, I felt sick.

Despite knowing they were just trying to get a reaction out of us, I felt a true tremble of fear shiver up my spine. These creatures were powerful. Even if they were joking now, what if they decided to act on it later? Here, trapped on this ship, I would be helpless to stop them.

Before I could step in, I felt Navan break away from me, moving rapidly in their direction. A cry went up as he struck Nestor in the stomach, the coldblood buckling at the knees. Cristo leapt to his comrade's defense, baring his teeth as he hurled himself at Navan, his sharp fangs ready to bite into the ashen flesh of the man I... cared for.

Kalvin joined the fray, his hands balled into fists, and punched Navan hard in the face. Navan reeled, staggering backward, but he was lunging forward again in no time, striking Kalvin in the neck.

"Navan, stop!" I yelled, but he either couldn't hear me, or wasn't listening.

The shifters shrank back as the coldbloods battled one another in a blur of limbs and fangs. Navan was strong, but it was hard for him to hold off all three of them at once in such cramped quarters. They barely had any space to lunge! He was doing a good job of it, ducking and diving beneath blows, but I could see he was struggling to keep an eye on everyone. They moved so fast, even I was having trouble keeping up from my spot on the periphery of it all.

"All of you, stop!" a voice roared from somewhere behind them.

Lazar had reappeared, just in the nick of time. Kalvin had Navan by the throat, with Nestor and Cristo pinning his arms behind his back. He was fighting back, his muscles straining against his captors, but I knew he wouldn't have lasted much longer, had Lazar not interceded when he did.

Immediately, the coldbloods released Navan.

"We were just discussing sleeping arrangements," Kalvin said casually, brushing blood from his lip. "I made it clear that Navan and Riley couldn't stay together in a pod, since they can't be trusted." He pouted, drawing backward like a wounded animal.

Lazar turned to where I stood, an apologetic expression on his face. "I will be the one to watch over them. The rest of you, I suggest you keep your distance," he warned. "I'm the highest-ranking officer on this ship, and if there's so much as a peep from any of you, Orion will be the first to hear about it."

"Don't blame me when the lovebirds escape," Kalvin grumbled, with the other two coldbloods reluctantly agreeing with Lazar's words.

"This way," Lazar said, leading Navan and me away from the main room of the *Asterope*, and down a very narrow hallway to the left. Navan's shoulders barely fit the width of it.

A second later, he stopped in front of one of the three doors that led off from the corridor. These were, presumably, the pods Kalvin had been speaking about. Pushing the door open, Lazar ushered us inside. Beyond was a tiny room with one bed and a makeshift cot pushed up against the curved wall. Aside from that, and two lamps, the room was bare.

"You should remain here as often as you can, during our journey," Lazar suggested, his eyes darting out to the hallway. "They will do you no harm while there is breath in my body, but they can't be trusted. I'm sorry you had to endure that," he said, turning to me.

"It's okay," I lied, still shaken by the words they had spoken.

"Navan, I trust you will keep your temper in check, in the future," Lazar continued, his gaze shifting to his nephew.

Navan's eyes burned with angry fire. He still looked confused about the double life his uncle was leading, and how he had come to be here, on Earth, with a rebel band of coldbloods. Perhaps Navan didn't believe his uncle to be any more trustworthy than the coldbloods out in the main room.

"Unless I'm provoked," Navan muttered.

"Well, try not to be provoked then," Lazar said. "Rest up. We've got a long flight ahead of us, and you are going to need your strength when we land," he added, his tone softening.

Without another word, Lazar ducked out of the room and shut the door behind him. Immediately, Navan crossed the space and pressed a button that glowed against the wall. There was a soft beep, before silence fell, leaving only the gentle thrum of the ship's engine to underscore the moment.

Uncertainly, I wandered over to the bed and sat down on the edge, my eyes looking up at Navan, waiting for him to join me. He did so a moment later, though I could feel the fury pouring off him in waves. His fangs were still half bared, glinting sharply. Curious,

I lifted my fingers to touch them. His expression was surprised as my fingertips ran along the smooth edges of the elongated canines.

As I pulled away, I smiled nervously. "They're pretty impressive," I said, my heart still pounding from the fracas outside.

"That's one word for them," he muttered.

Wanting to make Navan feel better, I put my arms around him and pulled him down onto the bed, wrapping myself up in his arms, feeling the strong contours of his chest beneath my head, and the steady beat of his heart within. He nuzzled into me, kissing me gently on the lips, just once. It was long and lingering, and though I wanted to enjoy it, I held back, knowing it wasn't the right moment.

Fear wasn't exactly an aphrodisiac, and I didn't like the thought of the coldbloods cackling outside, listening in. No, this was a moment for safety and security, and Navan had that in spades. Here, with him, I felt like nobody could get at me. We were in each other's arms, heading for a nightmarish world—I needed him just to hold me, to make things start to feel better again.

Although, maybe even his arms weren't capable of that.

The next three days went by in a blur. As much as I wished we could go after the pod containing my blood that was still drifting its way through space, Orion's orders to Lazar were that capturing the pod was only to happen *after* our mission on Vysanthe—as some sick incentive to ensure we performed well and got out alive, no doubt.

And so, there was nothing to do but wait. Navan and I tried to stay in our pod as much as possible, as I didn't want to face those pigs again and neither did Navan. Whenever I needed the bathroom, Navan would escort me, not wanting me to get caught in the corridor alone. During the brief periods we were out of our pod, Lazar made an attempt to talk to Navan if he was passing by, but for the most part, Navan was successful at avoiding him too.

On the evening of the third day, however, Lazar came to Navan in our pod. Navan let him in, eyeing him stonily while Lazar greeted him, then walked over to a small box in the far corner that I hadn't paid much attention to, and pressed a button. The lid popped open, and Lazar took two cushions and a box from within. Setting them down on the floor, with the box in the center of the two cushions, he beckoned to Navan.

"I bet it has been a while since you've played Periculum," he said, a tentative smile tugging his lips.

Navan frowned. "I haven't played that since I was a kid... With you, actually—that was the last time."

"Feel like a game? We'll be arriving soon, so this might be our last chance."

His words sent a shiver down my spine. *Arriving soon.* Although this journey was not exactly comfortable, a part of me wished it would last forever, so we never had to reach our destination. I was also surprised that it had gone so quickly. I hadn't asked Navan exactly how long it took to travel between Earth and Vysanthe in his *Soraya*, but I hadn't gotten the impression that it was this fast.

I watched Navan's expression, which looked as tense as I felt. "Your rebel tech is more advanced than I gave you credit for," he said after a moment.

Lazar shrugged. "Orion has quite a large pool of great minds at his disposal." Then he paused, watching Navan and waiting for an answer to his question.

I watched Navan too, wondering what he was going to say. I *had* wanted them to have a moment in which they might repair the broken links in their relationship, but only Navan could decide when and where that might happen.

"I guess a game couldn't hurt," he muttered at last, taking the cushion opposite his uncle.

A look of secret delight flitted across Lazar's face for the briefest moment, seen only by me. Perhaps there was hope yet of the two of them saving their relationship.

Intrigued by the game they were playing, I wandered over and sat on the edge of the bed, tucking my legs under me. I peered over Navan's shoulder to watch what was going on. It looked something like a game Roger used to try to get me to play, though this one had different quadrants on a board shaped like a map, and various objects of different sizes stacked up in a smaller box to either side of each player. After watching them set up, each putting a team of small figures into position, I soon realized that the aim of the game was to dominate the board, taking over each quadrant, until it was entirely filled with your color.

Of course it is, I thought to myself bitterly. *What else would Vysantheans play?*

It was a game of intellect and skill. I watched intently as Navan moved the figures across the board, storming through sections that were colored in the light blue of Lazar's pieces. He was good, his mind working in ways mine never would when it came to sneak attacks and sacrificing pieces in return for more space on the board. They were engrossed, the pair of them, and for once I could see the family resemblance, in the way their brows furrowed.

"By the way," Lazar said after a few minutes, "have you thought about how you will explain my presence to the queen? I'm not sure if Orion briefed you on that."

"I've thought about it," Navan murmured, his eyes fixed on the board. "If she asks for details, I'll tell her my own ship broke down —which is why I haven't arrived back on it—and that I sent out a distress signal. You answered it, given that you were in the vicinity, doing whatever weird research it is that you supposedly do for your alchemy projects..."

Lazar sighed, but smiled wanly. "I believe she'll buy that."

Feeling unsettled again at the reminder of our imminent arrival, I left them to the game. Seeking another distraction, I allowed my curiosity to lead me to the box Lazar had delved into to fish out the board game. There were other things inside. I sat down beside it, rummaging around for anything interesting. After plucking out a scroll that grabbed my attention, I unraveled it to find a map of space, etched across the wide piece of waxy material.

Only, it didn't look like any map of space I'd ever seen. There were familiar planets, dotted across the surface, but there were some I had never seen either. In one section, there were clusters of curiously named planets, each with a species listed beside it. *Aliens, everywhere.* I almost felt like laughing—all this time, Earth had thought aliens a mere theory, but here they were, written down in black and white. My eyes lingered upon the sight of my solar system, noting the lines that had been drawn between it and Vysanthe. Put on paper like that, it didn't seem all that far.

Feeling fear begin to prickle through me once again, I placed the scroll back in the box, stood up and walked over to the door of the pod.

"Where are you going?" Navan asked, his head snapping up.

"Just the bathroom," I said.

"I'll come with you—" he began, but I cut him off.

"Navan, it's okay. I'll go on my own this time. Lazar did make it clear on the first day that no one should mess with us... I'll scream if I need you."

Navan glanced between me and the game board, then finally grunted and nodded reluctantly.

I found the narrow hallway empty, much to my relief, and hurried along to the bathroom at the far end. Catching my reflection in the mirror, I splashed my face with some water, hoping it might bring some life and color back to my tired, dull features. At least we'd been provided with fresh clothing—plain, dark outfits that were surprisingly warm—which must have been arranged by Orion. It would have looked too fishy arriving in Vysanthe in our old tattered clothes, not to mention they'd be stinky as hell.

After I'd finished my attempt at freshening myself up, I returned the way I'd come... only to pull up short just before reaching the doorway to Navan's and my pod.

Kalvin was striding through the corridor, coming in the opposite direction. Knowing there was no place to run, I steeled myself against meeting him, and pressed on.

As I tried to pass him, however, I felt his hand grip my arm, pulling me back. Opening my mouth to scream, I jolted as no sound came out. Kalvin's hand had clamped across my mouth, silencing me.

15

I tried to bite his hand but nearly broke my teeth in the process. A rookie error, I discovered; coldblood skin wasn't like human flesh. It was shockingly tough.

"If you promise not to scream, I'll let go," Kalvin said, his tone surprisingly gentle. "I don't mean you any harm. I just wanted to apologize for my behavior the other night."

Wary but curious, I relaxed my jaw, nodding slowly. A moment later, I felt the hand around my mouth slacken, before it moved away entirely. Kalvin stepped back, his brow furrowed, like he expected me to do exactly what he'd asked me not to. Instead, I remained quiet, knowing I could always shout out if I needed to now that his hand was gone.

"Why should I trust a word you say?" I asked, folding my arms across my chest.

He smiled. "Because I'm a nice guy, really."

I didn't believe him, but he'd caught my attention. I wanted to hear what he had to say for himself. The horrible things the trio of coldbloods had said still haunted me.

"I doubt that," I remarked.

"I am, really. I just... I get carried away sometimes," he said... almost sheepishly. His dark brown gaze dropped to the floor. "It's bravado. You know, something to impress the other guys."

Why was he telling me this? Surely, if any of those "guys" heard him speaking like this, he'd be mercilessly teased, if not worse. Admitting it to me seemed like a weird thing to do, but then, what did I know of the inner workings of Vysanthean minds? Nothing, that's what.

"Say I did believe you. It changes nothing. I don't trust any of you," I said coldly, wanting to be back in the safety of my pod.

He nodded. "I can understand why. I just wanted to come by and see if you were okay. This mission is a crazy one, right? I can't even imagine how you're feeling about it. You've left your world behind, to head into the unknown—you're a braver person than me." He flashed me a grin.

Was he... flirting with me? It certainly felt like it. Perhaps this was a ruse to try to bring down my defenses. And yet... it appeared oddly genuine. There was a sincerity on Kalvin's face that hadn't been there the other day, and it was confusing the hell out of me.

"I'm a bit concerned, as anyone would be," I replied, not wanting to give too much away. Besides, he didn't know that I *had* to be here, thanks to Orion's chip.

"I just figured you might want to talk about it, since we're all in this together. I know it didn't seem like it the other day, but we are. We know it's going to be tough, and I wanted to make sure you were doing okay," he continued.

I frowned. "You think we're some sort of team?" I said, stifling a tight laugh.

He shrugged. "It's what we've been put here to do. We all behaved like idiots the first day, but you should know we've all got your back." I could barely believe my ears. "Plus, I've heard what Navan's like from his uncle—he never talks about anything. So I figured you might be in need of a shoulder to vent on."

Of all the people in all the world, Kalvin was the last person I'd feel like pouring my heart out to, and yet there was something compelling about him when he was being serious like this. He was trying—I could see it in his face.

So I decided to humor him.

"Well, I'm worried. I've never so much as left my country, never mind the planet," I said. "I don't know what to expect. Everyone and everything sounds so cold and harsh on Vysanthe, so I'm not exactly looking forward to it."

Just then, I felt a hand on my shoulder, pulling me sharply away from Kalvin. I jolted backward, almost losing my footing. Turning, I saw Navan's face looming above me, his slate eyes glowering in the direction of the blond-haired coldblood.

"What do you think you're doing?" he said, though I didn't know if he was talking to me or Kalvin.

"We were just having a friendly chat," Kalvin replied, his tone returning to the taunting lilt I'd heard a few nights ago. "Getting to know one another, before the big day."

A low sound growled from the back of Navan's throat, but I was standing between the two coldbloods, preventing Navan from lunging forward. There would be no more fighting while *I* was around to stop it.

"We really were just talking, Navan," I said softly, and placed a hand on his arm. "Come on, why don't we go and find something to eat?"

"Fine," he muttered, his eyes still on Kalvin. I led him down the narrow hallway and out into the main space of the *Asterope*.

There were several boxes of supplies stacked up in the far corner, and I made a beeline for them. Inside, there were several containers filled with metallic vials, and a few plastic boxes filled with what I'd discovered over the past few days was astronaut food. I picked up a pouch, then gestured to Navan for him to pick up some vials.

"You can't trust any other coldbloods, Riley," he said as he bent down to the boxes, clearly still preoccupied with Kalvin. "I thought you knew that."

I shrugged. "He wanted to apologize for the things he said the other night, so I was letting him. We're in this together, after all— we may as well be a team," I said, echoing Kalvin's earlier words.

Navan turned and widened his eyes at me. "It's all a game to them, Riley!"

Before I could reply, a loud siren tore through the ship.

Immediately, the *Asterope's* interior lighting dimmed down to a low, flashing red. Lazar came running out into the corridor, sprinting so fast he was almost a blur. He barreled through the main room, heading for the door at the far end which slid open, and he disappeared inside.

I looked at Navan, bewildered. "What is—?"

I didn't get a chance to complete my question as a screen embedded into the ship's wall flickered to life. After a few moments of white noise and crackling, an image appeared. Staring through the display was a woman with gleaming copper hair, shot through with bolts of brightest white. Her sharp, almost silver eyes pierced through to where I was standing, though I was pretty certain she couldn't see me. She was beautiful—astonishingly so —with cut cheekbones, dark red lips, and effortlessly arched eyebrows that seemed perpetually scornful.

"This is Queen Gianne of the planet Vysanthe. You have entered the airspace of my queendom, without my permission. Your ship is not one my system recognizes as due for arrival." Her silky voice boomed through the speakers. "I demand to know who you are, what you want, and why I shouldn't blow you up right here and now. I have ammunition aimed at your ship as we speak, so do not try anything foolish."

Blood pounded in my ears, and my gut clenched. We had reached Vysanthe.

I had known we would face Queen Gianne eventually, but I hadn't imagined what she might look like—or how poorly our arrival might be received. On screen, her expression remained fierce and unforgiving. I glanced at Navan, who looked just as shocked to see her as I did, his jaw clenched.

He strode toward the cockpit, and I followed, careful to keep to the shadowed sides of the room as I entered. It was even tinier than the ship's main space. A command module lay up ahead, where Lazar was frantically toying with various buttons and levers. Beyond that, Queen Gianne's face loomed, stretched across the ship's front.

"Let me," Navan insisted, and his uncle stepped to one side. With the press of a button, a smaller screen appeared beside the first, showing Navan's face. "I am Navan Idrax of the Explorer's

Guild, son of Jareth Idrax. I come bearing news for you, Your Highness."

I watched his face on the monitor, impressed by his calm demeanor. Queen Gianne studied him for a moment before speaking again. "Navan Idrax?" she asked, her tone suspicious. "The last I heard of Navan Idrax, he had gone to the far reaches of the universe. Why would you be here now?"

"I returned as quickly as I could, Your Highness," he said. "You see, early on in my exploration, I was betrayed. I had Jethro and Ianthan Plexus aboard my ship, but they sought to turn against you, Your Highness—they wanted to feed information to your enemies, the rebel forces. They changed the coordinates of my ship while I was sleeping, and took us to a rebel outpost. I realized in time to stop them from speaking with the rebels, but not before we had landed." He spoke quickly, and I could see Queen Gianne's face contorting with each word.

"Jethro and Ianthan Plexus?" she remarked icily.

Navan nodded. "I was forced to carry out their execution for treason. They wanted to smuggle rebels back, to create a weak point in your queendom, Your Highness."

"At a rebel outpost, you say?"

"It was only a small one, on a forgotten planet a few days' travel from here, Your Highness," Navan replied smoothly, his voice never faltering. Even I would have believed him. "There were a handful of rebels there, but they seemed disenchanted with the whole rebellion idea. I think the real rebel base had forgotten them, too. After seeing the execution of Jethro and Ianthan, they begged me to bring them back to Vysanthe, where they might offer you information on the true rebel base, in exchange for immunity... They know their true leader is you, Queen Gianne, and they would seek to be your citizens once more."

"This rebel base, is it close?" Queen Gianne asked, her eyebrow raised.

"The outpost is a bit under a week away, though the rest of the rebels scattered. Those I brought with me hold the information you seek."

"How many of you are there?" she demanded, peering closer into the screen, as though she could pick every crew member out.

"Eight, Your Highness," Navan answered swiftly. "Myself, four other coldbloods—including my uncle Lazar, who helped me out of a spot of trouble I had with my own ship—two creatures called Carokians, and my personal slave, of an unknown race."

I wondered if Carokians were a real thing. If they weren't, would the shifters just make something up? Time would tell.

For a few minutes that seemed to stretch on forever, Queen Gianne said nothing. Instead, she simply looked through the screen, studying Navan's face on the monitor. Surely, if she knew Jareth Idrax, she knew his son, too? From what I'd gathered, Navan was supposed to be close to the queen. Though, by the looks of it, she wasn't convinced of his loyalty.

"Perhaps your story is true," she sighed, breaking the tension with her crisp voice. "In these times, I cannot take any unnecessary risks. Stay precisely where you are while my border force comes and investigates your ship. If you move an inch, I shall shoot you from the sky—is that understood?"

Navan nodded curtly, and I could see him letting out a slight breath. "Understood, Your Highness. We'll await them."

"Very well, let's see if you make it through, shall we?" she said softly, before the screen flickered off.

Navan whirled around. "Hide everything, immediately!" he shouted, running out of the cockpit and back into the main space. "We've got Impalers coming, boys! Hide the weapons. Hide everything we don't want the border guard finding!"

I sprinted after him in time to see Nestor, Cristo, and Kalvin come hurtling out of the hallway a moment later, clutching handfuls of guns and boxes of weapons. Their eyes were wide in fear. The shifters followed soon after, carrying stacks of items.

"What are Impalers?" I gasped, heaving a particularly heavy trunk up into my arms.

"The Vysanthean border guard—well, Queen Gianne's border guard, anyway," Navan explained rapidly, tossing a bag of rifles to Kalvin, who was running past. He caught them with lightning-fast reflexes.

"Why are they called Impalers?" I pressed, following Navan toward Lazar. He gave me a look, making me realize it was probably a stupid question, and I shuddered.

"You, shifters, change into something vaguely Carokian!" Navan instructed, confirming that it was a real species. The two shifters looked at one another uncertainly, their skins unchanging.

An air of panic bristled through the ship as Lazar led everyone to a shimmering square in the wall of the *Asterope*, his hand seeking out a secret button that opened a hatch, invisible to the unknowing eye. Without a moment to lose, everyone shoved the boxes and trunks of weaponry into the hatch, making sure there wasn't a single box of ammo left out in the open. The only thing that stayed out were the metallic vials and boxes of supplies. After all, it had to look like a ship that had been lived in for a short while —the journey from the fake rebel outpost was a week-long journey, after all. I did what I could, throwing containers and bags at whoever was ready to catch them, until there was nothing left cluttering the narrow hallways of the *Asterope*.

A knock rapped at the front door.

The sound echoed through the confined space, filling me with dread. Everyone whirled around, their eyes on the spot where the gangway slid out. I didn't doubt these Impalers could have knocked the door down if they'd wanted to, but for now they seemed eager that we should open the ship up to them. A gesture of cooperation.

Lazar lunged for the button that concealed the invisible hatch, the façade sliding down with a rapid swoosh. To my surprise, I could see no hint of the square storage space in the wall's smooth surface once the screen was down. We had stashed everything just in time.

The Impalers were here.

avan opened the door to the *Asterope*, allowing the border guard in. The moment the door swung up, I was petrified of being sucked out into the darkness of space, but it seemed the Impalers had brought some contraption with them that attached to the outer wall of the ship, creating a tunnel through which they could move from their ship to ours.

Instantly, it was confirmed to me how they'd earned their nickname. They loomed in the doorway, brandishing large pikes with sharp, golden tips, the metal and the staff streaked with red. They reminded me of the spears I'd seen the rebel coldbloods using back at the hidden compound, the weapons crackling and fizzing, as though electricity pulsed through them. I wouldn't like to be on the receiving end of one of those. The spears had looked torturous enough.

The Impalers wore black and red, with streaks of greasepaint on their faces, making them look even more horrifying than they would have without it. The leader stepped forward, his blue eyes scrutinizing the ship, and everyone gathered in the main space.

Panicking, I turned to see that the shifters had morphed into green-skinned beings with bulging scarlet eyes and webbed feet, their backs hunched over, their mouths gaping open. They looked amphibian, and frankly repulsive... though perhaps not more repulsive than their natural form.

"Stay here while we search your vessel," the lead Impaler instructed, ushering his colleagues into the small space.

There were ten of them, some male, some female, though all equally terrifying. Branching out from the main space, they flooded the corridors, entering the pods. I could hear the sound of things being thrown around, the whole place being ransacked in search of contraband.

One of the large male Impalers stopped in front of me, his eyes boring down into mine. Quickly, I dropped my gaze, taking on the role of subservient underling. He sniffed me, jabbing my shoulder with the end of his pike. The tip bristled, but no shock of electricity jolted down my arm. He was just testing me, checking to see if I'd react. I didn't, keeping a cool head, playing the part I'd been assigned.

"What are you?" he growled, his breath hot on my face.

I shook my head. "Nobody, sir," I breathed.

"You got that right," he sneered, before pulling away, evidently satisfied that I wasn't harmful. Even so, my heart was pounding in my chest, my lungs barely able to catch a breath. Now, more than ever, I didn't want to be here. I didn't want to be on the edge of Vysanthe, with no choice but to land or die. I wanted to be home, wrapped up in the safety of familiarity. Even the comforting sight of Navan's eyes, watching me closely, couldn't take the all-consuming fear away.

Once or twice, several of the Impalers walked past the spot where the hatch was hidden away, but the design was too clever, foxing them. They didn't seem to notice anything amiss, their eyes barely glancing over the invisible panel as they moved on to more obvious hiding places. They turned over all the food boxes, pulling out everything, only to cast each item aside once they realized what it was. In the cockpit, I could hear a few of them rattling around. They exited, shrugging at their leader with disappointed expressions on their faces.

They hadn't found anything.

"Remain here. The queen will be in touch shortly," the leader said, once he had regrouped his troops. With that, they left the ship, the outer door sliding shut after them. I could still hear the sound of their heavy boots on the walkway they had connected from their ship, but that soon faded, leaving the *Asterope* in uneasy silence.

I was about to ask a question when Navan lifted his finger to his lips. "In case they've stuck bugs on the ship," he whispered.

I nodded. The last thing I wanted was for those terrifying individuals to return because of something I said. Instead, my eyes flicked to the invisible hatch. Lazar was standing beside it, his arms folded across his chest. With the Impalers' surveillance uncertain, it was clear nobody wanted to open the hatch... just in case. It would have to wait until we were on the ground.

Several minutes later, the sound of the ship's siren blared in my eardrums, the red light flashing once more. Queen Gianne was calling.

Navan immediately hurried toward the cockpit door, disappearing inside. This time, I didn't follow him. Instead, I stayed in the main space of the ship, watching as the screen flickered to life again on the far wall.

"It seems you passed my test, Navan Idrax," Queen Gianne said, smiling coldly. "Your father will be *so* happy to see you've returned."

"Thank you, Your Highness," Navan replied, his tone tight. "I look forward to an audience with you, so we might exchange information."

Queen Gianne laughed. "We'll see," she murmured, before the screen went dead. In place of Queen Gianne's face, a message appeared. *Permission to dock*, it said, flashing repeatedly.

Lazar moved away from the others and entered the cockpit, with me following close behind. I sat down on one of the chairs in front of the command module and let Navan and his uncle get to work, flicking switches and moving levers to bring the ship down to the planet of Vysanthe.

"Would you like to see?" Navan asked, turning to look over his shoulder at where I sat.

I nodded, though I wasn't sure whether I wanted to see this new planet or not. He pressed a button, and the shimmering façade of the ship's front fell away, revealing the expanse of space beyond the glass. In front of my eyes lay a dark planet with two icy tips at either end—the planet's bitter poles, no doubt. Across the surface were glowing lights, a sign of the cities and towns there. It was strange to see a new civilization rising up in front of me, with people milling about below, going on with their lives, oblivious to our presence above them.

It did not look like Earth, with its welcoming blue and green, its swirling white clouds streaming across the atmosphere. This was its gloomier, darker twin. This planet was far larger than Earth, though I could make out expanses of black water tinged with the pale blue of ice. There were certainly no welcoming vibes. In fact, everything about it screamed a warning to turn back, and run as far from it as possible.

Unfortunately for me, that wasn't an option.

"It's... something," I said, unable to find the right words for my fear and awe.

"A savage beauty," Lazar murmured, his eyes drawn to the sight of his home planet. "Just like its queens," he added, almost to himself.

Slowly, the *Asterope* began to descend, the planet drawing closer. The stars disappeared as we powered through Vysanthe's atmosphere, following the Impaler ship that flew ahead of us, its engines glowing blue in the darkness.

We seemed to be heading for mountainous terrain, with not a city in sight. I thought it a little strange, but I didn't even know what strange was anymore. Everything was weird. A vast peak rose up, the apex topped with snow, the sky around it stormy. Rain lashed against the windscreen of the ship, the water running down in fierce rivers. Thunder rumbled in the distance, and a crack of lightning shot out across the bruised storm clouds, lighting everything up for just a moment with its angry glare.

After navigating through a wide, gaping entrance in the side of the snowcapped mountain, Lazar landed the ship a short distance away from where the Impaler ship docked. We were in some sort of cave, though it wasn't the usual kind—the floor was polished stone, and there were monitors and screens everywhere, running through diagnostics of the ships beside them. Coldbloods wandered around, helping ships to land and fixing any that might be broken, their heads buried inside the bellies of these mechanical beasts.

Some of the ships looked like ours, superficially—with the same shimmering, almost liquid surface—while others were far bulkier and less sleek. That was good, because it meant the *Asterope* could blend in, and they hopefully wouldn't notice that, under the hood, it was more advanced than their ships. I realized this must have been how Navan had managed to keep his advanced ship, *Soraya,* a secret—he'd made the exterior blend in with other regular Vysanthean ships.

"Are you ready for this?" Navan asked, as two clamps extended from the cave walls and gripped the *Asterope.* A jolt told me it had been secured.

I shook my head. "Can I go home if I say no?" I half joked.

"I'm sorry, Riley," he said, looking crestfallen.

With a smile that belied my terror, I walked over to him and looped my arms around his neck, not caring that Lazar was there. Gently, I kissed him on the cheek, and looked up into his eyes. "You have nothing to be sorry for, Navan."

He exhaled, taking my hands in his. "Stay close to me."

He then led me out of the cockpit and into the main space, where the rest of the team was waiting. There was a nervous energy in the room that was hard to ignore, but I did my best as we headed for the ship's exit.

As the door slid up, we stepped out into the cave. The cold hit me like a slap to the face, but that wasn't the worst of my problems.

Coldblood guards swarmed us in an instant, brandishing the electrically charged pikes and spears they seemed to favor. One grabbed me, pulling me roughly to one side. Navan tried to keep hold of me, but another guard stepped forward and slammed the staff of his spear down on my wrist, forcing me to recoil from Navan's touch.

All around me, the other members of the *Asterope* crew were being manhandled, pulled and pushed in every direction by the armed guards. It all happened in a blur.

"I demand to know what you're doing!" I heard Lazar call out.

"We're taking you for interrogation," one of the guards barked back, hauling him toward the exit of the cave.

"Stop!" Navan shouted. "I will keep my slave with me, or you will answer to Jareth Idrax. She is my property. I will not allow her to be sullied by your hands!" I wasn't sure I liked the way it felt to be called his property, but I knew he was doing it to keep up appearances. I was supposed to be his personal slave, after all. Besides, I knew it pained him to have to use his father's name to get something.

The guard holding me relaxed his grip slightly. "Boss?" he asked, turning to one of the other guards, who was evidently their leader. On his face, he bore a tattoo, just below his eye. It was a fanged animal of some sort, though it wasn't a creature I recognized.

"Keep the girl with Idrax," he muttered, clearly disliking having to bend to superiority. "We'll leave it to Kiel to decide."

With the decision made, my guard shoved me toward the vast door that yawned at the far edge of the cave. It led into a long tunnel, which branched out into several smaller tunnels. The guards took us along the one at the very end of the passageway, stopping in front of a hallway of doors.

I watched as Lazar, Nestor, Cristo, Kalvin, and the two shifters, still shaped like Carokians, were pushed through doors. These were interrogation rooms. They couldn't be anything else. I gulped, realizing we were all going to be questioned separately. I knew enough of the plan to muddle through, but I was convinced I'd get some part of it wrong.

Navan and I were held outside one particular door. The guard holding Navan knocked once, and it swung wide open. There was a squat, barrel-chested troll of a coldblood standing on the other side, his muddy brown eyes peering curiously from me to Navan, and back again. This must be Kiel.

"Commander Kiel, we have Navan Idrax. He insisted he bring his pet along—do you want us to put her in with someone else? Grillo might like a go at her," the guard said, his tone menacing.

The pugnacious coldblood raised a bushy eyebrow, looking thoughtful for a moment. "Send her to Grillo," he said, flicking his wrist down the corridor.

Navan strained against the man holding him. "She can't be interrogated alone, not by a Vysanthean. She's too weak—she'll faint... and she'll be useless to you and me, if that happens," he added frostily.

"What is she?" the coldblood named Kiel asked, stepping closer to inspect me.

"Unknown species; I never thought to ask," Navan said. "A weak, feeble little race, way off in the Severn Quarter. I could have wiped them all out with my bare hands—they break so easily, not much use to anyone. Couldn't resist stealing this one away, though.

I mean, could you?" I felt a little sick, hearing Navan speak like that about me, despite knowing he had to.

It seemed to please Kiel and the other guards, who laughed raucously. The guard holding me even brushed his hand across the curve of my neck, making me shudder. I was already shivering from the cold, but that creature's touch added to it.

"How does she taste?" the guard asked.

Navan shrugged. "Not too good. Still, she's a fun thing to have around."

Another splinter of vile laughter echoed down the hallway. All I could do was stand there and listen, helpless to stand up for myself.

"Well, you'd both better come in here then," Kiel said, and the two guards roughly shoved us both into the room, which seemed to be hewn from the cave itself.

Inside, there was a desk and two chairs and not much else, save for the rack of weapons that hung from the ceiling. The walls dripped, and the bitter cold began to seep into my bones, my body going into spasms. Navan flashed me a look of apology, but I didn't respond, not wanting to give myself away.

"Do you think you could have some blankets brought? My slave isn't used to the cold," Navan said.

"What do you think this is, a hotel?" Kiel replied.

"She'll die if you don't, and I'm not finished with her yet," Navan retorted.

Kiel sighed. "Fine," he muttered, poking his head back out of the interrogation room to ask a passing guard to bring blankets.

In that brief second of time, Navan reached over and took my hand in his, lifting it to his lips for one daring kiss. It was a bold move that could have gotten us into a lot of trouble, but the small act warmed me. It steeled me against what was to come, knowing I had Navan by my side in all of this.

"You sure you're an Idrax?" Kiel asked, turning back to the room.

Navan smiled coldly. "Last time I checked."

Kiel pulled a face. "I've never known an Idrax to show sympathy to anyone, let alone a feeble specimen like this... however pretty it might be," he sneered. I sucked in a breath at the suspicion burning in Kiel's eyes. Clearly, the queen had told him not to trust Navan, despite his high status.

"Can we just get on with this?" Navan said tersely.

Kiel's mood shifted in an instant. Grabbing a golden blade from the rack of weapons, he stormed toward Navan and shoved him into one of the chairs, resting the sharp edge against his neck. I started forward, but a look from Navan held me back. The blade crackled and pulsed, Navan's eyes going wide as a bolt flew from the weapon and into his skin. His fingers curled over the armrests of the chair.

"Who are you?" Kiel demanded.

"Navan Idrax," Navan replied, his voice thick with pain.

A second bolt flashed from the blade. "Why are you here?" Kiel asked.

"I have information... information about the rebels... I need to tell the queen."

"Who are the people on your ship?"

"Rebels who have... come over to my side. I... convinced them to join me. They... wish to tell the... queen everything. They... want to... tell her... where the rebel base... is."

"What happened to Jethro and Ianthan Plexus?" Kiel ventured, sending another bolt through Navan's skin.

"They... betrayed the... crown!" he yelled, forcing the story from his lips. "They... wanted to... tell Queen Brisha... all of Queen Gianne's... secrets. They wanted... to mount a... rebellion. They wanted... to get the... rebels to... fight for Queen Brisha. I... stopped them."

"Are you sure you aren't the traitor?" Kiel asked, reaching up to the rack of weapons for a strange, claw-like device.

"I'm sure!" Navan grated out.

"Are you positive about that?" Kiel smirked coldly before fixing the device into a slot in Navan's chair and adjusting it so that it was against Navan's chest, the sharp edges touching his flesh. The center whirred, a white glow emanating outward. Navan roared, his fangs flashing as he struggled to break free of the device.

"I am... no traitor!" he hissed, and every jolt he took, I felt. I could hardly bear to look at him.

Kiel grimaced. "We shall see," he said, before mercifully leaving the room. Though, somehow, I didn't get the sense that he was convinced by Navan's tale.

Watching the door intently, I could hardly believe he had gone, but here we were, Navan and I, alone again. I ran over to him, but Navan forcibly raised a hand to stop me. As my skin brushed his, I felt a bristle of electricity snap between our bodies.

"It... will... hurt you," he said, his chest heaving with the exertion of fighting against the device that Kiel had left in place. The glow had ebbed slightly, but I could see it was still causing him pain.

"Dammit, I want to get this thing off you!" I said, but he raised his hand again, pushing me away.

"No. Just... stand back," he snapped. I staggered back, obeying his request even though it went against my every instinct. He then drew in a deep breath as if to calm himself, his eyes settling on me. "Just keep it together," he said in a softer voice. "The queen is about to arrive."

17

*B*arely a minute later, the door opened again and three coldbloods entered.

The first was a thin-framed, wizened coldblood with half a wing hanging from his shoulder-blade and milky eyes that barely seemed to see anything. The second breezed in behind him, her elegant, ruby-tipped wings tucked neatly behind her back. I recognized the vivid copper hair and almost-silver gaze in an instant. Queen Gianne had come to interrogate Navan herself.

My heart beat faster as she stopped in front of him. "Navan Idrax," she announced, her intense gaze flashing to me. "And what are you?" Her nose wrinkled, as though she'd smelled something unpleasant.

"My... slave... Your Highness," Navan replied, still straining against the pain from the torture device.

Queen Gianne turned to Kiel. "Turn that thing off," she ordered.

Kiel jumped to action, pressing a button on the device, and Navan immediately relaxed. "Now then, that's better, isn't it?" she said silkily, taking the seat opposite Navan.

"You are too kind, Your Highness," Navan replied, getting his breath back.

She laughed, the sound strangely pleasant. "Now, everyone keeps telling me you've got a hell of a story, and I for one am *dying* to hear it," she said, her eyes fixed on his, to the point where it began to make me feel uncomfortable.

With a heavy sigh, Navan told his story again, including Jethro and Ianthan's betrayal, and how he discovered the rebel outpost.

All the while, I watched the shifting expressions on Queen Gianne's face. It was hard to tell what she was thinking. One moment, there was a smile upon her lips. The next, a bitter scowl. Although, it didn't always fit with the story. No, her expressions were on a journey entirely separate from the words Navan was speaking. However, throughout it all, there was fascination in her eyes, and she didn't speak until Navan was finished recounting his tale.

When he was done, the wizened old coldblood who had entered the interrogation room with the queen leaned down to whisper something in her ear. It was the first time I had seen him move or speak since they arrived. In fact, I had almost forgotten he was there, he blended so well into the background.

Queen Gianne nodded at whatever the wizened coldblood had said to her. "Thank you, Aurelius," she said softly, before turning to Navan. "And thank you, Navan Idrax," she said, standing with a bone-grating scrape of the chair. Without saying another word, she walked toward the door, Kiel hurrying after her, a confused look on his pugnacious face. This Aurelius guy didn't move a muscle, standing like a statue.

"Your Highness, what shall I do with him?" Kiel called after her, prompting her to pause on the threshold of the room, turning to look over her shoulder with a dramatic swish of her long copper locks.

"Alas, I hate to see such potential go to waste," she sighed, her silver eyes widening. "But, on this occasion, it must be done. Despite promising beginnings, enviable rank, and a father whom I would trust with my life, it would appear the apple has fallen woefully far from the tree... I can tolerate many things, Navan Idrax, but I can't tolerate lies. You've left me with no choice, as much as it pains me to see you destroyed—to have such a spec- imen as yourself put down, no better than an icehound. Such a shame."

Shock seized my muscles, and before I could even react, Kiel drew parallel to Navan with supernatural speed. He pressed the tip of a blade to Navan's temple, the sharp point nestling just to the side of his slate eyes. I cried out and jolted forward to try to stop him, but one sharp blow from Kiel sent me sprawling to the floor like a ragdoll.

His weapon thrummed with energy, like the rest of the Vysanthean weapons seemed to. Placing his palm on the butt of the knife, Kiel braced his shoulders, ready to push the blade through the skin and bone of Navan's temple.

Panic hit me like a tidal wave as I realized that would be it. As soon as the blade pushed through his skull, I would lose Navan, and I didn't need to be a genius to figure out my life would be ended soon after that. How long could I possibly last, alone on this planet, where even butterflies wanted to kill you? This couldn't be happening. I wasn't ready to die. There were still a thousand and one things I had to do, most important of which was protecting the human race. What would happen to Earth if Navan and I were killed? What would happen to Angie, Lauren, Jean, Roger...

My brain froze as Kiel drew his hand back, preparing for the killing blow—but just as he was about to drive his weapon down, Queen Gianne raised her hand and called out, her voice splintering through the tense atmosphere.

"Wait!" she said. Kiel brought his hand up short, his whole arm shaking with the exertion it took to stop himself, mid-momentum.

As I watched her walk over to Navan, I thought my lungs might burst out of my chest. In the chaos, I had forgotten how to breathe, my cheeks reddening, my eyes bulging. Relief crashed over me, the adrenaline leaving my system in one hurried rush, leaving me trembling. He was safe... for now.

Queen Gianne approached Navan, examining him with a bird-like curiosity, her striking eyes looking over him as though he were an exhibit in a museum. Her head tilted this way and that upon her slender neck, her long fingers tapping at the dark red pillow of her bottom lip. It wasn't an appropriate time to go to Navan, I knew, and so I held back, once again going against every instinct I had. Instead, I focused on Queen Gianne, despising her and loving her in equal measure, for halting Navan's execution.

"Looks like you've passed my little test, Navan," she chirped, her voice oddly cheerful. "I had to see if you were telling the truth. Nothing brings honesty out of a coldblood like a near-death experience, but it would seem there was no other tale to come trickling out of you."

"Perhaps you ought to question him again, Your Highness, just to be sure?" the half-winged advisor, Aurelius, said quietly, his raspy voice barely making it across to where the queen stood.

She shook her head, visibly irritated by his question. "Not now, Aurelius. Navan Idrax has proven himself worthy today, and that is all there is to it. If I feel like interrogating him again, one day in the future, then I will."

"As you wish, Your Highness." Aurelius nodded, backing off.

"Besides," Queen Gianne said, with a smile, "I think Navan might prove very useful in our fight against the rebels, given what he knows about them and their outpost. Plus, he must be *very* charming, to have persuaded so many to his way of thinking..." She stroked a fingertip down the side of his cheekbone, and I flinched at the contact, wanting to smack her hand away.

"I will tell you all I can, Your Highness," Navan replied, his face giving nothing away.

"Yes, perhaps I will make you my advisor on the subject," she said, a strange smile curving up the corners of her lips. Nearby, Aurelius shook his head. Clearly, he wasn't into the idea of Navan stepping into his shoes. "Oh, and I do hope you know where the main rebel base is, somewhere in that pretty little head of yours, considering the fate of your comrades is still uncertain. I may not keep them around long enough to gather anything useful," she added, tapping Navan's temple precisely where the blade had been about to pierce.

"They are your loyal servants, Your Highness," Navan assured her, a pleading note in his voice. I understood why. If any of the *Asterope* crew were killed, Orion's suspicions would likely be aroused, and that would signal pain and suffering, if not certain death, for me. I didn't know how exactly Orion would know if something had gone wrong—whether he was relying solely on one of our teammates reporting back to him, or he had some other trick up his sleeve—but I was sure he had his ways, and I wasn't about to underestimate him.

"At this moment in time, I can only offer freedom to the pair of you. Take it or leave it," she retorted. "I will decide on your comrades at my leisure."

"Please, Your Highness, take my word that they are as loyal to you as any of your most-trusted citizens. They are as loyal to you as my father—I would ask that you reconsider. There is so much they can tell you."

"*You* will have to tell it to me, if I decide to do away with them," Queen Gianne replied tersely. "Now, do you want your freedom or not? I don't have all day."

Navan glanced at me, our eyes meeting. I wanted him to refuse her offer—one for all, all for one—but I wasn't really sure we had a choice. Testing the queen's patience didn't seem like a good idea, given that Navan was still sitting in a torture chair, and from the resigned expression on his face, he seemed to think so too.

"We accept your generosity, Your Highness," he murmured.

"Then go, before I change my mind," she said crisply. "Aurelius, be a dear and help Navan out of his chair—then show them to one of our nicest state rooms," she called out. The wizened old man acquiesced, then followed us out into the hallway.

For a moment, the paranoid half of me thought it was a trap, but as we entered the corridor, there was nobody to shove us around or arrest us again. There was only Aurelius behind us, ready to take us to the room that Queen Gianne had promised.

18

From the rock-hewn labyrinth of the cave's underbelly, Aurelius ushered us onto a bullet train that was waiting on a platform, the carriages empty.

As I sat beside Navan, the engine thrumming to life beneath us, my mind drifted toward thoughts of Queen Gianne—was she interrogating the rest of our group right at this very moment, coming to her "conclusions" about their loyalty? What if it was bad news?

The negativity was forced out of my mind a moment later as the bullet train took off, racing through a network of tunnels so fast that everything beyond the small windows was a blur. I could feel the skin of my cheeks pulling backward, as though I were on a rollercoaster, my body being knocked from side to side and pushed back against my seat as the bullet train zipped around corners and zig-zagged through tricky terrain.

It slowed as we approached an imposing building that was cut into the side of another mountain. Lights glowed in the windows that had been carved into the rock, the radiance oddly comforting to my human eyes amid all the icy gloom that surrounded us.

We came to a standstill at another platform, where a few weary-looking coldbloods stood waiting, faces lit up in surprise at the sight of Aurelius in the front carriage. Apparently, he was something of a celebrity in these parts—no doubt because of his association with Queen Gianne.

Aurelius pushed Navan and me through the small crowd and into what looked like a service corridor, tucked away behind the banal structure of a ticket office. He hurried us down it, bringing us to an elevator at the very end. When he pressed the top button, the elevator instantly whizzed upward, my knees feeling even weaker beneath the pressure that swarmed in around me, threatening to crush me. Everything was more extreme here, I was beginning to realize—no wonder the coldbloods had tougher skin, and muscles as hard as concrete.

At least here, in this mountain, it was warmer. I had stopped shivering once we'd stepped off the bullet train, but I could feel gusts of icy wind blowing in through the thin gaps in the elevator doors, making me think we were shooting up the outside of the mountain structure.

When the doors pinged open, we had arrived at a circular foyer, with several rooms leading off from the central space. Aurelius led us up to one of the doors and unlocked it, before gesturing for us to head inside.

"You will be locked in, for now. Queen Gianne will decide if you will be permitted a key," Aurelius explained curtly, evidently displeased at being the errand boy. "Should you require anything, please call the concierge on the comm device in your room." With that, he closed the door, locking it before he left.

"I don't think he likes you, Navan," I teased halfheartedly. "Thinks you're in the running for his job."

Navan grimaced. "Don't remind me. Feels like I end up following in my father's footsteps, even if I do everything I can to go in the opposite direction."

"*Literally* in the opposite direction!" I said, wanting to get a smile to break the stern surface of Navan's face. It felt like we both needed a moment of levity after everything we'd just been through. "I saw that map of yours—you can't get any farther away from here than Earth."

A small smile played on his lips. "How do you think I ended up there?"

"I can see it now," I said, closing my eyes and pretending there was a giant map in front of me. "Eenie, meenie, minie, mo!"

"Something like that," he replied softly, coming over to where I stood. Slowly, he put his arms around me. I turned my head so I could nestle into his chest.

"What are we going to do about the others?" I asked, my playful energy fading as I remembered the torture they were likely experiencing, right at this very moment. Tears pricked my eyes once more, and I snuggled into Navan's embrace, feeling the safety of his arms around me.

It was Lazar I felt sorriest for—he was an older man, with so much to lose. How quickly could one of those devices break a man weaker than Navan? How many secrets would they reveal, if Queen Gianne played her execution trick on them? Even our tentative freedom could not be taken for granted—if they told the truth, we would all be done for.

"We'll get them back in one piece, don't worry," Navan said. "They're smart guys—they'll figure out lies that work. They won't give up the truth, not when they have so much to lose. That's the thing about rebels—they have a cause."

I smirked, picturing Navan as James Dean, his t-shirt sleeves rolled up, his hair styled back in a messy sweep.

He eyed me with curiosity. "What?"

"Reminded me of an old movie—*Rebel Without a Cause*?"

Navan smiled. "Don't think it's reached us yet. Anyway, these rebels *do* have a cause, and they won't give any of us up. I promise you. They might be morons, for the most part, but I think they genuinely believe in what they're doing here. I might not agree with it, but I have to admire their tenacity."

As Navan dipped his head to kiss me, a loud noise pierced through the quiet. It was coming from the corner of the room, where a blue light was flashing wildly. A moment later, a holographic image of a handsome older couple popped up. One, a brown-haired woman with high cheekbones, grinned prettily, while the other, a muscular man with dark hair, showed only a close-lipped smile. Above them, the words *Incoming Call* blinked on and off in bold white lettering.

"Navan? It's your mother and father," the woman's voice said.

Breaking away from me, Navan stormed across the room to where the holographic comm device sat, and punched the blue button so hard I thought he might break it. With a whoosh, the holographic image disappeared, leaving only the blank wall behind it. The Idraxes had gone.

He punched another button on the device, every light on the machine sputtering out as he powered it down. Now there was no way for his parents to get through.

I frowned as he returned to me with a face like thunder. What was it about his parents, his father especially, that he hated so much? I knew about his sister, Naya, and the terrible way in which she had died. His father had been responsible for that, after concocting the damaging elixir intended for Ronad that had ended up in Naya's system, killing her. It was enough to scar any man for life, and keep him at a distance from such a person. But, despite the reasoning behind it, Jareth Idrax had never intended to kill anyone. He had been worried about keeping up appearances, and it had resulted in a tragic accident that had no doubt scarred Jareth and his wife, too.

No, there had to be something more to Navan's dislike—I could sense it.

"Why do you despise them so much?" I asked.

"I told you about my sister," he muttered, his eyes flashing with hurt.

"I remember every word," I promised, "but there must be something else to it. What your father did was wrong and terrible, but it was an accident. An awful accident."

Navan's face turned sour. "You're siding with my *father*?"

"Of course not!" I said. "I think what he did was awful under any circumstances. He should have let your sister and Ronad be, but that doesn't change what happened. It's just that... Well, your hatred for him now seems to be as fresh as if something awful had *just* happened, and I don't understand why."

For a long time, Navan said nothing, just stared at the opposite wall. Finally, he replied, "That man has ruled my life for too long. Throughout my childhood, my adolescence, my adulthood, he has always been there, lording his superiority over me, cracking the whip to make me like him... to make me better, always better. Not long ago, it got to the point where I felt like my life wasn't my own anymore. I was a puppet, and he was pulling the strings." He paced in front of me, avoiding looking me in the eyes. I was proud of him for saying this much, given that he wasn't usually one for big displays of feeling or sharing.

"What did he do?" I asked.

Navan sighed. "My parents have always had 'ideas' about us all. Everything has to be set out, planned down to the tiniest thing. In their minds, nothing can be left to chance. After the incident with Ronad and Naya, they went into some sort of crazy parent mode. They didn't want any of us choosing partners for ourselves, since apparently we could no longer be trusted. It was either do as they say, or stay a bachelor, basically." He scowled, shaking his head.

I frowned, hoping he hadn't chosen the former. I'd never heard him mention a girlfriend back home on Vysanthe, but then again, I'd never asked about one either.

No, I told myself, *he would have told you if he had a girlfriend here. He wouldn't have kept that from you.* Looking into his earnest eyes, I knew it was true—he wouldn't deceive me.

"Couldn't you talk to them, and just... explain?" I asked, wanting to switch my line of thought. If there *had* been a chance he was seeing someone else, this was the moment he would have come out with it.

Navan exhaled, running a hand down his tired face. "Riley, I'm tired and really don't want to talk any more about my parents now.

I've been through enough for one day. Let's just... enjoy this time we have together."

"Of course. I'm sorry," I said, beckoning for him to join me on the bed. There were two of them in the room, but there was no way I was sleeping alone tonight.

He stood in front of me, cupping my face in his hands, my chin tilted upward so our eyes were locked in a steady gaze.

But I could barely focus on his eyes. By the faraway look on his face, I guessed he couldn't focus on mine either. There was just too much at stake here. One false move and the whole house of cards would come tumbling down.

"What if an interrogator manages to crack one of the guys? Or kills them?" I asked. "Do you think Orion would listen to us, or do you think he'd just activate the implant and take me out of the equation?"

With a sigh, Navan sat down on the bed with me and put his arm around my shoulder, leaning his head against mine. "I don't know, Riley. I just know I have to do whatever it takes to stop him from activating that *thing*," he said bitterly, his fingers tracing the curve of my neck, where Orion had implanted the chip.

"But what can we do?" I mused, thinking about the mission brief. We were supposed to find weaknesses in the queendom and send information back to the rebel base. We were supposed to send her on a wild-goose chase. "When we see the queen again, we can't leave it up to the rest of the crew. You're going to have to tell her where the rebel base is."

Navan looked shocked. "I can't tell—" he began, but I cut him off, realizing he'd misunderstood.

"The rebel base, a year away from here," I said, reminding him of the ruse. "If the others haven't told her yet, then what does it matter if you tell her? She'll likely go and look at the outpost first, anyway, seeing as that's only a week or so away. *That* buys us time. Besides, you can always explain that your rebels have more information she might be interested in—I'm sure they can come up with something juicy," I said, giving him a knowing look.

A half smile passed across Navan's lips. "Maybe you're right. I wouldn't be surprised if she sent teams to both, to scope out the area. A year is a pretty long time, though," he said. "Wouldn't want to be one of the poor bastards who gets that job."

I nodded. "Maybe you should speak with Aurelius tomorrow, get a better idea of how the others are," I said, knowing the half-winged advisor might be the perfect source of information, where Queen Gianne and the queendom were concerned.

Navan smiled. "Also a good idea," he replied, twisting a strand of my hair between his fingertips. "I'd like to show you the Observatory too."

"Sounds interesting," I said, still a little nervous about the idea of walking around Vysanthe, with coldbloods at every turn. I leaned my forehead against Navan's, letting our breaths mingle together. "You know, I'm almost glad that I'm here—with you. Even if it means..."

"Don't, Riley. I couldn't bear it if anything happened to you," Navan breathed, his voice suddenly thick with emotion. He pressed his lips to mine in a kiss that was slow and sweet, before he pulled back to look into my eyes. "We should get some rest for tomorrow," he said, his voice a little stronger, and I nodded.

Exhausted, I didn't bother to change out of my clothes from

the ship as I slipped under the covers. Navan took off his shirt, and my gaze traced his bare back.

"I've always been curious about your wings," I said shyly. "How do they feel? Could you...?"

A smirk returned to Navan's lips as he unfurled his dark wings in a gust of air, and joined me in the bed. He pulled me into the comfort of his arms and enveloped us in his wings. I felt their strangely smooth surface against my skin as I drifted off.

At least for tonight, I could sleep well.

19

*A*n icy dawn rose over Vysanthe, cold light glancing in through the narrow slats that served as windows. I awoke, smiling at the blanket of wings that enveloped me, only to jolt a moment later at the sight of Aurelius standing at the foot of the bed.

"The queen wishes to see you in her garden," he announced, at least having the decency to avert his gaze. I shuddered as I wondered how long he'd been standing there, watching us sleep.

Navan stirred, sitting bolt upright when his eyes settled on Aurelius. "Ever heard of knocking?" he growled, running a weary hand through his hair.

"I'll wait outside while you make yourself presentable," Aurelius said crisply, before turning and heading out the door.

Standing, Navan folded away his wings, before pulling on the black t-shirt he had cast aside the night before. I was still fully dressed, though sleeping in the clothes from the ship had left me feeling dirty and uncomfortable. Walking over to the wardrobe that stood beside the twin beds, I opened it and took a look inside.

The clothes weren't quite in keeping with human fashion, but they weren't that much different than what I was used to. I picked out a cream-colored sweater, made from the softest material I had ever felt, hastily took off the t-shirt I was wearing and pulled it on. I couldn't help but wonder what it might be made from—spun material from the backside of some savage, fanged creature, maybe? Pushing the thought away, I looked down at myself, liking the way the sweater looked. The jeans would have to wait, but even a fresh top made me feel better—less sticky and gross, at least.

"You should grab a jacket, too," Navan suggested, coming over to pick out a huge furry coat. He draped it around my shoulders, and I pulled a face. It looked like there was a dead animal hanging on my back—which, I supposed, there was. Only, from the limp fur and strange flaps that looked like ears, it seemed like it had been killed mere seconds ago.

"I can't wear this," I said sadly, realizing the remnants of a fluffy tail were hanging down one lapel.

Navan shrugged. "It's either this, or you freeze."

Not exactly thrilled with my new attire, I kept it on as we left our quarters and followed Aurelius to the same elevator we had used the previous day. This time, however, the elevator didn't seem to go down, as I'd expected. Instead, it zipped horizontally, the force still brutal against my human skin.

It stopped abruptly, causing me to stumble forward. Navan caught me by the waist, his reflexes sharp.

"Everything's so much more violent here," I breathed, regaining my composure, knowing I hadn't seen the half of it.

"You're not wrong," he muttered.

The doors of the elevator slid open onto a wide, open court-yard, a blast of biting wind gusting in, nipping at my cheeks. Instantly, I felt glad to have the furry coat, which was keeping out most of the icy wind. Not all, but most. At least I wouldn't be a shivering wreck when I was brought before the queen this time.

The courtyard itself was empty, save for a bare, skeletal tree that rose up in the center, its bark a jet black, streaked through with veins of pure white. It was strangely beautiful, its clawed branches curving skyward. Overhead, the sky itself was a silvery gray, with deep purple clouds swirling menacingly in wispy clusters. In the air, I could smell the metallic scent of ozone, like the atmosphere before a storm. I wondered if the scent, so close to the tang of blood, was always there.

We hurried after Aurelius, who was walking remarkably quickly. Passing through the courtyard, we reached a covered walkway that reminded me of church cloisters, the stonework a gleaming gray marble. Nothing grew here, except the odd twisting vine bearing the petals of a black flower or two, or bunches of vibrant red berries. Against the biting wind and the grim weather, I was surprised that even they had found the audacity to flourish here.

Before long, we reached a tall set of stone doors, embedded within a large building that looked somewhat cathedral-like in its grandeur, stained-glass windows glinting in the white sunlight. At the entrance, two guards wielded spears; their faces were streaked black and red, as the Impalers' had been. They nodded to Aurelius, saying nothing to Navan and me as the wizened old man, his half-wing dangling down limply, ushered us inside.

Beyond the vast doors lay a botanical garden, and the scent of unusual and exotic blooms bombarded my nostrils. A fine spray of water jetted out from the sides of the stone walls every few minutes, the mist floating down to rest on the flowers beneath.

Everything about Vysanthe felt gloomy and cold, but not this place. Here, there were flowers and bushes and trees of all shapes, sizes, and colors. I noticed a rosebush nearby, harboring the most beautiful rusty-orange roses I had ever seen, though the sight of them threw me for a second—how did they come to have roses on Vysanthe? Did they grow elsewhere in the universe? *Apparently so...*

Queen Gianne was standing at the far end of the gigantic space, tending to a tree that bore a lurid blue fruit on its branches. Her copper hair was tied up out of her face, her silver eyes focused on the task at hand. She was collecting a small basketful of the fruits, effortlessly reaching up to pluck them off.

She turned as we approached, still holding her basket of blue fruit. "Ambrosia?" she asked, turning one around in her elegant hand, before extending it out to Navan.

Navan shook his head. "Solid food doesn't sit well with me, Your Highness," he said apologetically.

"Well then, perhaps your little pet might like a taste?" She smiled coldly, her eyes snapping toward me.

Again, Navan shook his head. "I don't think her weak metabolism could take such rich flavor, Your Highness."

I struggled not to turn to him to ask if it was okay to try. On a planet like Vysanthe, where everyone drank blood, I was going to have to eat at some point. My stomach was already rumbling, the sight of the blue fruit making my mouth water. Back at the *Asterope,* we still had the sachets of astronaut food, provided the guards hadn't removed it, but I had no idea how far the *Asterope* was from here.

"She looks eager, does she not?" Queen Gianne remarked, coming up to me, offering the blue fruit. "Go on, have a taste."

I didn't feel as though I could say no. Navan might get away with refusing an offer from the queen, but an underling like me certainly couldn't. I took the fruit from her, eyeing it closely. It looked like a small apple, though the skin was dappled with light and dark blue.

"Bite it," Queen Gianne said.

For a moment, I felt like Snow White holding the poison apple in her hands. I could feel the burning glare of Navan beside me, but I didn't dare look at him. Keeping my gaze low, I bit into the fruit, feeling the juice run down my chin. Flavor burst into my mouth, awakening every sense like a firecracker going off in my head. It was the most delicious thing I had ever tasted, half sweet, half sour, the flavor vaguely similar to cream soda.

I went to take another bite, but the queen knocked it out of my hand. The barely eaten fruit rolled away across the polished flagstones, leaving a trail of blue juice on the ground.

"Enough now," she purred. "A taste is enough, for the likes of you."

"You are too kind, Your Highness," I whispered, though my insides were twisted with anger and embarrassment.

She sneered. "You boys love your meek little creatures, don't you? A pathetic specimen that won't fight back. Shame you miss out on the fire of a real, strong female," she mused, turning her gaze back to Navan. "And how are we this morning, Navan? I trust you slept well? It must feel good to be back on home turf again?"

"Oh, it's always good to be home," Navan lied. "And the room you provided was more than generous, Your Highness. I must thank you for your excellent hospitality."

"Glad to hear it—it's a pleasure to have my finest subjects back in the fold," she said, turning back to the ambrosia tree. "Oh, and you'll be pleased to know that your comrades have proven themselves to be honest, worthy citizens..." She flashed Navan a look over her shoulder. "I have released them."

When the queen turned her back again, I looked at Navan, and together, we breathed a sigh of relief. Our team was safe, free to meet up with us in Vysanthe, so we could get this mission over and done with. The pod with my blood in it was perpetually making its way toward Vysanthe—a ticking time bomb looming above us. If we were quick, there was still more than enough time to intercept it.

"Your benevolence knows no bounds, Your Highness," Navan said.

"I am always willing to forgive, when the mood takes me," Queen Gianne remarked. "Your friends were fortunate that I was feeling generous. I think, perhaps, the sight of the fabled Navan Idrax had something to do with it." She winked, turning my stomach.

Navan smiled tightly. "You are too kind, Your Highness."

"Nonsense! Your father has been my most trusted advisor for as long as I can remember, and that deserves a slice of magnanimity," she replied, flicking her wrist. "The wanderer has returned. Your father is very pleased to have you back—I think he has grand ideas in store for you, Navan." She chuckled, flashing him a knowing look that only served to confuse the hell out of me. Did she know something I didn't?

Navan sighed. "You are all too kind, Your Highness," he repeated, somewhat emptily.

"Indeed! So kind that I am throwing a great celebration in your honor tomorrow," she stated, and Navan's face fell. "It shall be a celebration of lost souls returning to the light. A salutation to my position as queen, and how I shall be the one to bring salvation to the rebels, returning them to my queendom."

Navan grimaced, though he was careful not to let Queen Gianne see. "I look forward to it, Your Highness. Might I be permitted to bring my slave along with me?" he asked, not looking at me.

A sour look crossed the queen's face. "If you must, though she won't sit at the table with the rest of us. She can stand and beg for scraps, like the bottom-feeder she is."

I wanted to smack the self-righteous look off Queen Gianne's face, but I held myself together, keeping my chin to my chest, my cheeks flushing red with fury. I would not rise to her taunts. Not here, not with so much at stake.

Navan nodded. "Of course, Your Highness."

"In the meantime, I'm sure you're itching to get back to your family in Plentha," Queen Gianne said. "I've had a Snapper brought around to the front of the gardens, so you may travel across Vysanthe at your leisure, reminding yourself of its beauty. Though, I should warn you not to stray too far. It should be waiting in the courtyard as you exit."

Returning to her task of picking the blue ambrosia fruit, she made it clear the conversation was over. Navan and I turned away from her and walked out of the strange cathedral-like garden, through the marble cloisters, and back into the stark courtyard.

There, sitting on the flagstones, was a small silver ship. It looked compact, big enough to fit two comfortably, with metal panels that curved over the front and a beacon flashing at the top, just over the windscreen. It reminded me of a deep-sea lantern-fish, the panels sharpening to points across the front screen and resembling biting jaws.

"This is a 'Snapper'?" I asked Navan, who seemed calmer now that we were away from the queen.

He nodded. "See those teeth? They give it the nickname," he explained. "They serve a purpose, though. Air flows up through the curved teeth, creating a barrier that keeps the rain off the windscreen. We get a lot of rain here; you'll probably see for your-self, soon enough."

Taking my hand in his, he led me to the back door of the Snapper and pulled a lever that opened a narrow door. As I stepped inside, I saw that the vessel was just one slightly oval pod, with two seats at the front, next to the command module.

Sitting down in the one that didn't have a load of buttons and levers in front of it, I let Navan take the pilot's seat. With the flick of a switch, he brought the Snapper to life, the engine thrumming softly. A look of excitement flickered across his face—an expression I hadn't expected to see.

With a grin, he turned to me. "Allow me to show you the sights, m'lady."

ith skilled hands, Navan took us up into the skies above Vysanthe. A city lay below, enclosed between the towering walls of several mountains, though there were buildings carved into every inch of the mountainside, their lights glowing like fireflies in the near distance. Houses and structures of all shapes and sizes were crammed into the mountains' shadow, huddled together like penguins, but every single one was sculpted in the same unusual style. I couldn't tell whether it was beautiful or not—the lines were so severe, the colors so uniform. Sharply sloping roofs glinted with black tiles, each one decorated with a silver weathervane that depicted a different creature.

At the far end of the city itself, where the edges of two mountain ranges met, was an enormous gulley, with two gigantic figures carved into the rock, protecting the entrance to the huge city. One was female, the other male, their hands extended upward, seemingly in worship. There were crowns atop their heads, made from what looked like pure gold, that gleamed in the pale sunlight of Vysanthe.

"What city is this?" I asked, awestruck. "And who are they?"

"This is Regium—it's the royal district," Navan replied, evidently less impressed by a sight he'd seen countless times before. "And those two are the old king and queen—Queen Gianne's parents. Talk about overkill," he muttered, allowing the Snapper to swoop low over a series of ancient-looking buildings, their silver spires glistening with jewels that resembled rubies, drawing my eye like I was a magpie.

"I think they're beautiful," I said.

"You wouldn't if you knew how many people died to build them," he countered, and I grimaced, their beauty fading somewhat.

"What's that?" I asked, wanting to change the subject. I pointed through the windscreen at the ancient buildings, with their twisting spires, curved walls, and rounded windows. It reminded me of pictures I'd seen of the architect Gaudí's work, in Barcelona, back on Earth, and it gave me a pang of homesickness.

"That's the university—I used to study there," he replied. "It's got one of the best libraries in the universe. Maybe we'll find some time to look around."

I smiled, wondering if there were books in there that could tell me about all these weird and wonderful species that kept crossing my path. I wanted to know all there was to know about the universe, until I knew as much as Navan. Still, time was precious, and there was so much we had to do.

"We should start gathering intel for Orion," I said. "Who knows when we might get a chance like this again."

Navan nodded. "We should go to the Observatory first, see what we can find out there."

He swerved the ship around, heading away from the worshipping figures of the old king and queen. I couldn't take my eyes off the city below. Every so often, the crowded buildings would give way to an expanse of open space, possibly a town square or what might have been a pleasant park, had the greenery not been so dark and gloomy. The trees were barely holding on to their curling leaves. Here, coldbloods walked, carrying on with their everyday lives.

I saw restaurants and cafés, with elegantly dressed Vysantheans sitting at tables outside, despite the freezing temperatures, sipping from various vials. Though I couldn't hear them all the way up here, I could see the telltale expression of laughter from time to time, and the animated gestures of intense discussion. If I squinted hard enough, I could just about pretend they were human.

And then the city gave way to a steeply rising rockface, though the houses were crammed right up against the sheer incline. We rushed upward, the pull of gravity making my body feel heavy, before swooping up and over the snowy peak of a jagged mountain. On the other side, the Snapper descended toward a building that lay nestled on a broad ledge, looking over a black lake that lashed against the slippery cliffs below. The Observatory was enormous, its walls seemingly made from pure crystal. From where we were hovering, I could see people milling around inside.

Navan landed the Snapper outside, in a designated parking zone, before we exited the ship. I wrapped the fur coat tight around me, grateful for its warmth as the brutal winds hurtled against me, nearly knocking me off my feet. Navan held me fast, stopping me from falling.

Within a few moments, we were inside the relative warmth of the Observatory. It was a strange building, looking remarkably high-tech, with monitors showing countless regions of Vysanthe flashing up every few seconds. I knew it was Vysanthe because I recognized the cathedral building where we had met Queen Gianne, followed by the ruby-encrusted spires of the university building. There were many other places I didn't recognize, belonging to different Vysanthean districts, with a number of cold-bloods monitoring the images that flashed up.

"This way," Navan said quietly, moving off to a vacant space around the perimeter of the crystal building. I followed him, surprised by the amount of attention he was getting. At least five coldbloods had said a warm "hello" to him in the five minutes we'd been inside the Observatory, and he had politely waved back and asked after their families. I just hoped he wasn't attracting too much attention. We were supposed to be acting covertly, after all.

As Navan seated himself at a desk, a young coldblood wandered over. He was younger than Navan, with dark brown hair and eager blue eyes. For a moment, he just hovered close to where Navan was sitting, hopping anxiously from foot to foot. I wasn't sure he even saw me.

"Navan Idrax?" the coldblood asked tentatively.

Navan turned. "Yes?"

"Vasily Smail, at your service," he gushed.

Navan suppressed a smile. "You know anything about recent breaches in the queendom?" he asked. "I am curious to know about even the slightest chink in security. Now that I'm back, I'm serving as an advisor to the queen—and you must understand, this is all top secret. You are not to breathe a word of this to anyone. If you do, the queen will be most upset."

Vasily's eyes went wide with awe. "Of course, sir. I'll bring you a copy of the transcripts from the last week or so," he said, excitement bristling from him. I almost felt bad for him—this boy was clearly a big fan of Navan's, and Navan was using that against him. Still, if it meant we got to go home again, I wasn't exactly against a bit of harmless manipulation.

"Thank you, Vasily," Navan replied. The boy looked like he might faint at the sound of his name coming from Navan's lips.

As Vasily hurried away, I made a tutting sound in Navan's direction. "Poor kid," I murmured, half teasing.

"He's too weak," Navan muttered sympathetically. "Coldbloods like him don't last long anywhere."

I shuddered, wondering what that meant. Everything about Vysanthe felt Spartan. It was all about strength, and violence, and brutality. Lazar had been right—it held a savage beauty, but it was more savage than beautiful.

When Vasily returned with a small, circular disc, Navan thanked him, leaving him to watch with hopeful eyes as we departed the Observatory and returned to the Snapper. I turned and gave Vasily a delicate wave of goodbye, but the boy's face twisted up in disgust as he saw it. It seemed few coldbloods were immune to the Vysanthean superiority complex, even if they were the runts of the litter.

"What's on the disc?" I asked.

"Any breaches from the last couple of weeks," Navan replied, pocketing it as we re-entered the Snapper and took off. "There should be a decent amount of information on here for Orion. I just need to find a way of sending it to him without alerting any security."

"Can you do that?" I wondered, deeply concerned.

Navan nodded and took us back over the lip of the mountain peak. "I've got tech in my old place which I can use to transmit to Orion. Before we go there, though, I'd like you to see a few more things. Might as well use the chance we've got," he said, giving me a smile.

"Where to first?" I asked, grinning.

"How about... the palace?"

"Sounds good," I said, leaning back in my seat, watching the city sweep away below me.

A short while later, we drew up in front of the most exquisite building I had ever seen in my life. Twisting towers and glinting pinnacles rose up, almost as tall as the mountain that surrounded them, every single one drenched in sparkling diamonds. Where the walls of the university had been curved and strange, this building was sharp, every edge and contour cut with precision. Glittering balconies edged out every so often, with dark trees and brooding blooms sitting out, absorbing the Vysanthean sun's cold light. The palace looked as though it had been carved from ice, like something torn from the pages of a dark fairytale.

It certainly suited the cutting demeanor of Queen Gianne. Yes, I imagined she felt right at home within a place like this.

"It's quite something, right?" Navan said.

I nodded. "I've never seen anything like it."

"You ready to see something else?" he asked, tearing his eyes away from the compelling, frosted walls of the palace.

"What else have you got up your sleeve?" It would take a lot to top this.

He took me to all of his old haunts, dropping the Snapper down wherever he wanted me to take a closer look at something from his past. We passed through a number of districts, though we never stopped at the place Queen Gianne had suggested—Plentha, the district where his family apparently lived. I could tell he was actively avoiding them after the way he'd violently disconnected the call the previous night. That was something I understood. Sometimes, parents just weren't the people you wanted to see.

He took me to a winding river with a beautifully carved bridge crossing it. Underneath, meandering below the surface, were vivid silver fish with eyes that bulged out of their heads, their skeletons visible beneath the translucent flesh of their bodies. They were eerie and striking, all in one. Navan seemed pleased by them.

"We used to feed them when we were kids," he murmured, his eyes transfixed by the fish. I had a feeling I knew who he used to feed them with, my heart aching for him. Being home must have reminded him of so much.

After a while, we moved on, heading for a park that he used to frequent, though it was nothing like the parks I knew back home. This was barren and unwelcoming, with coldbloods walking sternly around the edges. A few were walking with creatures that looked like dogs, only these were far more ferocious. They were jet black, their eyes red and their fangs razor sharp, and their wolfish heads snapped from side to side, taking everything in. As one passed by Navan and me, my insides constricted, and I found myself half expecting it to lunge for me and tear my throat out.

"Icehounds," Navan told me, putting a comforting arm around my shoulder. With the hood of my fur coat up around my face, it was hard to tell I wasn't a coldblood.

Wherever we went, Navan was recognized. I hadn't quite realized I'd fallen for such a Vysanthean celebrity. Down every street, and standing on every corner, someone would stop him and welcome him back, saying how glad they were that he had returned. How did they all know? I guessed news traveled fast when you were the son of one of the queen's closest advisors.

"There are two more places I want you to see," he said, as we got back into the Snapper. "They've shaped who I am more than anything else," he added, a grim expression settling across his face.

A foreboding atmosphere settled across the Snapper. Navan was somber, his brow furrowed, his mouth set in a determined line. Ahead, I watched the mountainous district of Regium give way to the flat plateau of Plentha—the next-door district. Here, I could see towns and villages sprawling across shadowy plains, their grouped lights glowing like will o' the wisps, keeping weary travelers on the right path.

He landed the Snapper beside a patch of woodland that was set apart from the nearby settlements. As I stepped out of the pod, I saw a chapel up ahead. It was small but perfectly formed, with a high steeple, the structure carved from pale gray stone. All around, a graveyard flanked the chapel. Although, it wasn't like any graveyard I'd ever seen. Instead of headstones, there were colorful orbs placed at the heads of the burial sites. Approaching one, I staggered back as a holographic image burst out of the orb, startling me. An old man played on a loop, a smile stretching his face.

Navan walked past me, heading for the farthest side of the

chapel. A willow-like tree with blood-red fronds dangling down stood there, and beneath it—a single, purple orb. Navan had stopped in front of it, his shoulders tensed.

Gently, I put my arm around him, and looked down to see the face of a beautiful young woman with raven-black hair, and eyes the same color as Navan's, staring back. She was laughing in the image, though the loop was silent. Underneath my palms, I could feel Navan trembling.

"Naya?" I asked quietly.

Navan gritted his teeth, visibly steeling himself. "She shouldn't be in the ground," he said hoarsely. "Look at her—she was the epitome of life. Everyone loved her. She shouldn't be in darkness, alone in there."

I held him tighter, feeling his whole body shake. "I'm sorry," I whispered, knowing the words were not enough.

"She should be with Ronad. She should be alive and happy, but instead..." He trailed off, his voice choked. "This is all my father's fault. His sick desire to pair us all off, damning anyone's *actual* feelings!"

I wasn't sure what to say, so I just held him, feeling him turn toward my embrace. I held him close, letting him grip me as hard as he wanted, until the worst of it ebbed away again.

"I miss her so much," he whispered, kissing the top of my head. The words sounded strained.

I looked up at him and recognized the twist of guilt on his face. "You're not responsible for what happened to her, Navan," I said softly. "It hurts, and it will always hurt, but you can't hold yourself accountable. This is on your father, not you."

"I just wish she was here instead of me." He heaved a sigh,

swiping roughly at his eyes. "She'd have loved you." A small smile crept onto his lips then, and I sensed the worst of it had passed. I couldn't begin to understand the loss he felt, but I wanted to be there to help him through it.

"I'm sure I'd have loved her too," I replied, knowing it to be true. This girl looked like she had been a firecracker, sputtered out long before her time. The silence of the hologram was frustrating —I would have loved to have heard her voice, just once.

"I've got one more place to take you to," Navan said finally, taking my hand and drawing away from Naya's grave, though his eyes lingered on the hologram of her face. "It's not something I'm proud of, but I feel you ought to see it."

Around us, the light had dimmed considerably, and the cold sun was making its descent behind the mountains, ushering in the bitter Vysanthean night. Navan had warned me that the days were short on this planet, and when night *did* come, not even the fur coat would protect me from the freezing temperatures. Coldbloods could endure it, but humans could not.

With so little time before sunset, I could only wonder where he was taking me.

21

*W*ith the sun setting in the distance and the ghostly sphere of a moon rising behind the mountains, the Snapper soared across the towns and villages that glowed below. Eventually, all signs of civilization faded away, leaving a vast expanse of barren wasteland, the glint of ice and frost showing on the surface, making it shine like a mirror.

Up ahead, a few dim lights appeared. A makeshift town rested in the shadow of a hillside, a glittering lake beside it, the water dark. Navan set the Snapper down, pulling me to him as we exited the vessel, heading in the direction of the ramshackle town. There was a high wall around it, with metal spikes pointing upward, but the guard on the door—a gruff, scarred brute—simply nodded to Navan as we passed.

"Nice to see you back, man," he grunted.

Navan nodded. "We won't be long."

Inside, there were leaning stalls selling vials, as well as structures with people inside calling out names and numbers at the tops of their voices. Coldbloods crowded around these particular stalls, brandishing what looked like money in their direction. I'd seen enough derbies to know they were gambling.

Navan didn't say a word until we reached the edge of a large pit. Coldbloods surrounded the perimeter, their eyes focused on what was going on below. I glanced over the muddy lip, and the sight shocked me.

In the gaping hole were several small arenas. Inside, bare-chested coldbloods lunged at one another, some bare-knuckled, some wielding weapons, some fighting off huge beasts with dripping jaws. The scent of blood and fear rose up, stinging my nostrils. Whenever one of the warring coldbloods landed an exceptionally nasty blow, a roar of excitement went up from the surrounding crowds. I stared at one arena in particular as a toned female coldblood in light leather armor swiped a scythe at her opponent, knocking his head clean off his shoulders. My hands flew to my face.

I turned to Navan, horrified. "What is this place?"

"These are the fighting pits," he replied solemnly, his eyes on the battles.

"Wh-Why have you brought me here?" I gasped, as a different coldblood lost his arm to the slash of an enormous broadsword.

"I was a champion here, before I joined the Explorer's Guild," he said, distracted. "I needed to get the pain out... and this was the only place I could do that."

"You *fought* here?" I whispered, watching two coldbloods circle each other, their knuckles drawn up to their tattooed faces.

He nodded slowly. "When Naya died, the guilt was unbearable. I felt like I should have done more to stop it... to stop my father. So I fought to ease the pain."

I pictured him in the pits, brandishing one of those deadly weapons, taking the life of a fellow coldblood. I saw his anguished face, the guilt weighing him down as he lashed out to rid himself of the ghosts that haunted him. Had it not been for Jean and Roger, I wondered if I'd have ended up on a similar path of destruction. Maybe not fighting, but definitely something bad. It ran in my blood, after all.

"Did you kill anyone?" I asked.

He grimaced. "No, not here," he said softly. "To be honest, I came here because... well, I thought I'd lose."

I stared at him, letting the words sink in. He'd done more than come here to ease the pain. He'd basically come here to commit *suicide*.

His grimace deepened at my alarmed expression. "I know," he said. "I'm not proud of what I did. It was the darkest period of my life... a period I'm determined to never return to. Nobody had trained me, so I was as good as dead, but by some miracle I won, and the crowds cheered my name, baying for the blood of the loser. I couldn't do it, but the voice that wouldn't shut up had gone. I fought a few more times, never killing my opponent, until the management asked me not to come back—I was bad for business." He smiled wryly.

"Is that how you got those scars?" I asked, thinking about the lines that crossed his chest, back, and, partially, his neck and jawline.

He nodded. "I figured you must have wondered about them

but were too polite to ask... They remind me of my penance. I would have gone mad without them."

"You didn't kill Naya," I reminded him gently.

"I may as well have," he replied miserably.

The night was setting in, and the bitter cold penetrated the warmth of the fur coat bundled around me. My teeth had begun to chatter; my fingertips had gone numb. Seeing my discomfort, Navan put his arm around me and shepherded me back to the waiting Snapper.

"You're missed in the pits," the brutish guard commented as we left. "Never seen anyone fight like that."

Navan flashed him a look. "Well, I won't be coming back anytime soon," he said. "Have a good night, Joden."

The guard nodded. "And you, boss."

The warmth inside the Snapper welcomed me like a longed-for hug, and I hurried to my seat in the cockpit, drawing the coat closer to my body. Despite the horror of the fighting pits, I was excited to see where Navan would take me next. A sliver of dusky sunlight still glanced over the hillside—there was still time.

"Where to now?"

Navan smiled. "Home."

Confused, I sat back as the engine roared to life. I didn't think he wanted to visit his family, and I sure as hell didn't know how they'd react to me. In the outside world of Vysanthe, I could get away with hiding my humanity and avoiding unnecessary attention, as long as I drew my hood up, but in the confines of a house I would be outed as an alien immediately.

Turning the ship around, Navan flew it back toward the spot where we'd visited the chapel. I expected him to stop there, so I was surprised when he continued on, the Snapper's metal base brushing against the canopy of an expansive forest. We reached a clearing in the trees, where he set the ship down.

Stepping out, I saw a low structure in the shade of the gloomy, dark-leafed trees. It looked like a hut of some kind, with long-dead hanging baskets dangling from a wraparound veranda. No lights shone from the windows. Whoever lived here, it was clear they weren't home.

"What is this place?" I asked, my teeth chattering.

"My 'man cave'," Navan replied with a smirk, leading me up to the front door. Opening it up, he ushered me inside.

It was simple, with a lounge to one side and a kitchen to the other—though there was no oven or fridge in sight. I guessed cold-bloods had no need for such things. In the back, there was a bathroom and a bedroom, with basic furnishings. Still, it felt homey now that I was inside.

Navan wandered around, lighting lamps, before disappearing into the back bedroom. He returned a minute later with a bag, a few clothes trailing out of the top. In his hand he held a black box, which he set down on the surface of his coffee table. I eyed it curiously, sitting down next to Navan.

"It's the device I was telling you about," he said, seeing my confused expression. "I'm going to upload the contents of the disc and transmit the information to Orion."

I watched with bated breath as Navan placed the disc into a small drive. A screen flickered up from the black box, showing the progress of the file. The blue line crept along the screen, taking its sweet time.

"This is going to take a while," Navan muttered. "Let's go somewhere while we wait for it to finish."

I nodded, eager to see more of Navan's world. Leaving the black box on the table, he rose and rummaged in a closet. He pulled out another bulky fur coat and wrapped it around me as a second layer, then led me out of the cabin. Clutching a flashlight that lit the way, he walked with me through the eerie trees of the forest. My ears were pricked for the curious sounds of creatures in the undergrowth. A rustle close to my arm made me jump back, but Navan caught me, an amused chuckle rising from his throat.

"There isn't anything bad in these woods," he promised. "The worst creatures live up near the mountains. Here, we're pretty safe."

Not entirely convinced, I clung to Navan as we continued through the shadows of the forest. It wasn't as cold here as it was out in the open, but I could still feel the bite of the Vysanthean wind on my face, nipping at any bare flesh it could find.

Before long, we emerged from the tree line into a tiny grove. I had never expected to see such color in Vysanthe, but the trees here were bright with vivid purple blooms and sunny yellow flowers. A pond stood in the center, with the same luminescent skeleton fish as before turning circles beneath the water. In the darkened sky, huge fireflies flitted to-and-fro, lighting up the air like lanterns.

"This is my favorite place," Navan said, pausing to admire the grove. As my eyes drifted across the scenery, I noticed a squat, glass igloo to one side of the pond.

Navan led me to it, urging me through the door. The warmth

within was blissful. On the floor was a pile of more furs, which I quickly sat down upon, wrapping myself up in the layers. Navan sat beside me, putting his arms around me as I nestled into him, feeling the cold in my limbs ebb away.

Staring up, I saw the twinkle of stars in the distance, the sky blanketed in constellations. With no light pollution for miles, it felt like I could see every single one. Galaxies overflowing with stars streaked across the black velvet of the night's sky. My eyes went wide in awe. A shooting star shot across the scene, but I had learned to be wary of such things. Where once I might have made a wish, now I prayed it wasn't a ship, come to steal me away.

Soon, I began to feel toasty in the shelter of the igloo. In fact, the heat was so intense that I began to feel sleepy. It was like coming in after playing in the snow, the glow of a fireside having a soporific effect.

My eyelids grew heavy, my body leaning into Navan's. He smiled, pulling me closer. Mumbling, I leaned up and kissed the curve of his neck, prompting him to lay me back down on the furs. He put one hand behind his head, while the other cradled me to him, my head resting on the smooth contours of his chest. It was the perfect pillow, his heartbeat my lullaby. Fighting with my need to sleep, I managed to catch one last glimpse of a beautiful, starry night, before it claimed me.

A pale dawn roused me from my slumber. My stomach was aching with hunger pains, making me realize I'd eaten nothing since that taste of blue fruit Queen Gianne had offered me, before cruelly swiping it from my grasp.

Navan stirred, smiling down at me. "Morning," he murmured.

"Morning yourself." I grinned, pushing thoughts of food from my mind.

"We should be getting back," he said, sitting upright.

I nodded, scrambling to my feet. Rain was pattering against the glass curve of the igloo, the droplets icy cold on my face as we left its shelter. Racing back through the trees, we stopped by Navan's cabin, but the crawling blue line on his device had yet to reach completion.

Navan cursed. "We're going to have to come back for it," he said.

"Can't we... take it with us?"

He shook his head. "We're remote enough here that the signal won't be noticed, but if I take it back to the palace, security will likely sense it. We're going to have to leave it, and send it when we return."

"Can't you program it to transmit once it's loaded?"

Again, he shook his head. "I need to check it first, make sure it's in one piece." With a disappointed expression, Navan picked up the bag he'd packed and headed for the door.

"Don't suppose you've got any food in there?" I said hopefully.

He grimaced. "Rask, I'm an idiot—you must be starving! I'll get something for you once we're back at the palace," he promised, gesturing for us to leave. With my stomach still growling, I followed him to the Snapper and got in, watching the fields and towns and wasteland disappear as we headed for Regium.

"So are you gonna finally tell me who Rask is?" I asked as we flew.

He smirked. "He comes from an old fable Vysanthean parents tell their kids—about an ancient god from the old days, when Vysanthe first rose from the ice. He's a god of mischief and balance, offering a trick or a treat wherever he goes. It's why we say his name when something good or bad has happened."

I suppressed a smile—finding it funny that what seemed to be one of their worst swear words came from a kid's fairytale. I looked out at the view, picturing a shadowy deity, lauding his power across the frosty landscape of Vysanthe.

It was only half an hour before we reached the imposing, glacial façade of the palace. Hurrying out, we headed for the vast silver doors that served as the palace entrance. Immediately, guards swarmed around us, demanding to know what our business was.

"Queen Gianne is expecting us," Navan announced, and we were ushered inside.

The palace interior was as impressive as the exterior. Cavernous halls chimed with a thousand dangling crystals, icy chandeliers lining the route, with statues scattered about the place, looking like coldbloods frozen in time. Tapestries hung from the walls, depicting great scenes of war and the beautiful Queen Gianne standing in various poses, usually dominating a conquered species. Beside every single door that branched off from the main hallway, a guard stood, wielding a crackling staff.

A moment later, we were taken through another set of huge double doors, into a grand room with a throne at the very end.

Queen Gianne was sitting atop it, an angry look on her striking face. She eyed us with tangible annoyance.

"And where the hell have you been?" she snapped, as soon as we were brought in front of the throne.

"Getting reacquainted, Your Highness," Navan replied coolly. "I visited some old haunts."

Queen Gianne glowered in his direction. "While I did tell you to explore, I didn't mean you could just go wherever you pleased, for as long as you wished," she growled. "I'm of two minds about whether I want to throw this celebration in your honor now."

"My apologies, Your Highness, I should have known to return sooner," Navan groveled—a disturbing sight to see.

"You were spotted near the boundary dividing the queen-doms," she remarked. "When my advisors informed me of this unfortunate news, I have to say, I feared the worst."

Navan looked up at her. "I would never cross the boundary, Your Highness. There were friends in a nearby border town I wished to visit. That is all," he assured her.

I frowned, wondering when we had reached this invisible boundary. I didn't remember seeing it. Although, now that I thought about it, there was something strange about the location of the fighting pits. They had been so far from any other settle-ment—perhaps that was where the boundary lay, just beyond the pits? I reminded myself to ask Navan later... if Queen Gianne allowed us a later.

The queen's eyes narrowed to two furious, burning slits. She approached Navan, lifting his chin roughly with her hand so he was forced to look her straight in the face. Rage poured off her in waves.

"Perhaps my first suspicion of you was correct, Navan Idrax," she snarled, her beautiful face twisting into something ugly. "Perhaps you mean to betray me to Queen Brisha, like Jethro and Ianthan wanted to? Maybe they were the true followers, and *you* are the traitor."

It was clear that news of those two men's betrayal had crept into the deepest parts of her paranoid mind. And I wasn't sure that I could blame her—being a queen must be tough, especially when everyone wanted you dethroned, or worse. After all, Jethro had been high up in her esteem, once upon a time, offering his engineering wisdom. She had clearly trusted him as a close associate, and now... Well, it would be enough to make anyone paranoid. Distrust lingered in the air.

Navan shook his head. "No, Your Highness. You are the one true queen—you have always been my queen. I would never betray you."

"My sister sends messages, you know, telling me there are spies in my midst," she hissed. "That changeling witch wants to frighten me. She wants me to doubt everything so she can swoop in and take my throne. She thinks she's better than me, but she has no idea. I know her better than she knows herself. She will *not* get to make the first move—you can be assured of that! I will kill everyone I have to before I let her take what is mine," she roared, shoving Navan's face away violently. I could see small marks where her nails had dug into his flesh.

"Your Highness, we were just exploring," Navan insisted. "I am no traitor."

Slowly, the queen's chest stopped heaving, and she calmed down, brushing an elegant hand through her copper locks.

Striding back up to her throne, she turned to glance back at us. A glimmer of cold amusement passed across her features.

"Good," she remarked. "Because, if you betray me, I won't stop at just killing you."

Her eyes flickered to me, and in that moment, I knew I was in trouble.

22

"**Y**ou!" she barked, looking right at me.

I lifted my head, trying to look innocent. "Yes, Your Highness?"

"You see that water in the fountain over there," she said, gesturing toward a gem-encrusted water fountain a short distance away.

I nodded. "Yes, Your Highness."

"Fetch a dish of it, and bathe my feet," she instructed. "They are sore from my morning endeavors, and I would like them soaked and refreshed."

I went to stand, but Navan's hand shot out and grasped me by the wrist. Torn, I crouched, half sitting, half standing, not knowing what to do. I couldn't very well disobey a direct order, not if I wanted to live.

The queen's eyes narrowed. "I said, fetch a dish of water and bathe my feet, you vile creature," she spat.

Again, I went to stand, but Navan's hand pulled me back down. I could see the bemusement on the queen's face, and longed to break free of Navan's grasp—for his sake, as well as my own. I didn't mind doing something degrading if it meant we could get out in one piece.

"Navan? Explain yourself," Queen Gianne bellowed, her face a mask of fury.

"She is weak, Your Highness," he replied. "The temperature of the water will freeze her hands."

A surprised laugh rippled from the back of her throat. "Why should you care if she hurts her pathetic hands?"

"She is my servant—there are things I wish her to do, and for that I require her hands," he countered, his cheeks flushing a pale shade of pink beneath the ashen surface. In any other situation, I would have giggled, but right now, I didn't think I'd ever have the courage to laugh again.

For a moment, Queen Gianne said nothing. My heart was thundering in my chest, and I was expecting her to lash out at his flagrant defiance of her wishes. I didn't mind bathing her feet, but I couldn't turn to Navan and tell him that without revealing our true relationship. In the world of these coldbloods, I got the feeling that servants never talked back to their superiors.

A look of amusement and surprise flickered across the queen's face. "Well, well, well, I'm sure Seraphina will be thrilled to find out that Navan Idrax *is* capable of some sort of affection, even if it's just for a silly little *pet*," she sneered. "Now, if you can learn to wean yourself off unworthy creatures, you might end up half the man your father is. A servant does not need your sympathy, need I remind you?" A disgusted look glinted in her eyes as she scanned me, judging me on the spot.

But all my mind could focus on in that moment was: *Who is Seraphina?*

"It is not sympathy, Your Highness, merely necessity," Navan replied, his head hanging low. He could not look at me, and I didn't know why.

Mentally imploring him to glance my way, I hoped she was his mother... And yet, there was a sinking feeling in the pit of my stomach that wouldn't go away.

"Fine, then I have no more use for you," Queen Gianne sighed, flicking her wrist in irritation. "Be off with you. And do *not* be late for tonight's celebrations. Do I make myself clear?"

Navan nodded, rising to his feet. "I won't, Your Highness."

"Good." She smiled triumphantly. "Oh, and your uncle was looking for you earlier—he is doing some work in the Atrium. I suggest you attend to him."

"I will, Your Highness," Navan replied.

A few moments later, we were out in the main hallway of the palace, heading for the exit. I was excited by the prospect of seeing Lazar again so we could update him on Orion's mission and see what the others had been up to, but I couldn't ignore the sense of dread niggling away at the back of my mind.

"Who is Seraphina?" I asked, after a long, tense pause.

Navan grimaced. "She's not important," he said, still unable to meet my gaze.

I sucked in a breath, unwilling to let this one go. I gave it another few seconds before trying again. "Navan... *who* is Seraphina?"

He lowered his eyes to the floor, his jaw tensing.

With every second of silence, my worry grew. "She's not your mother, is she?" I said quietly.

He shook his head.

"Then... who?"

Navan finally looked at me, everything on his face screaming discomfort. Pulling me behind a pillar that was sharpened to a point like an icicle, he took my hands in his.

"Seraphina is... my fiancée," he whispered, a look of misery in his eyes.

Instantly, I staggered back, my hands slipping from his grasp.

He was *engaged*.

And there I'd been, thinking he'd chosen the bachelor life. Ha!

Suddenly I felt incredibly stupid. *Of course* he wasn't a bachelor. Of course somebody like him was attached to somebody else —he was beautiful, charming, handsome.

The rational half of me could understand that this had to be his parents' doing, but the emotional half was stinging. Why hadn't he been upfront about this? I could accept this was an arranged marriage, but... suddenly learning your boyfriend had a fiancée was kind of a big deal.

Why had he kept it a secret from me? He'd had plenty of opportunities to tell me—he could have done so when the topic came up just yesterday.

And for how long would he have kept me in the dark, if the queen hadn't outed him?

Not to mention, who this woman even was and how *she* would feel if she found out she was being double-played. I might not be the biggest fan of coldbloods, but I was sure whoever this woman was had feelings. How would *I* have felt to learn my fiancé was cheating on me?

"Do... Do you know how sketchy that is?" I managed, taking another step back from him.

"Riley, please. I swear, this wasn't a match I chose for myself! This is my father's handiwork. It's like I was saying to you—he has these plans for all of his children, and my marriage to Seraphina is supposed to unite two well-respected coldblood families— "

"And you didn't think that was something I ought to know?!" I exclaimed, trying to keep my voice low, but, God, it was difficult.

I turned and strode toward the palace exit. Rask knew, I needed some fresh air right now.

"I don't want it, though!" Navan hissed, catching up with me. "I don't love Seraphina! I have no affection for her whatsoever except that of a friend. I don't want to marry her. Everyone thinks the marriage is going to be a disaster, and they're right—it is, because I'm not going to be forced—"

I breathed in deeply as I stepped out through the main doors, my eyes fixed on the Snapper as I tried to tamp down the intense feeling of disappointment that was threatening to overwhelm me.

"So when were you going to tell me? As you were walking down the aisle?"

"Look, I'm sorry, Riley. I should have told you sooner. I just—"

"Just what?" I asked. We'd reached the ship, and I grabbed hold of my side door and swung it open, flinging myself into the passenger seat.

Navan followed suit and closed his door behind him, sealing us inside, where we could finally be less controlled about our volume.

"I kept wanting to tell you the truth, but the moment never arose," he groaned, slumping back in his chair and running his hands down his face.

A laugh escaped my throat, a high-pitched thing that sounded close to hysterical. "Oh, bull! Yeah, we've had our hands full, but we've had plenty of downtime too. If you'd wanted to tell me, you *would* have found the time."

As I glared at him, he kept his face resting in his hands, though from what I could see of his cheeks, he was flushing deeply. This was clearly uncomfortable for him, but it was for me, too. I didn't let up my glower. I wasn't fond of surprises on the best of days, but this... This was seriously not cool.

He let out a long, tortured sigh, then finally removed his hands to look at me. His eyes were shrouded with disgust and regret, his mouth turned downward as if he'd just sucked on a lemon. "You're right," he said. "I didn't want to tell you."

I stared at him. "That's not exactly the answer I was expecting."

He exhaled again. "I know—because there are still things you don't know about me."

I bugged out my eyes. "Clearly."

"I'm a chronic procrastinator when it comes to things I'm very nervous about, okay?" he burst out. "That's all there is to it. I wasn't trying to pull the wool over your eyes, or deceive you. I was just being a damn coward. Things between us happened so fast—one minute, we were working together as partners, the next, we had kissed. And with all the other crazy things that were happening, it was all too easy to find reasons to push this unpleasant little tidbit to the back of my mind, telling myself I'd tell you later. You can ask Bashrik how bad of a procrastinator I can be and he'll tell you.

Hell, it's why I wasn't the one who kissed you first. I would have done it that night in Siberia, you know, when we were dancing under the stars after I got you back from that man-child Donnel— but nooo... Procrastinator Navan took over, and like the dumbass I am, I listened to him. So I'm sorry, Riley—I've done it again. You fell for a master procrastinator. But... if you'll forgive me, I hope I'll have finally learned my lesson, and promise to try to be less of one."

With that, he folded his arms across his chest and frowned at me, waiting for my response.

My heart felt like it had skipped more than a couple of beats as he'd talked, particularly at that kissing admission, but I let silence reign over the ship, taking my time to consider my response. I could tell he was nervous even now, judging by the unevenness of his breathing, and the way his lips twitched ever so slightly.

Truth be told, I'd found his ranty confession downright cute, and it had melted most of my annoyance. I could accept his excuse that he was a procrastinator because, well... if I was honest with myself, I could be one too, sometimes, and I understood how uncomfortable this subject was for him to talk about. But I wasn't quite ready to let him know that yet. There were still many things about this situation that concerned me.

I kept my face a passive mask as I looked back at him. "So... who is this woman exactly?"

"Just a family friend," he replied quickly, a flicker of relief crossing his face. "We've known each other since we were kids. She doesn't feel anything romantically for me either—I guarantee you."

"She wouldn't be at all hurt if she knew you were dating another girl?"

"No, she wouldn't," Navan said. "If anything, she'd be happy for me, because she doesn't want to marry me either."

"She wouldn't come stalking me and slit my throat in the night?"

"No!" he insisted.

I folded my arms, leaning back in my chair. "Hmm. So what's your plan, then, Navan? Your parents expect the two of you to marry. How will you avoid it?"

"Right now, the two of us are doing everything we can to delay it. The whole situation is... complicated, but we've managed to put it off so far, and I swear, I will not end up marrying her, no matter what. Even if you weren't in the picture, I wouldn't."

I let out a steady breath and took a long pause, running my tongue over my lower lip and giving him a considering look.

"And, one final question... How many Navans are there? Is there a Grumpy Navan, a Dopey Navan...?"

A relieved smile broke out on his lips, before he narrowed his eyes at me. "Now you're being mean."

I laughed, letting my mask break. "Yeah, but you deserve it, you big oaf. Seriously—imagine if you randomly found out that I had some guy waiting to marry me back home!"

He shrugged. "Simple. I'd hunt him down and rip his head off."

"Right, point made."

"So can I kiss you now?" he asked abruptly. I realized a look of deep longing had developed in his eyes, his gaze intensified.

I frowned. "What, to make up for not kissing me first before? Sorry, I scored that baby al—"

I didn't stand a chance against Navan's supernatural speed. Before I knew it, he'd leaned forward, his hands touching my face and drawing my mouth to his. His lips caught mine in a deep, slow kiss that forced my eyes shut and overwhelmed my senses.

"How's that for an... eighth first kiss?" he murmured after several heady moments, as he parted our lips.

"Has it even been eight times?" I asked weakly, still half intoxicated by his taste and the feel of him so close.

"I've lost count, but how was it?" He drew away with a smirk.

"It was good. But don't get too cocky—I'll always have one over on you."

"I guess I'll have to live with that." He chuckled, settling himself back into his pilot seat. "So, now that... all of that's out of the way, let's go see Lazar, shall we?"

As Navan took off, I couldn't deny that I felt better about the situation, but still, there was a knot of anxiety in my stomach. I hadn't even met this woman, and had no idea what she was like.

I just had to hope Navan really would be able to find a way out of the engagement, and that he was right in his assessment that Seraphina didn't care for him romantically at all.

Because otherwise, this was going to get awkward.

The Snapper headed across the city district of Regium, and before long, we arrived at a circular structure that lay in the very center of the city. Navan lowered the ship right into the middle, where other ships of a similar build were parked, looking like silvery beetles resting on the ground.

As we stepped outside the Snapper, I looked up and saw that the entire inner wall of the building was made from glass, revealing the coldbloods within. There were stacks of books on several floors, making it look like a library, while others looked like grand meeting rooms. On the lower floors were rooms that looked like laboratories, with black-coated individuals walking around importantly. A few glanced our way, but with my hood up, their attention soon waned.

We entered, with Navan walking up to the front desk, asking for Lazar's location. The man behind the desk pointed us in the right direction. From the hallways, I could see the courtyard with the ships neatly parked, but I could also see through to the other side, watching the coldbloods at their work. It seemed strange that a race so alien could have everyday jobs, just like humans.

After walking down several corridors, Navan and I reached the door we were looking for, and I took the lead, knocking.

"Come in," Lazar's voice spoke from the other side.

We entered to find Lazar standing beside the window, reading from a tome in his hands, while the other coldbloods in the room seemed to be doing very little. He turned toward us as Navan closed the door.

"Where have the two of you been?" he asked curtly, dispensing with the usual niceties.

Navan sighed. "Seems like everyone's asking that today."

Lazar frowned. "Is something the matter?"

"No," Navan replied quickly. "We're good."

"Well, that's good to hear—but you've put me in a bit of an awkward situation, Navan," he said grimly.

"How so?"

Lazar raised an eyebrow. "I've spoken with your father. He says you won't answer his calls, and your comm is switched off. Is there any particular reason you're avoiding him? I had to make something up about decompressing after your trip, but I'm fairly certain he didn't buy it."

"Of course there's a reason, Lazar! Naya died because of him," Navan growled, his bad mood returning. I sighed. Just the mere mention of his father seemed to flip him like a switch.

"But that was an accident," Lazar countered. "He loved your sister dearly."

Navan's eyes flashed angrily. "Even so, that doesn't excuse him of his crimes. *All* of this is his fault, Lazar," he said, gesturing around. "We wouldn't be here if it wasn't for him. Nobody would know about the immortality elixir if he hadn't been hell-bent on figuring out the solution—he has ruined everything. He just *had* to be the one to crack it. I can't even bring myself to look at his face, let alone speak to him."

Lazar walked up to Navan and placed a hand on his shoulder. "I understand, Navan. I won't force you to speak to him. However, I should warn you, he will likely be at the celebration tonight. You won't be able to avoid him forever."

Jareth Idrax was going to be at the celebration? Did that mean I was finally going to meet the man who had caused Navan so much heartache and devastation? A shiver of fear ran up my spine. Men like Jareth rarely got to where they were by being anything but ruthless. With Navan already in a grim mood, I could just imagine the exchange that might occur. I was going to have to keep a close eye on him.

"Was that everything? Queen Gianne said you were looking for us," Navan sighed, rubbing at his temples.

"I managed to pilfer some of those human food pouches from the *Asterope*—thought Riley could use one right about now," he explained.

Immediately, Navan's face softened. "Thank you, Uncle."

"Think nothing of it—can't have her starving to death," Lazar replied, flashing me a surprisingly sympathetic look. "Do you have anything for me?"

Navan nodded. "We got some intel from the Observatory, but I haven't been able to send it to Orion yet. It's safe, but it's still uploading."

"Excellent," Lazar said, his eyes lighting up. "Do let me know when it's sent, so I can see how much longer we have to stay in this hostile place."

"Will do."

"Now, I suggest the pair of you go and make yourselves look presentable," Lazar insisted, as he passed Navan a sack filled with the astronaut food. "I'll see you at the celebration later."

We left, and had just reached the end of the hallway when three figures sprang out of nowhere, cornering us into an annex that branched off from the main walkway. A shock of white-blond hair bobbed in front of my eyes.

Kalvin, Nestor, and Cristo stood around us, a hint of threat in the air. Their eyes were narrowed, and there were fading bruises on their faces. It seemed the interrogators had hit them much harder than Navan or me.

Kalvin pressed forward, looming over me, a leer in his eyes. Navan immediately stepped between us and pushed his hands against the coldblood's shoulders, forcibly shoving him away.

"About time you two showed up," remarked Kalvin, flashing a grin. "Thought you'd abandoned us."

"You'd be the first to jump ship," Navan retorted.

Kalvin rolled his eyes. "I was just wondering if you've managed to mess things up for us yet? You've been missing a fair while—I expect you've done something stupid."

"We've been keeping to the mission, instead of loitering in hallways," Navan said drily.

Kalvin stepped away, his brow furrowed. "You'd better not ruin this for us, Idrax. We've been waiting a long time for this moment, and if you slip up, there'll be hell to pay."

With that, the trio of coldbloods turned and stormed down the corridor, disappearing from sight.

"Idiots." Navan scowled, then glanced down at me. "You okay?" he asked, his tone softening.

"Yeah, I'm fine," I said. "Let's just get out of this hallway."

I lingered close to him as we made our way back to the ship. Lost in my own thoughts, I kept mostly silent during the journey back to the place we'd spent that first night on Vysanthe. I didn't know why we were going back there, but I presumed it had something to do with pleasing the queen. Not to mention the fact that I'd seen a few gowns hanging in the wardrobe—perhaps I could borrow one. It seemed unlikely, but what else were they for?

Docking the Snapper at the hangar below, we took the elevator up to the top floor and sought out our room.

When we arrived, however, we found the door swung open,

and the interior ransacked. Chairs and tables were toppled onto the floor, and the clothes from the wardrobe were slung all over the place. It looked like a bomb had gone off.

I began to panic, wondering if someone had been sent to search our room for the disc that Navan had taken from the Observatory. Did they know? Was someone onto us?

Then a cold laugh split the air, a shimmering motion revealing the two shapeshifters, who were lounging on the beds. They had camouflaged themselves to the color of the bedding, but now they were visible, their disgusting flesh pooling on the covers.

"Comfy digs you've got here," the female shifter remarked.

"What are you doing here?" Navan snarled. "Get out, before I throw you out!"

The female shifter exchanged a glance with her partner. "We had a hunch. Thought you might be trying to escape back to Earth. No evidence, as yet. But there's still time for your betrayal," she said coolly, flicking lint off one of her sacks of skin. "We have our eyes on you."

"Thought we'd enjoy these sweet quarters while we were at it," the male shifter cackled. I grimaced, wondering what they'd been up to while we were gone. Deciding it was better not to know, I pushed the thought from my mind.

"Suppose we'd better be off," the female shifter sighed. "Got to look like that fat toad, and the skinny, useless one."

I frowned. "Who?"

"Kiel and Grillo, I think their names were," the male shifter replied. "If I'd known old queenie was going to let us off anyway, we'd never have done away with them. Oh well, can't be helped now."

Without another word, they got up and waddled from the room, their skins changing from wormy pink to ashen gray within mere moments. As they exited, they had taken on the mantle of coldbloods—one of them looking the spitting image of our interrogator, Kiel.

I shuddered, wondering what they'd done with Kiel and Grillo's bodies. More than that, I feared what would happen if those bodies ever got discovered.

"I hope they disposed of them properly, where no one will find them," Navan muttered, voicing my own concerns.

"Yeah, well, I guess we don't really have time to worry about that now," I said, sighing. If we were going to get through tonight, we needed to make sure we were convincing. Navan was to be the hero, returning home after a trying expedition. And I was to be... his pet. I swallowed. "We should get ready. Tonight won't be easy."

Navan nodded. "You're right," he said quietly. "Everyone will be watching us tonight."

23

*D*ressed in a scarlet silk gown that I had taken from the wardrobe in our chambers, I couldn't help marveling at the transformation. With my hair curled and flowing past my shoulders, and a touch of Vysanthean mineral makeup I'd found in a drawer, I looked like an entirely different woman compared to the tired and faint girl I'd been a few hours ago.

Navan looked more handsome than ever in a high-collared suit that matched the color of his eyes—a deep, slate gray. It was hard to keep my eyes off him. Stealing glances at him, I found that he was looking at me too, his eyes wide with appreciation.

With us walking into the palace together, I even managed to forget about the knot in my stomach caused by the uncertainty that was his fiancée, Seraphina. For now, I could pretend every-thing was all right. He was here, and I was here, and that was all that mattered if we were going to get through the evening.

My jaw dropped as we stepped into the grand hall of the

palace. The extravagance was unreal. I wasn't even sure how they'd managed to put it all together in such a short amount of time. Sapphire-plated towers of vials in all sizes rose up, almost touching the ceiling, and there were glinting crystal glasses filled to the brim with a dark, ominous substance. I wouldn't be eating tonight, but the coldbloods could gorge themselves. Besides, I'd already wolfed down a packet of powdery casserole that had kept me from the brink of passing out.

All around the floor, elegant dancers whirled and turned, their flimsy gauze costumes floating, making them look like mysterious fairies. Jewels glistened on their ashen skin, the contrast striking. Melodious music trickled down from an orchestra set up at the head of the hall. The instruments weren't recognizable to my human eyes, but the sounds they made were beautiful. It was eerie and stirring all at once, almost making me want to take to the floor with the whirling dancers.

"What are those towers made from?" I asked, keeping my voice low. The stone was like nothing I'd ever seen before. It was opalescent in its sheen, but the stone itself was rippled through with veins of sapphire, creating an awe-inspiring marble effect. The same stone was draped around the necks of several revelers as necklaces, sparkling with every turn they made in the soft light of the hall.

"It's opaleine," Navan explained. "We mine it from a planet called Zai."

"Zai? Is it near?"

He nodded. "Near enough."

"Do people live there?"

He sighed sadly. "A race called Draconians live there. They're a humanoid dragon species, very powerful—not that it does them much good."

I frowned. *Dragons.* Another mind-blowing species to add to my list. "Uh, what do you mean, 'not that it does them much good'?"

"They could be the most ferocious race in the universe—they're towering, they breathe fire, they have twice the strength of coldbloods—but they're perpetual pacifists and highly religious. Their faith prohibits violence," he said somberly. "Opaleine is their sacred stone, used in all their rituals and celebrations, but the coldbloods have mined it mercilessly, knowing the Draconians won't fight back."

I felt a flicker of anger, though this wasn't fresh news to me. I knew the coldbloods were merciless plunderers, searching the stars for anything they could pillage and steal. Still, it didn't make it an easier pill to swallow. If they could rampage across a planet with such strong inhabitants, Earth would be a breeze to them.

"Opaleine has become more prized here in recent years, though," Navan went on. "The coldbloods stopped mining Zai after a strange plague started spreading across the planet, deadly to our immune systems. Since then, opaleine has become a cherished object—a symbol of absolute wealth and power. Only those rich enough, and formidable enough, have any left. As you can see, Queen Gianne has it by the bucket-load." He flashed a grim look at the gleaming towers.

"What caused the plague?" I asked, my curiosity piqued.

He shrugged. "Nobody knows. For a long time, the coldbloods suspected the Draconians had released it themselves—I suppose it doesn't count as violence if there's no bloodshed. Not to a coldblood, anyway." His tone was bitter, his eyes burning with a deep-rooted hatred for his home planet. Vysanthe was a planet that ran on greed and dread—in a way, it was its own plague, infecting the universe one planet at a time.

All around us, the best and brightest of Vysanthe had gathered. They were all beautifully dressed in elegant gowns and suits of a quirky style, with sharp edges and intricate patterns, and each one was clamoring for the attention of Queen Gianne, who was mingling, a glass of that red substance in her hand. Nobody was as exquisitely dressed as the queen, whose dress flowed out in several ruffled layers, leaving a long train behind her. On closer inspection, I realized that each layer was encrusted with opaleine, the heavy hem having to be hauled around by several attendants, who rushed to her aid every time she moved. Her copper hair was piled high atop her head, with opaleine-studded combs shaped like snowflakes protruding from her mass of curls.

Shimmery black shadow had been blended around her eyes, making her silver irises pop, and seem all the more deadly. On her lips, she wore a deep, sultry red, with powder brushed beneath the harsh lines of her cheekbones, so that they stood out even more. A savage beauty, indeed.

"Navan, there you are!" a voice called from across the crowded room. Navan froze, a look of dread passing over his face, as a handsome older couple made their way toward us. I had seen them before, in the image that had flickered up on the holographic comm device.

The Idraxes were moving toward us. There was no escaping them now. Beside me, I felt Navan tense.

"Mother, Father," he said tightly.

As they neared, I saw that Jareth and Navan shared the same facial structure, though he had his mother's slate-gray eyes. The latter was smiling warmly as she embraced her son, pulling him into her arms whether he wanted to be hugged or not. Jareth, far more restrained, offered a hand, which Navan shook politely.

"It's so wonderful to see you!" his mother cried, holding him by the shoulders so she could look at him properly. "Why didn't you tell us when you got back? We've missed you!" There was a hint of hurt in her voice.

"We didn't even know until Queen Gianne mentioned something about you returning with Lazar," Jareth added, sternly. "I spoke with him, since you seemed to be... out of range. He said you were 'decompressing.'" A disbelieving grimace passed over his face, though Navan's mother's expression never ceased to be anything other than delighted.

She was a beautiful woman, her smile coming easily, her lavender gown highlighting the color of her eyes. I wasn't expecting Navan to introduce me, because I realized he couldn't. I was a pet, a slave, an underling—I wasn't worthy of such an honor.

"Will you join us back at the house after the celebration?" she asked hopefully.

Navan shook his head. "I have too many things to attend to, Mother."

"Well, you'll sit with us, won't you?" she ventured. "Your brothers are here... though I think they're distracted by those dancers," she added, looking unimpressed. I cast my gaze over to a group of tall, striking coldbloods standing to one side of the dancefloor, admiring the sight of the flowing dancers. There were seven in total, all of them sharing Navan's dark features, though in my opinion, none were quite as handsome as him.

"I don't think so, Mother," Navan said. "I'm still recovering from my journey. I'm here to endure the celebration, and then I'm retiring for the night."

His mother frowned. "Would it kill you to indulge in our ways, just once? You've always been like this. This celebration is in your honor, Navan—you could at least try to enjoy it. Speaking of your brothers, where is Bashrik? I haven't heard from him in weeks. The pair of you... Honestly, it's like you *want* me to worry."

"He wanted a change of scenery," Navan replied, without missing a beat. "Asked me to drop him off at the colony on Daro— you know how he loves Darian blood. I'm supposed to pick him up on my way back out." A tight laugh emerged from his lips, as his mother chuckled. Apparently, there was some shared joke I was missing out on.

"He'll be the size of a house by the time we see him again!" Jareth commented sternly, though there was the slightest hint of amusement on his stoic face.

"Seraphina is here somewhere, Navan," his mother said suddenly. "I'm sure she's eager to see you. I think I saw her by the—"

"Not now, Mother. I really should be making the rounds," Navan interrupted. "I spotted some of the Guild here who will be eager to know what I've been up to."

His mother seemed disappointed, but if his father felt anything, he didn't show it. With an embrace just as awkward as the first one, Navan turned and walked away from his parents. I followed, feeling their eyes on me as we left. I guessed if Navan had stayed longer by their side, they would have asked something about me—where he'd picked me up from—but as it was, he didn't give them the chance.

I let out a soft breath. In the back of my mind, I'd expected we'd end up bumping into Seraphina here—this was Navan's party, after all—but I still wasn't feeling in the least bit prepared for it, despite Navan's reassurances that she wouldn't cause us any trouble. I wiped my sweaty palms on my dress and tried to distract myself with the scenery.

"Could have been worse," I said quietly, as we made a detour around the side of the main hall, and out into a connecting hall-way. The music echoed faintly through the walls, but there was nobody here.

Navan shook his head. "I doubt it. It's going to be impossible to keep my distance tonight."

"I'll create a diversion," I said, trying to get him to smile a bit.

"They barely even see you." He sighed. "That's the way of my people—they just dismiss anyone who isn't of their kind. I mean, how could anyone ignore you? Look at you, Riley! I've never seen anything more perfect in all my life, and they look down their noses at you, like you're something unpleasant they've stepped in," he ranted, slamming his hand into the wall of the palace hallway.

I felt my cheeks flush. "What's your mother's name, by the way?" I asked, eager to change the subject. I enjoyed the compli-ment, but not the anger that came with it.

"Lorela," he replied, his shoulders relaxing.

"That's a beautiful name."

He nodded. "I wish she was as beautiful a person. But honestly, it's my father who's the main problem—she goes along with whatever he says. Seeing them tonight... I'm worried I'll never be able to look at them in the same way again. They want to rule over my life with an iron fist, won't be satisfied until I'm exactly what they picture me to be. It's like they've learned nothing from their mistakes with Naya... absolutely nothing."

I reached out and took Navan's hand in mine—there was only so much we could do under the watchful eyes of the coldbloods, but I needed him to know I was there for him.

"You don't need to be what they want you to be," I whispered, lifting my other hand to his face, making him look at me. "Free will, remember?"

He grunted. "Have fun telling them that. I've told them time and time again I don't want to marry Seraphina, but it falls on deaf ears—they don't care about anyone but themselves. Our union is the only thing that will increase their standing in our society, and they're willing to pay the price, regardless of my or Seraphina's feelings." Exhaling, he looked me in the eyes, and the earnestness I saw there made my heart pound. "It's not fair to either of us, Riley. I want her to find a partner whom she loves completely, and who loves her the same way in return, the way I..." He paused, swallowing, and his gaze dropped to the floor. "Well, the way I..."

"Do you have a death wish?" A cold voice echoed down the hallway before Navan could finish. I hurriedly drew my hand away from Navan's cheek, realizing we had drawn far too close. It had probably looked like we were about to kiss, and... Well, if I was honest with myself, depending on how Navan had finished that last sentence, we might have been.

We turned sharply to see Kalvin striding toward us, a furious look on his ashen face. He was dressed in a maroon suit, the red contrasting starkly with his white-blond hair. He stopped beside us, pulling me forcefully away from Navan, just as a coldblood guard walked through the door of the hallway.

"Stop taking what's mine!" Kalvin barked suddenly as he noticed the guard, his eyes narrowed at Navan.

The guard eyed us curiously. Apparently believing it to be a Vysanthean tussle over property, he shrugged and carried on.

"Take your hands off her," Navan hissed, as the guard disappeared from sight.

Kalvin released me, but his eyes remained narrowed on Navan. "You're even more of an idiot than I thought," he snapped. "This... affair of yours could get us all killed, if the queen found out. You're breaking the law, falling for an outsider. If you cared at all for Riley, you wouldn't be acting like this—parading her around for everyone to see, swooning over her in the hallway of the bloody palace, for Rask's sake! How about you keep it on the ship, and in your pants?"

Just then, a figure emerged from the shadows of the corridor, holding a glass of red liquid in his hands. I didn't recognize him, and Kalvin and Navan didn't seem to know who he was, either. He was a tall, willowy coldblood, with faded gray wings and a frosty look on his angular face—and I realized he'd probably just heard every word of our conversation.

"Well, well, what *would* the queen say if she found out the son of Jareth Idrax was fraternizing with a... whatever you are," he said, a threatening note in his voice as he moved closer, glancing over me. "I'm sure it would open up a position at her side. I mean, your father would *have* to be punished too—she couldn't be associated with someone whose son had performed such a vile act."

"I have no idea what you're talking about. You caught us in a dispute over stolen property, nothing more," Navan retorted quickly. A little too quickly.

The coldblood smiled. "That idiot guard might have believed it, but he didn't see what I did. You were 'swooning over her', as your friend put it. Romancing that creature. I saw the look in both your eyes."

"Who are you?" Navan demanded.

"A loyalist. Unlike you, clearly," the coldblood replied sharply, his nose wrinkled up in disgust at the sight of me. "But I'm not an unreasonable man. If we can come to some sort of arrangement, perhaps I won't announce your betrayal to the entire party..."

Kalvin scowled. "You dare to blackmail us?"

The coldblood shrugged. "You've made it so easy," he purred. "Not that I'm interested in you. I don't even know who you are. It's Idrax I'm after."

Navan frowned, visibly struggling to keep his cool. "What do you want?"

The coldblood grinned, looking me up and down. "How about you give me the girl for an hour or two, and we'll call it even? I've never experienced her species before."

With the coldblood's attention turned entirely on Navan, he didn't notice Kalvin lunging for him until it was too late. Snatching a concealed knife from within his suit jacket, Kalvin plunged the blade through the back of the coldblood's neck, pushing so hard that the sharp point ended up coming out the other side. A sickening gurgle erupted from the coldblood's throat as dark liquid oozed out of his mouth. A few seconds later, his eyes went blank, the life gone.

Leaping to action, Navan tugged a tapestry from the palace wall and laid it flat on the ground, and Kalvin let the dead cold-blood fall onto it.

As they hurriedly wrapped up the body, Kalvin hissed, "That was too close, even for you."

For the first time ever, I saw Navan rattled. Pure fear flickered across his face. Our relationship had almost blown our cover, and I was beginning to think it was more dangerous than even I knew.

"We need to hide him, fast!" Kalvin whispered, pulling the tapestry toward the recess the cold-blood had been hiding in.

There was a door hidden in the shadows. Running toward it, I opened it, letting Kalvin drag the dead body over the threshold. Navan was out in the hallway, mopping up any evidence he could find with the edge of a curtain he'd torn away.

Beyond the door I'd spotted was a storage room. It didn't look like the type to be frequented much—there was hardly anything in here, except for a pile of boxes—but that didn't mean someone wouldn't come in and find what we were trying to conceal. Still, it was our only option for now. The outside world was too far away, and we couldn't exactly drag him through the main celebration hall.

Navan entered the room a moment later, and he and Kalvin

hid the dead coldblood behind a stack of boxes. The corpse couldn't be seen from the door, and discovering him would mean someone had to sift through piles of stock, but it did nothing to settle my nerves.

"We're going to have to come back for him after the celebration, when the palace is quieter, and dispose of him properly," Kalvin said. "Sooner or later someone will find him, especially when he starts to crumble."

I frowned. "Crumble?"

Kalvin nodded, wiping a sheen of nervous sweat from his brow. "When coldbloods die, their bodies crumble to ash. The scent is overpowering—like pure ozone. We've got a few days before he starts to go, but who knows when we'll have a chance to get back here."

"It'll have to do for now," Navan said, dragging another set of boxes in front of the makeshift burial site. "We'll be missed if we stay out here too long," he added, glancing tensely at the door.

Leaving the coldblood behind, the three of us stepped back out into the hallway and closed the door firmly behind us. After dusting ourselves off, we returned to the main hall, though I didn't think I'd ever be the same again. I was shaken, fear bristling in my veins, putting me on edge. Turning to Navan, I could see that he was feeling it too.

Kalvin hung back, and out of the corner of my eye, I realized he was discreetly forcing the knife through the soil of a nearby potted tree. He then covered it over, as though nothing had ever happened. A smart idea.

With that, we returned to the main room and headed for our

seats, with Kalvin moving away from us to join a different table at the far side of the hall. The dancers had gone, but the music was still playing, with several coldblood couples taking to the floor. Everyone seemed to be in a celebratory mood, clinking glasses of red liquid and downing the contents in one swift gulp. I couldn't help feeling disgusted, yet I couldn't stop watching.

I stood behind Navan since I hadn't been given a seat, and gazed out over the revelers, taking everything in. My senses were on high alert, suspecting everyone of knowing what had happened. It wouldn't take much for the coldblood to be discovered, and then we'd be done for.

Navan was sitting at a table with a dozen or so members of the Explorer's Guild, by the sound of their conversation. As much as I wanted to glean more knowledge about Navan and his prestigious position as a Chief of Exploration, I couldn't fully concentrate. Every moment that passed, I was convinced we were going to be found out.

"How about you, Idrax? Looks like you found at least one interesting thing on your travels," an older coldblood teased, glancing my way. My ears perked up.

"Not really," Navan said coolly, casting a casual glance my way. "Picked her up from a little nowhere planet. Weak race, weak blood. Could wipe them out in one go if I wanted."

"What is she?" another explorer asked.

He shrugged. "Need to go over the books in the library, see if she matches up to anything we've found before. Her blood tasted *awful* though—easily digestible, but made me feel queasy for a week." The table erupted into laughter, and I realized everyone's focus was on Navan. It was clear he was the "cool kid", with all these other coldbloods trying to win his attention.

As the minutes ticked by into hours, I began to feel myself relax. A few more hours, and we could be out of here, getting that body far away from where anyone could discover it. Just a few more hours. I could manage that.

I spotted Kalvin at the opposite end of the room, in deep discussion with some of the others at his table. As they lifted their heads, I realized they were Nestor, Cristo, and the two shifters, now in the guise of Kiel and Grillo. A risky move, bringing the two shifters here. What if their façade slipped? What if their façade slipped, *and* someone found the body? Two strikes, and we'd be out.

A scream went up from the crowd, startling me. My heart thundered.

"He's dead!" a coldblood waitress wailed, rushing into the throng, her hands covered in a dark substance.

All semblance of relaxation shattered.

Navan scraped back his chair and rose to his feet, as the rest of the room descended into chaos. People were screaming, everyone was running, and nobody seemed to know what was going on. Guards strode forward, brandishing their crackling pikes, their menacing eyes scanning the room for any sign of trouble.

"Who is dead?" a voice bellowed across the hall. Instantly, everyone fell silent. It was Queen Gianne, rising from her throne, her eyes livid.

The waitress turned, trembling. "There is a body in the stockroom, Your Highness. I was bringing out more glasses and... I found him!" she shrieked, sinking to her knees in front of her queen.

"Everyone, stay where you are! Anyone caught running for the exits will be killed on sight," the queen roared, clearly infuriated by the interruption to her party. "Guards, follow this waitress! Search the area for the killer. Nobody leaves until this vulgar beast is found!"

To the chorus of marching boots, the guards swarmed into the hallway we had come from, the doors swinging shut behind them, leaving us with the uncertainty of their return. I wanted to grasp Navan's hand, but I stayed put, knowing that any sort of affection would only get us into even more trouble. It was a waiting game, now.

In the distance, I saw Kalvin and the others get up out of their seats, deliberately keeping their gazes away from where Navan and I were standing. The looks on their faces didn't exactly fill me with confidence. There was terror written on every single one.

"What is the penalty for a crime like this?" I whispered to Navan.

"A very brutal, very painful, very slow death," he replied, his voice wavering slightly.

I froze, unable to speak. My mind was full of a thousand terrible executions. For myself, I knew it would be over with far faster than it would for the coldbloods, with their superior strength, but I wasn't ready to die. Nor was I ready to watch Navan die. There had to be a way out of this. They *couldn't* know it was us.

Ten torturous minutes later, the guards returned. One of them ran up to the queen, bending his knee as he neared her.

"Well, what have you found?" Queen Gianne demanded.

"Jora Razul, Your Highness," the guard replied.

Queen Gianne's cheeks flushed red with fury. "One of my most loyal subjects. A faithful friend to the one true crown!" she cried. "How did he die?"

"Knife wound through the neck, Your Highness," the guard explained. "We didn't find the murder weapon."

Immediately, Queen Gianne's gaze rested upon Navan, before floating down to me. Scanning the crowd, she sought out the faces of Kalvin and the others, too, her chest heaving with rage. "Fetch Navan and his pet to me, and those rebels too!" she roared, her voice shaking the crystal glasses.

The guards made a beeline for us, jabbing the tips of the bristling spears between our shoulder blades, the electric buzz driving us toward the queen. I felt like a cow on its way to the slaughterhouse, being cattle-prodded all the way. As we reached Queen Gianne, the guards shoved us downward, making us sink to our knees in front of her.

"How is it that there have been no murders like this committed since I have been queen—but, the moment you bring rebels across the threshold of my queendom, a loyalist winds up dead in a palace stockroom?" she asked, her words dripping venom, her gaze fixed on Navan's face.

"I don't know, Your Highness," he replied quietly, keeping his head down.

"You think it's a coincidence, Idrax?" she spat, her silver eyes burning with furious fire.

He shook his head. "I don't know, Your Highness," he repeated.

"It all seems a little suspicious to me," she hissed, dipping low to his face. She snatched his chin up to make him look at her.

"This was *you*, wasn't it? This was your plan all along. You thought you could frighten me by ruining my celebration, and picking off those closest to me—is that it? Did my sister put you up to this?" I could feel the anger pouring off her, sending terror through my veins.

"No, Your Highness," Navan insisted. "I had nothing to do with this. I don't know how that coldblood died."

"You got one of your little cronies to stab him, is that right? You want me to think my queendom isn't safe, yes?" she snarled. "Well, it won't work, Idrax! I will never be afraid. My queendom is solid, and shall forever stand, no matter how many rebels flock to my door, trying to take me down!" Her hand shot out and struck Navan hard across the face. His head jerked backward, the blow echoing across the silent hall.

Once again, it took everything I had to keep still, to stop myself from checking he was okay. A handprint was beginning to blossom against the ashen gray of his skin.

Queen Gianne was running scared; I could see it on her face. There was not only anger flickering across her features, but panic too. All of those things she had said were things she feared. It seemed the Queen was having a crisis of confidence, all smothered in a front of bravado. To me, it was crystal clear that she *didn't* believe her queendom or her crown were safe. She was downright paranoid.

Slyly glancing to his side, Navan flashed me an apologetic look that made my pulse quicken in despair. With a sinking feeling in my stomach, I realized he was going to own up to it, to save us all.

"Your Highness, I—" Navan began.

"It was me," a low voice interrupted, before Navan could say another word.

I turned sharply to see Kalvin kneeling at the end of the lineup, his gaze lifted to meet the queen's. "I did it, Your Highness. I killed Jora Razul," he said hoarsely, keeping his eyes on her.

Forgetting Navan, the queen whirled around and stormed toward him, bending low to his face. "Did my sister put you up to this?"

He shook his head. "Forgive me, Queen Gianne—the one, true queen of Vysanthe. Jora and I got into a fight about an old disagreement. I had stolen his girl, a long time ago, but he never forgave me," he explained, thinking fast. "I'd been away so long, I thought he'd have forgotten all about it, but he sprang on me in the hallway, and I fought back in self-defense. I didn't mean to kill him, Your Highness. He took me by surprise, and I retaliated. It was a stupid argument about a petty squabble, and it ended in tragedy—it was just the two of us, out there in the hallway, and I hid him because I was ashamed of what I'd done."

I stared in open-mouthed disbelief, both at Kalvin's swift-thinking mind, and at the realization that he was sacrificing himself for the sake of us. No, not us—Orion's cause. All of this was for the rebel cause. If nobody took the rap for Jora Razul's murder, then the mission stopped here. Still, I could hardly fathom how someone could believe so wholly in a cause that they would be willing to die for it. I had never been Kalvin's biggest fan, but I couldn't help but feel a deep, newfound respect for him. There was an incredible sense of duty in his character, even if it was tragically misdirected.

A sense of duty that I prayed had just saved all of our lives.

Queen Gianne seemed to consider Kalvin's words, conflict moving across her face in a grim shadow. With my eyes upon her, I prayed the queen would be merciful.

"This is the truth?" she asked, her features softening.

Kalvin nodded. "This is the absolute truth, Your Highness."

"Very well. A tragic accident, nothing more?" the queen mused.

"Nothing more, Your Highness. A silly mistake that cost a cold-blood's life," Kalvin replied, a glimmer of hope in his eyes.

"Two lives," she corrected, a cold smile on her face.

Kalvin frowned. "Two, Your...?"

The words died on his lips as a guard stepped up behind him. Queen Gianne flicked her wrist, and before my brain could even comprehend what was happening, the guard brought his crackling spearhead down, skewering Kalvin in one fell swoop. The sharp edges of the spear pushed straight through his spine and out through his ribcage. He gasped once in surprise, and then he was gone, his eyes fogging over.

As the guard removed the pike, using his boot as leverage to haul the weapon back out, Kalvin's body slumped forward on the ground, his limbs splayed out at unnatural angles. I willed him to get back up, to take another breath, but it was too late. Kalvin had given his life for the rebel cause, and that was all there was to it. No fanfare, no ceremony, no high honor, just a body crumpled on the ground, his blood pooling out around him.

"Everyone may leave! The celebration is finished!" Queen Gianne boomed, turning around. Her attendants lifted her skirts as she sashayed across the hall and out into a connecting corridor. The party was over.

I couldn't peel my eyes away from the sight of Kalvin, even as I felt the hot pressure of tears building behind them. I felt numb, the only thought running through my head being that he hadn't deserved to die like this.

He may have been vulgar, but he had proven himself to be braver than every single one of us.

In Vysanthe, it seemed, bravery wasn't rewarded.

25

Slowly, the revelers began to make their way out of the exits, their mood somber. A few cast glances back at the dead body on the floor, but none of them wore any mask of sympathy on their faces. They didn't know Kalvin—didn't know what he had given up, or why; they must have thought he was a miscreant who had wronged the queen.

As the crowd dispersed, leaving the crew of the *Asterope* in silent horror, one figure began to approach us. Jareth Idrax was making a beeline for Navan, who was rising to his feet, his eyes set on the crumpled figure of Kalvin.

"Navan?" Jareth said softly, resting his hand on his son's shoulder.

Navan flinched, turning. "Father," he returned flatly.

"I'm sorry for your loss. A terrible thing he did, but in days gone by, the queen would not have delivered such a harsh sentence," Jareth said, his tone unexpectedly empathic. "I'm sorry you were put in this position, so close to being blamed for his actions. The queen is... unsettled, to say the least."

My suspicions had been right. The queen was on edge, her mood and manner disturbed by word of rebels, and the threat to her throne. Even so, I was still reeling from what she had done. A long prison sentence might have been better, but then, I didn't know the judicial system here. Did they even have prisons? By the sound of what Jareth was saying, they didn't simply kill people on sight, without some sort of mercy. Vysanthe was full of surprises.

"She killed a man without trial, Father—I'd say she's a little more than unsettled," Navan shot back. "How can we trust a queen like her, if she can't control her impulses?" he added, lowering his voice so only Jareth and I could hear his treasonous talk.

"I'll forgive you for saying that, this once—you are evidently shaken, but you should not speak of her that way again," Jareth reprimanded. "Hopefully, with you as her advisor, alongside me, we will be able to guide her toward a more peaceful way of being... In truth, I've never seen her this bad. Even after I started intercepting the letters from her sister, her mood has continued to darken. It will be up to us to see her through this bout of paranoia."

For the first time, he looked at me. It was a real stare, instead of the cursory glance I'd been given before. Confusion furrowed Jareth's forehead.

"I think, perhaps, you should rid yourself of this servant," he remarked, waving a hand toward me. "The queen doesn't like it— she doesn't appreciate the presence of outsiders, given the current climate. It would be best for everyone if you took her back to where she came from, or simply dropped her somewhere nearby, so we can get on with things as a family," he stated.

I could feel Navan's hackles rise at the dismissal of me. But what could he do? He was on Vysanthean soil, and as long as he was here, his parents would continue to try to bend him to their will. I could see it on Jareth's face, how he longed to have his son beside him, advising the queen—a true family business.

"She's not going anywhere, Father," Navan said. "She is my servant, and I've grown used to having her around. She's useful."

Before Jareth could respond, another figure approached. My eyes went wide at the sight of her. I had never seen a woman more beautiful. She was tall and slender, with raven-black hair that curled around her striking face in long, elegant tendrils. She had the same ashen gray skin as the other coldbloods, but it suited her far better than any female coldblood I had yet seen. Her eyes were the color of burnished copper, bordering on red, her black lashes full and fluttery. Bitten-red lips turned upward in a polite smile, lighting up her stunning face. I was speechless.

This was Seraphina. I was sure of it.

"Excellent timing, Seraphina!" Jareth remarked, confirming my thoughts. I had a feeling he'd planned the whole thing. "We were just about to discuss possible dates for your unity ceremony, now that we've coaxed him back into the fold." He chuckled, putting an arm around Navan's shoulder. Navan stiffened immediately.

"Lucky I arrived when I did, then," Seraphina replied, her voice sweet and kind. Although she smiled at Jareth's words, the good humor didn't reach her unusual eyes. So, Navan was right—Seraphina wasn't into this marriage, either. I could see it all over her face, and it brought me a much-needed dose of relief. "It's wonderful to see you again, Navan. How were your travels?" she asked, directing her attention to Navan. It was a friendly, platonic exchange. She was keeping her distance.

"Interesting, but I'm back in one piece," Navan replied.

"I'm sorry about your friend," she said softly, looking toward the body on the floor, which had yet to be taken away.

Navan nodded. "Me too."

"And who is this beautiful creature?" she asked, looking warmly at me.

A small smile crept onto Navan's lips, but he quickly suppressed it. "This is Riley," he said simply.

She flashed him a knowing glance, before moving to take my hands in hers. Clasping them tightly, she gave me a huge smile, her copper eyes gleaming in admiration. "You are the most exquisite thing in this room," she gushed, "though don't tell Queen Gianne I said so."

"I won't," I murmured awkwardly, finding my tongue.

"That voice! What an exotic accent," she marveled. None of her words felt insincere. Every single one sounded warm and genuine, and her hands squeezed mine in delight. "I hope you've been taking good care of her, Navan."

He grimaced. "I've been trying."

"Well, she looks to be in one magnificent piece." Seraphina grinned, though her smile suddenly fell as her eyes came to rest on the side of my neck. "Except for these... How did you end up with these wounds?" she asked quietly, her tone so low that Jareth couldn't overhear, and I realized with alarm that she had spotted the faint marks caused by the chip in my neck.

"An accident," Navan interjected, before I could speak. "Nothing that won't heal."

Seraphina paused for a moment, continuing to eye them with a furrowed brow, but then she pulled away, resuming her straight posture. "Well, it's a pleasure to meet you, Riley," she said, the smile returning to her lips. "Perhaps we will see each other again. In the meantime, keep him out of trouble. He attracts it like nobody's business." She smirked, though I could see she was only half joking.

Despite my initial feelings about this woman, I was shocked to find that I actually liked her. There was a vibrant warmth to her that made it almost impossible to dislike her. Plus, she had treated me with grace and respect, which was more than could be said for the rest of the coldbloods I'd met. Jareth still wouldn't look me in the eye, or even acknowledge me personally. I might as well have been an inanimate object to him.

"So, when shall we set the date?" Jareth chimed in, pressing the subject.

Seraphina turned, placing her hand on his arm. "There's no rush. Navan has only just returned—how about we let him get his bearings again, before we discuss such heavy matters? I know I'm in no hurry. We can wait awhile, until everyone is feeling up to it," she suggested, passing me a discreet glance of sympathy.

I raised my eyebrows. How did she know? Was it that obvious what Navan and I meant to each other, even when we were just standing together? I hoped not, or else we were in big trouble. On second thought, maybe it was only obvious to those who viewed me as an actual equal.

Whatever the case, from the detached way Seraphina was talking, I was thoroughly convinced that she didn't have any romantic feelings for Navan whatsoever. Her approach made it feel like a business transaction—a necessary evil that they could keep putting off. There was reluctance in her voice, and I was more than glad to hear it.

"There's no time like the present," Jareth insisted.

Seraphina sighed. "I would love to stay and discuss it, I really would, but my parents will be waiting for me outside. My mother was quite troubled by the events of this evening, and I think she would prefer to have me close by. Another time, though. No doubt my father will be in touch with you shortly." Her eyes flickered with faint sadness as she leaned over to air-kiss Jareth on both cheeks, then gave Navan's arm a friendly pat.

"Soon," Jareth repeated.

As she passed me, I noticed her glance briefly at my neck again, before smiling once more and heading off.

"I should probably get going too, Father," Navan said. "There are many things I need to get in order."

"Promise you'll visit your mother," Jareth replied. "She worries about you."

"I'll swing by the house as soon as I can," he muttered. I wasn't sure if he was lying.

With that, Navan turned on his heel and headed for the exit, with me following close behind. Outside, the sky had darkened, and a bitter wind whipped up around us as we made our way toward the spot where Navan had left the Snapper. With no coat to protect me from the icy blast, I began to shiver uncontrollably. A moment later, in the shadow of the vessel, Navan wrapped his arms around me and pulled me tight, before ushering me onto the ship. A stolen embrace.

As soon as we stepped into the Snapper, I knew something was wrong. It was a sensation I'd felt before, back on the ship we'd abandoned outside the rebel compound on Earth. An unsettled vibration hung in the air, as though someone was watching.

Something leapt from the wall of the ship. A split second later, I felt cold, fleshy hands on my neck. It was the shifters. Out of their coldblood guise, they were back to their original forms, and I felt my stomach turn at the sight of them. The female shifter had me by the throat, but the male shifter hadn't dared lay his hands on Navan, who was eyeing the pair furiously.

"We've got a message for you," the male shifter hissed.

"Oh?" Navan remarked sardonically, lunging for me. Instantly, the female shifter let me go, backing away toward the exit, allowing Navan to grab me and take me in his arms.

She nodded. "We've spoken with Orion," she said coldly. "He says that if one more of his rebels dies because of you, then your lives will be forfeit."

Navan and I exchanged a glance. In all the chaos, I'd practically forgotten to consider what the repercussions of Kalvin's death would be in regard to Orion. A shiver ran down my spine as the shifters scurried out of the vessel, disappearing into the darkness.

"I suppose tonight could have been worse," Navan said, tightening his hold on me. His eyes passed over the chip in my neck, and I nodded. Kalvin's death was a tragic one, but at least there hadn't been any further retribution for his loss. We'd already suffered enough for one night.

We just had to be more careful in the future.

I pressed a gentle kiss to Navan's cheek. "You were right about Seraphina," I said softly. "She really doesn't seem into you."

Navan smiled. "Told you so. Now, we just need to figure out a way to keep delaying the marriage until—"

I never got to hear what he was going to say, as a tap at the door of the Snapper diverted our attention.

The female shifter had reappeared in the low light of the entrance. "Oh, and one more thing," she said, her tone unsettlingly sweet. "Orion sends his regards. This is for Kalvin."

As the shifter darted away, pain hit me in a savage wave, agony rippling through every vein, exploding every cell in a bolt of white-hot torture. It centered in my left leg, the pain there growing so unbearable I thought I might be about to die. Instead, my knee buckled, bringing me down with a hard crash. I collapsed, crying out in agony, tears streaming from my eyes. Blinking furiously, I realized I couldn't clear away the fog of the tears. I couldn't see anything at all.

Every part of my body felt as though it belonged to someone else. Pain shot through each limb and muscle, causing spasms that reached down to the very bone. I had lost control of myself, and I couldn't grasp that control back. My mind was hazy, my eyes were blind, and my body was not my own.

As I collapsed, I felt Navan's strong arms around me. "Breathe, Riley, you have to breathe," he whispered, his voice panicked as he bundled me against his chest. "You're safe, you're all right! I'm here. You have to breathe. Breathe for me, Riley. Please. You're okay, I promise."

With his arms to brace myself against, the trembling in my

body ebbed. Navan's body was stabilizing my own, preventing me from doing myself any real damage. With every whimper of pain, I felt his lips kiss my face, trying to bring me back from the edge of delirium. Slowly but surely, the pain and shivering began to die down. At last, they subsided completely, leaving me limp in Navan's arms, and although I was the one trembling, from the look in Navan's eyes we were both equally shaken.

He swallowed hard, and his voice was hoarse as he spoke the words we both knew to be true. "We can't piss off Orion again."

26

I slept late the following morning, my body aching, my eyelids heavy. I felt like I'd gone twelve rounds with a heavyweight, and now I was feeling the effects. My left leg was the worst, a dull throb there pulsing constantly.

"How are you feeling?" Navan asked for the millionth time. I appreciated his concern, but I was in an irritable mood thanks to the pain, and it was starting to get annoying.

"Better," I lied, wanting him to stop asking.

"Do you feel up to an outing?" he asked, packing a few things into the bag he'd brought from the cabin. I was picking at the remains of a packet of biscuits and gravy, the thick, clumpy mixture making me feel even more nauseated.

I nodded, eager to be out of the stuffy room, which held so many nightmares. I couldn't stop picturing the shifters on our bed, lounging back with their fleshy pouches pooling on the covers, and the cold sensation of the female's hands on my neck. Flashbacks of Orion's punishment exploded in my mind, forcing me to relive the pain and the shock of it. More than that, I was haunted by the dead-eyed corpse of Kalvin, the pike skewering him like a kebab. I needed fresh air and a change of scenery.

"The cabin?" I asked. Surely, the intel would have uploaded by now. If it had, it meant we'd have something concrete to send back to Orion, to get him off our backs. Hopefully, it would mean I could go home, and get this awful thing out of my neck, once and for all.

"As long as you're up for it," he replied, his tone laced with concern.

"I'll be fine," I said, infusing my voice with more confidence than I felt. "I'm feeling better."

"As long as you're sure..."

I grimaced. "I'm sure. Now, can we go, sometime before Vysanthe thaws out?"

He chuckled. "Coldblood humor—I like it," he commended, slinging the bag onto his shoulder and heading for the door.

The flight to the cabin seemed to whiz by faster than it had the last time, with us reaching the woodland within half an hour of leaving the confines of Regium. I smiled as the dark trees approached, remembering the night Navan and I had spent asleep under the stars, cozied up in the warmth of the igloo. I thought of the skeletal fish, twisting and turning beneath the water of the pond, and the beautiful fireflies glowing in the darkness.

The good feeling didn't last, however. When we set the Snapper down in the glade where the cabin sat, I was surprised to see another ship already sitting there in the open space. Panic shot through my veins, and I started hyperventilating. I was already on edge from the effects of the chip—I didn't think I could cope with another surprise.

"Who is it?" I whispered, feeling foolish as I realized the owner of the ship couldn't hear me from the passenger seat of the Snapper.

Navan frowned. "Lazar," he answered, his eyes narrowing on the vessel.

"How do you know? Is he supposed to be here?"

Navan shrugged. "I left a message with him saying we'd be coming here today. I guess he thought he'd wait for us."

"Don't mind another man in your man cave?" I said, allowing myself a moment of levity as relief washed over me.

"Who said I didn't mind?" Navan replied, a smile tugging at his lips. "He was supposed to wait outside."

Lazar opened the door to greet us as we made our way across the glade toward the entrance to the cabin. His shoes were off, and he was wearing what looked like furry slippers. Navan eyed them, a glimmer of irritation passing across his face. It looked like Lazar had made himself a little too at home.

"Well, you took your time!" Lazar said, as Navan and I stepped into the warmth of the cabin.

Navan moved toward the black box he'd left on the coffee table, ignoring his uncle's comment. As he reached it, however, a long string of expletives erupted from his throat. I hurried over to where he stood, just as he snatched up the box and shook it, hard.

"Useless piece of crap!" he yelled, shaking it once more for good measure.

"What's wrong?" I asked, trying to get a look at the progress screen. Two words flashed up, in neon-blue letters: *Data Corrupted.*

"Did you do this?" Navan snapped, whirling around to look at Lazar.

He shook his head vigorously. "Of course not! It didn't say that five minutes ago, I swear—it was hovering at ninety-nine percent."

"Then that little suck-up must have given me a faulty disc," Navan growled.

"I doubt he did it on purpose," I said, feeling sorry for the little fanboy who had been so excited by Navan's presence at the Observatory.

"Is there nothing we can use from it?" Lazar asked, wearing an expression of disappointment.

Navan exhaled, running a hand down his face. "I don't have the tech here, and I don't want to risk transmitting from anywhere that's not remote."

"How about we take it to the palace, extract what we can from the disc, and have a good look around while we're waiting for it to upload again?" Lazar said. "Even if there is intel on there, it won't include the palace—we should check for weaknesses there, do some multitasking. Then, we could come back here and get everything we have sent off at once."

Navan scowled. "I really don't want to go back there."

"The queen will no doubt be expecting you to drop in on her at some point, thanks to your father's meddling," Lazar replied apologetically. "He's calling you his deputy-chief advisor."

Navan's expression dropped in horror. "He's not!"

"Oh, he is." Lazar nodded. "Although, it's probably not a bad idea for you to go and see her today—keep her sweet after last night's debacle, smooth things over, you know."

I nodded. As reluctant as I was to go anywhere near that queen again, Lazar's suggestion made sense. "She's terrified of losing her crown," I said. "A little pep talk could be just what she needs to get her back on track. The last thing this place needs is a mad queen, executing people left, right, and center. And, if people doubt her, things will start to fall apart... Civil war would destroy this place."

"You had me at 'mad queen'," Navan muttered, stuffing the black box into his bag. I just hoped we'd be able to get something off it before Orion started to lose patience.

Zipping back across the harsh landscape, with Lazar crammed into the Snapper with us—since he'd decided it would be better if he kept his ship at the cabin, as a getaway vehicle, if necessary—I thought about home. If everything went well, I'd soon be returning, with plenty of time to intercept the blood-pod on the way. Glancing at Navan, I wondered what he'd do when this mission was over, and the blood had been retrieved. Would he come back with me to Earth? It was something I had assumed in the back of my mind but never asked. Given his hatred for Vysanthe, I hoped he would.

The icy palace came into view, and the Snapper descended into what felt like our usual spot. We got out and walked through the vast entrance, the guards letting us past without so much as a grunt or a gruff word.

Everything looked so different now, compared to the previous night. All the decorations had been torn down, the walls and ceilings looking strangely bare, and the grand hall had been cleared of all party evidence. There were no opaleine towers bearing vials upon vials, no crystal glasses with red liquid inside, and no chairs and tables. It was one big expanse, devoid of festive spirit.

Crossing the empty floor quickly, Lazar led us down the same hallway that Queen Gianne had disappeared through after Kalvin had been executed. It was broad and wide, ending in a familiar set of double doors. This was the throne room, where Navan and I had visited the queen. Frowning, I guessed several corridors must lead here.

Navan stepped up to the door and rapped hard on the metal surface. A moment later, a guard came to the door and poked his head out.

"What?" he barked.

"I'm Navan Idrax, here to see the queen," Navan said. "I think she might be expecting me."

The guard shook his head. "Not today, she's not."

"What do you mean?" Navan frowned.

"Queen Gianne isn't seeing anyone today," he replied tersely. "She doesn't wish to be disturbed, and I'm here to ensure she gets her privacy. Now, I suggest you scoot back the way you came, before I'm forced to throw you out."

Navan pulled a face, and I knew it mirrored my own. This guard was half the size of Navan—there was no way he'd be doing any throwing out. But, of course, it wouldn't come to that. The queen had given her orders.

"Do you know when she'll be receiving visitors again?" Navan pressed. If the queen was isolating herself, it had to be bad. Paranoia was a leech, and I had a feeling it had taken hold of Queen Gianne.

"Yeah, of course, let me just whip out the queen's diary," the guard scoffed. "No, I don't know when she'll be receiving visitors again, but it's definitely not today!" With that, he slammed the door shut in our faces.

"Well, he was rude." I whistled.

"Small man syndrome," Navan muttered, though the humor didn't reach his eyes. I could tell he was worried about the queen, too. Jareth had already admitted she was becoming crazier, and this only proved it was getting worse.

As we walked back through the palace hallways, Navan pulled us away from the corridor that led to the exit, and into a side room. It looked out onto a courtyard filled with white blossoms that fell to the ground like snow. Here, monitors and screens beeped and thrummed, and two bulky coldbloods sat in front of desks, looking bored out of their brains.

They turned as we entered. "Navan?" one said, a look of surprise on his face.

"Idrax!" the other, a female, cried. "Thought you were on the far side of the universe!"

Navan smiled. "Had to come back sometime, right? Hafar, Kwen, it's good to see you guys." Leaving Lazar and me, he walked over to them and patted them both on the back as they embraced him warmly.

"What brings you here? You in trouble again?" the male cold-blood, Hafar, asked, pulling away and flashing a glance of suspicion.

"No, no, nothing like that—for once," Navan laughed. "My father has made me his, uh... deputy-chief advisor, and he wants me to look through some files. The queen's worried about rebels, so we're checking the perimeters for any breaches. I got this disc from one of the guys up at the Observatory, but I think he was a newbie. The thing keeps saying the data is corrupted."

The female, Kwen, nodded. "The tech up there is ancient, man! They're always losing important stuff," she said, grimacing. "You want us to take a look at it for you?"

Navan grinned. "I was hoping you'd say that. Although, my father will kill me if he finds out I've lost all that data, so if you could keep it on the down low, I'd be eternally grateful."

Hafar laughed. "Say no more. Leave it with us, and we'll have something for you in a couple of hours."

"Thanks, guys, I owe you one," Navan replied, giving Hafar a playful punch in the shoulder.

"Hey, you owe us *many*!" Kwen pouted.

"And, one glorious day, I will pay you back," Navan promised, before turning to leave the room.

As we all returned to the hallway, I looked up at Navan in surprise. "Who were they?" I asked, curious.

"Old friends," Navan replied with a chuckle. "Let's just say we were all a bad influence on each other when we were younger. How they landed jobs here, I'll never know, but I'm certainly glad they did."

I smiled, picturing Navan as a younger man, in his early teens, running amok in the palace, no doubt causing his father endless hassle. It was always nice to see the relaxed, funny side of Navan— I hadn't had much chance to see it, here on Vysanthe. Home put him in an almost perpetually somber mood, and while I under- stood why, I still loved to see a glimpse of his happier self.

"Let's roam around the gardens for a while. I hear they're beau- tiful this time of year, and I'm sure the queen won't mind," Lazar suggested with a wink, plucking out a curious, pen-shaped object. Only, it was longer and wider than a normal pen, and didn't seem to have a discernible nib of any kind. When he pressed a button on the side, the object glowed a dim purple. And as he flourished it in the air, a trace of blue followed the path of the pen, before dissipating.

"What's that?" I asked Navan. We headed through another network of corridors, following Lazar's lead.

"It's an Escribo," he replied softly. "It creates an image that stores itself inside the pen. Lazar is creating a map with it."

"Woah. Cool."

The icy wind snapped at my face as we stepped out into the gardens of the palace, forcing me to draw my coat closer to my chin. My eyes watered, but I tried to look around at the flowers and trees that blossomed in such adversity. Most were twisted, gnarled things that looked half dead, but there was the occasional surprise as we walked between walled gardens, exploring the grounds. A bush filled with spiny red flowers sprang up, its petals unfurling as we passed. Pausing, I bent to take a closer look, only to be yanked backward by Navan's firm hand.

"Don't get near those," he warned. "They shoot out deadly barbs if you get too close."

"Well, that's nice."

I decided to stick to the center of the garden path after that, where I hoped I wouldn't come under any direct attack by flora or fauna.

Navan noticed, and chuckled.

"Welcome to Vysanthe," Lazar said, shaking his head. With every step we took, he was lifting his Escribo to the air and drawing the shape of whatever he was looking at, whether it was a wall, a window, a fortification, or a fence, flicking the pen discreetly, in case anyone was watching. He traced a few images of the flowers too, undoubtedly to create the impression that he was simply committing the beautiful blooms to eternal memory.

As we turned a corner on the garden path leading up to a large lake, with several bridges spanning the water, a young male cold-blood dressed in a dark green uniform came running up to Lazar, clutching something in his hand. By the time he reached us, he was breathless, pressing a hand to his chest as he held out a small square of glass.

"A message... for you... Lazar," he panted.

Lazar took it, and the messenger lurched away again. He pressed a tiny button on the side of the glass, and the screen blinked to life, though I couldn't see what the note said. The words were only reflected on the side that Lazar held up to his face. I watched his expression intently, hoping to gauge something from it.

He blinked in surprise, and looked at me. "Riley, did something—" he began, only for Navan to cut him off mid-sentence.

"Aurelius!" Navan hissed suddenly. I looked up to see that he had spotted the queen's advisor moving out from behind a bit of topiary shaped like a wolf. He was walking away from the palace at breakneck speed.

"He's heading for the military compound," Navan said quietly, nodding toward a squat gray building that sat behind the palace grounds, overlooking the lake. I supposed it made sense that the queen would have her army at hand, for whenever she might need them.

"We should go after him," Lazar said at once, distracted from whatever it was he had just read. "This could be the perfect opportunity to gain precise intel on the queen's military."

That definitely made sense. Finding weaknesses in the walls was all well and good, but finding weaknesses in the actual army was a huge step up.

If we could do that, Orion would be sure to let us go.

$\mathcal{W}$e quickly found ourselves trailing Aurelius, and, fortunately for us, he didn't feel the need to turn around to check whether anyone was following.

We slipped through the compound entrance, sticking to the shadows. Ducking down behind a stack of crates, I peered around the corner in time to see Aurelius come to a halt in front of a group of fearsome-looking coldblood soldiers. He looked them up and down, a disgusted expression crossing his face.

"What do you think you're doing?" he barked. "Do you think this is some sort of recreation? I don't expect to come to the training ground and see the queen's soldiers lounging about, doing nothing! Look at you—you're the most pathetic excuses for soldiers I've ever seen!"

Suddenly, Navan got up and wandered over to where Aurelius and the soldiers stood, leaving Lazar and me gawking at him from behind the crates, wondering what the hell he was playing at. I'd thought we were supposed to be stealthy.

"Aurelius!" he called confidently.

The wizened, half-winged coldblood turned. "Navan... what a pleasant surprise," he remarked, frustration still written across his wrinkled face.

"I was just wondering if you'd seen Seraphina today," Navan said. "I wanted to make sure she was okay after last night."

Aurelius frowned, and a flicker of emotion that I could've sworn looked like jealousy crossed his face. "No, I haven't seen her today," he replied bitterly, making me wonder what his gripe was, exactly. It was quite clear to me that Aurelius disliked Navan, but... Aurelius was too old to be with Seraphina, and yet... Was that it? Did the old man have a thing for Seraphina? I shuddered, thinking of the beautiful woman, and what she would look like on Aurelius's arm. I would almost rather have seen her marry Navan than this old coot.

Almost.

"These guys giving you problems?" Navan asked, turning his gaze to the nervous recruits. "Seems like we've been having a few issues with new blood in the army, of late. Not even close to the caliber of our regular squadrons, eh?"

Aurelius grimaced. "These new recruits are all incompetent," he muttered. "They have no basic training, they'll never match up to the rest of the army, and the queen won't put any more time or money into the resources these idiots so clearly need. It's that bloody immortality elixir—if she could just forget about it for one second, and think about something other than stockpiling resources, we might actually be able to replenish our army with viable soldiers," he ranted, more to himself than anyone else. I listened, rapt at the information he was giving away. However, realizing he may have said too much, Aurelius immediately paused and glanced suspiciously at Navan. "What makes you an expert on it, all of a sudden?" he asked, his tone wary.

"It's this new job my father has roped me into," Navan explained, keeping his eyes on the recruits. "I want to make sure I know as much as I can, so I can offer educated advice to the queen. I'd hate her to think *I* was an idiot."

Aurelius frowned, studying Navan's face. "You won't last long at the palace, Navan," he muttered after a moment. "You're not made for it, the way I am... You're better off as far from Vysanthe as possible."

"Ah. That's a shame. Well, I guess I'd better stop chatting with you, and keep searching for Seraphina—I could have sworn she said she'd be here today," Navan mused. "If you do see her, let her know I was looking for her!"

Aurelius looked like he was about to burst a blood vessel, but only Lazar and I could see the look of sheer hatred that the wizened old coldblood was sending toward Navan's back. Navan, meanwhile, walked straight past us, evidently not wanting to draw attention to our hiding spot. He didn't stop until he was out of the compound.

Crouched behind the stack of crates, we waited until Aurelius and the new recruits had gone inside the compound before hurrying after Navan. He was waiting for us at the edge of the lake, a perplexed expression on his face.

"Do you think that's enough to satisfy Orion?" he asked as we neared.

Lazar frowned. "What do you mean?"

"Well, we know the new recruits are terrible. They have little training, and, with the queen sending the best troops out into the universe to steal and plunder, that means her half of Vysanthe will be left exposed," he said. "Orion would only need to wait until the main corps were otherwise engaged, the squadrons dispersed to every quarter of the universe."

"And, we have what is left on that disc, as well as the map you've made," I added, the idea of home drawing closer.

Lazar shook his head. "The Vysanthean army is the most fearsome in the universe. Even if the new recruits are terrible, the rebels wouldn't be able to fight the true army off if they answered the queen's call for help."

"That's Orion's problem, not ours," Navan said irritably. "We've found the intel he asked for, and now it's time for us to leave."

Lazar sighed. "Well, we can certainly send it and see what he says... which brings me to what I wanted to say before," he said, returning his focus to me.

"About *me*?" I asked, frowning.

He nodded. "That message I received... it was from Seraphina."

"Seraphina?" Navan said, his eyebrows rising in surprise.

"She sent a letter regarding the marks on Riley's neck," Lazar explained. "I presume she saw them when the pair of you were introduced last night. Anyway, she is concerned that you might be in danger, Riley, and she has asked me to ensure that the offending item is removed."

Navan and I exchanged a look, my brow furrowed with panic. Nobody was supposed to know about the chip. How could Seraphina know what was under my skin? Curiosity bubbled away inside me, but I knew I couldn't ask how Seraphina knew about the chip without revealing the presence of the one in my neck.

"Seraphina was involved in a kidnapping several years back," Lazar went on, apparently reading my mind. "The people who took her implanted a chip in her neck that could control and immobilize her if she didn't do as she was asked—or if her parents didn't answer the ransom. I found her when she fled her kidnappers, and it was me who removed the chip before they had the chance to set it off," he added, eyeing me curiously.

"Poor Seraphina," I murmured lamely.

"Seraphina is worried you have a chip in your neck, Riley," Lazar said pointedly. "Is she right?"

I shook my head defiantly. "No, I have no idea what she's talking about," I lied, lifting my coat collar to cover my neck, making a show of shivering violently.

"Well, I could... remove it, Riley," Lazar said. "I just need to see exactly where it is. If you tell me, I can get rid of it before anyone suspects a thing."

"She said she doesn't know anything," Navan growled, coming to my defense, and I was grateful. I had always been a terrible liar.

"You would let her keep that thing inside her, Navan?" Lazar reprimanded, turning on his nephew. "Do you know what those things can do?"

Navan grimaced.

Lazar sighed heavily. "I am guessing you've already experienced a taste of its power, but if Riley is still standing, it means you haven't seen the worst of it. You need to tell me where it is, so I can remove it."

All I could think about was the threat Orion had made before we left Earth. It had not seemed like an empty one. But he would kill me if Navan or I so much as uttered a word about the chip to Lazar, I just knew it. Glancing at Navan's face, I could see that he was apprehensive too.

"There is no chip, Uncle," Navan maintained, but Lazar still wasn't letting it go. Why, I wasn't even sure—what difference did my wellbeing make to him?

"You don't have anything to fear, Navan," he explained. "The only thing you have to fear is what will happen if you leave that thing in Riley. Now, I'm guessing Orion put it there, but I was assigned to watch the pair of you closely. Orion won't hear about the missing chip unless I tell him, which I'm not going to. He can activate the chip from afar, but he can't see what's happening through it—it's not a camera. He has to be told when and where to activate it, and I won't be breathing a word of its absence."

I stared at him. "Why... Why would you defy him? Aren't you supposed to be one of his best men?"

A sad smile crossed Lazar's lips. "While I agree with the vision that Orion has, I don't always agree with his methods," he admitted quietly. "There are times when I find myself wondering how the two of us ever came to work together—we are so different, and yet so similar, at the same time. Regardless, I refuse to put my nephew's soulmate in danger because of Orion's need to control, using whatever terrible means he sees fit to use."

I flushed at the term "soulmate", but it was especially confusing coming from Lazar. Not so long ago, he had flat-out refused to help us, and now he was offering to remove a chip that had been placed in my neck by his leader. I couldn't wrap my head around it. The only thing I could assume was that, without sons of his own, Lazar's protective instincts of his nephew were taking over. I wasn't arrogant enough to believe that Lazar gave a damn about me, but he cared for Navan—it was clear in everything he did. And, if Navan cared about me, then maybe, just this once, Lazar's bubble of protection would extend to me.

"There is no chip, Uncle," Navan replied faintly, the conviction gone from his words. I could see he was mulling over what his uncle had said, and the potential power the chip held over me. We couldn't trust Orion not to push the proverbial red button, and what we really needed was to make sure we got the chip out before he had a chance to activate it again.

"Keep up the pretense all you like, but if you want that chip removed, meet me tonight, at the *Asterope*," Lazar said finally. "I have instruments there that will ensure the safe removal of the implant. I did the same thing for Seraphina, all those years ago—I have not forgotten how."

"Why would you help us?" I asked.

Lazar sighed. "I meant what I said before about not always agreeing with Orion's methods, and Navan is my nephew. But I suppose you could also call it morbid curiosity, if you like. I'm a medical man by profession, though I haven't been able to do much since the war ended. I dabble here and there, but I'm excited to get my hands dirty with something innovative again—you know, to keep the mind fresh. Removing that chip will be just the booster I need to feed that little whisper of excitement."

I swallowed. I wasn't sure how I felt about being an object he could "dabble" with, but if this bit of surgery could potentially save my life, then maybe it was worth the risk.

"Now, I must return to the others," Lazar said softly. "I'll leave you to make your decision in peace, while I go and tell them the good news."

"Good news?" Navan asked.

Lazar nodded. "Assuming our data satisfies Orion, we return to Earth in a few days."

I blew out, relief washing over me. Never had sweeter words been spoken. And yet... we were in a bind regarding this whole chip issue. Who was to say that, as soon as I set foot on home soil, Orion wouldn't just pull the trigger anyway? Then again, what if Lazar was wrong—what if Orion could sense the removal of the implant and activated it while it was being removed? Or worse, what if this was all just a twisted ploy by Orion to see if we would betray him? What if Lazar was in on it? It would certainly explain his sudden change of heart.

Navan glanced at me but remained silent, clearly believing I had to be the one to make this decision, without pressure from him either way. It was my life on the line, after all, not his.

So many thoughts raced through my mind at once as we watched Lazar walk away, but after several minutes, there was one voice in the back of my head that broke out louder than the rest.

It was a veritable cacophony, ringing in my ears. It was the voice of Roger, and Jean, and Angie, and Lauren, and everyone who might be missing me. It was a beacon, calling me back to Earth. Silently, I thought of home, and Navan, and I knew what my answer had to be.

*L*azar left us to think about his proposal, but I'd already made my mind up—I had to let him remove the chip. If the surgery was successful, we would have taken power away from Orion, and I wouldn't be in constant fear of dying unexpectedly. I was convinced that I stood more chance of surviving and getting back to my family without that thing in my neck.

Now all we had left to do was wait.

"I'm just not... completely sure this is a good idea," Navan said, standing by the window as the Vysanthean sun began to set. We had tried to keep busy throughout the day, but all we'd ended up doing was a lot of pacing around our room, the tension crackling. I agreed with him, but I just wanted the chip out of my neck. For the most part, I believed Lazar when he said Orion wouldn't know, even if a niggling doubt remained.

As darkness fell, we left the chambers, heading down in the elevator to the underground station that rested below the mountain. There were guards everywhere. Knowing we'd have to avoid being seen, we hovered behind a pillar until the bullet train pulled up to the platform. Darting from our hiding place, we jumped onto the emptiest carriage, with me pulling the hood of my coat around my face so nobody would see the pale, human color of my skin.

The bullet train clattered as it shot through the tunnels beneath Vysanthe, before screeching to a halt ten minutes later. The doors slid open, and, stepping cautiously out, I recognized the station where we'd arrived.

Following the route to the ship hangar, we clung to the shadows, wary of being spotted. Even though we had free rein of the place, thanks to Queen Gianne, I was fairly sure this part of Vysanthe was still out of bounds. The queen was likely still paranoid about us making an escape attempt.

Seeing that the corridor ahead was clear, we raced down it, seeking out the cave with the *Asterope* inside. As I rounded the corner, a couple of steps in front of Navan, I froze. A guard stood right in front of us, mere yards from where I'd come to a halt, my muscles twinging with the strain of pulling myself back. Navan almost barreled into me, stopping himself at the last moment.

The guard had his back to us, polishing the deadly edge of his pike.

I glanced at Navan and gave him a signal to move backward, as silently as possible. He nodded, carefully stepping away, moving back around the corner. I followed, holding my breath. My heart was pounding, the blood rushing in my ears.

Seeking out a recess in the hallway, we drew into the shadows, Navan pulling me close, camouflaging me in the darkness. We waited, listening for the sound of footsteps on the polished stone floor. Before long, the guard turned the corner and passed by without noticing us, whistling as he walked.

That had been too close. Way too close.

As my blood pressure slowly returned to normal, we snuck out of the recess and headed for the cave hangar. Surprisingly, there were no guards here, only a few late-night mechanics toiling away at their appointed vessels. With their focus elsewhere, and most of their heads buried in the metal entrails of a ship, they were easy to skirt past. Our goal was the *Asterope*, which stood to the far side of the hangar, gleaming elegantly.

Keeping alert, we approached, pausing at the spot where the gangway usually slid out. Tentatively, I knocked, hoping for a response.

Lazar answered a moment later. "You came," he said softly, his tone not exactly surprised.

I nodded. "If you can get this thing out of me, I'm all for it."

"Then we should get started," he replied. "This won't be easy for you."

We followed him into the belly of the ship. His words haunted me. Would it hurt? I scolded myself—of course it was going to hurt. Orion wouldn't have implanted something that was easy to remove.

We moved to the right of the ship's main space and entered a narrow hallway that I hadn't seen before. Walking to the very end, Lazar led us through a low doorway, into a tiny, metallic room that smelled of sterile chemicals. I guessed it was the medical bay, though, with no previous reason to use it, I hadn't had the opportunity to explore this side of the *Asterope*.

In the center of the room, there was a surgical table, with bright lights shining down upon the cold, chrome bed. Screens flickered to life around it, a monitor beeping in a single flat line. When I was hooked up to it, I hoped it wouldn't end up showing that same image.

"Get up onto the table," Lazar instructed, as he began to search through several drawers that were tucked away in the ship's walls. He drew out a pouch of sharp-looking instruments and laid them flat on a nearby tray, waiting for me to obey.

Removing my coat, I lay down on the table, the metal icy against my back. Anxiety coursed through my veins, reminding me of doctor's visits and dentist appointments from my childhood. I hated hospitals at the best of times.

Lazar sat down on a stool close to my head, scooting the wheeled tray with the instruments closer. I took a deep breath, my nerves calming slightly at the sensation of Navan's hand holding mine. Looking up, I saw his comforting face, and allowed myself to relax slightly. I was never going to be totally at ease, but his presence helped.

"I'm just going to make an incision," Lazar said, cutting down the fabric of my t-shirt to expose the bare flesh he needed. I could hear the scissors cutting the material, the sound a chilling one, so close to my ear.

"Wait, what about painkillers?!" I asked, looking at him in alarm.

"I don't have any painkillers suitable for humans on hand, I'm afraid," Lazar replied in a low tone. "If I gave you the stuff we give coldbloods, it'd probably wipe you out for seventy-two hours... if not permanently."

Remembering the effect that silver root stimulant had on me, I didn't find that hard to believe. "Oh God," I groaned, glancing again at Navan.

He swallowed, his brow creased in concern. "You don't have to go through with this, Riley," he whispered.

I shook my head, steeling myself. "No. I have to."

"Will you be all right?" Lazar asked.

I nodded, biting my lip. "Let's just get this over with."

I braced myself, expecting a sharp pain. At first, that was all there was—the nasty, uncomfortable feeling of something cutting my fragile skin. That was enough to make me moan and break out into a heavy sweat, but then the scalpel blade hit a foreign object, and the agony that followed was *not* what I'd signed up for. A jolt of pure torture shot down my entire body, my muscles going into spasms. I bucked against the table, every cell ablaze with the force of the electric shock. Something was wrong.

"Is this supposed to happen?" Navan hissed, his hold on my hand tightening.

Lazar nodded. "The chip sends out miniature tentacles that embed into the nerves surrounding it. It gives a direct line to the brain's pain center."

I couldn't bear it, a cry erupting from my throat. My body felt like it was on fire, my brain searing hot, my eyes fogging over, speckled with black dots. I gripped Navan's hand as hard as I could, but nothing helped. He was just an anchor, grounding me in this sea of agony.

"Maybe we should stop," Navan urged.

I shook my head violently. "No! Get it out!" I gasped, biting down on my lip, a trickle of blood meandering down my chin.

Above me, I saw Lazar's eyes home in on the scarlet rivulet, but I didn't care. Right now, if he wanted to devour the very life from me, I wouldn't stop him. I just wanted the pain to be over.

Lazar returned his attention to the task at hand, snatching up a pair of sharp-edged pliers. I whimpered as I felt something cut inside me, the sensation unbearably weird. Tears were rolling down my face, my lungs burning with the strain of trying to draw in breath.

"Only eight more," Lazar said, his tone soothing.

"Can you speed up?" I hissed through gritted teeth, another jolt of electricity tearing through my veins.

Lazar nodded, and I felt another cut. Everything felt strange and messy, the world around me bending and swirling. Delirium was setting in, and the pain grew so fierce I was sure I was about to pass out.

Drifting in and out of consciousness, I felt cut after cut after cut, the snipping sound grating against my senses. My brain pulsed against the confines of my skull, feeling as though it were about to explode from its bone prison. My eyes bulged and my tongue swelled, my body breaking with every moment that passed. I couldn't take it anymore, but I knew I couldn't ask him to stop either—if I gave up now, there was no telling when another opportunity would present itself. Orion was under no obligation to remove it.

"One more," Lazar promised.

The snip of the chip's last tentacle rattled through me, making my teeth chatter. And then, the agony was gone, disappearing as quickly as it had arrived. I lay back, panting, still gripping Navan's hand... It was over.

With a clink of metal on metal, Lazar deposited the chip into a basin beside him, before taking up a strange-looking gun. As he pressed the muzzle to my neck, a cold sensation trickled through the wound on my skin, soothing it.

"What's that?" I wheezed.

"It will clean and seal the wound to prevent infection," Lazar explained, lifting the gun away.

I waited, expecting more. When it didn't come, I sat up on the table and turned to Lazar. "Is it out?"

He nodded, lifting the basin so I could see the offending article. A small, square object lay at the bottom of the metal dish, covered in blood and scraps of flesh. But it was there... It was no longer inside me, looming over everything we did.

Slowly, still doubting my pain receptors, I swung my legs over the edge of the surgical table and stayed there a moment. Navan moved toward me, enveloping me in his firm embrace. I nestled against his chest, feeling tears of relief trickle down my cheeks. I couldn't speak, but I didn't need to—Navan was here, his arms were around me, and we were safe from Orion's threat.

I turned to Lazar, who was cleaning the soiled instruments in a small basin at the side of the room. "Thank you," I gasped, finding my voice. The words were croaky, my throat tight, but the sentiment was clear. I had never been more grateful.

"It was nothing," he muttered, avoiding eye contact and turning quickly back around. I frowned, finding his reaction odd. But knowing I wasn't in my right mind, I brushed it off. I had more important things to focus on right now.

"Will there be any side effects from the chip?" I asked anxiously, needing to quell my fears.

Lazar shook his head, his back still to us. "No, the chip is out. There should not be any further repercussions," he replied, his tone strangely flat. Was I imagining things, or was Lazar acting weird? At the very least, he looked uneasy. Perhaps he was having doubts about crossing Orion? I imagined that had to be it. The two of them had been in cahoots for so long, it couldn't be easy to go against his wishes, even if Lazar didn't agree with his chosen methods.

"Are you sure?" Navan pressed.

Lazar turned, a forced smile on his face. "I am certain. Seraphina has never felt any aftereffects. Now, we ought to get going before someone discovers us, and you ought to get Riley to bed—she has been through an awful lot this evening," he said, putting the tools away.

It appeared the conversation was over. This was all the comfort I was going to get. Still, with that thing out of my neck, it felt good enough for now.

We left the *Asterope*, and Lazar accompanied Navan and me as we hurried back through the hangar toward the underground station. My legs still felt weak, but I had Navan to hold on to as we ran. A bullet train was waiting at the platform, the carriages empty, nobody else around. Quickly, we boarded, just as the doors were about to close.

Reaching the station at the other side of the tracks, we moved stealthily through to the elevator before heading up to the chambers Queen Gianne had given us. I was surprised to see that Lazar was coming with us this far—I'd expected him to turn off in a different direction.

As we reached the door to the chambers, he pulled Navan

aside. "Might I have a word with you, before I retire?" he asked, his gaze intense.

Navan frowned. "Sure."

I hovered on the threshold, not knowing whether to go into the chamber without Navan. "Do you need me?" I asked.

Lazar shook his head. "It's just Navan I need to speak to," he insisted, a note of apology in his voice.

I went into the room, wanting to pause by the door and eavesdrop, but knowing I shouldn't. Frustrated, I walked over to the window and gazed out into the Vysanthean night, my eyes drawn to the pale crimson moon gleaming above. What were they talking about out there? I had the unsettling feeling that it wasn't anything good.

Navan strode back into the room ten minutes later, a perplexed expression on his face. He walked straight over to me, taking my face in his hands and leaning his forehead against mine. He was breathing heavily, his manner strange.

"I need you to promise me something," he whispered, planting a delicate kiss on my face.

"Huh, what?"

"I need you to promise that, when the time comes, you will do what is best for your survival and trust me. As much as I love how headstrong you are, I need you to not be stubborn about this—I need you to just do what I say, when I say it, okay?" he explained rapidly, kissing me over and over, in between words.

"What? Wait, wait," I spluttered, pushing him back so I could look him in the eyes. "Navan, what is this? What's going on?" I asked, feeling a prickle of alarm. Navan's façade of calm had fallen, and it scared me.

"I've got a plan to get us all out of Vysanthe safely," he went on, his words hardly any less cryptic, "but it requires complete trust in what I say. When things begin to snowball, I need you to go along with it."

"What do you mean? What did Lazar say to you?"

Navan sighed, running a hand through his hair. "Orion has given us permission to leave Vysanthe soon," he said. "Lazar wanted to discuss our departure, and while I was with him, I came up with a plan. I don't want you to worry about it now—you've got enough on your plate." His eyes dropped worriedly to my neck. "Honestly, I don't know when the moment will come for you to leave, or the exact circumstances, but I'm going to be on the lookout for it. When the moment arrives, it should be obvious, and I need you to promise me that you'll take the chance."

Worry and confusion still gripped me—I had no idea what he meant by "take the chance"—but after the strain of the day, I found I didn't have it in me to argue or push him further. I just nodded, and hoped whatever Navan had planned wouldn't end up putting my safety before his.

29

I awoke the following morning with a throbbing pain along my neck, the dull ache running all the way down my shoulder. Still, it was nothing I couldn't handle after the agony of the night before. No doubt it was just my body getting rid of whatever traces the chip had left behind.

I rolled over in the bed to find Navan gone. My first instinct was to panic, and I sat up and looked around, just in time to see him come through the front door of the chambers. He smiled as he saw me, coming to sit at the edge of the bed.

"Morning, sleepyhead," he said softly. "How are you feeling?"

I let out a sigh and leaned back. "Groggy."

"Any pain?"

"Just a few aches, nothing I can't cope with," I replied. After the secret discussion with Lazar the previous evening, I was curious to know where he had been. "What have you been up to?"

"I went to pick up the disc from the guys at the palace," he said casually, taking a seat in a chair.

I was about to ask him further questions about last night, but, realizing I desperately needed to pee, I got up to go to the bathroom. On reemerging a few minutes later, I found Navan's chair empty.

I glanced toward the front door to see him standing there, in the middle of closing it. He turned to face me with a grim look.

"That was a messenger—the queen has invited us to breakfast," he said sourly.

"I'm guessing we have to go? I mean, it's not as if I can eat anything," I muttered.

He sighed. "Be rude not to."

Fearful of what the queen might want us for, I dressed quickly, and we left the room, all other thoughts evaporating into the ether. Taking the Snapper across the familiar route, we headed for the palace. After parking, we hurried through the palace in the direction of the throne room, where Queen Gianne was waiting for us.

A circular table covered in a cloth of deep plum velvet had been positioned in front of the silver throne, and there were plates laid out at every seat, with an assortment of vials placed on top. At one seat, however, was a very surprising sight—a bowl full of fruit had been set out, the colors vivid. I didn't recognize any of the fruit pieces, but my mouth was watering regardless. I couldn't wait to devour something that wasn't from a plastic packet.

Nestor, Cristo, Lazar, and the two shifters, morphed back into their Carokian forms, were already sitting at the table, their eyes flickering toward us as we approached. Queen Gianne was speaking with some guards on the far side of the room, but as she saw us take our seats, she swept across the floor to join us. She was dressed in a flowing gown of pure white, with an opaleine brooch clasped to the neckline.

With a flourish, she sat down at the table, removing the stopper from one of the vials in front of her and downing the contents. A trickle of something silver ran out of the corner of her mouth, before being hastily brushed away. Taking it as a signal, we all began to eat—or drink, in everyone else's case. I descended upon the fruit bowl, a burst of flavor exploding in my mouth, the sugar rushing straight to my head. Some flavors were familiar, but most were brand new, exciting my senses. I hadn't realized until that moment just how much I missed real food.

"You're probably wondering why I've brought you all together this morning," Queen Gianne began, after finishing off a second vial.

As a group, we looked up from what we were consuming and let our collective gaze rest on her. I thought she looked paler than the last time I'd seen her, with dark circles under her eyes, almost hidden by deftly applied makeup.

"It was a surprise, Your Highness," Navan said first, the silence having stretched on a moment too long.

"No doubt I frightened you?" she prompted, giving a slightly manic laugh.

"Not at all, Your Highness," Navan replied, though I detected a note of unease in his voice.

Queen Gianne looked disappointed by this news. "Well, never mind. I've got you here now. You see, I thought we might take a moment to discuss the rebels. That is, after all, why you were permitted to remain in my queendom," she continued. "I wish to know what you know, since intelligence was your bartering chip."

Another silence stretched across the table, though it was Nestor who broke it this time. "What would you care to know, Your Highness? We can tell you everything we have at our disposal," he said calmly.

"Where is the rebel base?" she asked, diving straight in with the big question.

"It's situated a year's travel from Vysanthe. I traced a map while I was there—I can bring it to your private study, if you would like, Your Highness?" Nestor offered.

She smiled. "That would be excellent. I am eager to send a portion of my army to seek them out as soon as possible, and destroy their base before they can gather numbers and strike us first," she explained, a glimmer of fear flickering in her eyes. "This outpost, is it on your map too?"

Nestor nodded. "It is, Your Highness. I made a note of everything we discovered at the outpost, and I would be more than happy to share it all with you, my queen."

"Do they plan to strike Vysanthe?" Queen Gianne wondered, her voice wavering ever so slightly.

"Those we found felt abandoned by the rebels, Your Highness," Navan cut in, gesturing to the others at the table, who nodded vigorously. "The last they'd heard, the rebels were trying to piece themselves back together again, but had no immediate plan to retaliate."

"Indeed, Your Highness, nor did they appear to have the numbers, by all accounts," Lazar spoke up. "At least, that's what I gathered from talking with these ex-rebels during the journey back to Vysanthe in my ship. A plague had set in among many of them, similar to the one that ravaged Zai, and I believe their forces took a hefty blow as a result. Nestor and Cristo here were left behind at the outpost because they were showing symptoms, though it didn't amount to the full-blown infection."

"Are they still infected?" Queen Gianne cried, horrified.

Lazar shook his head. "No, Your Highness. The plague never took hold of them. Indeed, it's why I have taken a medical interest in them—I was curious to sample their blood, so I might experiment with a cure for the Draconian plague. If we could cure it, we could begin to mine opaleine again," he said, tempting her.

"That would be a fine thing indeed," Queen Gianne murmured, before another wave of anxiety rippled across her face. "And you are certain the rebels don't mean to strike anytime soon?"

Navan nodded. "They are a year away, Your Highness, and none of our Explorer ships have picked up anything strange on their travels. Lazar took the liberty of checking the records himself, to make sure no anomalies have been spotted. Thus far, they are staying under their rock."

Apparently satisfied by Navan's words, the queen scraped her chair back and rose to her feet. With a sinking feeling, I watched her gaze flit to Navan, where it stayed. "Navan, would you come with me please? I would like a word in private," she said sternly, her tone brooking no negotiation.

Navan rose to his feet and followed her across the throne room. They disappeared through a side door, leaving the rest of us sitting around the breakfast table, twiddling our thumbs. There was no telling when either of them would be back, but I couldn't eat a bite more until I knew he was safe. I stared at the rest of the fruit, pushing it around the bowl.

Nobody spoke much, as the seconds ticked by into minutes, and those minutes became an hour. A nervous energy clung to the group, everyone consumed by their own thoughts and worries. Even the shifters seemed perplexed. Navan had been gone a long time, and that couldn't be a good thing, where Queen Gianne was involved.

"Screw this, I'm going for a walk," the male shifter grumbled, getting out of his seat. "Shout for me, or something, when the two of them decide to come back."

"I could do with stretching my legs a bit too," Nestor agreed, pocketing a vial for the road.

"They're probably not even coming back," Cristo muttered, flashing a glance at the door they'd disappeared through.

The female shifter said nothing, simply got to her feet and followed the male shifter out of the throne room, the two coldbloods trailing close behind. I wanted to call them back, knowing it was a bad idea to leave the table, but they wouldn't have listened to me even if I'd tried. To them, I was just a pathetic human riding on Navan's coattails. I had no authority here.

I looked to Lazar, but he didn't seem to think much of it. With the rest of them gone, he and I were the only ones left at the table. It was strange not to have Navan beside me, bridging discussions with his uncle, and I wasn't really in the mood for small talk.

As it turned out, Lazar wasn't either.

As soon as the others had disappeared from sight, he turned to me, resting his hand on my shoulder, just below the spot where he'd removed the chip. An earnest look spread across his face.

"Navan and I have discussed a moment such as this, Riley," he said, his voice suddenly urgent as he looked to each door of the throne room. "We agreed that, should a window of opportunity present itself, you should try to escape. I think this is one such opportunity."

I stared at him blankly.

"Our escape will be infinitely more hazardous than yours, Riley. Here, we are known, but you aren't," he continued, holding me tightly by the shoulders now. "We may have to endure things that you simply will not be able to—not because you aren't strong, but because you are human. You are vulnerable, Riley. If you don't go now, you will be putting everyone's lives at risk... That includes Navan."

I sat for a moment, trying to process what he was saying. He wanted me to leave... *now?* I thought back to what Navan had said the night before, about trusting him and doing what he told me to do, when the time came. But it wasn't Navan telling me to go. It was Lazar. I eyed him suspiciously—I still hadn't managed to shake the memory of his strange behavior after the surgery. Could I really trust this coldblood?

"I've attached a pod to your room, Riley," Lazar carried on, his hands shaking me gently, urging me to listen. "I had it arranged once the queen called me to this meeting. If you go there now, you can escape before anyone even knows you're gone. I've programmed it to fly automatically to certain coordinates in space, where Navan and I will pick you up later. It will be easy—as simple as being a passenger on a ship."

Navan's words kept playing in my head, but, again, he wasn't here to tell me that the moment had come. He wasn't here to tell me to trust Lazar, and there was something about the lean old coldblood that made me doubt everything. What if all of this was a ruse to get me out of the picture? What if Lazar was leading a third life, on top of his other two? What if he was in cahoots with Jareth, and this was his opportunity to get me away from Vysanthe? All of this ran through my head in a matter of seconds, bringing me no closer to a decision.

"I need to hear it from Navan," I replied finally, looking Lazar in the eyes. Even now, his gaze contained a shiftiness that set my nerves on edge. "I'll go, but I need Navan to confirm you're telling the truth—that the two of you did discuss this."

Lazar shook his head in irritation. "You have to go *now*, Riley. You are running out of time!"

"I need Navan's confirmation," I repeated.

"After everything, you still don't trust me?" Lazar countered.

I stared at him defiantly. "I don't, Lazar. I'm sorry, but I don't. What you're asking me to do is a pretty big deal. I made a promise to Navan to do as he told me when the time came, but you never came into the equation. If now is the time, I need to hear it from Navan." I just hoped I wouldn't live to regret those words. No matter how hard I tried, I couldn't bring myself to believe Lazar's motives were pure. Something fishy was going on, and I wasn't about to leave Navan on the brink of uncertainty.

"Riley, listen to me," Lazar pleaded. "Navan needs you to go, now. His life is on the line if you don't—you will hold him back. He will try to protect you, and it will undoubtedly get him killed. Is that what you want?"

I shook my head. "No."

"Then go, now!" he hissed.

Just then, the sound of footsteps reverberated around the throne room. From both sides, two parties approached—the rebels on one side, Queen Gianne and Navan on the other. Meeting in the middle, they all sat back down, and Queen Gianne called for dessert to be brought. She didn't seem to mind that the rebel cold-bloods had gone for a wander. Nor did she seem particularly perturbed by the fact that one of the Carokians was missing—the male shifter—his seat standing empty too. Which was good. I didn't feel like witnessing another one of her tantrums.

As dessert was served, I could feel Navan's eyes on me, forcing me to look up and meet his gaze. And as our eyes locked, I realized I must have made a mistake. He looked unsettled, if not outright shocked, to see me still sitting at the table.

Apparently, that moment with Lazar had been my window of opportunity after all. A window I had just slammed shut.

30

"What happened?" Navan asked, as he and I arrived back in our chambers. After finishing the meal in intense silence, Queen Gianne had dismissed us and we had abandoned the palace (though not before Lazar had narrowed his eyes at me and told Navan, "I think you and Riley may need to have a few words...").

"Uh, I was about to ask the same of you," I said, gesturing to the small, silvery pod now hovering outside our bedroom window. "You were expecting me to just take off with Lazar like that?"

"What happened exactly?" Navan asked, eyeing the pod.

I exhaled. "When Queen Gianne took you out of the room, the rebels all left too, except for Lazar. It was just me and him in there, and he told me that this was my moment to escape—that he had already triggered a pod to wait outside my room, and I had to climb into it and it would shoot me off into space, alone, and you would apparently come floating out to find me at some unspecified point in the future... That was really your plan?" I raised my eyebrows, hoping he realized how sketchy that must have sounded to me at the time, especially coming from Lazar.

Navan grimaced. "Well, not exactly—it's been hard to predict the exact moment we'll be able to get out of here, with so many moving pieces. But I told Lazar to be on the lookout for escape opportunities, too—so yeah, you should have done as he asked."

"You know, it would have been really helpful if you'd told me *that* last night, instead of the cryptic gibberish you gave me. I promised you I'd jump when you said—not when Lazar said. I didn't know if I could trust him about something as big as this!"

Navan sighed. "Seems like we really need to work on our communication skills."

I widened my eyes at him. "Excuse me, *our*?"

"Okay, mine."

"I mean, honestly. Is this one of those 'Procrastinator Navan' things again?"

He sighed. "Miscommunicator Navan. Gets ahead of himself when he has a lot on his mind and presumes others understand things he hasn't actually explained."

"Sounds about right. He and his twin brother are probably enough to drive me crazy." I was starting to realize coldblood men really weren't that different from human men.

"I shall endeavor to stick to Sexy, Amazing Communicator Navan in the future."

I suppressed a smile. "I'd love me some of *him*... But, seriously, what now? I'm fine to leave this place as long as you're close behind. Also, what did the queen talk to you about?"

Navan winced. "She wants me to depart with several

squadrons tomorrow, to lead the attack mission on the rebel planet... I may need to keep up the pretense a while longer, or else she'll suspect foul play. Once we're far enough away from Vysanthe, I'll do what I can to escape, and join you when I can."

"So you're not escaping with me?" I gasped, wondering what the hell that meant for the both of us.

"I don't know what else to do, Riley," he replied in frustration. "She wants me to leave the rebels behind, too—she doesn't trust them enough, and she wants to see what other information she can extract from them. If I leave now, their lives will be forfeit. Lazar's, too."

"What am I supposed to do?" I asked, terrified by the prospect of drifting alone in the gaping vacuum, God knew how many millions of miles away from home.

"Lazar would arrange a pickup to take you back to Earth," he said. "I would keep Lazar in the loop regarding where I was, so he could pass messages to you, and then I'd join you when I could. I would never leave you alone out there, Riley. I'd find a way to get to you."

I still couldn't believe what I was hearing. In theory, if all went according to Navan's plan, I could make the journey back by myself, but I'd be a nervous wreck. Not only at the idea of the ship breaking down or any number of other things going wrong, but also because I didn't want to leave Navan here, not knowing what might happen to him. What if, somehow, he *couldn't* get away?

I opened my mouth to speak, but the words froze on my lips as a cry rang out, piercing the air. It was coming from outside, just beyond the door of the chamber. Whirling around, I glanced back at Navan, my nerves shot.

"You heard that, right?"

Navan nodded, brushing past me to reach the door. He flung it open, and a second later, Lazar tumbled into the room, collapsing on the floor, his arms reaching out for us. Dark blood smeared his face and soaked his clothes. His features were battered and bruised, one eye closed up entirely.

"Lazar!" I cried, running to his aid. With Navan's help, I hauled him up onto a nearby chair. As I ran to get water to sponge some of the blood away, I could hear him croaking out words.

"The queen... She knows," he said, his voice strained. "Soldiers are... coming."

Navan paled. "Now?"

Lazar nodded, wincing in pain. "I... just managed... to get away... in time."

"How does she know? Does she know everything?" Navan pressed, as I returned, dabbing at the horrific wounds on Lazar's face and torso. From the looks of it, something—or someone—had ripped him to shreds. Deep gashes lacerated his entire body, the skin torn off, hanging in ragged ribbons of dripping flesh.

Again, Lazar nodded. "Shifter was... caught... contacting Orion," he said, before a wracking cough halted his speech. Blood bubbled up over his lower lip, trickling from the corner of his mouth.

"Where's the shifter now?" Navan demanded, a cold look in his eyes.

"Tortured. Forced information from... him," Lazar choked. "Then... they killed him. You... have to go... now."

I looked at Navan, not knowing what to do. We couldn't just leave Lazar here, to the mercy of the queen's soldiers. My gaze turned toward the little pod ship, still bobbing outside the room. That was our way out.

"Lazar, you have to come with us," I said, gesturing toward the vessel. "We can all get out of this."

Lazar shook his head. "I will... stay, and fight... the queen's guards. It will... buy you... time," he replied firmly.

Navan took his uncle's hand. "Look at you! You can't stay and fight anyone in this condition. You're coming with us." He leaned down to lift Lazar's arm over his shoulder, but Lazar pulled back with surprising strength.

"Take Riley... and go!" he demanded.

"We're not leaving you," I cut in.

Lazar turned to Navan, pulling his face down toward his. "If you... don't leave now, without... me, you will never... get out of... here alive," he warned. "If you want... her to live, you have... to go!"

Navan looked at me, his face a vision of torment. Neither of us felt right leaving Lazar here, but the threat of the soldiers loomed over us. Through the still-open door, I saw the lights on the elevator flash, and heard the telltale thud of boots coming up the stairs to the side of the landing. They were almost here.

"I'm sorry, Uncle," Navan said, running to the door. Just as the elevator pinged, he slammed the door shut and turned the lock, before returning for me. He grabbed my hand, pulling me toward the bobbing ship, pushing me out of the window onto the narrow ledge outside. He followed straight after, his hand reaching up for the side of the vessel.

With a whoosh, the back door slid open and a gangplank shot out. Behind us, I could hear someone breaking the door down. Every thud made my heart pound harder. Would we make it out in time? Glancing through the window, I saw Lazar rising from his chair, raising a gun to the door.

"Go!" Navan shouted, forcing me into action.

I leapt for the gangplank and hurried into the ship's belly. Navan was close behind me, his hand slamming down on a button that shut the vessel's door after us. Without pausing for breath, he headed for the pilot's seat and brought the command console to life. It flickered and beeped, ready for his instruction.

As I sat down in the seat beside him, my ears still pricked for the sounds of a battle, he took hold of the controls and lifted the ship upward. It rose with a jolt, soaring into the air. Without looking back, though my thoughts were with Lazar and his last stand, we zipped across the landscape, the vessel moving at breakneck speed over familiar territory.

Just then, red lights began to flash, and a siren blared inside the ship. This pod wasn't anywhere near as advanced as the *Asterope*, but they shared some technology. A translucent screen slipped across the windshield, the words *Incoming Message* blinking furiously.

"Do we answer it?" I asked, already fearing whose face I would see.

Reluctantly, Navan pressed another button on the console. After a crackle of white noise, an image appeared. Queen Gianne was staring right at us, her eerie silver eyes practically popping out of her head. Her cheeks were flushed an angry red, and a burning fury ignited her gaze. With her teeth bared, her fangs flashing, she leaned closer to the camera.

"I'm going to blast you out of the sky!" she screamed, the sound shattering my eardrums. "You won't escape me, traitors! I will follow you to the ends of the universe if that's what it takes! *Nobody betrays me!*"

Navan quickly shut off the transmission, but it was too late— the fear had already set in. The thing was, I believed every word of what she had said, and it chilled me to the core. Queen Gianne would not stop hunting us, and if she would not stop, then... my hopes of returning to Earth had become little more than a distant dream. If we went back to Earth now, Queen Gianne and her entire military force would follow us, putting my home planet in untold danger. I couldn't risk that. Not to mention, we'd have to reach the *Asterope* first—this little pod wouldn't go the distance.

The sound of splintering glass suddenly ricocheted in my ears, the windshield exploding inward in a hailstorm of glinting shards. I ducked as the debris rained down on me, while something much larger shot straight past my head. I covered my head with my arms, sliding down beneath the command console, praying for it to stop.

"Navan, get down!" I yelled, but he was still focused on getting the ship to move faster. We were sitting ducks out here.

A split second later, something blasted through the destroyed windshield, hitting Navan square in the shoulder. He cried out, clutching his arm. A crackling arrow had embedded into his skin, the point piercing clean through muscle and flesh. Blood poured from the wound, the bristle of the arrow's electrical charge sending shocks through his body.

"Riley," he gasped, nodding at the console.

I jumped up, knowing it was down to me now. Taking over the controls, I tried to remember the flight lessons I'd had in the Fed ship—it had been easy enough then, and this ship didn't seem so different. It was small, with controls that responded in the same way. I tested it, seeing if the pod would rise with my instruction, while dodging the artillery flying through the window. To my utter relief, the ship shot up as I moved the controls.

Keeping focused, I moved the ship forward, accelerating quickly. I had thought about lifting the ship upward, toward the planet's atmosphere, so we could punch through into the emptiness of space, but now we had a broken windshield—and in any case, I knew there was no point trying to leave the planet now. If the queen and her army were only going to follow us... that left only one option.

"We have to head north," I told Navan, swerving the ship in the opposite direction and building up speed.

Grimacing through the agony in his arm, Navan looked up at me, an alarmed expression on his pained face. "North? We can't go north!"

"We're going north," I replied firmly.

"That's insane, Riley—we *can't* go north," he said, wincing. "The only thing waiting for us there is Queen Brisha."

I shook my head. "The only way to stop Queen Gianne's army from shooting us down is to go toward enemy territory," I said. "The truce is already teetering on a knife edge, but Queen Gianne won't want to be the one to cross it, not even for us."

"Trespassing on Queen Brisha's side of Vysanthe will probably land us in even deeper trouble," Navan warned, though I could see he agreed it was our only choice. Whichever way we turned, death appeared to be waiting for us—and I knew I'd rather take my chances with Queen Brisha than Queen Gianne. I just hoped I wouldn't live to regret the decision.

I forced the accelerator into overdrive, and we shot across the sky so fast everything became a blur, my movements on the console allowing us to evade the ships soaring toward us, firing at the pod. Lazar had picked the perfect vessel—it was small and quick, just the right kind of ship to avoid a horde of soldiers in.

With Queen Gianne's fighters still tailing us, and the wind whipping into the ship so violently I thought my face might fall off, we reached the border. I could see it now, shimmering in the near distance, jutting up between the ridges of a jagged mountain range. We had just passed the spot where the fighting pits had been, so I knew I was going the right way. Holding my breath, I kept the pod going, not knowing what the shimmering barrier might do to it—or us, for that matter.

"Will the border hurt us?" I asked frantically, as we approached at a rapid pace.

Navan swallowed, his eyes trained on the barrier. "I don't think so."

"You don't *think* so?"

I squeezed my eyes shut as we barreled through it, only to open them again a moment later. We emerged on the other side, unscathed. Beside me, Navan leaned over and pressed a large white button on the console, and flashing lights went off around us.

"What's that for?" I asked, my whole body shaking.

"I'm flying a white flag," he said, "letting Brisha know we're a neutral party."

I frowned. "Will that work?"

He shrugged, grimacing in pain. "I hope so."

Suddenly, the rattle of gunfire went off, making me duck for cover once more. I stayed under the console for several moments, covering my ears every time another assault peppered the air with loud explosions.

"It's the border control, shooting down Queen Gianne's ships," Navan said, reaching for my hand, bringing me out from under the console. "They're not shooting at us."

I watched through the rearview monitors as flaming balls rained down from the sky, tumbling to the ground below—the remnants of those soldiers who had dared to cross the border in ships built for military action.

They wouldn't be returning to Queen Gianne's side of Vysanthe. Then again, neither would we. The only way for us now was forward, into the uncertain embrace of Queen Brisha.

At least she hadn't shot us down. That had to be a good sign... Right?

*a*s the ship's siren erupted again, the message screen flickered to life. For a moment, I jolted, thinking it was Queen Gianne, but as the image focused, I realized I was mistaken. This woman had long, curling hair, a paler shade of copper than her sister's—more strawberry blond than vivid bronze. Her eyes were of the same intense, silver shade, but they didn't hold the same manic expression that Queen Gianne's did.

No, this was definitely Queen Brisha.

"Well, this is a pleasant surprise," she said, her voice clipped and charming. "Navan Idrax, in the flesh."

Navan frowned in bemusement. Evidently, he hadn't expected the queen to be so cordial, or half as welcoming as she seemed. "Queen Brisha," he said formally. "I wish to request an audience with you."

"Such fortuitous timing, Navan," she replied with a smile. "You've been on my mind an awful lot lately. Indeed, there are several important matters I wish to speak with you about. How excellent that instead of having to track you down myself, you have come to me with open arms!"

There was something eerie about the delight in her tone, and the joy that sparkled in her peculiar eyes. I felt a twist of concern in the pit of my stomach, wondering if I'd have to beat away a queen's flirtatious advances toward my boyfriend, after everything I had already gone through with his parents and the betrothal.

"So, we may have an audience with you, Your Highness?" Navan asked, uncertainly.

"We?" Queen Brisha replied.

Navan nodded. "I have a... friend with me. I would prefer not to leave her in the ship while we discuss matters."

She laughed, the sound genuine and oddly sweet. "Of course, the more the merrier! I shall be expecting you in my palace shortly. Follow the coordinates I am sending you, and my guards will escort you to me. I look forward to our meeting," she said softly. With that, the screen disappeared, Queen Brisha with it.

"So I'm going to be your friend here instead of your slave?" I asked, frowning.

Navan nodded. "I'm tired of putting on that show—I'm hoping we can get away with more on this side of the border."

I fell quiet, turning my thoughts to the queen's words, and finding them strange. From what I'd gathered, "the more the merrier" wasn't exactly Queen Brisha's motto, and I couldn't shake the fear I felt at the notion of her and Navan discussing "important matters." What were these important matters? How could she be so familiar with him?

Following a flashing beacon on the screen, I lowered the ship to the given destination, obeying Navan's instructions for landing the vessel. With only a minor bump, we reached the ground and parked in a deserted expanse of frosted grass. Around us stretched an endless mountain range, the tips white with snow, along with shimmering, frozen lakes nestled in harsh valleys.

Ahead of us, several armed guards dressed in silver and green emerged from a darkened tunnel in the rockface of a large mountain—along with a tall coldblood woman in a black dress. They all smiled as they approached, and Navan and I moved forward to meet them.

"Welcome to Queen Brisha's queendom. I am Pandora—I will be your guide throughout your stay here. Anything you need, let me know," the woman said warmly, her eyes only slightly curious as they glanced over me. "Our queen is most anxious to meet you."

"Thank you," Navan replied, still clutching his arm, his hands covered in blood.

She raised her eyebrow. "We should get your injury seen to, though I don't wish to keep the queen waiting. I'll send a medic along as soon as I have delivered you to her," she promised.

She was a striking woman, with broad shoulders and an elegant neck. Her purple-tinted hair was tied up in a ponytail, with golden ornaments woven through her locks. I wondered what they signified, seeing that the majority of the guards wore similar accessories in their hair too. Her sea-green eyes were kind but stern, and I could tell she was the kind of woman nobody would want to mess with.

Navan grimaced. "That would be good," he said, his palm not quite stemming the flow of blood.

Turning, we followed Pandora into the tunnel, where darkness enveloped us. Flashlights lit up the shadows, casting terrifying figures on the walls as we walked. I shuddered, feeling the cold of the atmosphere clinging to my bones. In our panic to leave, I'd forgotten to pick up my fur coat, and now I was facing the full effects of the Vysanthean weather.

As if reading my mind, Pandora came toward me, brandishing a coat one of the guards had been carrying. It was made of a leathery material, the inside lined with thick, dense fur.

"You'll need this," she said, draping it around my shoulders.

"Thank you," I replied gratefully, wrapping it around myself to keep out the bitter chill.

Five minutes later, the tunnel gave way to a stone walkway that looked out on a glistening city. I gasped in awe at the array of exquisite sandstone buildings that shone with golden tiles. Crystal-encrusted towers glittered in the sunshine, and coldbloods were smiling out in the open piazzas.

The most striking building of all, however, was Queen Brisha's palace—not quite as striking as Queen Gianne's fairytale-like home, I had to admit, but still stunning. It rose up like a trident, three minarets forming the prongs. Each one was dusted in crystals and rubies, and the whole structure sparkled like a Christmas ornament. Statues of sculpted coldblood males and females adorned the fortifications, their bodies twisted like dancers, wielding shining weapons and holding various objects in their hands. One held a scale. Another, a book. A third, a flaming torch, the flames real.

Descending a flight of steps, we were led through a series of gardens, with trees and bushes bearing more fruit and flowers than Queen Gianne's. Here, there were water fountains and ponds with meandering fish, though the fountains had frozen mid-pour, the effect stunning.

After leading us through a grand entrance around the back of the palace, Pandora and her guards walked us the length of an exquisite hallway, the tapestries showing images of Queen Brisha's people, in various scenes. Some were picking fruit, while others were dancing in one of those beautiful piazzas. Nowhere was Queen Brisha present in the pictures—a stark contrast to the hall-ways of Queen Gianne's palace, where her face was everywhere.

Here, I felt like a guest instead of a prisoner, which was a welcome change. Even so, I couldn't help feeling uneasy. Even if Queen Brisha seemed amiable enough, she was still a ruling cold-blood—not a woman to be trifled with—and I didn't trust her motives for treating us like this. Something was definitely amiss, reminding me of one of Roger's favorite phrases: "If something seems too good to be true, it probably is." I felt sad, thinking about my adopted dad, but I pushed it away—now wasn't the time for such worries.

I dared a glance at Navan to try to gauge how he was feeling, but the look on his face only escalated my fears. There was worry and regret in his expression, too. I desperately wanted to speak with him, to find out what was on his mind, but with the guards around, I didn't have a chance. Maybe we would have been better off getting shot down by Queen Gianne after all, instead of entering this strange, unknown territory. A place that was not only new to me, but to Navan too. Even before the planet had been divvied up between the sisters, I got the feeling he hadn't spent much time in the north.

We paused beside a tall set of golden doors, but were ushered quickly inside. My heart was racing, my nerves on edge—we were about to meet Queen Brisha.

For a moment, however, I forgot my fears, as we found ourselves entering a giant library. It was not what I had expected, having become accustomed to being shoved into throne rooms and dank cells. A soft gasp escaped my throat as I took in the endless stacks of leather-bound books, standing row upon row. In the center of the room was a roaring firepit, with high-backed chairs arranged all around it. There, Queen Brisha was sitting, her nose buried in one of her tomes.

She got up as we neared. Even in this small movement, I was taken aback. Where Queen Gianne wore opulent dresses with expensive adornments, Queen Brisha's tastes were far less lavish. She wore elegantly tailored black pants, with a silver stripe running down the leg, and a loose-flowing blouse of the same silver shade. A choker adorned her neck, a small cluster of opaleine in the center, but that was the extent of her finery. Even her feet were bare as she walked over the carpet toward us.

"Welcome, honored guests," she said, holding out her arms. "Pandora, please fetch a medic to see to Navan," she added, though Pandora was already on her way out the door to do just that.

"Absolutely, Your Highness," she replied, before disappearing from sight.

"Now, make yourselves comfortable. We have much to discuss," Queen Brisha said, gesturing to a trio of high-backed chairs by the open firepit. "I thought your friend could use somewhere warm for our meeting. This Vysanthean climate doesn't agree with her."

Navan frowned. "No, indeed, Your Highness... though your guard was kind enough to give her a coat to wear," he said, his tone tense. I figured he shared my sudden fear—*does she know what I am?*

"Even so, a coat is no match for a good fire—come, warm yourself. Get the Vysanthean chill out of your bones. If you don't, it'll stay there for good," she joked, sitting down in one of the chairs, a look of expectation on her face.

"Thank you, Your Highness," I replied, taking a seat. She was right: the roaring flames' warmth was a welcome feeling after the bitter cold of the outside world.

"Such a pretty voice!" Queen Brisha remarked. "What are you, if you don't mind me asking?"

"Riley is an unknown species—we're still figuring out what she is," Navan cut in, before I could say a word.

The queen smiled. "*You* might not know, but she surely does?"

I had to think fast. "Kryptonian," I said, picking the first planet that came to mind. Thankfully, Earth franchises didn't reach these parts of the universe.

"Not familiar with it myself. Whereabouts is it?"

"At the far edge of the Drax Sector, Your Highness," Navan answered, a tiny flicker of amusement in his eyes.

Again, the queen smiled. "Does he always answer for you?" she teased.

"I didn't know there was a world beyond mine, Your Highness," I replied anxiously. "So it means very little to me—Navan is better equipped to tell you where I'm from. We are not as advanced as you are. Indeed, it has not been long since we first discovered how to forge metal," I lied, trying to come up with something convincing.

"Well, this place must be quite the culture shock!" she said.

I nodded. "It does take some getting used to."

"And how are things run where you hail from? Are there king-doms, queendoms—who controls things around your neck of the woods?" she asked, her tone genuinely intrigued. I could see a light in her eyes, too, gleaming with curiosity.

I shrugged. "We don't really have kingdoms anymore, where I come from. Dictatorships aren't exactly in style," I said, smiling slightly. Something about this woman lured me into a sense of security, though whether it was a false one or not, only time would tell.

Queen Brisha chuckled with amusement. "How fascinating! What a history you must have."

Despite myself, I found the woman intriguing. She was almost soft-spoken, with no tinge of paranoia in her voice to sully her words. Everything about her suggested a sharp intelligence... The stacks and stacks of books were a giveaway to the intellect that lay beneath her striking surface.

My mind trailed toward thoughts of Jethro, and what he'd said about wanting to be on Queen Brisha's side when a civil war inevitably erupted on Vysanthe. Now I understood why she was the obvious choice—she didn't seem volatile or impulsive like Queen Gianne. She was more cerebral. It explained why she took time to decide whom she allowed into her queendom, carefully considering each case to determine what was best for her people. I was sure there *was* a hint of paranoia, with her believing outsiders could be spies, but unlike Gianne, this queen didn't radiate a sense of chaos.

I also realized that, in her eyes, we were defectors. We had come across the border, and, in doing so, sought out her refuge. I remembered Navan telling me that, in order to gain Brisha's favor, defectors had to offer something exceptionally valuable to her to prove themselves trustworthy beyond all doubt. Would she expect that from us? If so, I had no idea what we could trade. I was sure Navan wasn't about to try the whole "rebel" charade again with this queen, after it had backfired so badly with Gianne.

"And you, Navan, how does it feel to be back on home soil?" Queen Brisha asked warmly, as if they were old friends who had just met up after a long absence. "I hope you haven't suddenly gone against the idea of dictatorships?" she teased.

Navan shook his head. "Not yet, Your Highness," he said, teetering on the edge of sarcasm. "It's always nice to be on my home planet."

"And how is your father doing with the search for blood? I would certainly enjoy a taste of that elixir, once it's complete." She grinned, catching Navan off guard. I could see the concern on his face.

"How do you—" he began, but she cut him off.

"I have eyes everywhere, Navan. I like to keep ahead of the curve," she explained kindly, no hint of threat in her voice.

He shrugged. "My father rarely shares his work with me, and I have yet to find a suitable blood for his requirements."

A glimmer of intrigue crossed Queen Brisha's face. "Is that so? Very well. At least that gives me a chance to find it first." She chuckled. "Now, you must be wondering why I've asked you here, instead of blowing you out of the sky?"

Navan and I nodded in unison.

"I'm not an unreasonable woman. I like to give chances, where I see potential," she explained. "And so, I wanted to bring you here, to give you the opportunity to win me over. First, you can begin by telling me what has brought you here to my side of Vysanthe. Second, I'd be very interested to know how my sister is doing, and what she is up to. I trust you won't mind telling me a few things in return for shelter and safety?"

I glanced at Navan, who looked back at me. It appeared we were standing at a crossroads, with fairly few options ahead of us. We couldn't leave for Earth without the *Asterope*—or Queen Gianne's fleet following us—and we couldn't remain here without telling Queen Brisha something. The only problem was—did we tell the truth, and risk everything? Or lie, and hope we could get away with it?

"You needn't feel any responsibility toward my sister," Queen Brisha continued, as I wondered what we were going to do. "I know better than anyone what she can be like. She rules with fear, believing it to be the only way to control people. If you have come across the border, especially in the manner you did, with so many ships on your tail, I have a feeling you did not leave on the best of terms. I am simply interested in why—why run from the South?"

Neither of us said a word, prompting Queen Brisha to frown. It was clear she didn't like to be kept waiting, but there was something else, as well. There was a look of pity in her eyes, as if she knew something we didn't.

"Gianne used to be a kind, artistic creature," Queen Brisha went on. "The crown has twisted her up inside, and made her a shadow of the woman she once was. I warned her this would happen—I told her not to let her paranoia get the better of her, but she has taken my words in a manner they were not intended, and I fear it is doing her harm. From what I hear, she is terrified of everyone—she suspects everyone and everything of betrayal, but only has the threat of execution as a means of controlling her populace. She is teetering on the edge of madness." The sad note in Queen Brisha's voice surprised me. Although a tentative truce existed between the two sisters, Queen Brisha clearly still cared for her twin. Well, perhaps she didn't exactly *care* for her, but she certainly pitied her.

"I think you may be right," Navan said unexpectedly. "Queen Gianne is not herself. She is using greater force than ever before, and has become less tolerant of infractions against her rules." I wondered where he was going with this. Surely, telling Queen Brisha that her sister was on the edge of a breakdown would only push the civil war forward? Then again, if it was imminent anyway, it was merely accelerating the inevitable. Perhaps Navan was thinking we could escape during the turmoil that would follow such a battle? It seemed like a longshot, but I wasn't sure what else he could be thinking.

"Ah yes, your father is her chief advisor, is he not?" Queen Brisha asked, though it was clear she already knew the answer.

Navan nodded. "It's why our misdemeanor hasn't gone down at all well with your sister. I think she is terrified of what people would think, if she made me an exception to one of her most concrete rules. She might have thought about it, given whose son I am, but not even my father could talk her into it."

"Misdemeanor?" Queen Brisha asked, raising an eyebrow.

"It's why we're here, across the border," Navan continued. "We're seeking amnesty in Northern Vysanthe, because of... well, because of my feelings for this woman here." He looked at me, a smile lighting up his ashen face. As much as it warmed me, that felt like an unnervingly bold move, to reveal our romance like that. But I knew Navan must have been damned confident that Brisha wouldn't blow up like her sister would, or he would never have risked it.

Thankfully, Queen Brisha's eyes lit up. "Oh! A tale of star-crossed love. Well, this is an extraordinary turn of events!" She was evidently delighted by the idea. Looking at her collection of books, I found myself wondering if she had a few choice romances in there somewhere, for when she needed a spot of escapism. "Although, surely you knew what would happen when you brought her to Vysanthe?" she added, making my stomach lurch.

"I brought her here because I had nowhere else to take her," Navan replied smoothly. "Her species isn't used to the tempera-tures in this part of the universe, and I didn't want to leave her on some unknown planet where anything might happen to her. I was planning to seek out her homeland in a week or so, after I'd completed some repairs on my ship, but I needed somewhere to keep her in the meantime. I thought I could pass her off as a slave I'd taken, but it... didn't really work out."

"How so?" Queen Brisha pressed, licking her lips in antic-ipation.

"We were caught kissing in a corridor at a party the queen threw in his honor, Your Highness," I chipped in, flashing her a shy smile.

Queen Brisha chuckled. "How delicious. But what made you think I'd be any less harsh on this affection the two of you share?" Her delight ebbed for a moment, her stare intensifying.

I took a deep breath as Navan replied, "I know your view on inter-species relationships isn't one that will result in the death penalty, Your Highness. So, I suppose we were hoping you might look kindly on our love, and accept us into the fold, so to speak... It's a bold assumption, I know, but we didn't have many other options. It was run to you, or die."

I watched Queen Brisha as she mulled over our tale, but no matter how hard I tried, I couldn't read her. Despite her apparent warmth, in that moment I honestly had no idea which way she would swing when it came to our judgment. Not for the first time, I wondered if we'd made a horrible mistake in coming here. What if she spoke to Queen Gianne and realized that our story was made up? It appeared she had a lot of intel on what was going on in the southern part of Vysanthe—what if her spies, whoever they were, fed back the reality of our escape? I couldn't help feeling we'd simply jumped out of the frying pan and into the fire.

After a long pause, Queen Brisha spoke. "While I love a tale of tragic romance, and I sense that what you are telling me is the truth, given the way you look at one another... I can't just offer you the amnesty you seek. As with all defectors, you must prove yourselves to me beyond all reasonable doubt before I can take you under my wing. I will not put my people at risk by inviting miscreants into our midst... as adorable as I think the pair of you are." She smiled then, her cold mask breaking.

"What can we do to prove ourselves to you?" Navan asked. I noticed his jaw tense slightly.

"I trust you know Gianne's palace?" she replied.

Navan and I nodded. "It's a beautiful place, Your Highness," I said, remembering the glacial surface and the striking towers.

She sighed, lounging back in her chair. "It is beyond beautiful, little Kryptonian," she remarked. "I imagine it blew your mind, given where you've come from."

I nodded. "I have never seen anything quite like it, Your Highness," I replied, meaning it.

"Your brother was the architect, was he not?" Queen Brisha asked, turning her attention to Navan.

He smiled proudly. "Indeed, Bashrik was the lead architect, Your Highness." I knew he'd said his brother's name for my benefit, given the number of brothers he had. Still, it surprised me. I had never thought of Bashrik as an architect.

"I remember when it was being built," Queen Brisha murmured wistfully. "I sent spies to check on its progress, and the images that came back took my breath away. It could have been the most exquisite building in the entire universe, but my sister's tastes have ruined the interior. It's only a matter of time before the outside starts to go, too. And those gardens! For a coldblood whose passion is supposedly horticulture, she's done a terrible job of them." A rueful smile passed over Queen Brisha's deep red lips.

"I'm sorry, Your Highness, I don't follow," Navan said blankly. I didn't either. What did this have to do with us?

She chuckled. "I want a building that will rival Gianne's palace, only my feat of architecture will not be used for something as trivial as housing a throne and a mad queen," she explained. "I want a building designed that will house a new alchemical laboratory, purely used for research into the immortality elixir. The best and brightest alchemists from across my queendom will reside there, working around the clock to find the key to cracking this elixir. It will be a building that coldbloods will come from far and wide to see."

"And for that, you need... Bashrik?" Navan asked quietly, a crestfallen look on his face. It flickered there for only a second, before he covered it with a polite expression of interest.

The queen nodded. "He is the only one who possesses the skill I need, to design something truly worthy." She sighed thought-fully, and I imagined she was envisioning her vast laboratory. "However, I know he is loyal to the South... so that's where you come in."

"You want me to bring him over to your side, Your Highness?"

She smiled. "Now you're getting it. I want you to invite him here, to the palace, and ensure he comes. I'd invite him myself, but since he would most likely refuse a personal invitation from me, I thought you could do it. He is far more likely to listen to his brother."

Navan sighed heavily. I could see he didn't like the idea of getting his younger brother involved in this whole mess, but what choice did we have? If he refused Queen Brisha's request to wrangle Bashrik, then we were back to square one. And, now that we were in the heart of Northern Vysanthe, we had nowhere to run.

Of course, I didn't know how we'd even *contact* Bashrik at this point, let alone get him here, but... one step at a time.

"I will do as you ask, Your Highness," he said after a few moments of silence, his brow furrowed.

"Excellent!" Queen Brisha said, her eyes glittering with excitement.

"Now, Your Highness," Navan replied, "if I may, I would like to seek medical attention. I'm beginning to feel a little queasy." In all the tension, I'd forgotten about his arm, and the medic that had never come. It seemed Queen Brisha had, too.

"Goodness, your arm! I'm sorry, I completely forgot," she said. "That's not like Pandora—perhaps someone held her up on the way to the infirmary. Anyway, if you go outside, one of the guards by the door will assist you."

Navan smiled weakly. "Thank you, Your Highness." With that, he rose. I got up too, moving to follow him to the door.

But Queen Brisha spoke again. "I'm not quite finished with *you* yet, little Kryptonian," she said, her tone eerily light.

Navan turned, his hand protectively closing around mine. "Your Highness? I was under the impression you had given us your request for proving ourselves."

Queen Brisha shook her head. "That was *your* mission, Navan, but I need *both* of you to prove your worth to me. I have something else in mind for your dear love, but I would speak with her in private about it. It is not for your ears."

"I would rather not leave her alone, Your Highness," Navan replied tersely. "I trust you, of course, but if you have something to say, you can say it to both of us."

"Excuse me?" Queen Brisha rose sharply from her seat, her eyes flashing with annoyance. I imagined nobody ever spoke back to her like that, and I wasn't about to let Navan get on her bad side. We needed to keep her sweet if we wanted to get out of here alive.

Navan tightened his hold on me. "Either I'm staying, or she is coming with me, Your Highness. I'm not leaving her alone," he repeated slowly, the unspoken words "with you" hanging in the air.

I had to step in before a fight could start—or Navan ended up on the end of a pike. Turning toward him, I looked him dead in the eyes. "Navan, I will be fine," I said, trying to sound calm in spite of my pounding heart. The *last* thing I wanted was to be locked in a room alone with this queen. "If the queen requires me to do a task, then I will do it. If it means we can be together, without living in fear, then it will be worth it. Now, go to the infirmary."

To say Navan didn't look pleased would have been an understatement, but I sensed he wasn't going to argue. Leaning down to drop a chaste kiss on my lips, he pulled me into a tight hug even as his injured arm hung limply by his side. He looked like he was going to say something else as he drew away, but thought better of it.

"Just be careful," he muttered, before turning and walking out of the room.

"Protective, isn't he?" Queen Brisha remarked, her tone amused. "Borderline stifling, if you ask me, but I know it's personal preference. I, myself, can't stand a partner with a hero complex, but I can see the appeal."

I was surprised by her casual manner, her former irritation fading as quickly as it had appeared. In its place, her warmth had returned. I sat back down, wrapping myself up in the coat that Pandora had given me, as the flames danced higher in the firepit. I was shivering, though not from the cold.

"Now, let's get down to business," the queen said softly.

33

"What sort of planet is—what was it called again?" Queen Brisha asked, diving straight in. I had a feeling she was trying to catch me in a lie.

"Krypton."

She nodded. "Yes, what sort of planet is it?"

I shrugged. "It has land and sea, and there are mountains and deserts," I said, not knowing how much to give away, and how much to keep to myself. Was there a way of figuring out the name and location of a planet just by the description? I hoped not. "My people live in small towns and villages, making a living mostly by farming land and scouring the seas. We're subsistence farmers and foragers, mainly." The half-truths poured out of me, my pulse racing.

"And your people, do they all look like you?"

I shrugged again. "More or less. We come in different colors and sizes, but the basic foundations are the same."

"You are the dominant species?" she pressed.

"I believe so," I replied, ever conscious of her intense stare upon my face. Somehow, it felt as though she could see right through me, gazing into the privacy of my head.

"Interesting," she mused.

"It is, Your Highness?"

She smiled. "Oh yes. You see, Riley, I received word from a coldblood named Jethro, not long ago, that he had collected a special blood sample, and was sending it straight to me. He wouldn't tell me which planet he was on, only that he had found some blood that might prove extremely useful in the immortality elixir research."

I paled, as realization dawned on me like a pile of bricks. "Wh- Why wouldn't he tell you where he was, Your Highness?" I asked, desperately hoping I could find a way to wriggle out of this corner she was backing me into.

"For good reason, I suppose," she replied. "He feared the message might be intercepted by my dear sister, and she might try to go after the pod herself to steal the sample within."

I began to panic, horrified that she knew about the pod's existence. I had known about Jethro's deceit in sending the pod, but I hadn't known that news had reached Queen Brisha. All this time, she had known it was on its way to her. We had been so convinced we could intercept it without anyone getting their hands on it. But now that hope had been dashed. Now there was nothing to stop her from heading out to retrieve the sample, and putting my blood to her own awful uses.

"You're surprised?" she noted.

"Just cold, Your Highness," I managed. I still didn't know

exactly how much she knew, and I wasn't about to help her out, with my stupid face giving the game away.

She smiled coldly. "I must say, it's quite the coincidence that Navan happens to be traveling with another species, considering the last time I heard news of him he was traveling with Jethro himself," she began, twisting the knife. "Don't you think that's a strange coincidence that Jethro was traveling with Navan, came across a strange blood sample, and now you're here, at Navan's side? Even stranger that nobody can get in contact with Jethro..." A warning flickered in her silver eyes.

"A very strange coincidence, Your Highness," I whispered, my voice gone.

She gave a tight laugh. "I'm not an idiot, Riley. I know your presence has something to do with this blood sample Jethro was supposed to be sending, and I'm hoping you can tell me why the pod's tracker stopped beeping several days ago?"

I gulped and shook my head. "I don't know anything about a tracker, Your Highness." It wasn't a lie. I *hadn't* known there was a tracker on the sample pod, and I had absolutely no idea where it might have gone, if what Queen Brisha said was true. In fact, the very idea of it going missing filled me with a renewed sense of dread. What if someone had taken it? I wasn't sure who else might have known about it, but that didn't mean it wasn't possible.

"Jethro assured me the cargo would be safe on the journey, given the pod's stealth mode. He warned me in his last message that the tracker would only start flashing on my monitors once it was a certain distance from Vysanthe, to keep the location of the sample's origin a secret. So, I was delighted when it *did* begin to flash, just under a week ago. Given my current need to rally troops,

I couldn't spare any to go on a lengthy mission after it, figuring the pod would come to me in good time. Each evening, I would trace its path, and delight at the thought of its arrival. But then, it stopped, and it hasn't started again." She sighed irritably. "As you can imagine, this has brought me no end of frustration—these things are usually so reliable, which is why it is beyond me how the pod has managed to disappear off the face of the universe."

I shrugged. "I... I can't help you, Your Highness. I don't know anything about a tracker, and I don't know anything about the pod's disappearance. Do you at least know where it went missing?" I asked. If someone had taken the pod, I wanted to know where they had snatched it from.

She frowned. "Somewhere out in the Severn Quarter, close to the Ferrite System. But, that's beside the point. I want you to tell me what you know about this blood sample before I start going off on any wild-goose chases," she demanded, her friendly tone all but gone. It was clear she had run out of patience.

I thought about lying to the queen, but knew it would do nothing to help me gain her trust. Right now, we needed that more than keeping the pod's secret, especially if it had gone missing somewhere in the depths of space. Navan and I could worry about that later, once we were away from the confines of Vysanthe... *If* we ever got away.

"The sample... It *is* from my home planet," I finally replied. "But I'm telling the truth when I say I don't know anything about the pod going missing, or the tracker suddenly disappearing. Is the Ferrite System far from here?"

Queen Brisha frowned. "Just under a fortnight from here."

That seemed a long time compared to our journey from Earth

in the *Asterope*, but I had to remind myself that the queens didn't have the same advanced technology yet. "So, that's still a fair distance away?"

She nodded. "I suppose so."

"Well then, all I can say for certain is, if it vanished so far away from Vysanthe, it's highly unlikely that your sister intercepted it," I said. "From what I could gather while I was in the South, and from Navan's father, they are no further along with making a break-through in the immortality elixir. They don't have the right blood, and nobody has found any with potential... who hasn't switched to your side at the last minute," I said pointedly, letting her know I knew about Jethro, and the promises that had been made.

A wave of relief washed over Queen Brisha's face. "I suppose that does make sense. Only Jethro and I knew about the pod, aside from yourself and Navan, by the looks of it. Perhaps I will send a small team after it to see what has become of it. Maybe it has simply malfunctioned."

I nodded. "That could be the case."

"Alternatively, you could tell me where to find your planet," she said suddenly. "I would only seek to take some samples—I would not interfere with, or harm, your people."

My stomach knotted. Neither queen was supposed to have technology advanced enough to travel the distance to Earth yet, but once she knew my planet's location, I had no doubt that she'd pour all her resources into ship development, and it would only be a matter of time before she cracked it. If Jethro and Orion's group had, others could.

I shook my head, trying to remain calm and choose my words carefully. "With all due respect, Your Highness... I'm not going to tell you where my home planet is. I trust you, and I believe you when you say you would only take samples, but I can't risk others finding out its location. I'm worried about the coldbloods who might be watching you, just as you are watching them. Imagine if I told you where my home planet was and you set out for it. Within minutes, your sister could have put a tail on your ships. You said it yourself—she's paranoid and on the edge of madness. She will do anything to seize ultimate power, and that includes going to extreme lengths to obtain the immortality elixir first."

"I will worry about my sister. Just tell me where your home planet is," Queen Brisha pressed. I could tell I was testing her patience, but I felt I had firm ground to stand on. Everything I'd said was true... except for the part where I said I trusted her. These sisters *were* embroiled in a constant game of one-upmanship. Of course Gianne would follow wherever Brisha went, out in the universe.

I sighed wearily. "Your Highness, you of all people must under-stand the idea of loyalty to one's home planet, the desire to protect one's people. Surely you can understand why telling you might not end too well for my species? Coldbloods are ravagers and plunderers—you move from planet to planet, taking what isn't yours and leaving chaos in your wake. You wipe out resources so you can take them for your own needs," I said, unable to prevent the words from tumbling out. I had been harboring them for a long time. "You don't care about those you take from—and in this instance, that resource *is* my people."

Queen Brisha's eyes glittered with anger. "You know nothing of our people, little Kryptonian," she snapped.

"I know enough, Your Highness," I countered, trying to main-

tain my cool. "However, it seems you're mistaking my intention—
I'm just trying to point out why telling you where my planet is
would be a disaster. I still want to prove myself to you."

This seemed to surprise Brisha, her features softening at the
revelation. Instead of fury, hope sparkled in her eyes.

"What do you suggest?" she asked, leaning forward.

I sucked in a deep breath, knowing that what I was about to
say was insane, but the queen had backed me into a horribly tight
corner, and in this moment I didn't feel I had any other choice.
"Instead of revealing my planet's location to you... why don't I give
you a sample of my own blood? The same blood Jethro was
sending to you."

A broad smile stretched across Queen Brisha's face, her eyes
positively glittering with excitement. "An excellent alternative,
Riley," she said softly. "As I suspected, you're far cleverer than you
look. Stay here while I get one of my guards to fetch a medic—
there's no time like the present for an extraction!"

As Queen Brisha headed for the door, I felt my heart shrink to
the size of a pea. I'd *had* to offer her something valuable to divert
her attention from Earth's location, and giving her a small sample
of my blood was a million times better than telling her where to
find my planet, but I was terrified where this would lead. For all I
knew, that small sample could release a horde of immortal coldbloods on the universe. Regular coldbloods already caused so
much damage; it didn't bear thinking about how much harm
immortal ones would bring.

The medic arrived two minutes later, accompanied by the
queen. He was a short, slim coldblood with a pair of sallow wings

that hung limply at his back. He carried a bag under his arm as he approached me.

"This is the subject," Queen Brisha said, gesturing toward me. "I'd like you to take a sample of her blood."

The medic nodded. "How much, Your Highness?"

"A vialful," she replied.

"Very good, Your Highness," he mumbled, before moving toward me.

As he lifted a dampened cloth that smelled intensely of chemicals to the side of my neck, I was reminded of Jethro drawing blood from me. He'd done it with his fangs—they must have been able to suck up blood like syringes—and I hoped this old guy wasn't about to use the same method.

As he pulled out a hypodermic needle from his bag, I realized that he wasn't.

I also realized that this was actually happening. Really, truly happening. A Vysanthean queen was finally obtaining my blood.

Even though my heart was pounding, every fiber of my being begging to pull away, I sat still, allowing the medic to cleanse the side of my neck. He lifted his needle to the fragile flesh. Without warning, he sank it into my skin, and I felt the scrape of it, though it lasted only a moment. An unpleasant pulling sensation rippled up the veins in my neck, and then, barely a minute later, it was done.

"Take that to the alchemists, will you?" Queen Brisha instructed, as the medic shoved his tools into his bag. He was careful with the vial of my blood, placing it into a secret pocket, hidden in the bag's lining.

"I'll do it right away, Your Highness," he promised, giving a nervous little bow before scurrying out of the library.

Queen Brisha sank back down into the chair opposite me, a pleased look on her face. "That was a very brave thing you did, Riley," she said softly. "And I, for one, am extremely grateful."

"How long will it take until you can use it?" I asked, my throat raw.

She shrugged. "That depends on how long it takes my alchemists to synthesize it. Naturally, each new species is its own beast when it comes to blood and how we coldbloods absorb it. But I estimate... hm, several weeks. My alchemists' processes are thorough."

Several weeks? Then maybe, just maybe, that gave us a window of opportunity. I wasn't sure where we would go from here—I needed to talk to Navan and tell him about what I'd done—but knowing we had some time, more time than I'd expected, gave me a flicker of hope. It wasn't much, but I was grateful for it.

Because at this point, I needed all the hope I could get.

$\mathcal{A}$fter the meeting with Queen Brisha, Pandora returned to escort me to the chambers that had been arranged for Navan and me. They were situated at the top of the third tower of the palace, overlooking the glistening city below. The room was plush and elegant, with red velvet chairs and a brocade chaise longue in front of a roaring fire. To one side, there was a four-poster with gauzy, golden fabric hanging down and shrouding the comfy-looking bed. To the other, there was a small kitchenette, which had been fully stocked with vials as well as food I could eat. There were fruits and vegetables of various forms, and hopefully none would kill me.

I supposed it was the queen's way of welcoming us to the North. Lying down on the bed, I was glad of the soft mattress beneath me sapping away the aches and pains of the last few days.

It appeared to be the only plus side of Queen Brisha's arrangement. At least here, Navan and I didn't have to hide our relation-ship. She knew about it and didn't seem to mind. In fact, she seemed intrigued by the forbidden nature of our love.

Navan arrived about half an hour later, just as I was drifting off to sleep, comforted by the roaring flames and the soft bedding. His entrance stirred me, and I sat up, taking in the sight of his bandaged arm. At least he wasn't bleeding anymore, and there was a delirious, playful quality to his face—which I guessed had some-thing to do with Vysanthean painkillers.

"Navan, how are you feeling?" I asked, getting up to go over to him.

"Fine," he replied with a crooked smile.

"They give you something for the pain?" I teased, though my heart wasn't in it. My mind was elsewhere, thinking about what I had done and how Navan was going to react. I could still feel the sharp sting of the needle where it had pricked my neck.

"Oh yes. They gave me soren root," he explained, as if that was supposed to mean something to me.

"What's that?"

"Painkiller. Think they might have given me a bit too much." A goofy laugh bubbled up from his throat, forcing a genuine smile to my lips. Taking his hand, I led him over to the couch and sat him down, feeling regretful that I would have to burst his happy bubble with my news. Before I could speak, however, he cut in. "I've spoken with Bashrik," he said, a deranged smile on his lips as his eyes struggled to focus.

I frowned in surprise. "Already?"

"Why yes." He nodded. "I had some time in the infirmary,

thought I'd put it to good use. That brawny woman gave me her comm device." He started absently picking at the edges of his bandages, and I reached out to remove his hand, keeping it firmly in mine to prevent him from unraveling the whole thing. I presumed by "brawny woman" he meant Pandora.

"What did Bashrik say?" I asked in disbelief. Everything was happening so fast.

"Says he's on his way." Navan sighed, collapsing back into the comfortable cushions of the loveseat.

My eyes bugged. "He's on his way?! How... How can he be on his way?"

"He and Ronad managed to intercept a rebel coldblood ship. Won't be long until old Bashie gets here to build a big lab that will ruin everything." Another stupid laugh pealed from his throat.

"What about the others?" I asked, gripping his shoulders and trying to shake some sense into him.

"Ronad's staying on Earth. He's no longer a coldblood, remember? Can't have him coming to Vysanthe—a coldblood with no wings, imagine that!" He heaved a sigh. "Wish I was back there with him. I like Earth."

"What about Angie and Lauren?" I pressed, feeling a twist of guilt in my stomach. I'd left them to cover for me, and I couldn't help feeling like I'd abandoned them. I couldn't even begin to explain how much I missed them. I just wanted to see their faces again, even for a moment, to get a grip on reality again. Being here, it was easy to think I might never return home—especially now, under the watchful eye of Queen Brisha.

"Didn't say." Navan shrugged. "But you know what else I like?"

he added softly, his gaze filling with such adoration I thought my heart might melt.

"What?" I murmured.

"You," he announced, sitting up to take me in his arms. He was smiling, his hands reaching up to cup my face, before his lips grazed mine. His mouth tasted oddly metallic, with a hint of sweetness—the soren root, I guessed, praying the trace wouldn't affect me too. Not wanting to get too carried away, especially given what I had to tell him, I pulled away slowly, keeping my arms around his neck. "Hey, come back," he said, chuckling as he tried to lean in to kiss me once more.

Gently, I pushed his shoulders back. I had to get my news out of the way.

"There's something I have to tell you," I said. Now was probably a better time than ever, with him in his slightly muddled state —hopefully it would soften the blow.

"Is it how much you want to use those herbs on the bedside table and let me have my wicked way with you? I can work around this," he chuckled, nodding toward his strapped arm as he stroked my cheek with the thumb of his good hand.

I frowned. "Herbs?"

He nodded. "Spotted them as soon as I walked in. Queen Brisha must have left them for us, the little minx. They'll keep us safe if we decide to... you know." He winked, though the soren root had addled his coordination, causing both eyelids to flicker at once. I stifled a laugh, flushing.

I glanced toward the bedside table and saw a crystal bowl filled to the brim with the herbs he was speaking about. I blushed harder. I'd thought they were some sort of Vysanthean potpourri, not a coldblood contraceptive. But now wasn't the time. Aside from the fact that I had grave news to deliver, I didn't want our first time to be while Navan was under the influence of painkillers—I had no idea if he'd even remember it.

Holding back Navan's advances once more, I shook my head. "No, it has to do with what Queen Brisha and I discussed while you were at the infirmary... Navan, I did something bad." I lifted his chin so he was forced to look directly at me. For a moment, his woozy façade faded, his eyes coming into focus, his brow furrowed in concentration.

"What... What happened?"

"I gave her my blood," I said quietly, the words stinging as I uttered them aloud. "She knew about the pod and its contents, but Jethro wouldn't tell her where it came from. The only problem is, the pod has gone missing somewhere near the Ferrite System, and she wanted to know what I knew about it. I couldn't lie to her, not if we wanted to gain her trust. So I offered her something I knew would prove our loyalty—a sample of my blood to make up for the one that never arrived." I pulled down the neck of my shirt to show him the needle mark in my flesh.

For a long time, he said nothing. However, I could see from his expression that the effects of the soren root had all but disappeared in the face of my news. It would have sobered up an alcoholic on a three-day binge.

"Can you say something, Navan?" I muttered, squeezing his good hand in mine.

"I just... I... can't believe you did that," he whispered, his brow knotted in a disturbed frown. "I understand she backed you into a corner, but... what's the point of any of this, if you've just gone and given them what they want? What was the point in me trying to keep Earth safe, if you've handed it to them on a silver platter? She won't stop at one meager sample, Riley. Once she finds out it works, she'll want more, and she'll torture you until she gets the answer she's after!"

I sighed, knowing this reaction was inevitable. "I would rather give her some of my blood now, than give away Earth's location. Those were my two options, Navan. When she wants more, then... I'll just have to deal with that when the time comes." I noticed I didn't say "if", because the thing was, I knew Navan was right. One sample wouldn't satisfy Queen Brisha, not if the synthesized blood worked in completing the immortality elixir's full potential.

He swallowed hard, then went silent for another minute. "You bought yourself and your planet a bit of time... nothing more," he said finally, frustration drawing deep lines in his forehead. "As for the missing pod, let's just hope it's fallen into the hands of someone who doesn't know what they've got. We could do with a break, right about now," he added sourly.

"I'm sorry, Navan," I muttered. "If I'd seen any other way, I would have taken it." I could see he was angry—not at me, but at the situation—though there wasn't a lot more I could say.

"I'm going to bed. This has been one hell of a day," he grumbled, getting up off the seat and moving over to the bed. He lay down on the left side, his back facing what would be my side of the bed.

I followed a short while after, curling up into a fetal position next to him, though I didn't try to snuggle. I'd just dropped a bombshell on him, and he needed time and space to process it.

I turned my back on him and faced the opposite wall, my eyes falling on the bowl of special herbs by my bedside. I sighed and shut my eyes, trying to force my thoughts elsewhere, until finally sleep claimed me, bringing with it dreams of tangled limbs and missed opportunity.

35

*D*ays passed, with Navan still downhearted about the arrangement I'd made with Queen Brisha, as well as the prospect of Bashrik being dragged into this mess. Still, with so much time on our hands—between waiting for Bashrik to arrive, and waiting for the blood to be synthesized—we were given some freedom to explore Northern Vysanthe.

Pandora followed us everywhere we went, but she kept her distance, making it feel as though we were two tourists wandering around and seeing the sights. From time to time, we'd spot her in the crowds or at the corner of a street and remember we were being watched. Regardless, I was determined to find some enjoyment in this wretched place, and I was hell-bent on bringing Navan into the bubble of my enthusiasm too. I'd had enough of Mopey Navan.

"Look at these statues!" I cried, grabbing his hand and pulling him across a semi-crowded piazza to gaze at the frieze in the center. Dancing nudes twisted and turned atop a water fountain, raising their arms to the sky, their wings outstretched with such majesty it made my jaw drop.

He shrugged. "I've seen better."

"How about we stop for something to drink?" I suggested, moving toward a series of cafés that were set up around the piazza.

"You won't be able to drink anything," he replied morosely.

"Fine, how about we go to the botanical gardens and see some of those twisty fish you like so much?"

"I don't think they have any," he said stubbornly.

I rolled my eyes and beckoned to Pandora, who approached us through the throngs of coldbloods. "Pandora, can you please take us to the botanical gardens?"

"Of course, though I don't think they're open today," she replied.

"Is there any way we could still visit them?" I asked sweetly. Normally I wouldn't have pushed for it, but I needed to thwart Navan's negativity. I cast a discreet glance in his direction, and she seemed to catch on.

"Umm... All right. I'll let them know you're the queen's guests —it shouldn't be a problem," she said, restoring a little bit of my faith in this alien species.

That was something I'd noticed about the coldbloods in Northern Vysanthe in general. They didn't treat us as pariahs, nor did I have to wear a hood to fit in. I could wander around as I pleased, holding Navan's hand if I wanted to. Aside from a few odd looks, they let us be, some of them uttering a casual "hello" or a pleasant "good morning". Indeed, nobody seemed frightened or morose here. It was a million miles away from Southern Vysanthe, where everyone appeared to be frightened of their own shadow and a smile was a definite no-no.

Here, life seemed to be a little slower, a little happier, a little brighter.

At the botanical gardens, they let us in without needing much coercion, leaving us free to walk around the glass-domed structure and marvel at the bright flora and the creatures that fluttered about the place. As a strange butterfly with see-through wings and an albino body passed my shoulder, I jerked back. Navan caught me before I fell into the fishpond behind me.

"It's just a butterfly," he said, a flicker of amusement on his face.

"I thought it might have been one of those... hurty butterflies, or whatever they were called," I said sheepishly, though I was secretly glad to be back in Navan's arms.

"Horerczy butterflies," he corrected, his tone warming. "But no, that is just an Arcan butterfly—they come from the hot springs of our moon, Arcan."

"Is that why it's so hot in here?" I asked, feeling flushed. There was a humidity in the air that made it difficult to breathe, like sucking syrup through a straw.

He nodded. "Nothing in here could grow without this heat."

As we strolled around some more, he kept his arm around my shoulder, my body nestled into his. Tenderly, he placed a kiss on top of my head, and I knew he was on his way to recovery. He couldn't stay depressed forever.

At the edge of a vast pond, we watched the skeletal fish Navan loved so much twist and turn beneath the water's surface, and his expression grew wistful. Here, he turned and lifted my chin, pressing his lips to mine. He kissed me slowly, his hands trailing through my hair before resting at the sides of my face.

"I'm sorry I've been a jerk," he whispered, parting our lips.

I brushed my fingers against his cheek. "Don't be. I get it. I know how hard you've worked to keep my species a secret, how much you've sacrificed..." He'd even taken *lives* for the sake of keeping my planet safe. To suddenly learn that all of it might have been in vain was a crushing blow, and it only deepened my affection for him to see how much he cared. He might be a coldblood, but there was a humanity to him that was greater than most humans' I knew back on Earth.

The emotion welled up in me as I leaned into him again, catching his lips in mine and pulling myself flush against his chest. I kissed him softly, tenderly, wanting him to feel how much he'd come to mean to me, until movement to our right distracted me.

We drew apart to see Pandora passing our way. Instantly, an embarrassed expression crossed her features.

"I'm sorry to interrupt," she murmured. "Shall we... um... head back to the palace for lunch?"

I could have stayed in Navan's arms much longer, but my stomach was growling. Navan and I glanced at each other, and then he nodded, as if he'd read my thoughts. "Yes, let's head back," he said, taking my hand.

With a relieved expression on her face, Pandora took the lead, guiding us on the invigorating walk back to the palace.

In the hallway, however, she turned. "Would you mind if I left you to find the dining room on your own? Ask one of the guards if you get lost—there is something urgent I must attend to," she explained.

"Not a problem," Navan said.

"Thank you," she replied solemnly, before disappearing into the belly of the palace, leaving us alone.

Before we could enjoy the solitude, something moved out of the corner of my eye, causing me to whirl around sharply. A masked figure had slipped out from behind a pillar and was making a beeline for us. Navan immediately stepped in front of me, his eyes narrowed.

"Bashrik?" he whispered in disbelief, as the figure came to a halt in front of us.

It shook its head, gesturing to a room three doors along on our right. We glanced uncertainly at each other, but curiosity got the better of us both. We hurried through the door he'd pointed to, into an annex on the other side. The figure locked the door behind itself before turning to us. A moment later, it removed the mask.

It was a lycan. And not just any lycan...

"Galo?!" I gasped, in utter disbelief. How could he be here? The last time I'd seen him he'd been deep in rebel territory, with little hope of escape.

The elderly lycan smiled tightly, an oddly sullen expression in his lime-green eyes. Whereas before his lined face had been bright and relaxed, his gaze twinkling with some untold joke, now it sagged, as if it bore a heavy weight.

"Indeed," he muttered.

I frowned. This wasn't the Galo I remembered.

"What are you doing here? How did you find us?" Navan asked, his eyes narrowed and glinting with suspicion.

"It wasn't difficult," Galo replied. "I found a way to sneak into Vysanthe's orbit and simply followed the trail of chaos. As fortune would have it, I picked up Queen Brisha's transmission to you and improvised from there," he added, with a shrug.

Navan frowned. "That makes no sense, but even if that were true, what are you doing here? The Fed have no purpose here."

Galo smiled, a hint of sadness creeping into his eyes. "I bring a message from Orion." There was a note of remorse in his voice, a flicker of the old Galo shimmering beneath the cold, strange surface.

I felt a chill run down my spine. "Orion?" I gasped, utterly confused.

Galo nodded. "Now that the situation has changed, Orion's demands have duly adapted. Since you have failed to deliver on the previous information he asked for, he has decided that he would like something else instead—you must steal any and all of the immortality elixir research from Queen Brisha, and send what you find straight back to him." He paused, dragging in a heavy breath. "He says that if you don't comply with his wishes, he will kill off humans one by one, on Earth... starting with your parents. You have one month to complete this task, before he begins his executions."

I felt as though he'd just punched me in the stomach. "My parents? H-How would he even find them? How did he find *us*?" I asked, breathless.

"I don't know exactly how he'd find your parents, but I have a feeling you don't want to test his skills when it comes to tracking people down," Galo said. "As for you... Orion didn't just implant a chip so that he could control you, Riley. He planted a tracking device in you, too, so he could follow your progression from the moment you both left for Vysanthe. He has been tracing your every move."

Realization dawned on me. Lazar had removed the chip that could end me, but he had willingly left the tracking device in there. I wasn't foolish enough to believe he knew nothing about it. Even if he hadn't known initially, after cutting me open he would have seen it. Anger bristled through my veins—I had known there was something amiss after the surgery. I had seen it on Lazar's face. I just hadn't known what it was, at the time. Guilt.

Furious at his actions, I felt stupid for not pressing the matter when I'd had the chance. True, Lazar didn't agree with Orion's violent methods of getting what he wanted, but Lazar still wanted the mission to succeed. Of course—it all made sense now. He didn't want me to be hurt by the chip for Navan's sake, but he still wanted Orion to be able to keep tabs on us. *That* was why he'd left the tracker in me.

"After all the trust I put in him," Navan hissed, his hands balling into fists. "If I ever see that traitorous lizard again... He won't get away with this!"

Galo glanced down at a watch on his wrist, and his face morphed into a mask of panic. "Drat," he breathed, the emotion in his voice returning him to a semblance of his former self. "Listen, Orion has me on a timer, and I have less time—much less time— left than I thought. You need to find one of the Fed outposts in deep space and warn them about Vysanthe's quest for immortality. Seek out allies, build a viable force that can take on the might of the coldbloods. Do this, or we are all destined for destruction!" He spoke rapidly, his eyes wide with alarm. "The star—" he began to add, but he was cut off mid-sentence. His body convulsed in violent spasms, his limbs flying out at all angles, his head snapping back as his eyes rolled into his head.

Blood filled his mouth, a sickening gurgle rising up his throat, before his knees buckled and his body crumpled to the floor. He stilled, his limbs splayed out unnaturally, his eyes suddenly glassy and blank.

"No," I gasped, hurrying to his side and kneeling by his head. I clutched him in my arms, shaking him hard. But as much as I willed it, he didn't come back to life.

I choked back a sob as Navan dropped down next to me. I hadn't known Galo very long, or very well, but I felt his loss more intensely than words could explain. He had been kind to me when no one else was. He had guided me through what were possibly the darkest hours of my life, when I'd been all alone, without even Navan to help me. Galo's voice had been there, steady and soothing. If it weren't for that old lycan, I wouldn't even be here today.

As I pulled his head up to hold him closer to me, I noticed the scars of three triangular dots on the side of his neck. I felt a hollow in the pit of my stomach. I knew those scars. I had the same ones. They couldn't be anything else.

"Oh, Galo," I whispered, tears pricking my eyes.

Orion had implanted a chip in him too. Even so, Galo had tried to give us a final warning, and it was up to us to make sure that it wasn't in vain.

*a*fter wrapping Galo's body in a curtain we dragged down from the window in the annex, and tying some weighty metal paperweights to his ankles, Navan picked him up. We managed to get away from the building unnoticed, and Navan carried him gently in his arms to the nearby lake that lay on the far side of the palace gardens, in the shade of the mountainside. Here, dark green, willow-like trees trailed the still water's surface with their spiny tendrils, and bug-eyed creatures crept from the darkness of the bordering woods to sip from the icy water.

With his mouth set in a grim line, Navan went toward the water's edge, his muscles flexing as he prepared to throw Galo's body into the dark liquid. I called out, stopping him.

"Wait!"

Navan turned anxiously. "Is someone coming?"

I shook my head. "I just... want to say goodbye," I said softly, tears rolling down my cheeks. I couldn't bear the idea of Galo alone under the water, with nobody saying a word over him. It didn't seem right that he wasn't surrounded by his kinsmen, being buried in the lycan way—whatever that was. Instead, he was here, on a planet that actively hated his kind, being tossed into a lake like a piece of garbage. I couldn't handle the grief, feeling it clench at my heart like a vise. He didn't deserve this. He was good, and kind, and gentle—and Orion had killed him.

Navan laid the lycan down on the bank and stepped back. He dipped his chin to his chest, his eyes closed in a private reverie.

I drew in a deep, shuddering breath. "I didn't know you very well, but you were always kind to me," I began, letting the words come. "You felt like a grandfather... It sounds silly, but that's how I saw you. I'm sorry this has happened to you, and I'm sorry you're so far away from home. I know what that feels like. I... I hope you find your way back to people you have loved and lost, and I hope they are there to greet you with open arms. I hope you can rest now, and know that your life was not lost in vain. We will do what you asked. We will heed your warning—so you can rest in peace, Galo. As painful as those final moments must have been, we will make sure they were worth living."

"You were a brave warrior, Galo," Navan spoke suddenly, taking me by surprise. "You will be avenged." It was a simple statement, but it was powerful. "Is there anything else you want to say?" he asked, turning to me.

I shook my head. "No, I think I've said everything," I said quietly, trying to keep myself together.

With a nod, Navan picked Galo's body up once more, and waded into the icy lake. Once he was up to his chest, he let go of Galo, the lycan's body resting on the surface for a moment before it floated down below the surface, never to rise again. I watched as the dark water enveloped him, forcing myself to remember this moment, no matter how painful it was. It would spur me on in times to come, when things got difficult. I had to believe that.

As Navan re-emerged from the water, I wrapped my arms around him, not caring that he was soaking wet. His body was bitterly cold, but still I clung to him, pressing my face into the curve of his neck, wanting to feel the comfort of him. He held me tightly, laying a tender kiss on my forehead.

"I just can't believe he's dead," I whispered.

"I know," Navan murmured against my hair. "Even when you don't deliver the killing blow yourself, the ghosts can still haunt you." He sighed. "I know Ianthan's ghost still haunts me."

It had been a long time since I'd thought about Ianthan, not realizing how much his death might have affected someone like Navan. The more I got to know him, the more human he began to seem. I barely noticed the ashen skin anymore, and he'd rarely had the opportunity to spread his wings since we'd arrived on Vysanthe. His grief was etched across his face. The two of them had been friends, after all, before Ianthan allowed himself to be swayed by his father's endeavors.

"You cared about him a lot," I observed softly.

He nodded. "He was my best friend—someone I thought would always be there, would always have my back. That doesn't go away, even through betrayal." He exhaled, his eyes taking on a faraway look. "I miss him."

"I'm sorry," I said, tightening my hold around his waist, as both of us stared out toward the placid water, where Galo's body now lay.

I wondered what the pair of them used to do together, before life got in the way. They'd known each other for a long time—through all the firsts, no doubt. It made me smile to think of the two of them as coldblood kids, flapping about and causing trouble. Still, it didn't seem like Navan wanted to say any more on the subject, so I left it. His pain was tangible.

"What are we going to do about Orion?" I asked, changing the subject. The icy chill of fear returned as I recalled his threat. *My parents. He said he would hunt down my parents.*

Navan's eyes grew steely. "We should listen to Galo, but we're going to have to play the long game while we're stuck here in the North," he said bitterly. "There will be no escape with Queen Brisha watching us. At least, not for the time being."

"What, so we report back to that monster?" I spat, hating Orion with every cell in my body.

"For now," Navan replied. "We can start small, feed little pieces of information back to Orion that don't really help him out. While we're doing that, we can think of a way to get out of here, to fulfil what Galo told us to do."

I nodded. "Will the Fed in deep space be easier to persuade than the ones on Earth?" I asked, remembering how reluctant they had been.

He shrugged. "Different factions are run by different species. If we can find a more proactive headquarters, we might have a shot. They need to be powerful, too, if we're going to amass allies in our fight against all those who would see the immortality elixir completed."

I thought about the final words the lycan had tried to get out, before the chip had cut him off so brutally. He had been about to say something important, I was certain of it.

"What do you think Galo was trying to say?" I murmured.

He shook his head, his face perplexed. "I've been wondering the same thing, but I can't come up with anything. He might have been about to give us a location, or coordinates, or something useful... I can't say, honestly. I wish I had the answers."

"Me too." I grimaced, hating that it had come to this. "And now... we continue to be pawns in this intergalactic power play."

"Until we can come up with something else," Navan said. "Once we have another viable option to get out of here and get to a Fed base, we go for it. It will happen—it's just a matter of time."

I tried to take comfort in his words as we returned to the palace, knowing that people would likely have started to look for us. Pandora had left us over an hour ago, and since we hadn't turned up for lunch, I had a feeling we'd been missed. I just hoped Pandora didn't get in trouble for our absence—she was growing on me. She didn't say much, but there was a steady strength to her that I warmed to.

However, as we arrived back at the palace, seeking out the dining room, it appeared they had bigger things to worry about than a few missing defectors. We had only reached as far as the grand hall, with its sweeping chandeliers and marble floor, the cream color threaded through with veins of gold, when we came across a large group of Queen Brisha's soldiers. They were crowded around something—or someone—though I couldn't make out who or what.

I did, however, recognize Bashrik, who was standing in front of

Queen Brisha, flanked by two armed guards, his face animated, his hands gesturing wildly.

"I didn't bring them deliberately, Your Highness!" he shouted, stepping away from the tip of a crackling pike. "I didn't even know they were on board. I'm not even sure *how* they got on board!"

"Bashrik," Navan breathed in surprise, and I frowned, wondering what was going on. Apparently, Bashrik's ship had arrived while we'd been by the lake, and, despite his invitation to come here, things seemed far from cordial.

"You expect me to believe they are stowaways?" Queen Brisha asked. "You expect me to believe that two inferior creatures managed to sneak past you and get aboard your ship, without you realizing? You've been traveling for days, have you not?"

Bashrik nodded reluctantly. "I have, but—"

"So, explain to me how they have not wasted away from thirst and starvation? What, did they sneak past you again, and rummage through your supplies? I am no fool, Bashrik. I will not be lied to."

"Look, I'm not lying, Your Highness!" Bashrik exclaimed. "I don't know how they did it, but somehow they have. If I had known about them, I would *never* have told your border control agents that I was alone on the ship—I would have declared them as passengers. I know how stringent your security checks are!"

Just then, the circle of soldiers broke slightly, allowing me a glimpse of the figures within. My heart sank. Angie and Lauren were sitting on the floor in the center of the armed guards, their faces terrified, their hands covering their heads, as though they expected the soldiers to strike them at any moment.

I rushed forward, shoving the guards aside to get to my friends.

The guards, however, had other ideas. They pushed me back roughly, sending me flying backward, and I landed in an awkward heap on the floor.

"Don't touch her!" Navan yelled at the guards, as he helped me to my feet.

Instantly, Queen Brisha's attention switched to us. A look of surprise passed over her features, her eyes curious. Slowly, she descended the stairs where she was standing, and came toward us. She placed a gentle hand on my shoulder, flashing me a concerned glance.

"Are you hurt?" she asked.

I shook my head. "No, Your Highness. Only, I know these girls —they're my friends. If Bashrik said he didn't put them on the ship, then I believe him. If you'd just let me speak with them, I'll find out what happened," I pleaded, trying to keep the panic out of my voice. If Angie or Lauren said a word about where they were really from, we were doomed. I had to get to them before Queen Brisha had the chance to probe them.

She paused for a moment, thinking. "No need. Your 'friends' have already told us their tale... though they refused to tell me which planet they have come from—which, perhaps, I should have expected after your own caginess." I let out a soft sigh of relief, while she gave me a pointed look. "Your 'friends' informed us that they snuck aboard Bashrik's ship, which was why Bashrik didn't declare them, but I didn't believe them. I do not like surprise guests in the North—even guests as interesting as Kryptonians— and I was concerned about why Bashrik would lie to me about them. Naturally, if he is to join our fold, I need to be able to trust him. Now that I hear confirmation from your lips, however, I am more inclined to think he is telling the truth..." The queen paused, casting a long, intense look over at Bashrik, before returning her eyes to me. "Saying that, my rules change for no one. If your friends are going to stay, they will have to prove their loyalty to me. And I think you already know exactly what I will ask of them, given their refusal to tell me the location of your planet."

An amused glimmer flashed in her silver eyes, and my stomach dropped.

"I require samples of their blood, so that I may synthesize them along with yours," she continued. "It will give us more to work with."

I nodded slowly. "A... fair exchange, Your Highness," I managed, knowing I had no other option but to agree. "But first, please allow us a few hours together, so they can recover from their long journey. If they have traveled this far without food and water, they will be too weak to have blood taken—even a small amount."

Queen Brisha smiled. "You are a smart one, aren't you?" she murmured, though I sensed it wasn't kindly meant. "Very well. Pandora, please escort our newcomers to suitable chambers."

"All of them, Your Highness?" Pandora asked, approaching as she glanced at our motley crew.

The queen nodded.

"Thank you, Your Highness," I said.

"I shall send for you and your friends later this evening, once they are rested," Queen Brisha promised, a hint of warning in her words.

I nodded. "Of course, Your Highness. I'll prepare them and make sure they know what's going on."

"See that you do, little Kryptonian... See that you do," she remarked. With that, she turned away, heading toward a door on the far side of the main hall. It slammed shut, the echo ricocheting in my ears, sending a shiver down my spine.

"If you would all join me," Pandora said, gesturing toward a different door.

With the help of Navan and Bashrik, I got Angie and Lauren up off the floor. Nobody spoke as we trailed after Pandora, who strode ahead at an uncomfortable speed. Navan and Bashrik didn't have a problem, but it was tough for us Kryptonians to keep pace, so she stopped every so often to allow us to catch up.

At last, Pandora deposited us in a vast apartment just as exquisite as the chambers Queen Brisha had given to Navan and me. There were several en-suite bedrooms branching off from a main lounge area, where comfy sofas had been arranged in front of a fireplace, and there was a kitchen and a main bathroom to one side. Bookshelves stood against the vibrant plum walls of the apartment, with countless leather spines facing outward, enticing the reader in. It saddened me that they would likely never get read.

"If you need anything, let me know," Pandora said kindly, before taking her leave. No doubt, she had matters to attend to with the queen after the kerfuffle that had just taken place. I was just glad Bashrik and my friends had arrived with their lives intact.

As Pandora left, an awkward silence descended on the room. I had yet to greet my friends properly, or even give them a hug, but still I hung back, feeling strange—it was weird to see them on Vysanthe, when they were supposed to be safe and sound at home. Secretly, a part of me wished they hadn't come. They were in danger here. Not only that, but they were putting us all in more danger too.

Then again, there was another part of me—a much larger part —that was thrilled to have them back. Seeing them again, I realized just how much I had missed them.

Angie walked up to the fireplace and turned around dramatically, her hands on her hips. "Well, is someone going to tell us what the heck has been going on, or are we going to stand around like dorks all day?"

*G*rinning, I rushed to greet my friends, throwing my arms around them and pulling them close.

"We thought we'd never see you again," Lauren said softly.

"We had no idea what had happened to you," Angie added, with a hint of a reprimand.

I smiled sadly. "I'm sorry, guys—it all happened so fast. I'm still not even sure *I* know what's going on, and I've been living it. But enough about me for a second. How are you two?" They had looked genuinely shaken by their run-in with the guards, and I wanted to make sure they were okay.

"It's all kind of a blur, to be honest," Lauren replied, pushing her purple glasses back up onto the bridge of her nose.

"Yeah, I seriously wasn't sure I'd come out of all that with dry pants," Angie said.

I smirked. "Let me know if you need a change of undies."

"Speaking of a change of undies," Bashrik interjected as he glared at Angie and Lauren, "what the hell were you two thinking? You almost got me killed!"

My friends suppressed a smile, sharing a conspiratorial glance.

"Sorry about that, Bash," Angie said, before turning to me. "After we got the call from Navan, it didn't seem right allowing Bashrik to leave us in Texas. I mean, what were we going to do? Sit around, twiddling our thumbs, while our best friend was stuck on a planet on the other side of the universe, and potentially in mortal danger? We would have gone insane. So, we made an executive decision."

"*Angie* made an executive decision," Lauren corrected. "I didn't have much choice in the matter."

"But aren't you glad you came?" Angie asked.

Lauren grimaced. "Ask me in a few days."

"As much as I hate to break up this charming reunion," Navan interrupted, "we really should brief you all on what has been going on before Queen Brisha sends for you again. We have a very fragile position here, and we've been forced to tell a few tales to ensure we didn't end up dead. So you're going to have to get up to speed pretty quickly. Bashrik, I know I told you some of what Queen Brisha wants from you, but you'll need to know the ins and outs of things, too. Hopefully by the end of this everyone will have the whole story instead of little fragments."

Bashrik nodded, though his sapphire eyes were still flashing with annoyance as he glanced across at Angie and Lauren. "I still can't believe you snuck on board my ship," he muttered.

"No harm done though, right?" Angie said sweetly.

He scowled. "I'm sending you my medical bills."

Navan coughed, diverting everyone's attention, and I sat beside him, my hand on his. Once the whole group had gathered on the sofas, he began to tell the tale of what had brought us here. He told them all about the failed rescue attempt at the hidden rebel compound, and the promise we'd had to make to get out of there alive, which had led us to Vysanthe. I chimed in here and there, and together, we explained all about the chip, the undercover operation to garner intel for Orion on Queen Gianne's queendom, and our escape over the border into Northern Vysanthe.

"Hence the arm," Navan noted, lifting his bandaged limb.

"I was wondering about that," Bashrik noted. "It's not like you to get injured."

"A lucky shot, nothing more," Navan retorted.

Ignoring their brotherly banter, I pressed on, explaining Queen Brisha's rules, and the need for outsiders to prove themselves. Here, we got to the grim part. Looking at Angie and Lauren, I went into detail about the blood and what she expected of them. Predictably, their faces twisted up in disgust.

"I hate needles." Lauren shuddered.

"Yeah, and I'm not letting some nasty grayskin near me with something pointy!" Angie said.

Bashrik flashed her a look. "I've asked you not to call us that."

She sighed. "I didn't mean *you*. I meant the evil ones who want to take our blood."

"Even so, could you not?" Bashrik remarked frostily. Not waiting for her response, he turned to Navan. "What about the pod with the blood sample in it? Do we know where it is?"

"Vanished," Navan replied. "It had a tracker inside it, programmed to start flashing only when it reached a certain point, to keep the location of Earth secret, but the beacon went dead a few days ago outside the Ferrite System."

Bashrik frowned. "Weird."

Navan nodded. "Very weird. We just have to hope it's broken down, or has been snatched up by someone who just wants the parts."

"Do we really have to have our blood taken?" Lauren asked, bringing us back to the matter at hand.

Before I could answer, alarms erupted all around us, the sound piercing through my eardrums with a deafening shriek. It screamed in a very particular pattern, starting quieter before reaching earsplitting levels of loudness. Navan and Bashrik looked at each other, fear paling their faces. Lauren and Angie were looking at me like I ought to know what the sound meant, but I was just as confused as they were. The only thing I *did* know was that I had never seen Navan so frightened. He was truly rattled, his eyes wide in panic.

"What's going on?" I asked frantically.

"It can't be…" Navan whispered.

"Navan, what is it?!" I pressed, grabbing him by the face and forcing him to look at me.

"They're air-raid sirens," Bashrik hissed before Navan could reply. "We're being attacked!"

A second later, Pandora burst through the door, wielding two crackling sabers in her hands. On her back, she had two silver rifles, and at her hips were four silver pistols, flanked by pockets of ammo. She looked intense, to say the least, but I knew she might be just the woman to get us the hell out of here.

"Follow me!" she roared, before darting out of the door again.

We ran after her, Navan suddenly returning to himself as he sprinted out of the room and down the hallway, following Pandora's lead.

She took us to the end of the corridor, pausing in front of what looked like an ordinary wall. Bracing herself, she heaved a booted foot against the surface of the wall, kicking it with all her might. Something finally gave with a deafening crack. The wall crumbled, revealing the shape of a door that had been concealed by a layer of plaster. It was ajar, and Pandora slammed her shoulder against it, pushing it wide open.

"This way!" she bellowed, disappearing through the doorway.

It led to a series of winding staircases, which we thundered down, the rickety metal frame trembling beneath our weight. My heart was pounding as we hurried farther and farther down into the darkness, the way lit only by the dim glow of emergency lighting that clung weakly to the slick walls of the secret passageway.

After what seemed like a lifetime of running down stairs, we emerged in a brightly lit cavern. My eyes blinked furiously, getting accustomed to the light again, and I realized we were in an underground bunker, deep beneath the foundations of the palace. It was gargantuan in size and hewn from the rock itself, much like the hangar in Queen Gianne's realm, but there were no ships docked here.

Instead, there were hordes of military personnel running around, barking orders. Others sat in front of glowing blue screens, watching a series of images and camera feeds while their fingers danced across smaller screens laid flat on their desks. They were jotting down what they saw, I realized. Where we would have had a keyboard, they had these small screens instead.

It was then that I understood what this place was—we were in a command center. This was the hub of security activity for Queen Brisha's queendom. I gawked at the extent of her military operation. No wonder she knew so much. There were cameras everywhere, watching everything.

I turned as I heard the queen's voice shouting above everyone else's. She was dressed in black military fatigues, her hair swept back in a bun, her silver eyes moving between the enormous screens that hung from the ceiling of the cavern. Although she spoke with authority and intense volume, her voice was calm, her manner even more so. Every movement she made, and every word she spoke, was carefully deliberated—I could see it in her face. I had never seen a woman more powerful and awe-inspiring, staring at her where she stood giving orders atop a marble plinth. Even Pandora paled in comparison, and I had just watched her kick a wall down.

"Evacuate Lyceum, Vergar, and Nocta to the community bunkers!" she boomed, her mighty voice carrying across the length and breadth of the enormous underground chamber. "Rygel, Horvat, and Scahva can follow. Get every civilian out, now! Send the cargo ships to pick up any remaining civilians in the villages and hamlets surrounding the cities. Take anyone who is left and get them to the nearest bunkers!"

Up on the screens, I watched as a fleet of military ships took off from various hangars dotted around Northern Vysanthe. In other images, I saw soldiers and pilots sprinting around loading bays, gearing up their vessels for the fight ahead. Enormous troops of infantry marched into the bellies of gigantic gunships, where they strapped themselves in, the metal doors left open. In a moment of panic, I wondered how they would get down to the ground to fight... and then I remembered. They had wings. Perhaps they didn't even fight on the ground at all.

Beside the large blue screens that were hanging down from the ceiling was another large screen, though this one was tinted red. On it, I could see the approach of Queen Gianne's ships, her colors —black and red—streaked onto the outside of the vessels. They swarmed like a great metal mob, coming forward in seemingly endless numbers, with more ever-present on the southern horizon.

Palace staff were being ushered through several doors that branched out from the main command center, before being herded toward a large section at the back of the cavern, which held rows upon rows of small wooden huts.

It seemed like Queen Brisha had been preparing for this moment for a long time. But, although she was moving around her post with a calm demeanor, it was evident that this move had taken her by surprise. Even so, she was proving herself a worthy queen by getting her subjects out before the worst of the assault hit. Somehow, I doubted Queen Gianne would do the same.

Feeling as though I had just summoned the devil herself, Queen Gianne's face suddenly appeared on every screen at once, looming large above us. Her expression was a smug one. At the sight of her, Angie and Lauren huddled close to me, while Bashrik and Navan looked up, their faces showing their rage at what she was doing.

"Dear Sister, I'm very sad it has come to this," she purred

coldly, her voice booming through every speaker in the cavern. "Unfortunately, you have only yourself to blame for this attack. I'm afraid you have forced my hand."

Queen Brisha pressed a button on her wrist, causing a small screen to flicker up with her face on it. "Whatever makes you sleep better at night, Sister, knowing how many innocents you have slaughtered for the sake of your own paranoid delusions," she retorted bitterly, though she was doing an impressive job of keeping her cool.

Queen Gianne glowered. "This is all on you, Brisha. I could have continued to keep the peace, but then you spurned our species by giving asylum to criminals like Navan Idrax and his little pet. You are not fit to wear a crown, Sister. You have lost your way—you have lost *our* way of living. What are we, if our race is not the most superior in the universe? If you spoil the blood by mixing species, where are we going to end up? No, Sister, I will not allow it. This is all on you."

"You don't know what you're talking about, Gianne," Brisha said evenly. "I rule with a fair hand instead of an iron fist, and my people love me for it. *Your* people wish to dethrone you because they are terrified of you. You're running scared, and you're lashing out—you've done it all your life. Now, if you would just come to the palace and talk to me, I'm sure we can figure this out without the need for bloodshed."

But it was clear Queen Gianne was way past that. There was a mania in her eyes that terrified the living daylights out of me.

"I can see them!" Queen Gianne said sharply, her finger jabbing at the screen. "Those traitorous cretins! And... Bashrik Idrax?! The whole family is rotten! See, you let defectors and traitors into your midst! You shelter them. You aren't fit to be queen!"

I glanced at Navan, feeling panic rise in my throat. Queen Brisha still thought that Navan and I had run to her because of our illicit romance, but if Queen Gianne were to expose us as traitors now, revealing our connection to the rebels, then it would all be over. This war between sisters wouldn't matter to us, because we wouldn't be alive to see it. Angie, Lauren, Bashrik... all of us would be doomed.

To my relief, Queen Gianne skipped over the details, choosing to simply call us every expletive under Vysanthe's sun. She stared straight at us with her enormous eyes, blown up to epic proportions on the screens in front of us, her rage palpable, even though she wasn't actually in the room.

"You think I'm not fit to be queen?" Queen Brisha scoffed. "Look at yourself. You're a quivering wreck. You think you can send every ship you have at us and hope to win, but there's no strategy there—there's no skill or intellect involved in anything you do. You rush in headfirst, cause a huge mess, then run off with your tail between your legs, leaving everyone else to clean up after you."

Queen Gianne looked like her head was about to explode. "How dare you," she breathed. "You've never even seen any action, because you don't take any risks—you're a coward, with your head always hidden in a book. Even your subjects think you're a pushover. They don't like you—they think you're weak!"

"Better a kind queen than an incompetent, mad one," Brisha shot back.

"You've always thought you were smarter than me, Sister, but we'll see about that," Gianne remarked, her eyes narrowing to almost reptilian slits. "You think you've got the upper hand when it comes to the immortality elixir, but you're wrong. It is slipping away from you as we speak. While you have been chatting away, I've been busy." She smirked. "We will see who wins this race, Sister."

A split second later, the video feed ended, the screens switching back to images of the fleets taking off and the townships that were coming under fire.

"I want security at maximum to prevent any more hacking!" Brisha demanded.

"No!" Navan suddenly bellowed.

Everyone in the cavern whirled to look at the screen his eyes had turned to. In the image, bombs were being dropped on a striking building, and I realized what it was. It was the only place Gianne could bombard that would hit Brisha where it hurt—her alchemy lab.

For a moment, Queen Brisha's cool, calm façade slipped. An almost innocent look of terror flickered across her face, her eyes burning with a bright rage. She recovered fast, turning to her military personnel.

"Why weren't those ships stopped once they got over the border?!" she roared. "Get them shot down, NOW!"

Her team jumped to action, barking orders through their comm devices to the military leaders and skilled pilots on the other end. On the screens, I watched as Brisha's ships maneuvered into position, blasting the enemy ships out of the sky... but the damage was already done. Blinking on a broken feed, I saw the remains of the alchemy lab, plumes of black smoke rising up from the debris. It was a pile of rubble now, nothing more.

Queen Brisha's eyes lingered on the image, her face contorting into a mask of pure hatred. "This is an act of war!" she cried. "We will retaliate, and we will be smart about it! We will use strategy, and we will show Gianne what true triumph looks like! We will not allow this to stand!" As she shouted, her team whooped and hollered below her.

Indeed, it seemed her sister was wrong—Brisha had the full support of her people, by the looks of things, and now she was mad.

"Bashrik!" she barked, taking him by surprise.

"Your Highness?" he replied, hurrying to meet her as she approached.

"The alchemy lab I require of you, in return for Navan's place in my realm, must be built a few weeks from now," she demanded. "I had hoped we might have months, to make it truly perfect, but as you can see... we don't."

Bashrik looked aghast. "A few weeks? That's impossible."

Queen Brisha glared at him. "Nothing is impossible, Bashrik."

He sighed, clearly not wanting to argue with the queen. "Well... I will do what I can. But I can't promise beauty, Your Highness."

"Then promise me practicality instead."

"That I can do, Your Highness," he replied.

With that, she turned to Navan. "My sister took me by surprise this time, but she will not get the chance to do that again. For that, I want your help," she said sternly. "I need more bodies on the ground. I need more soldiers, Idrax, and we're going to start with you. From this moment on, I am drafting you into my army. You are strong, you are fast, and you are smart—the perfect combination. I don't doubt that you will become a great leader one day, but you will begin with the rank of infantry soldier. Your training will start soon."

I gazed desperately in his direction, but his eyes were focused on Brisha. I could do nothing to stop this runaway train. It was out of my hands now—Brisha's word was final, but where did that leave us? With him drafted into the army, and Bashrik engaged in building the alchemy lab, how were we ever supposed to find a way to leave Vysanthe now?

*P*andora took us into a large hut at the side of the cavern, but I could barely speak as we made our way toward it. Navan put his arm around my shoulders, pulling me to him. I leaned against him, feeling dizzy. In the space of a few minutes, everything had changed, and I didn't know how to fix it. If Navan was being drafted into Queen Brisha's army, what did that mean for our plan?

The whole day felt surreal, and unbelievably long.

"I'm starving," Angie said as we entered the bare hut, breaking the tension.

"I'll fetch something you can all eat," Pandora said, before disappearing back out of the hut.

We sat around in silence, all of us entirely shell-shocked. I guessed this wasn't what Angie and Lauren had been expecting when they snuck to Vysanthe—for a bombing to break out just hours after they'd landed. I wanted to hug them tight, letting them know it was all going to be okay, but I couldn't. I didn't know that it would be.

When the food came—Pandora and a few servants bringing it in—we descended upon it, filling up plates of fruit and steaming root vegetables I didn't recognize. Angie and Lauren eyed it curiously, but I assured them that it was safe. Meanwhile, Bashrik and Navan approached a tray of warm bowls filled to the brim with a smoking red liquid, a look of confusion on their faces.

"What's this?" Navan asked Pandora.

"Ferakor blood stew," she explained. Whatever *that* meant.

They each curiously dipped a spoon into the mixture and lifted it to their lips. Apparently finding it not unpleasant, they began to eat, devouring the strange concoction. I guessed it wasn't what they were used to in the South.

As Pandora departed once more, we sat down on the wooden chairs that had been set up. Angie, Lauren, and I snatched up furry coats that Pandora had brought for us. Wrapping ourselves in them, we glanced nervously at one another. It appeared nobody wanted to be the first to speak, after the events of the day.

"What are we all going to do?" I asked, breaking the tense silence. Someone had to, and I couldn't bear another moment of it. "We can't just sit around doing nothing," I added, gesturing to Angie and Lauren.

Angie nodded. "I've been thinking about it... and I'd like to help with planning for the new alchemy lab. My dad's an architect, so I'm familiar with blueprints and architecture. I figure I could be of some use, and it'd be something I could keep myself distracted with," she explained, not addressing Bashrik directly.

Bashrik's eyes widened, and he shook his head sharply. "Um,

no. You'll only get in my way and slow me down. I can't afford any distractions—not when Queen Brisha wants it built in a few weeks."

"I used to help my dad with his projects all the time," Angie retorted. "I'm a good assistant when it comes to things like design, and I'm pretty handy, too. Trust me, I'm not saying this to get in your way—in case you think I'm *that* petty. Your job just happens to be where I'd do best, and hey, if I'm not useful, you can fire me."

"Give her a chance, Bashrik," Navan muttered, rubbing his temples, clearly not in the mood for arguments.

Bashrik pursed his lips. "Fine. Just don't start crying when I let you go."

Angie rolled her eyes. "Please. As if I'd shed a tear on you."

"Lauren?" I prompted, turning to my other friend.

She pushed her glasses back up onto the bridge of her nose. "I don't know," she said quietly. "I'd like to be useful, but I'm not as brave as the rest of you, and I don't have the physical strength you guys have, either... I'm honestly not sure where I can help." There was a sense of dejection in her voice, her gaze dropping to the floor.

I smiled, knowing exactly where Lauren might fit in. "The queen has a huge library. If you could get permission from her, you could help research more about the immortality elixir. I'm sure you could find something in there that nobody has found before—a different perspective, maybe? If anyone can find something new, it's you. You're the smartest girl I know."

A smile spread across Lauren's face, her eyes brightening behind the lenses of her specs. "Sure... I could do that. I'll read every damn book if I have to."

That only left me. Bashrik already had his work cut out for him, and I knew what Navan would end up doing, though I couldn't bring myself to utter the words aloud. He would be headed into certain danger, and I couldn't bear the thought of it. His fate hung heavy over the group, remaining unspoken.

"You're going to end up dead, Navan," Bashrik said suddenly, voicing my own worst fear.

He grimaced. "You know I always appreciate your positive outlook on things, Bashrik—but in this case, I'm good."

Bashrik gripped Navan's shoulder. "Seriously, man. This is Queen Brisha's army we're talking about. The chances of you making it out alive are slim to none."

"How is that helpful, Bashrik?" I sighed. This was already hard enough for me to deal with without Bashrik being a bundle of nerves.

"What about you, Riley? What are you going to do?" Lauren asked, thankfully changing the subject. Only, the question was one that had been plaguing me. I had an idea, but it wasn't something I wanted to admit to the group just yet. It was risky, and potentially downright dangerous, but it was the only thing keeping me sane.

"Uh... I'm not sure yet," I hedged.

Navan looked at me suspiciously, his brow furrowed. It was clear he knew I was thinking something I shouldn't be.

"Anyway, that's not important right now," I continued, before he could start interrogating me. "We've got a bigger problem."

"What?" Lauren asked, a note of alarm in her voice.

"We need to find a way to secretly send information to Orion, or he's going to start killing more humans... starting with my parents." I had delayed bringing them up to speed about that particular aspect of Orion's latest torment. It was painful to think about, let alone talk about.

My friends gasped.

"*More* humans?" Lauren whispered.

"Your parents?" Angie murmured in disbelief. "How would he even find them?"

"I don't know, but that's his threat, and I don't feel like testing it." My thoughts returned to poor Galo, who had given me that advice.

"We'll gather info from our respective positions in Queen Brisha's ranks, pool it together, and figure out a way of transmitting it," Bashrik said, finally on a more productive train of thought.

"There are a few remote spots that might work," Navan added, though his eyes were still on me. "If one of us can get hold of a comm device, we should be able to hack it and do this without anyone finding out."

A somber mood descended across the group once more, the news of Orion putting a damper on things. It was almost amusing, where we'd ended up, and in any other circumstances I would have laughed at the ridiculousness of it all. Navan and I were still somehow spying for the rebels, but now we were betraying an entirely different queen.

"I need a shower," I said finally, wanting to extricate myself from the group. There was something I needed to do, and I couldn't do it with everyone's eyes on me. Slowly, I got up, and I was thankful that Navan left me to my privacy as I stepped out of the hut and headed in the direction I'd last seen Queen Brisha.

Before I could reach the main section of the command center, however, I almost ran headfirst into Pandora. She was rushing in my direction, her head down, not seeing me until we almost collided.

"Rask, I'm sorry! I was in a world of my own," she said, skidding to a halt.

I smiled. "No problem. In fact, you might be just the person I'm looking for," I said, realizing she might be able to help me. Queen Brisha was preferable, but Pandora was her righthand woman, which was more than good enough.

"Oh?" Pandora said.

I drew in a deep breath. "I want to join the queen's army," I said, voicing my plans aloud for the first time. There was no going back now that it was out of my mouth. "Either that, or train with them, at the very least," I added, hoping for a positive reaction.

Pandora's face was blank for a moment, and then an expression of disbelief settled over her features. She eyed me curiously. "I hope you don't think me rude, but your species is weak—you would be of little use in the queen's army."

"Well... if you gave me the chance, I think I might surprise you. I'm good with knives. Even Navan was impressed by my throwing abilities. Besides, I'm stealthy—that could be of use to the queen. More importantly, I don't want to sit around doing nothing while your queendom is being attacked. I refuse to." I folded my arms over my chest, determined to stand my ground. I didn't want to say it out loud, but I hoped that my proactive mentality might get me on Queen Brisha's good side, building a bridge of trust between us. If she could learn to rely on me, that could give us the freedom to escape in the future.

Of course, my motives for joining the army were not entirely for Queen Brisha's benefit. I knew that if I could be part of the soldier training I would be able to spend more time with Navan, and keep an eye on him. Also, it would mean I could grow stronger, and learn more about coldbloods' weaknesses and how to defend myself better against the species. I also couldn't help but think of Orion, and how I might exact my revenge on him if I ever got the chance, for all the torture he'd put us through—and for how he'd killed Galo.

Pandora looked thoughtful, though a strong trace of doubt remained in her expression. "Well... I suppose we *are* about to begin a fresh round of training soon... I should warn you, though, it won't be easy. You will struggle and find it difficult to fit in. Everyone will think the same about you that I have, regardless of your skills."

I knew she was right, but I wouldn't be put off. My mind was made up.

I shrugged. "I don't really mind what others think of me. I'll show them I've got guts enough to be there."

Pandora sighed. "All right. Then I look forward to seeing you on day one. I'll send word when you are expected."

"Thank you, I appreciate it," I said, giving her a smile. "Is it safe to go back into the palace now? I, uh, kind of really need a shower."

She nodded. "Gianne's troops have all retreated since the alchemy lab bombing—it's fine to return. I'll be passing your group; would you like me to tell them to meet you in the apartment?"

I shook my head. "Thanks, but I just need a moment alone," I admitted.

She smiled warmly. "Of course, Riley. If you take the staircase over there it should take you up to the right tower," she instructed, nodding to one of the doors in the side of the rockface. "I'll see you again soon." With that, she excused herself, heading toward the hut area at the side of the underground chamber.

Feeling a sense of relief at the small period of freedom that lay ahead of me, I hurried toward the staircase she'd gestured to and ran straight to the very top. As I reached our floor, I was breathless, my lungs burning, but I knew I was mere minutes away from standing beneath the comforting cascade of hot water. The thought spurred me on, leading me into Navan's and my chambers.

I froze when I saw the figure standing in front of the roaring fireplace, his back facing me.

"Navan? What are you doing here?" I asked, surprised. Then again, this was exactly like him—he must have known where I'd be headed, and here he was, waiting for me.

"Where did you go?" he asked, his eyebrows raised as he turned to face me. "When you mentioned taking a shower I thought I'd come and join you, but when I went to the showers at the back of the hut village, you weren't there... so I thought I'd wait for you here in case this was where you meant."

I blushed. The thought of Navan and me in the shower together was just the kind of image my mind needed right now, after the turmoil of everything else. It beat solitude any day. Still, he was going to need an explanation for what I'd been up to, and I had to tell him, even if it meant distracting him from that delicious idea.

"I was talking to Pandora," I said, biting the bullet. "I asked to join the next round of army training."

Navan's jaw dropped, his face aghast. "Why... Why didn't you say anything? Couldn't you have at least run it by me first?" he replied, a look of horror on his face. "Do you have any idea how hard it's going to be—and how dangerous?!"

I sighed. He sounded just like Bashrik when his voice rose like that. "I knew you'd have been against it if I'd tried to speak to you about it. Besides, who says I have to ask your permission for everything I do?" I pouted at him. "Now that we're here on Vysanthe for the foreseeable future, I can't rely on you to always be there. Army training *will* ensure we're as close to each other as possible, but it will also teach me to be a strong fighter. I'll end up more capable of protecting myself, which is what you want, right?"

Navan's features softened, his disbelief fading. It surprised me to see him accepting my words so quickly, but I was glad for it. Perhaps Navan was finally learning to trust my Earthen judgment. It made me smile, his acceptance of me making him even more attractive in that moment.

"You're right that it will make you a stronger fighter," he said, taking a step closer to me. "And I want to be close to you, too... Plus, they'd never put you on a *real* battlefield—I'd make sure of that."

That promise calmed a lot of my nerves about the idea. I wanted to learn to be a soldier, but the idea of actually *being* one didn't really sit well with me. I didn't think I had it in me to actually kill someone.

"Please don't be afraid to talk to me, though, Riley," Navan said, closing the gap between us. He took my hands in his, gazing down into my eyes. "I want you to feel like you can tell me anything. I know I'm not always the best at... communication, but I promise I'll try harder to listen to you first before freaking out over things."

"You mean you'll be Sexy, Amazing Listener Navan?" I asked.

He smiled. "With emphasis on the Sexy."

I grinned, allowing his arms to slide around my midriff, while draping my own over his shoulders. It seemed we were making progress, Navan and me. Although the universe's future looked stormy and uncertain, *our* future seemed to be burning brighter.

He leaned in, pressing his cheek to mine, and I closed my eyes, enjoying the rough stubble of his jaw.

"Now, how about that shower?" he whispered huskily in my ear.

"Sounds like a plan," I breathed back.

He moved in to kiss me, and as his lips caressed mine, all the pain and suffering of the past two weeks ebbed away, my world becoming what I could hold in my hands. My skin tingled as his hands traced my waist, and I trailed my hands through his hair, drawing our kiss deeper.

In this room, with him, I could imagine we were anywhere. Vysanthe didn't exist. Orion didn't exist. The queens didn't exist. As long as we were in here, alone together, then the bubble of bliss wouldn't burst. Outside, I knew the uncertainty of a dangerous future loomed over our heads, wielding a pin that could dissolve our bubble with one jab, destroying it forever.

But for now, for this moment, we were safe inside it.

EPILOGUE

PANDORA

I waited until darkness fell, and the hallways of the palace grew quiet. After the events of the day, Queen Brisha wasn't likely to sleep tonight, but I knew she wouldn't call for me again until morning. I had told her I was retiring to bed, which was true… But there was something I needed to do first.

I made my way to the old galleria. Dustsheets covered the aging statues and portraits from the days of Queen Brisha's parents, the pale shapes looking like ghosts in the dappled moonlight.

Reaching the small broom cupboard at the back of the hall, I glanced over my shoulder once, then shut myself inside. Another door lay ahead of me, hidden behind rows of forgotten cleaning equipment. I opened it softly, emerging at the top of a winding stairwell. I swept down it, careful to keep my footsteps light, then drew out the set of keys in my pocket and unlocked the metal door at the bottom.

Stepping out into the crisp night air, I inhaled deeply, allowing myself to pause as I looked around. The gardens were shrouded in shadows and silence, the icy stillness almost unnerving. It was hard to believe that just hours ago the city had been under attack.

The shriek of a throat-tearer broke the calm, causing my heart to skip a beat. As the large bat flapped out from the branches of a nearby tree, I took it as my cue to keep moving.

Spreading my own wings, I took to the air, soaring high over the grounds. I flew until I reached the tallest tree that stood on the perimeter of the royal property, where I descended and settled myself among the sharp leaves. My eyes drank in the sprawling view of the city, falling briefly on the ruins of the bombed alchemy lab. Then I drew my wings around me like a shield, blocking out the harsh gusts of wind, and focused on the task at hand.

I reached for one of the two comm devices attached to my belt and switched it on. Punching in the only code I used with this device, I waited. It dialed. Once, twice, thrice.

And then a familiar baritone voice answered, infused with expectation.

"Pandora?"

I drew in a deep breath, knowing this conversation wasn't going to be easy.

"Orion, we need to talk."

READY FOR MORE?

Ready for the next part of Riley and Navan's story?

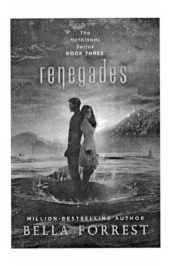

Dear Reader,

Thank you for reading *Coldbloods*.

On to Book 3 of the series: *Renegades*! It releases **February 10th, 2018.**

Visit: www.bellaforrest.net for details.

I look forward to seeing you back in Vysanthe!

Love,

Bella x

P.S. Sign up to my VIP email list and I'll send you a personal heads up when my next book releases: **www.morebellaforrest.com**

(Your email will be kept 100% private and you can unsubscribe at any time.)

P.P.S. I'd also love to hear from you — come say hi on **Twitter** or **Facebook**. I do my best to respond :)

HOTBLOODS

Hotbloods (Book 1)

Coldbloods (Book 2)

Renegades (Book 3)

THE GIRL WHO DARED TO THINK

The Girl Who Dared to Think (Book 1)

The Girl Who Dared to Stand (Book 2)

The Girl Who Dared to Descend (Book 3)

The Girl Who Dared to Rise (Book 4)

The Girl Who Dared to Lead (Book 5)

THE GENDER GAME

(Completed series)

The Gender Game (Book 1)

The Gender Secret (Book 2)

The Gender Lie (Book 3)

The Gender War (Book 4)

The Gender Fall (Book 5)

The Gender Plan (Book 6)

The Gender End (Book 7)

A SHADE OF VAMPIRE SERIES

Series 1: Derek & Sofia's story

A Shade of Vampire (Book 1)

A Shade of Blood (Book 2)

A Castle of Sand (Book 3)

A Shadow of Light (Book 4)

A Blaze of Sun (Book 5)

A Gate of Night (Book 6)

A Break of Day (Book 7)

Series 2: Rose & Caleb's story

A Shade of Novak (Book 8)

A Bond of Blood (Book 9)

A Spell of Time (Book 10)

A Chase of Prey (Book 11)

A Shade of Doubt (Book 12)

A Turn of Tides (Book 13)

A Dawn of Strength (Book 14)

A Fall of Secrets (Book 15)

An End of Night (Book 16)

Series 3: The Shade continues with a new hero...

A Wind of Change (Book 17)

A Trail of Echoes (Book 18)

A Soldier of Shadows (Book 19)

A Hero of Realms (Book 20)

A Vial of Life (Book 21)

The Breaker (Book 2)

The Chain (Book 3)

The Keep (Book 4)

The Test (Book 5)

The Spell (Book 6)

BEAUTIFUL MONSTER DUOLOGY

Beautiful Monster 1

Beautiful Monster 2

DETECTIVE ERIN BOND (Adult thriller/mystery)

Lights, Camera, GONE

Write, Edit, KILL

For an updated list of Bella's books, please visit her website: www.bellaforrest.net

Join Bella's VIP email list and she'll send you an email reminder as soon as her next book is out. Visit: www.morebellaforrest.com

CPSIA information can be obtained
at www.ICGtesting.com
Printed in the USA
LVOW08s1204070218
565498LV00003BB/741/P

9 781947 607224